ROGUE WARRIOR: TASK FORCE BLUE

"Heart-pounding, white-knuckle, pure adrenaline action. . . . A great book."

—*The Beaumont Enterprise* (TX)

ROGUE WARRIOR: GREEN TEAM

"[A] fast-paced yarn with vivid, hardware-laden detail."

—*Booklist*

ROGUE WARRIOR: RED CELL

"A chilling, blood and guts, no-nonsense look into clandestine military operations told like it should be told. It doesn't come more powerful than this."

—Clive Cussler

Acclaim for Richard Marcinko's explosive autobiography—
the #1 *New York Times* bestseller!
ROGUE WARRIOR®

"*Rogue Warrior* leaves Tom Clancy waxed and booby-trapped."

—*Los Angeles Times Book Review*

"Fascinating."

—*The New York Times Book Review*

"Profane and asking no quarter: the real nitty-gritty, bloody and authentic."

—*Kirkus Reviews*

Other books in The Rogue Warrior® series:

Rogue Warrior

Rogue Warrior: Red Cell

Rogue Warrior: Green Team

Rogue Warrior: Task Force Blue

Rogue Warrior: Designation Gold

Rogue Warrior: SEAL Force Alpha

Rogue Warrior: Option Delta

Rogue Warrior: Echo Platoon

Rogue Warrior: Detachment Bravo

Rogue Warrior: Violence of Action

Rogue Warrior: Holy Terror

Also by Richard Marcinko:

Leadership Secrets of the Rogue Warrior

The Rogue Warrior's Strategy for Success

The Real Team

ROGUE WARRIOR®
VENGEANCE

RICHARD MARCINKO

AND

JIM DeFELICE

POCKET STAR BOOKS
New York London Toronto Sydney

A Pocket Star Book published by
POCKET BOOKS, a division of Simon & Schuster, Inc.
1230 Avenue of the Americas, New York, NY 10020

This book is a work of fiction. Names, characters, places and incidents are products of the author's imagination, or are used fictitiously. Operational details have been altered so as not to betray current SpecWar techniques.

Originally published in hardcover in 2005 by Atria Books

ISBN-13: 978-0-7434-2277-2
ISBN-10: 0-7434-2277-5

This Pocket Star Books paperback edition May 2006

10 9 8 7 6 5 4 3 2

Cover art and design by Carlos Beltran

Manufactured in the United States of America

For information regarding special discounts for bulk purchases, please contact Simon & Schuster Special Sales at
1-800-456-6798 or business@simonandschuster.com.

Dedicated to the 180,000 Homeland Defense employees who are faced with new challenges every day, and all the first-responders who must be prepared to function if and when they fail. They all fully understand the 24/7 demands.

Part One

MOI?

"Decline the attack unless you can make it with advantage."

—FIELD MARSHAL MAURICE COMTE DE SAXE,

MY REVERIES, 1757

1

It was your basic freight train: big, slow, and ugly, springs squealing like a pig in a Missouri hog pen. The sound didn't make any difference to the fine, upstanding middle-class citizens of Lenaza, a few miles outside of Kansas City. Hell, nothing made much difference to most of them, because they were snoring in their beds. The train had crept into their dreams forever: it rolled through every night at two A.M., give or take.

Tonight, it was a bit on the take side. But me and my guys were about to even the ledger out.

Guys and *gals*. Never let me forget Trace Dahlgren. At that exact moment she was leaning off the side of an AH-6 Little Bird helicopter as it swooped down toward the freight train in question. I was leaning off the other side, doing my best to pretend I was the patient type. This was necessary because the helo pilot had a hell of a time matching the speed of the train, a useful prerequisite to our immediate goal: disembarking from the aircraft onto the roof of one of the diesels. The train had picked up speed as it started downhill, and to complicate things just a little, the weatherman had screwed up again, and the calm, clear night I'd ordered had turned windier than hell and misty to boot. I swore to myself that next time I'd play hobo and hop on the damn thing if I wanted a ride.

"Can we at least get over the damn train?" groused Trace. "All I see here is dirt." Normally dependable and crystal clear, even the discrete-burst communications system we used was having a hard time of it; it croaked and crackled, distorting her voice.

The helo rocked hard right and we zipped over the train—but instead of hovering over the engines, we were above one of the chemical tankers. Jumping off onto the car wasn't particularly convenient—if you can't figure out why, find one of those mega culvert pipes and spread your legs over it. Our pilot had flown with the 160th SOAR once, the Army's dedicated special operations airborne taxi squad, but either once was a long time ago or this just wasn't his night.

The tankers were the reason we were here. They happened to be all filled with the same basic ingredient: cyanide gas, or more technically speaking, Chlorcyan, another name for cyanogen chloride. Left alone, Chlorcyan is "simply" riot gas: beats shit out of your eyes and chokes you, maybe to death, maybe not. Heat it so it starts to break down and let some of it come into contact with water and you get hydrogen cyanide, which is best known as the gas used by the Nazis in their quest to exterminate a good hunk of the human race.

The exact effect of blowing up a dozen cars of

the stuff would depend slightly on luck; if the charges were placed willy-nilly, all you'd get was really wretched smog and an ecological disaster unmatched since Chernobyl. If you knew what you were doing when you blew them up, you could kill half the population in the state.

My goal wasn't to blow them up, not really. The train was starring in a little Red Cell II exercise I'd worked up to test the procedures of the regional Homeland Security alert system and its various dependent and not-so-dependent agencies. The train was supposed to be under their guard and jurisdiction, well protected from terrorists and maniacs, to say nothing of airborne hobos with improvised explosive devices and attitudes to match.

"We need to be over that front locomotive," I told the pilot. "Before the tunnel."

"I'm trying, Skipper."

"Try harder."

Finally the helo flitted forward and a relatively flat stretch of diesel engine appeared below my boot. I clicked the fancy French snap on my safety harness and stepped off as naturally and easily as if I were hopping off the last step of a mall escalator.

And if you believe it was *that* easy, I have some swampland for you to take a look at.

I felt like a cat pouncing onto the seat of a wet motorcycle moving about sixty miles an hour as I stepped off. My feet started to slide out from under me, but I managed to grab the edge of the roof I'd landed on. Trace came off just like the lady she is. Catlike and nimble, she stepped, twirled, and gave me a look that seemed to say, *So what's the big deal?*

There were three diesels, all facing forward. Trace and I were on the first, both of us just ahead of the dynamic brake fan, which is the large cooling area in the center of the locomotive. As a general rule, the people who design locomotives don't give a hell of a lot of thought to people riding on the top of them, which means moving across them and getting down while the train is doing sixty or so is not particularly easy. The fact that the top of the engine had been slicked with the rain made it even more interesting. Trace slipped and fell spread-eagled out across the top. Instead of gloating as I probably should have, I grabbed her leg to save her sorry butt and slipped myself. All I could find for a handhold was the side of the engine. I managed to grab it just as we roared into the tunnel.

If I hadn't been hanging on to Trace by a couple of fingernails, the rest would have been easy: a quick slide around and I'd have plopped down on two feet onto the catwalk outside the engine cab. But between Trace and the wind of the tunnel and the slippery slime of the moistened grit I was perched on, I found it possible to slide in every direction but the one I wanted. If you've ever tried to catch a greased pig in the middle of a mud flat while a hurricane rolled through, you'll know what I mean. Trace suddenly slid over the side. Thinking she was falling, I threw my other arm out to grab her and flew off the side of the top of the locomotive.

I expect most of you reading this book know who the hell I am better than I do, but let's do a quick review for the nuggets among us who have wandered into *The World According to the Rogue Warrior* without a map or the proverbial pot to shit in, and more important without having read the books that should be on everyone's MUST READ NOW list, starting with *Rogue Warrior* and ending with *Violence of Action.*

Yesterday—well, it *seems* like yesterday—I kicked commie slimebag butts and slit throats in the jungles of Vietnam. Pretty little hellhole there, as detailed in *Rogue Warrior.* Fast-forward through mountains of shit and red tape and you get to the part where I started SEAL Team Six, the Navy's preeminent counterterrorism force—Delta Force with fins and finesse. After three years as CO on Six, I finally pissed enough people off that the powers-that-were found a way to shaft me off to the sidelines. Not that I stayed shafted too long—I managed to *really* irritate people with a little operation called Red Cell. This was conceived as an exercise in kicking the Navy in the pants—alerting the brass, swabs, ship drivers, and everybody else top to bottom to the very real danger terrorists posed. Today it's damn obvious what terrorism can do, but in 1984, very few people understood the danger posed by maniacal slimebags who believe religion greenlights murder and mayhem. Not that knowing any better has helped all that much in terms of improving security, but that's a topic for another day.

Red Cell got attention for a couple of reasons—"blowing up" nuclear submarines and Air Force One were just the start. All of this attention led inevitably to the ultimate revenge of the nerds: I got railroaded on a set of trumped up charges into a federal home for the absurdly unappreciated.

And then things got *really* interesting. It turned out that, once I was officially out of favor, my services were indispensable. I guess the secret to getting ahead is to get screwed by the right people in life.

Bullshit on that. I took no prisoners and gave no quarter; the secret to my success was the good ol' American secret to success: work twice as hard as everyone else. But I go into all this stuff in my other books, so we'll just skip up to the very recent past, say the three weeks that brought me to Lenaza.

Over the years, I have gained a certain reputation and maybe even a certain fame as a guy who knows the color of his shit when it comes to dealing with terrorists and security issues. And while I admit to rubbing a percentage of people the wrong way—I like to say I'm one hell of a brain surgeon, but I do flunk bedside manner—another percentage of people realizes that if you want to improve your security problems, the person to call is Demo Dick, whose talents and private firm are available for the proper considerations. Which led Rich Armstead from the Homeland Security Office to pick up the phone and jingle yours truly at Rogue Manor one fine early-spring morn. He explained that his department was working with local agencies to improve antiterrorist security. I immediately got the picture—Rich wanted Dickie to do a rerun of Red Cell.

"No," I told him. "I'm out of the pissing-people-off business. Now I just kill them if they get in the way."

Rich laughed, but I wasn't kidding. Certainly not about testing defenses BS. Showing people how dumb their security precautions are makes them mad, and, unfortunately, usually doesn't help improve them much.

Look at it this way: if the organization were smart enough to take constructive criticism, they wouldn't be so fucked up in the first place.

Rich didn't give up, though. He laid on the your-country-really-needs-you crap and dropped the President's name and insisted I ought to talk with him in person. And just in case I forgot the way, he'd detailed a limo to pick me up.

So that's what the honking was in the driveway.

The day Rich called had been a particularly bad one for the office PR wise, with some dinky newspaper named the *New York Times* burying a story on page one about security lapses in the nation's rail industry. What really pissed Rich off about the story was that for once the news hounds had actually gotten their facts right; if any terrorist hadn't had a blueprint for ruining a lot of mornings in America, they sure as hell had one now.

Rich covered his feelings pretty well, smiling and shaking hands and even trying to flatter me by talking about what good shape I looked to be in. That's the dead giveaway, I guess, when they start asking if you're still benching five fat ones every day. (I am.) He smiled and nodded and slick as a carnival hawker moved onto a sob story about how fucked things were security-wise across the country. This of course naturally led to asking if I'd do my bit to straighten it out. There were violins in the background, and just as he finished, the strains of the Star-Spangled Banner seeped in from the outer office.

I may not be wiser but I'm definitely older since the days of Red Cell. I offered to provide Rogue Warrior services overseas for the proper fee, no holds barred and no questions asked. Hit the scumbags where they live and head off the trouble was always what I was best at, and I told Rich it made a lot more sense in the long run, in the short run, and in every run in between. Uncle Sam has seen fit to contract out for a variety of services which for one reason or another can't be handled in-house, and I'm always happy to work with Uncle on what needs doing.

Rich stood up, grinned, and shook my hand as if we'd agreed.

"Call when you're ready to start," he said.

"Don't sit by the phone."

He grinned as I left. The phone calls from old pals started five minutes after I was out of the office and continued nonstop. It was good stuff: duty and honor, responsibility, need in a time of crisis. Tears in my eyes—you get the picture. The clincher was a five-minute conversation with the President of the United States that went roughly like this:

"We want you, Dick."

"Yes, sir."

So I agreed. It was my only option anyway. So many damn people were calling I couldn't use the fucking phone even to order a pizza.

Rogues never do learn, I guess. I rounded up some of the usual suspects, made plans to hire a few new ones, picked up a Rand McNally of the U.S., and off we went.

Which was how I came to be surfing a diesel locomotive roaring through the Missouri countryside, pretending to be a scumbag terrorist bent on kicking mud in the face of the world's only superpower.

Or rather, I came to be flying off said diesel locomotive, looking at becoming just another piece of tunnel trash.

I jammed my right hand out against the side as I went over, hoping I'd grab part of the pipe that ran back along the side of the engine. In my mind, I saw myself swinging down Tarzan-like and hopping onto the next platform.

That was in my mind. In real life, I missed completely. My chest and chin smacked against the side of the locomotive. My hand bashed against something else and I grabbed it desperately, sure that gravity had finally managed to find a way to kick my butt.

It hadn't, fortunately, though it kicked just about every other part of me. I'd snagged the side support of the metal ladder running up to the cab, jamming my arm between the corner of the rung and the side. I smacked against the side of the locomotive a couple of hundred times, flailing to stay upright as we emerged from the tunnel. After what seemed like a hell of a long time, I managed to get myself on the ladder—upright, bruised, but unperforated.

And where was Trace while all this was going on? Mangled to shit back in the tunnel?

No, laughing, I think. She managed somehow to slide across the back of the cab, roll over me, and end up on the tiny platform at the rear above the coupling assembly. Just like a woman—you save her butt and then she walks all over you.

"You done fucking around over there or what?" she squawked in my ear as I met her on the walk-around ledge that circled the locomotive's waistline.

"I'm ready," I grunted.

"What?"

That's what she said, but I couldn't hear it, and in fact I had trouble seeing her mouth it in the dim light. My microphone had snapped off somewhere in my tumble, though I didn't realize it at the time. We made our way to the front locomotive without further adventure, perching near the cab door.

If we'd been real terrorists, we might have popped a concussion grenade inside, killing the two crewmen. Or maybe we'd've sprayed them with our MP5s; hard to say what sort of terroristic mayhem might have occurred to our crazed minds. But Red Cell II fielded only *considerate* terrorists, and to avoid injury we had equipped ourselves with pepper gas, actual weapons tucked beneath our black clothes. The stuff was environmentally friendly, too, approved by the EPA and conservationists for terrorist use around the world. Even Greenpeace endorsed it.

I gripped the handle to the door. It pulled open easier than I expected. Trace flew through the opening.

"Homeland Security!" she shouted. "Stop the fucking train."

There were two men in the cab. The first one looked at her like he was about to have a heart attack.

The second pulled a gun.

Staring down the business end of a firearm never becomes routine. You can train to deal with it, and after a while it does lose *some* of its shock value, but a gun's a gun and death is death. Every so often they come together in the form of a small piece of lead propelled at high speed. So when it happens, you deal with it right away, no questions asked. Stop to ask questions and you may not be alive to hear the answers.

So Trace reacted and I reacted, and the result was one very teary-eyed engineer.

Which served the asshole right, because he actually managed to get off a shot.

Colonel Jeff Cooper—a serious, A1 pistolero and instructor—drills his people to conjure a "flash sight picture." The technique ensures a takedown shot in very close quarters and extremely tight situations. Had the engineer shot off a few zillion rounds with the esteemed colonel, no doubt this tale would have had a different outcome.

Still, you have to give him points for trying. The first bullet flew by close enough to change the press in my pants. There was no second bullet because by then, Trace and I had the man down on the floor. I felt damn lucky I didn't get bitten by a ricochet in the cab. It wasn't the engineer's fault that he shot, really. We hadn't told him that it was an exercise, and if someone had tried to hop my train in the middle of the night, I'd probably do the same.

Well, not exactly the same. I take Colonel Cooper's advice very much to the heart.

Both trainmen got faces full of pepper spray. The shooter began rolling around the cramped cab, screaming and carrying on. The other man fainted. This didn't keep his face from shading purple as tears streamed from his eyes, but even so, it was probably the most logical reaction to the situation.

Trainmen secure—we cuffed them with those nifty plastic garbage bag ties you've seen on EPWs—we now owned the train. Imagine how much ten tanker cars, their cargo, and three diesels would have fetched on eBay. But cash flow was just fine that month, and as thievery wasn't the point of the exercise, I checked our position on the GPS, then backed down the throttle and eased on the brakes.

Trace pulled out her cell phone and sent a signal to the second half of the team, which was waiting down the tracks. Then she pulled a bottle of water from her vest and gave it to the trainman who'd tried to kill us, telling him to swish it over his eyes. Obviously we cuffed him with his hands in front of him to ease discomfort and the potential of him beating himself up trying to get balanced as he tried to stand up.

"This is just an exercise," Trace told him. She dumped the bullets from his pistol—it was a Colt revolver, a short-nosed job once favored by detectives—and stuck the weapon in his belt. "We're sorry if we hurt you."

He grumbled something that I couldn't quite make out over the squealing of the brakes, though I gathered he wasn't completely accepting of her apology.

As we stopped the train, Danny Barrett and two other members of the Rogue Warrior team had turned onto a nearby service road and were driving along the tracks in a pickup truck. They carried a dozen IEDs, or improvised explosive devices, which had been armed with small radio receivers. Under other circumstances, the business part of the packages would have had C-4 explosive or something similar. C-4 is your basic plastique dynamite substitute; the stuff is so stable that I swear you can set it on fire and it won't explode. Of course, I wouldn't jump up and down on it to put the fire out. In the interest of avoiding a really spectacular catastrophe, we'd substituted less potent but nonetheless showy fireworks in its place.

I know what you're thinking: Dick, you can get C-4. Hell, you can get anything you want. You trot over to the annex at the NSA (No Such Agency), whip out your credit card, and they'll fill the shopping cart for you. You know what? You're right. So, just to show what real *Tangos*—another word for "terrorists"—could do, we had obtained real C-4 for the operation the day before, courtesy of the bomb squad of a nearby county law enforcement agency, which shall remain nameless for reasons that will soon become obvious. Said bomb squad used real C-4 as part of its training sessions to give the people who were supposed to work with it a bit of realistic experience. No problem there; commendable, in fact. But they kept it at headquarters. In my experience, one of the least secure places in most local municipalities is the local police headquarters, and this proved the case here. Danny and two other team members, Sean Mako and Fred "Hulk" Goddard, conducted an exercise long on deception and short on exertion—just the sort of thing Danny learned to love during his days as a detective back in the D.C. area.

Sean and Hulk were new shooters, recruited as cannon fodder by yours truly, with the help and cooperation of Danny and Trace. Sean had become a SEAL when he was just twenty—not a record, but close. He served with Teams Two and Six, then graduated to freelance for our Christian friends—Christian as in "Christians In Action," otherwise known as the CIA—in Iraq and someplace in Central America; even Sean's not sure where it was. Past affiliations are no testament to character, fortunately, because Sean proved to be a perfect fit with Red Cell II and extra handy in this case. Before joining our little party he'd worked on a tactical squad in Missouri and attended a program put on by the agency in question. He not only knew about the C-4 but where it was kept.

Hulk is one of those real maggot ex-SEALs who thinks it's funny to mouth off about how the old farts ought to stand aside and let the young guys take charge. I used to threaten to put him over my lap and give him a good paddling with a baseball bat. I'd have to whack him on the side of the head with it first, though, because Hulk stands about six-ten and if he weighs less than 280, the action hero he was named after wears lady's underwear.

Danny and Hulk went into the station posing as painters, claiming the lieutenant had asked them to come around the day before and give an estimate. Sean came in a minute later to ask about a gun permit he was having trouble with, backing them up and providing diversion if necessary.

The estimate gag has to be the oldest trick in the book. It was the lieutenant's day off, of course, but the cover story itself had been selected carefully. The local newspaper had reported that the county supervisors had authorized a fresh paint job for the office building and would be accepting bids in a few weeks. Danny had called the day before, leaving two messages "from the painters" with the receptionist and the lieutenant's secretary, so that if anyone had raised questions, she could have scratched her head and said, "Oh yeah, them." But no one asked any questions. Danny pulled out a clipboard, Hulk took out a laser ruler, and they started measuring the offices as if they were preparing a bid.

It took nearly five minutes for them to reach the locker area where the bomb materials were kept. I'd like to say that there they were met by armed guards whom they had to subdue. My guys won only because of their determination and grit; from that point, they blew their way into the safe holding the weapons and made off with the goodies.

I'd like to say that, but, of course, it's not true. Stealing the C-4 involved walking to an open metal shelf, bending down slightly, and scooping the material into the tool bag Danny had brought along.

When Danny told me all this later on—and we watched it on the mini–digital video cam they brought along to document the operation—Danny insisted the entire operation had been among the most hazardous he had ever been involved on: bending so far forward could easily have thrown out his back.

Not wanting to mess up the department's budget, we returned the C-4 a few hours later, depositing it on the desk of the organization's head man with a little note on how we had obtained it. This half of the caper was carried out by the prettiest looking cleaning lady you'll ever see wield a duster: Trace. She left the explosives but came back with two shiny badges—a fair exchange, if you ask me.

As for the detonators, real terrorists might have gone on the Internet or the Slimebag Home Shopping Network and bought high-tech stuff, but we're a government operation, so we went the cheap-o route: local Radio Shack gladly sold us the equipment, thinking we were using the transmitters for our radio-controlled airplane. The most difficult part of the transaction was remembering which phony phone number to give the guy behind the counter so they could put us on their "Must Call at Dinner Time" telemarketing list.

As the train pulled to a stop, Danny and his guys got the video camera in the truck rolling, recording the scene for training purposes. Then they ran up and hoisted themselves about the tanker cars, setting their charges. Me and Trace, along with the two railroad people we'd detained, got out of the diesel and marched toward a nearby strip mall on the other side of the service road. During our intel gathering we'd spotted a Dunkin' Donuts here, complete with a set of picnic tables at the side of the parking lot around back. I couldn't have asked for a better field headquarters. I bought the two trainmen coffee and heart-stoppers, snapped off their plastic handcuffs and sat them down at the tables to watch the rest of the proceedings. Half of the donut shop had been turned into a Baskin Robbins ice-cream place and Trace came out licking a cone piled high with scoops of dark chocolate.

"That's going to cost you two extra miles in the morning," I warned her.

"It'll be worth it." She just about purred as she licked her tongue across the ice cream. I smiled at the way the engineer's eyes just about popped out of their sockets.

The wind had died down and the clouds were breaking up; the moon supplied enough light so I could see down the track without my night goggles. About three-quarters of the way through my Big Gulp, my cell phone vibrated on my belt. I flipped it open and found myself talking to Al "Doc" Tremblay, one of the original plank holders from Red Cell.

"Hey, Cock Breath. Doom on you," said Doc. Doc's eloquent turn of phrase was part of our normal greeting etiquette, but in this case he was telling me he had spotted the first of the emergency vehicles sent to check out the situation.

Like to see someone figure that out with their secret decoder ring.

"Got it," I told him. I hopped off the line and got Danny on the radio, telling him to snap it up. Within a half minute, our pickup truck began sending dust up from along the railroad tracks.

The two sad-sack trainmen tried to smile as the

first red light glimmered in the distance. I felt a little sorry for them; not only were their eyes reamed but this was going to make them the butt of jokes for weeks. Danny, Sean, and Hulk came over just in time to watch the fun. I saw how Hulk bulked up—he had a dozen donuts, all Boston creme, and he wasn't sharing.

Doc drove up a few minutes later, completing the party. His walruslike mustache twitched, and he walked with the same swagger I recognized in his stride some twenty years ago when he played an important role on the original Red Cell. Doc's put on a few pounds since those days—but only a few—and he was a skinny SOB to start with. More than likely his wife gets the credit for him staying in shape. Donna is all the motivation any man should need to stay in shape, and how Doc was lucky enough to hook up with her in the first place remains one of the universe's unfathomable mysteries. He came over and plopped down on the bench. "Who's got two-thirty-three?" asked Doc, sitting down nearby.

"Me," said Trace.

"Don't tell me you guys started a pool on the response," I said.

"Not on the response," said Doc. "On the fireworks."

"Don't tell me any more. I don't want to be unduly influenced." I'd taken out the detonator and was waiting to launch the IEDs—improvised explosive devices, if you're new to pyrotechnics—at the most propitious moment.

Just as I was about to push the button Danny spotted Colonel Richard Telly's car tearing down the highway. Telly was the Department of Homeland Insecurity regional director—the bigwig whose domain we were peeing all over—and I didn't want him to miss any of the show. So I waited until he pulled up next to the first tanker car to touch off the Roman candles.

The show they put on was pretty impressive, even if I do say so myself.

Colonel Telly may have agreed. I know his dry cleaner sure did.

We heard the shrieks and screams all the way over where we were sitting. We were still laughing ten minutes later when the first squad car pulled up near the donut shop, lights and sirens blazing. Before I could even offer him a coffee, two more black and whites had pulled in behind him.

"Looks like they almost have us surrounded," snickered Trace.

"Drop your weapons," said one of the cops over his loud speaker.

"Comic relief," said Doc.

"Watch it, this ice cream is loaded," laughed Trace.

One of the doors to the police cars opened. An officer slid down behind it, gun drawn and aimed in our general direction.

The 9mm Beretta is a very serviceable pistol, reliable, accurate enough in trained hands, and relatively inexpensive—all definite selling points for a police department. It does suffer from something of an image problem, however. You see so many of them that they tend to lack the coolness factor needed to impress your hardened bad guys, let alone your smart-ass

Rogue Warrior team. Which may explain why Trace laughed so hard she dropped her ice cream.

"Now I'm going to have to get another," she said between guffaws. I don't think I've ever seen that woman laugh quite as hard as that—and, of course, her laughing got us laughing even more. The cops, more than a little confused, stood up slowly and looked around, very possibly wondering if we'd hijacked a truckload of nitrous oxide in the course of our evening festivities.

We might all still be laughing if a Crown Vic hadn't screeched to a halt in the lot at that very moment. A little red light revolved on the dashboard. Colonel Richard "Dick" Telly (Ret.) had arrived.

If I weren't so politically correct, I might suggest "Ret." stood for retarded. But by calling Telly that, I would be slandering a lot of otherwise fine though mentally challenged individuals.

"What the fuck is going on here Marrr-sink-o?" he yelled.

It was a struggle getting serious. "You tell me, Dick," I managed finally.

I tossed away the cup I'd been drinking from and the cops all snapped their weapons back to firing position. I was now liable to be arrested for littering. I made a show of smiling and holding my hands out at my side in as nonthreatening a manner as I can muster at three-thirty or so in the morning.

"Marrr-sink-o, do you have any fucking idea of what you're fooling with here?" demanded Telly.

"Tell me, Dick," I repeated.

"Cy-cy-cyanide," he sputtered. "You know what this could have done if it blew up?"

"As a matter of fact, I do. How technical do you want to be?"

Telly's mouth moved, but nothing came out.

"Cy-cy-cyanide," mimicked Trace. The girl can be a real devil when she wants. Twenty-eight years old, five-eight, and built rock solid, her Achilles' heel is a sarcastic sense of humor that never knows when to call it quits.

Must be why I love her so much.

"Well, let's see," I told Dick, trying to throw a professional blanket over the situation. "Hydrogen cyanide and cyanogen chloride—that was car one and two respectively—belong to a group of so-called blood gases. Now these are not your typical beer farts. They interfere with the body's utilization of oxygen; basically, they're strangling you from the inside. Cyanide and its related compounds also have a particularly nasty effect on the central nervous system, kind of like drinking a lot of really cheap gin. Which is why I personally stick with Bombay Sapphire. And I'd advise you to do the same."

As I was talking, I had walked all the way over to Telly, so we were now standing face-to-face, separated by his car door.

"Of course, what exactly would happen in this case depends on several factors," I continued, "including whether we decided to simply blow up the train cars, or to get really fancy, maybe had a way to mix a little sulfuric acid in and turn the town down the tracks there into a giant gas chamber. Not much of a wind tonight," I said, bending to the ground and picking up a few strands of grass. I tossed them up as if to check which way it was blowing, though

I knew damn well it was blowing straight out Telly's fat ass. "Light wind. Might dissipate in a few hours. First responders are dead, by the way. I apologize if I'm wrong, but I don't see any hazardous material trucks or any of that sort of thing, no MOP-4 chem suits, not even raincoats. Colonel, you have some serious butt kicking to do to get your people in gear. I do see some television trucks, though," I added. "You'll probably want to go down and talk with them yourself."

"Fuck you, Marcinko. Fuck you."

"Wow, he put you in your place," said Doc as Colonel Dickless Telly hopped back in his car and whipped out of the lot.

"Cy-cy-cyanide," mocked Trace, and those of us who weren't laughing already just about collapsed in convulsions.

There are a lot of folks in Homeland Security who are dedicated, hardworking, and intelligent—and a surprising number are all three at the same time. But none of them work for Tell-Me-Dick. He's carefully weeded out anyone smarter than him, which accounts for the fact that he's so understaffed. I'd suspected it prior to our encounter, but there's nothing like seeing a wild animal in his native habitat to truly understand the beast.

"TV truck at two o'clock," said Danny as the police cars beat a hasty retreat. He pointed down the road to an approaching van with a satellite dish.

"Time to move on," I told the team. "Sean and I will grab the video cams from the bridge and the crossing. We'll meet the rest of you back at Diggers."

Diggers, being our temporary headquarters (aka the most convenient area bar), complete with pool table and a bartender as generous as her chest was bountiful.

As we drove toward the video cams we'd left to record the event for training purposes, Sean fired up a handheld Sony to get a new angle on the response. Calling it fucked up beyond belief is being polite. The HAZMAT team had not yet arrived, there was no secure perimeter, and neither Tell-Me-Dick nor his equally clueless underlings had established a proper command post. If this were a real disaster, they'd all have killed themselves by now. Which I guess would have made the argument that it wasn't a disaster.

Danny had set up the video cams earlier, posting them on small tripod stands and marking the locations with flag poles and reflectors so they'd be easy to retrieve. The cams are smaller than the digital jobs you see in stores. They can take and store over six hours of low-light video and can be equipped to uplink to satellites or to feed into a radio or even a computer network. The resolution is a bit grainy and the action choppy, but we weren't looking to show what we'd recorded at the local cineplex. An outfit called Law Enforcement Technologies Inc. out of Colorado Springs developed them and made them available to me on a trial basis. Besides the tickets to the annual shareholders' barbecue, it's one of the benefits of sitting on their board of directors. I can get what I need without going through the normal two hundred and sixty-seven reviews, audits, and opinions a government purchase order would require, or the non-export customs agreements and security checks even a private agency needs to clear.

As Sean jumped out and grabbed the first unit, an enterprising television crew drove up and asked if we were part of the Homeland Security operation.

"You want to talk to Colonel Telly," I told them. "He's in charge."

"He doesn't seem to know anything," said the reporter.

I couldn't really argue with her, so I just shrugged. The crew gave me a sympathetic look, then drove off down in the direction of the train bridge, about a quarter of a mile away. We had one of our video cameras there, so we headed in that direction ourselves. A police car belatedly decided to find out what all the excitement was about.

The van stopped near the creek that the bridge spanned and the reporter and her driver/cameraman got out. Sean and I decided to put the Ford's heavy-duty suspension to the test, clambering over the railroad tracks to get closer to our unit. Not coincidentally, this put us farther from the reporter and gave us a clear shot at the nearby highway. I got out of the truck and hustled down the embankment like I was making a pit stop, working across the cut and then up the side of the bridge, which was a steel-frame job with thick girders and peeling paint. The camera had been taped against one of the beams by Doc, who'd used enough duct tape to hold the entire bridge together. I had to hack through it with a knife to release the camera. As I did so, I happened to glance down along the tracks, which were nearly at eye level on my left. Out of the corner of my eye I saw a snake humped over one of the tracks in the distance. I stared at it for a half second, wondering what the hell a snake was doing on a bridge.

Then I realized it wasn't moving. And that it had to be one of the longest snakes in history. My eyes followed it off the side of the track to the grid work below. I climbed up onto the bridge and started walking out over the span. After a step or two, I realized I wasn't looking at a snake, but it still took a few more seconds before I saw the satchel charges rigged to blow up when the train went over the bridge.

Satchel charges. Old suckers rigged the way someone might have been taught back in the old days. The trigger mechanism had been hooked into a thick wire stretched across the rail that would be severed by the steel wheel of a locomotive, a kind of reverse switch that I guess you might have considered kind of clever if you're into grading those sorts of things. Clever or not, it was definitely armed—and it wasn't ours. I swung under the bridge, examined it with my keychain flashlight, and gingerly disarmed it.

Then again, there are only two ways to disarm a bomb: a) violently, by blowing the sucker up, hopefully on purpose, or b) gingerly. If b) doesn't work, see a).

Meanwhile, the cops and the reporter started jawing back near the track. The police officer did not appreciate the reporter's recitation of the Constitution and its amendments, specifically the one entitling the press to pee on any damn picnic they pleased. At first glance, the reporter hadn't looked like much, but out of the truck—where you could see her short dress and sturdy legs, the curve of her breasts and her shoulder-length blond hair—I wouldn't have minded having a spirited conversation with her myself.

As a matter of fact, I was just considering whether I might want to offer my services as a negotiator when someone nearby shouted, "Holy fuck!"

It was the cameraman, who had wandered near the streambed on the other side of the train bridge to take a leak. I crossed over the tracks and looked down toward the water as he switched on his camera light.

A body floated against the rocks. The cameraman was getting some good video, but it was pretty clear he wasn't going to use much of what he shot. The body was there, but the head wasn't. Neither were the hands.

2

These developments delayed my arrival at Diggers considerably. Telly was convinced the charges were part of my operation, despite my assurances to the contrary. I think he wanted to pin the body on me as well. As it turned out, though, the headless, handless man helped divert attention from his own little fiasco. The local TV station went on the air immediately, reporting that the corpse had been found "during a Homeland Security exercise" and gave no details at all about what had happened to the train.

Besides the pull on my patriotic heartstrings and the rewarding feeling of doing something for ol' Uncle Sam, Rich Armstead had dangled one other incentive before the eyes of yours truly to get me to launch Red Cell II: Karen Fairfield.

Karen heads Homeland Security's Office of Internal Security Affairs (OSIA). She and I had worked together thwarting a plan involving a suitcase nuke.* Along the way we'd developed a certain fondness for each other, one I definitely hoped to continue and enhance. Karen is one of the few people in Washington who understands what the words "I promise" mean, and dealing with her pro-

* See *Violence of Action* for the entire story.

fessionally would actually restore the deepest cynic's faith in government. It even restored mine.

Dealing with her personally, well, all I can say about that is: HANDS OFF!!!

Karen had helped set up the Red Cell II operation and provided necessary support within the government, functioning basically as a cutout. Dealing directly with Rich Armstead would have inevitably subjected me to the chain of command, along with its associated dweebs, bean counters, and general fuckups. The audit trail would have grown steadily until it drowned me in red tape and emails. It would have been only a matter of time before the operation was given its own budget line, office, car pool, expense accounts, GSA overseer, congressional liaison, lawn maintenance agreement, and government pension plan.

Having a cutout meant everything I did stayed off the books, unencumbered by bureaucratic bullshit. Having Karen as the cutout meant I would be dealing with someone I trusted. It also meant I could wake her up at four in the morning without having to apologize.

"Dick, where are you?" she said sleepily.

I expressed my regret that I was not alongside her, then filled her in on what had gone down.

"They chopped off his head?" she asked when I finished.

"And his hands."

"Jesus. Why?"

"I'd say the obvious reason was to prevent an ID. The local police types aren't sure that it's related to the bombs I found, but it's awfully coincidental if it's not."

"He probably wandered by and saw something he shouldn't have."

"Maybe, but if that were the case, why go so far as to chop off the guy's head and hands? They're trying to keep him from being identified. He had to be involved somehow—if it's connected. Listen, Karen, there's an FBI agent involved, and he was telling me they have no hard information on terrorist cells operating out here. You think they're that incompetent?"

"Maybe. Or maybe there are none."

More likely they felt they were protecting their turf from a Homeless Insecurity doofer, but I didn't bother arguing with her. "I'm supposed to be in Iowa the day after tomorrow, but I think I ought to hang around and see if we can come up with anything," I said. "Can you rearrange that for me?"

"All right, Dick. Whatever you want."

"*Whatever* I want?"

There was a long pause. "Whatever you want," she said finally.

The assistant DA and a homicide investigator knocked on my hotel room door around six A.M. to go over what I'd seen and to arrange for interviews with the rest of the team. I was as helpful as I could be considering the hour, even suggesting they join me for a little morning PT, known in some parts as physical training and in others as ass whipping. They declined politely, and I joined Trace for the two-mile warm-up designed to get my blood flowing. To my way of thinking, they made a serious mistake in not coming along. The sight of Trace in formfitting spandex and a judiciously trimmed sweatshirt would add years to anyone's life, and it certainly helped me speed through the run. But it's the stretching that really pumps the heart. To see Trace Dahlgren in a hurdler pose, leg taut, chest thrown forward, is to have tangible, undeniable proof that there is a God.

Anyone who has read *Violence of Action* knows that Trace and I have been fraternal in the past. But the physical stuff was just that—past. There was just no way to conduct a physical relationship and continue working together in close proximity on the Rogue Warrior shooting team, so we mutually agreed on a no-fuck policy.

Not without some regrets, I might add, especially during trunk rotations. We hustled through a Level 5 SEAL workout in the hotel gym, and by the time we hit the pull-ups that signaled the home stretch, we were both sweating like pigs. The Level 5 workout is typical SEAL fodder during BUD/S. When you're young and frisky, it's almost easy. When you reach a certain stage of maturity, however, you grin and bear it. If it hurts, I must be doing it right.

Repeat that over and over. If you can, then you're not working hard enough!

Trace must have been feeling a little tired herself, because she kept the four-mile cardio run that topped off the workout down to an eight-minute pace. We showered off and rendezvoused with the rest of the team in the hotel restaurant at ten A.M. A chorus of groans greeted the information that we would spend the afternoon answering questions at the DA's office. I told the team the interviews might provide a chance to pick up some reciprocal information. Danny—who'd worked as a homicide detective back in D.C. before hitching up with yours truly—was eager to put his police skills to work, as was Sean, so I made them the point men in the informal investigation.

As the meeting was breaking up, Doc pulled me aside. "Anything strike you funny about the charges that were set on the bridge?" he asked.

"Everything strikes me funny about it," I told him. "Which part exactly did you have in mind?"

"The satchel charges. From the way you described the explosives, they were C-3. Right?"

"That's what they were."

"Odd stuff to be screwing with in Kansas, don't you think?"

He had a point. Let me back up just a second for you youngsters: C-3 is a yellow-tinted explosive, and most folks think of it as an earlier version of C-4. It's on the volatile side, but it is a good choice for a water environment. Still it's an *old* explosive, something that a geezer like me or Doc might be familiar with but unlikely to be the firecracker of choice for anyone younger. And, in fact, I wouldn't have used it myself; C-4 and its newer cousins are much easier to get hold of and generally safer to use. But let's face it: your average terrorist is not going to get too hung up on how fashionable his bomb materials are. What's important is that they go boom, which the satchels certainly would have.

"A terrorist wannabe could have found a recipe for it on the Internet," I told Doc, citing C-3's one actual advantage. "It's not exactly hard to make. You could cook it up in the average kitchen. Just don't put it in the Cuisinart when you're done. What about the body? An accomplice?"

"Doubt that's related," said Doc. "Probably floated downstream."

I made the mistake of mentioning that I thought the autopsy might tell us; Doc responded with a filibuster on autopsy methods. Doc wasn't a real doctor. His nickname came from his skills as a Navy corpsman. (He was also a sniper.) I'd guess he knows enough medicine to do a heart transplant with a penknife and chewing gum.

I'm exaggerating. He'd need a combat knife at least.

Anyway, the short version of Doc's lecture was: don't count on the autopsy to tell you anything you don't know before you go in. Especially in this case.

The two FBI investigators and the local detective shared more or less the same opinion when we met later on. The one piece of information I got from them: the hands and head had been taken off with something like a small power saw, probably portable, easier to handle than a chainsaw and capable of making a smoother cut. The rest I had already guessed: it was unlikely that the murder had taken place there, and most likely the victim had been drugged or killed before being mangled. You didn't exactly need a degree in forensic science to know this: there was no blood on the banks of the stream, and chopping off body parts in a raging torrent of water seemed dicey at best.

Information exchange over, I spent considerable time convincing the policemen that I had nothing to do with setting the explosives on the bridge. One of the G-men accused me of it flat out, claiming I had "motive and opportunity."

The polite portion of my response was: "Fuck you, I had motive."

"Makes you look good," he replied.

Some things are so stupid you can only snort in response, and that's what I did.

"Dick Telly is screaming" was how Karen greeted me that afternoon when I called to check in. "He says you're a murderer and a saboteur and a felon, and that you nearly wiped out half of Kansas by almost blowing up a train full of cyanide."

"Did he say I spit in old ladies' eyes, too?" I asked.

"He may have. What was this about stealing a helicopter from a Guard unit?"

"We didn't steal it," I told her. "We piggybacked onto its readiness certification test. It had to fly *sometime* this month, and so did the pilot. I was saving the budget. You know how much it would have cost to rent a chopper? Those things are expensive. And most pilots won't fly at night without serious incentive, which means double-time pay and a couple of bottles of gin. Plus most of them went to college, so you can't foist the well brands off on them."

"You flashed a gun to get the helicopter pilot to take you?"

I pled the Fifth. I hadn't, actually; there was no need to. The pilot and the maintenance people had cooperated to the max, but we had concocted a cover story in case the heat came down. I had no problem keeping their asses covered; I might need those butts down the line. "What's the big deal?" I told Karen. "We're supposed to be running realistic simulations here. If last night wasn't realistic enough, next time I'll set off the C-4."

"You're not listening to me, Dick," pleaded Karen. "Telly is screaming. He wants you the hell out of Dodge."

"Who's going to investigate the bomb on the bridge and the body?"

"The FBI, the local police, the sheriff's department, the state troopers—"

"But who's *really* going to investigate it?"

"It's not your problem, Dick. Honestly, it's not your problem. Your job is to see where there are deficiencies."

"And that's it?"

"Yes, that's it. Why don't you go on to Iowa? Stick with the program."

"Karen, do you have any idea what would have happened if those charges on the bridge had gone off last night? Let's say by some miracle that a cloud of gas hadn't formed. You know what the effect on the drinking water in town would have been? The town wells are located ten feet from the stream."

"We have people working on it. We're going to improve security. You did a hell of a job. Richard thinks so."

I grunted something. Even a dumb Slovak

knows that when someone's trying to make nice, you should make nice back. Still, there are limits. . . .

"Your original mission is very important," Karen said. "That's the greater threat."

"All right. We'll stick to the original agenda. Only for you."

"Thanks."

"We're supposed to be back up in Illinois next week," I told her. "That's Telly's territory, too, right?"

"Maybe things will cool off by then."

"Unlikely. I know his type."

"Dick. Please."

When Karen says the word *please*—well, the only thing to do was change the subject.

"So how you been?" I asked.

"In need of a good massage," she said. "And maybe an executive session in a hot tub."

"I'd like to take care of both right now. Grab a flight and meet me in Kansas City."

"I wish I could." Her sigh filled my hotel room.

My contact person in Iowa was a sawed-off female spark plug named Cordella Hunt, who had just been put in charge of a special antiterrorist task force under the Iowa Department of Public Safety. I'd call Cordella a bitch, but I'm not in a generous mood. She's the kind of a woman who thinks she has to curse twice as hard, fight three times as dirty, and drink five times as much as any man she meets, just to prove she's in the game.

Yup, my kinda gal. A *brorilla*—half broad, half gorilla.

Hunt's professional resumé began in New York City, where she worked as a street cop for a couple of years before her husband's job took her to the heartland. She wangled a spot with the Iowa State Patrol, moved over to the Des Moines Police Department, got herself into undercover work, then took a detour into the tactical squad, hostage negotiations, and back into investigations. She moved on to become a special agent for the Department of Public Safety's Division of Criminal Investigation, and from there started working with the FBI on some local investigations. You wouldn't think there'd be enough crime in a beautiful state like Iowa to keep people like Cordella Hunt earning a steady paycheck, but you'd be surprised. There's a darkness that lurks under the surface of Middle America, as the honor roll of troopers and police officers who have fallen in the line of duty unfortunately attests.

I met Cordella in a nondescript office building not too far from the Des Moines Area Community College Urban Campus. The offices were low-key to a fault, the only signs announcing the presence of a Web imaging company, a misdirection play to confuse terrorists who hadn't done their homework. The security inside the building was very good; without really assessing the situation, my guess is it would have taken SEAL Team Six a whole ten minutes to get inside without being detected.

"So you are the infamous Rogue Warrior," said Cordella, welcoming me into her office.

I gave her the glad-handing routine and the shit-eating grin people have come to expect. Everything's show business these days, even SpecWar.

"You say that like you have a chip on your shoulder," I told her.

"Let's just say that your reputation precedes you," she said, folding her arms. "So you're here to make us look bad, huh?"

"No, ma'am. I'm here to kick you in the butt so you get serious about security," I told her. "I'm here to make it easier for you to get what you need from the powers that be, because you're going to be able to point to a list of things that need to be improved, and that can only be improved with a serious commitment. Some of that will involve money; more of it will take elbow grease and attitude."

"I have plenty of elbow grease. Attitude . . ." Cordella frowned and stood up from behind her desk. Five-six, five-seven, she weighed maybe one-sixty, and a lot of it was in her shoulders and arms. She had the look of one of those pioneer women who spent the day bustin' the sod and whuppin' the cattle before tying on her apron at night to cook dinner for the family. Hearty stock, not to be messed with. "Unfortunately, there are a lot of folk around who don't take things seriously. The World Trade Center and the Pentagon are a long way from Iowa."

"They're not as far as you think."

"You don't have to tell me that, Mr. Marcinko."

"Call me Dick. Or worse, if you feel the need."

Cordella finally smiled. "I appreciate what you're up to. But I have to say, I don't like the idea of getting my butt kicked."

"Good. Then it'll be more fun."

She held out her hand. "Luke Cox says you're all right."

Cox—the puns are too easy, so we'll give him a pass—was another Homeland Security honcho. He coordinated domestic intelligence for the agency. As a blind to Congress and maybe the terrorists, his office was titled Threat Data, Polling and Logging: "Tadpole." Whether this confused terrorists, I don't know; it sure as hell confused people his office dealt with, like those in the CIA, who wanted to know why pollsters were asking for code-word-level information.

As for Congress, hell, Congress people are *always* confused.

"You know Luke?" I said, as if Cox and I were old buddies. Our acquaintanceship amounted to a few waves in the hallway. He didn't get in my way; that was all I really knew about him.

"Eons ago, I was in the Coast Guard," she said. "Then I wised up. I talk to Luke from time to time, usually when he thinks Tadpole has something worth looking at. Most of what he sends me isn't worth much, but he's trying."

We set out the ground rules, which basically were that there were no ground rules. Our Red Cell II team would, however, limit its activities to a particular geographic area, to be named by Cordella herself. This was fine by us. Having people know more or less where we were going to strike didn't hamper us at all and took away much of the grounds for griping.

In the interest of not embarrassing the locals there too much, we'll call the place she chose "Hometown, USA." It's a nice, smallish city of roughly twenty-five thousand people with a pleasant downtown, a lot of green grass, and more "good mornings" and "how do you do's" per square mile than anyplace else on earth. About the last spot in the world a terrorist would think of attacking.

Which of course made it an extremely likely target.

We chatted for a bit longer, fencing really, as Cordella tried to get me to be a little more specific about what we do. Finally I started smiling and nodding and not saying anything. She realized what was going on and conceded by getting up and sticking out that shovel of a hand she had.

"Fuck you very much, Demo Dick," she told me.

"And fuck you, too, Cordella."

"We'll see about that."

Something about a woman in uniform gets my blood going, even if the uniform in question was just a simple denim shirt and crisp khaki pants. But maybe it was the spit in her eye that was so damn attractive.

"Tell you what, after my people kick your people's butts, we'll get together for dinner and whatever to discuss the need for improvements informally," I told her.

"Skip dinner," she said. "I'll take the whatever—after my people kick your people's butts."

We shook hands on it, and I'm not lying when I say I had to count my fingers to make sure I had them all on the way out.

Hometown, USA, straddled a river, and you could easily put the whole town in a frenzy by destroying one of the three bridges that crossed it. The supports on the oldest had been admirably over-engineered, which meant that you'd have to use a lot of explosives to take it out. But a U-Haul filled with fertilizer would have probably buckled the roadway sufficiently to close it. I doubt either of the other two bridges would have survived a concussion grenade, let alone a serious bomb or fertilizer-laden truck. Three trucks, three bridges—would a more or less simultaneous attack like that get national headlines, you think?

Okay, let's say you don't like bridges. Same explosives, same number of trucks—just put them in the center of town. The explosion would create more than enough chaos to get the national media parachuting in. Fertilizer is not exactly difficult to obtain in Iowa, and while there certainly has been more awareness of its potential uses following Timmy McVeigh's Oklahoma nightmare, it's still relatively easy for it to end up in the wrong hands.

As tempting as it was to close down all arteries into and out of the city at what passes for rush hour in the Buckeye State, we decided that play was too easy. I definitely believe in the old KISS principle—"Keep It Simple Stupid"—but my troops are creative types and need to be pushed. We spent the morning of our arrival playing tourist, scoping out the municipal building and other government installations in town. Two dozen state troopers and members of the National Guard arrived in the meantime, their presence duly noted by the local newspaper, which reported that Homeland Defense and something called the Antiterrorist Awareness Task Force would be conducting a readiness test that week. I think we were supposed to be the ATATF, though personally I preferred the name Red Cell II.

Technically, the news story was a serious breach of the ground rules—the test was not supposed to be made public—but having the good citizens of Hometown, USA, suspicious of outsiders worked in our favor. This is because—unlike the extra troopers, policemen, assorted Homeland Security folks, and Guardsmen—we didn't *look* like outsiders. We wore jeans and faded shirts and scuffed up sneakers you can find in any Wal-Mart. And our token nonconformist, Trace, found the perfect cover in the news story: she was a reporter from back East in town to cover the exercise. Reporters need photographers, so Sean was pressed into service. Dummying up credentials involved a quick visit to the local library, which had a color Xerox machine, and then a trip to the mall where she found a U-Laminate-It booth. Anyone who had bothered to check the number on the business card would have gotten a machine at Rogue Manor set up to sound as if it were part of the National News Desk of the *Washington Times*. No one bothered.

I suppose you can give Trace's legs some of the credit. Those aren't the legs of a terrorist, though they do strike terror in the heart of many a man.

Her cover allowed Trace to get a behind-the-scenes peek at the city's defenses. Within a few hours she had toured every post in the city, and we had digital photos of every conceivable bastion of insecurity in the berg. The operation kicked off at precisely 2200 hours that night, when a pair of suspicious types bought themselves a pair of beers at a watering hole across from the police station and retired to the corner near the shuffleboard table. Their conversation was mostly unintelligible, but at some point the word "school" was heard by at least one of those nearby. By happenstance, the person with the sharp ears was a National Guard captain enjoying a little downtime with his men. Shortly after the suspicious types left the bar, the captain sprang into action, and before dawn the high school was surrounded by a company's worth of Guardsmen and police officers. When the district buses went out to pick up the kiddies, each had two members of the task force aboard and was shadowed by a car with two plainclothes policemen inside. Snipers were posted on the roof of the building. Two helicopters provided constant surveillance overhead.

It was great fun for the kids.

At 0555—for variety's sake we decided on a late start—a call came in to the local police station that a middle-aged man was having a seizure outside the library. By the time an ambulance responded, a mustachioed passerby had stopped to render assistance. As luck would have it, the good Samaritan turned out to be a doctor, who quickly diagnosed the ailment not as a seizure but a full-blown heart attack. A second call was sent for the ambulance, though by now it was already on its way. The truck arrived a few minutes later, siren wailing and tires squealing. Like so many other emergency squads in small cities, this one lacked the cutting-edge equipment to deal with a coronary at the scene. Therefore, the man was packed into the ambulance under the watchful eye of the doctor, who jumped in with his briefcase to help the attendants care for their stricken patient.

Thirty seconds after the doors shut, the patient rose from the stretcher. Not only had he regained his vim and vigor, but he had somehow obtained a weapon—a haughty looking H&K P7M8, as a matter of fact.

I wish we'd had a camera aboard. Doc thought he'd be dealing with a *real* heart attack any second, so he quickly explained to the two attendants that this was just part of the drill. The attendants looked at each other and then started laughing. Nervously, but laughing just the same. We didn't let the driver in on it; the compartment was closed off from the cab, and it was easier and more realistic to carry on as we were. Within a few minutes, we were backing toward the doors at Good Samaritan Hospital, exactly as if it were a bona fide emergency. Sean was just coming up toward the door with a limp, having called in his bum knee a few minutes before. Had the security officers given us any problem, he would have pasted little stickers on their heads telling them they were dead. He didn't have the chance, however, as the security people were too busy admiring the new nurse who had just reported for ER duty—Trace, who fills a nurse's uniform in a way that the Surgeon General advises is seriously dangerous to your health. Poor girl couldn't seem to get the ladies' restroom key to work. Considering how far she had to bend over to get the key into the lock, helping her was definitely a job for both officers.

We had the emergency room taken over within two minutes. The only holdout was the clerk assigned to take down the insurance information from people on their last legs before admitting them for treatment. It took three stickers across his fat mouth to get him to shut up and stop asking for our provider cards.

Sean lost his limp and rendezvoused with Hulk out front at the main entrance, where the two security officers were stickered and trussed before they could even look up from their coffee cups. (They thought the cuffs were a joke until they tried to get out of them.) The last officer on duty was up in the security office, where he was supposed to be watching the surveillance cameras, but was found involved in a very hot game of computer solitaire instead. He was easily surprised by Trace, who had brought a gun with the donuts she took him. Being in a generous mood, she let him handcuff himself—and keep the donuts.

We could have made the whole exercise more interesting by cutting off the phone lines and electricity, but that might have put real people at risk. We also let the doctors and nurses go on with their everyday business, though I have serious doubts that Tangos would have.

But we did have *some* fun. Even though they were only handcuffed, the security people took a while before realizing that they could use their phones and call out for help. When they finally did, it took the National Guard and police a good ten minutes to respond. A small blue smoke bomb exploded as the first troop truck went up the drive. A red bomb went off under the second, and—you guessed it—a white one under the third. Iowa had put Dickie in a patriotic mood.

The smoke really came to the fore as the laser lights whipped through it from the simulated .50-caliber machine gun we'd set up on the knoll near the parking lot. Hulk and Sean had spotted the laser at a club the previous evening, and we decided to borrow it for our own purposes. This involved borrowing a generator as well. Fortunately, the local police department had volunteered one, along with a trailer and vehicle to tow it. Whether they realized they volunteered these items was not recorded in the official report.

While the responding troops danced the tango, we exited stage right down the hill and away from the hospital, having demonstrated that we could take and hold it long enough to blow it up, or, if we were feeling truly perverse and destructive, merge it with HealthSouth.

We had a plan to sneak away if necessary: Danny had "borrowed" an ambulance earlier and left it in the driveway. But there was no need for stealth. We simply walked down the hill opposite the laundry entrance, scattering eight and a half minutes before the first trooper car came up to close off the area.

Damn straight I timed it. Got it on video, too.

Cordella was a good sport about the whole thing. To be honest, the security lapses here were no worse than those anywhere else in the country, and if we really had decided to hit the school instead of the hospital—well, I'd have to say that they might have held us off for almost five minutes, if not six. I gave her an informal report on some of her organization's shortfalls, then collected on our bet.

3

Five o'clock in the morning, you're having the wet dream of your life, and the phone on the bed stand rings. You know absolutely that you should not answer it, but your lifelong military training makes you roll the fuck over and reach for the handset. Even as you pick it up you know it's a mistake. But you tell yourself . . . maybe . . . maybe it is Karen . . . or someone . . . really . . . important.

Ha!

"This will not happen again!" shouted Colonel Tell-Me-Dick Telly through the phone. He shouted some other things, but my subconscious was back in the middle of the dream and I had a hard time getting focused on the meat of the conversation.

"What time is it, Dick?" I asked, trying to get my eyes to focus on my watch.

"Who the hell cares what time it is? This will not happen, Marcinko. I will not be embarrassed by you. I don't fucking care if you are in bed with Armstead. It will not happen again!"

"Well, it's dark in here, but I do believe I'm in bed all alone," I told him. "What won't happen again?"

Telly repeated for the third time that it wouldn't happen again and then proceeded to read me the riot act about no longer embarrassing the locals. I say *read,* but in his case you have to understand that's a figure of speech. If Telly can read anything more challenging than a toothpaste label, I'm dropping dead tomorrow.

Now, I've had my ear chewed by some world-class chewers, starting way back in basic about a million years ago. Admirals have beat their swords into ploughshares on my skull. Far worse, I've had the hairy soles of a Navy chief walk up and down my backside getting my shit squared away. Compared to any of those ass chewings, Tell-Me-Dick's hysterical squawks registered somewhere below mosquito bites on a rhino's rump.

But fuck-all, the thing is—he was an A1 serious dickhead, and if I have to get woken up at two bells, as the old sailor dogs say, then at least make it something fucking important. Unless your personal attributes measure 36-24-36 or thereabouts, and you're doing it in person.

"I know you're in Illinois, Marcinko. I know that's where you are. Don't screw with me. This will not happen again."

"So tell me, Dick," I said finally. "You figure out who put those charges on the bridge yet?"

"Don't change the subject, Marcinko."

"What about our Topless Tango? You figure out who he is?"

"I said, don't change the subject on me."

"Next time these guys plan an operation, we may not be there to stop it," I told him.

"You go ahead with your little fucking operation. Just don't screw with me."

"Gee, thanks, Colonel Telly," I said.

"Don't thank me, you asshole. You don't embarrass the local forces, you understand? You don't embarrass this department. This is the United States Government we're talking about here."

And on and on he sputtered. It made me feel a little nostalgic, as if I were back in the Navy. I waited until the asshole paused for breath, and then I said:

Nothing.

Not a word. I didn't yell or scream or use any of those naughty words he had. I didn't kick the wall or throw the phone across the room. I didn't threaten to punch him out or even wrap the cord around his neck like a noose.

I just breathed. Softly. Very softly.

"Fuck you, Marcinko," he finally yelled over the phone. "Fuck you."

Imagine if I had a dollar every time someone said that to me?

I thought Tell-Me-Dick had set his alarm clock especially so he could wake me up, but further intelligence proved that this had not been the case. Apparently the alleged Homeland Insecurity meister had been woken himself an hour earlier by some yahoo at *Good Morning America*, who wanted him to rush over to a studio. There, he would appear live nationwide, explaining why Homeland Security's Red Cell II team was exposing security lapses all across Middle America. Any Washington player with a pound of smarts—a small group, I know—would have grabbed the opportunity and turned the appearance into a lobbying effort for more of whatever it was he wanted more of. But Tell-Me-Dick had only a quarter-pound of smarts, which led him to bark "no comment," stew for a half hour or so, then track me down. This wasn't particularly difficult, as I had called his office the afternoon before, explaining that we had found our way to Springfield, Illinois, and would incite the citizens to terror at our earliest scheduled opportunity.

The laws against prank calls are very lax in Illinois, and so I merely replaced the phone on the hook, hanging up on Tell-Me-Dick and grabbing a few more winks of sleep before starting the day. I was sweating a few piles in the motel room gym an hour or so later when the cell phone rang. It was Karen. Tell-Me-Dick had ruined her sleep, too, and was taking a fair stab at ruining her day as well.

"You're not going to like this," she said, starting off the business end of the conversation.

"Then don't tell me. You're the cutout for a reason."

"Dick."

I knew what was coming. The truth is, this exercise bullshit had already worn a little thin. We'd been doing it for a few weeks now, and—while most of the locals reacted more like Cordella than Tell-Me-Dick—we were still about as welcome as skunks in church. I didn't mind their reactions so much as the fact that what we were doing was so damn *easy.* If you're going to have a war on terror—

HAVE A FUCKING WAR ON TERROR! I prefer the offensive to the defensive—that's what SpecWar is all about—but geez, Louise, get serious. High school kids could have taken over that hospital as easily as we had.

But I'll get off my soapbox. The short and long of Karen's phone call was that henceforth and from now on, Red Cell II would have to submit our plan of attack in advance like any self-respecting group of fucking maniacal madmen bent on destroying the world's greatest country would do.

"I'll be back in D.C. tomorrow," I told her.

Karen urged me not to pull the lever on the flush toilet.

"Far as I can see, it's already been flushed," I told her. "Come on, Karen, I'm not going to waste my time and the government's money out here. Get somebody else to pull their pud in the Midwest."

Karen started lecturing me on how I wasn't going to get any sympathy. I told her I wasn't looking for any. As my ol' friend and fellow SEAL Boomerang used to be so fond of saying: "*Sympathy* is between *shit* and *syphilis* in the dictionary."

There were, however, other things I was looking for.

"Meet me at the airport and we can have a nice little dinner," I suggested. Cooking is one of my unadvertised secrets. "Shrimp scampi, a little wine."

"You can't pull the plug on the operation. These exercises are important. The people in Iowa are very appreciative," said Karen. "Just cool it with Telly, and we'll work out the rest of this with Rich when I get a chance to talk to him."

"There's no way to cool it with Telly. He wants something that will make him look good," I told her. "Karen, between you and me, the whole country is a disaster waiting to happen. It's as if no one's learned anything since 9/11. Nothing."

"That's why we need you."

"Then we do it my way. I'm not sticking with this if the local bozos are calling the shots," I told her. "I went easy on the people in Iowa. I went easy on Telly the other day. But if you want me to bend over for him, you're soaping up the wrong asshole."

"Now, there's an image."

We threw a few more words back and forth, basically because we both wanted to put our lips to much better use. Happiness for the Rogue Warrior that morning came in the form of a very cold shower.

The team reacted with the predictable four-letter words when I related the morning conversations.

All except for Trace. Her Apache eyes twinkled and she broke into a grin.

"So when do we put it in his face?" she said.

"How so?" asked Danny.

"We tell him what we're going to do, and then we go and do it, anyway."

Straight from the Rogue Warrior playbook. That's why I like her.

"Is that what you're thinking, Dick?" asked Doc.

I hadn't been, but it did make a lot of sense. Fitting, too—shit one last time on the asshole's parade before packing it in.

"I don't see why not," I told them. "Red Cell I

played by the rules every so often. Here we'll just tell them the time and the place and see what happens. That's what he wants."

"How much of an advantage can we give them?" asked Sean.

A lot, as it turned out.

Since the in-your-face bit had been Trace's idea, I tapped her to go and talk to Tell-Me-Dick. I figured it this way: he wasn't going to buy me presenting him with an olive branch. And as disciplined as I can be, I'm a crappy liar, especially when it comes to sucking up to assholes. Call it a pucker problem: my lips refuse to assume the anal position.

Trace donned her Class A uniform—tight sweater, short skirt, heels like knives—and went to meet Tell-Me-Dick at his headquarters. She returned with our assignment: strike a truck depot in nearby Mudville the following morning at nine A.M. sharp. Tell-Me-Dick even gave her a map of the area. It showed that the only access into the truck depot—which covered roughly twenty acres—was down Water Avenue, one of the two streets in town with a stop sign.

Mudville—the police chief's a pretty good guy, so we'll use only a nom de guerre—is a middle-class town about ten minutes outside of Springfield, assuming you hit traffic on the highway. It's filled with solid middle-class houses, the ones you used to be able to afford when the words "Made in America" were found on something other than antiques. Back then, the center of town was dominated by a large cutlery factory—knives, forks, that sort of thing—

and most people around either worked there or at the brick factory near the town line. Between those two places were machine shops, a couple of hardware stores, a guy who fixed radios, and a bank where the teller not only knew your name but would give you a call on the phone before letting your account get overdrawn. They're all long gone now, except for the bank, which is owned by some outfit in Singapore making a fortune investing the local late fees in chintzy toy factories in Red China. Things are so slow in Mudville that they only open the office Tuesdays and Thursdays. There are three ATMs, which charge two dollars and fifty cents a transaction, unless you're a bank customer, in which case your account gets you a twenty-five-cent discount.

The fork business went out twenty years ago. Part of it was torn down and another part turned into storefronts. Every fourteen or fifteen months, somebody new comes in fired up about selling candles or cookies or ladies' underwear, but the only business that's ever stuck is the used bookstore in the corner unit. If you ever get to Mudville, go in and check the bookcase all the way on the right. That is the Rogue Warrior's real John Hancock on the title page—just so you know.

I know about the bookstore because it's right across the street from the entrance to the truck depot, which Tell-Me-Dick assigned us to test. Which meant that it was a good spot to observe the security officer who was observing Danny as he pretended to scope the place out.

The security officer had been alerted by a pair of small video cameras arranged on telephone poles out front. These cameras fed into a security station via a cable back into the complex. The person monitoring the system was reasonably awake. Danny managed to saunter up and down across the street only twice before they sent someone to check. Two minutes after the man on foot came out, a second guard came around in an unmarked car. I say unmarked, but it was a dark blue Chevy Caprice with a pair of whip antennas on the back and a spotlight to boot, so I can't imagine anyone but Tell-Me-Dick not realizing it was some manner of official vehicle.

In the meantime, my pocket scanner picked up the communications signal. It was scrambled, but my goal at the moment wasn't to listen in. I hit one of the presets and recorded the dedicated frequency. The geek gear from my buds at Law Enforcement Technologies would help us figure out the encryption and break it later on.

Assuming that much work was necessary.

TV cameras covered the entire perimeter of the depot, with the poles set back from a razor wire–topped fence. A pair of guards were posted at the front gate to inspect incoming trucks. While they were doing a so-so job of it that afternoon, I figured that by tomorrow at nine A.M.—our designated "event" time—they would have set up the portable X-ray machines they'd brought in on pallets earlier in the day. Two companies of National Guardsmen had been trucked in for the exercise and were augmenting the local police and security teams. I watched them arrive and get waved right through without so much as a glance at the driver's dog tags.

Danny, Sean, and Hulk continued to test the defenses over the course of the next few hours. We have a few tricks to set off sensors and watch how the security people respond, but most of the work really comes down to observing and interpreting. How many men to a sentry position? What happens if two trucks come up? How many holes are there in the fence? (You'd be surprised!) Are bicycle riders treated the same as trucks? Are women searched? Kids? And on and on. Watching and thinking, thinking and watching. Success in SpecWar requires the ability to use the most powerful weapon in the human body—the gray one atop your neck.

"We can go in as Guardsmen," suggested Doc at the afternoon planning and pizza session around three. "We can walk in the front gate, right?"

"No, we save the uniforms to walk out," I told him. "I have something fancier for getting in. Besides, they may actually check IDs tomorrow—on the way in, since they know we're coming. What they won't do is check them on the way out." I turned to Danny. "They're putting the Guard up at the Holiday Inn on the highway. Think you can charm a few out of their uniforms?"

"I can give it a shot," said Danny. "We can wait until they go to dinner, then break into the rooms."

"Sean and Hulk will back you up." I turned to Trace. "When you presented Colonel Tell-Me-Dick with the plan, did you agree to go in through the front gate?"

"I didn't say anything. He gave me a map and showed me where the gate was."

"No agreement on our part to use the gate?"

"No."

"I don't see how we're going to get into the place at nine A.M. if they're expecting us," said Sean.

"Who says we're going in at nine? Trace, did you say anything about going *in* at nine?"

"Telly said he would expect us at nine."

"Sure, expect us. We will be there. We will even go *through* the gate at nine. But we'll be leaving, not entering. We'll make a night jump into the depot, set up our charges, and leave via the front gate. All we need is an aircraft. Problem is, my C-130's in the barn being painted," I told them. "We may have to contract out."

Actually, the closest C-130 belonged to the Air Farce's Air Morbidity Command and was down in Texas. I'd toyed with the idea earlier of requesting a drop from a C-141B out of Scott Air Force Base (there just happened to be one there; I'd checked), but Tell-Me-Dick had gotten the word out banning any flights involving me and Red Cell II. I have enough friends and strings to pull that I could have arranged it, but the crews' arses would have been exposed later on, and naked Air Farce butts are not a sight for sore eyes.

Besides, Trace had come back from her meet and greet with Tell-Me-Dick's personal credit card. I thought it might be poetic justice to charge the plane ride to him.

How many people do you think you can cram into a Cessna StationAir?

Well, the specs say six, but six is an awful lot of

people for any single-engine plane, especially when it's taking off from a grass runway, which is what Sky Acres turned out to be. Even four was tight when you toted up the gear we were lugging, but the way I drew up the plan we needed three people inside: Sean, Trace, and myself. Doc put his piloting skills to good use and I would say we cleared the fence at the end of the runway by a good six inches, if not seven.

"Next time we opt for the Turbo," muttered Doc, referring to the deluxe model. We hadn't been able to get it in under Telly's credit limit, unfortunately.

Jumps into an urban environment are not among the easiest ways to while away the nighttime hours, even going out of a C-141 or an MC-130 with high-tech locator gear and a handpicked air crew. The fact that we were jumping on a moonless night meant it would be hard for the security people below to see us, but that amounted to our only real advantage. The service ceiling on the Cessna is listed as 15,700 feet. Doc pushed her all the way to 18,000 feet to make sure the plane could not be heard from the ground. That kind of altitude is tough on a little engine, but the Cessna was up to it, inspired no doubt by Doc's mutterings and growls.

The airplane hadn't been configured for jumping, which made it difficult for us to go out all together. Sean and Trace leaned forward in what you might call a winged-frog pose before disappearing out of the cabin. It wasn't the prettiest jump ever, but it did accomplish its main purpose, which was getting the hell out of the aircraft. I followed about a half of a half tick behind, head down and arms back in a delta.

Sixteen thousand feet doesn't qualify as a high altitude jump, but it does give you time to think about where you're going. Depending on how fast your terminal velocity is, your free fall can last a minute and a half, which is a decent amount of time to kill. Some people have been known to roll over on their backs and count the stars on the way down. Gravity is an easy boss to work for; she doesn't give a shit whether you're facing ass upward or downward, just so long as you fall.

I spun back around and got myself oriented around five thousand feet. The truck lot was easy to see; it was the only thing in that part of the state ringed with floodlights. I was off course a bit, but with another delta and slight nudge of the shoulders, I had myself just about dead-on as I came through three thousand feet. I spotted a chute opening on the left about five hundred feet below me. I hunted to the right, watching for the second.

And watching. And watching.

It wasn't below me, either. Or above anywhere that I could see.

Shit.

A wave of relief shot through me as I spotted a black shadow on my right a few dozen feet above me, which was surprising, though technically not impossible. By now, I was at two thousand feet and it was time to pop the handle on my own rig. I did and got a perfect inflation above. But as I scanned the cells with a small Maglite I realized that the shadow I'd just seen was moving very quickly to my right. It looked to me like the lines had either twisted or started to twist. The thing to do in that situation is to try to untangle until, say, 2,000 feet, then break away and pull your reserve.

That's what you should do if you're an experienced jumper and can see what you're up to. Sean had neither advantage, and his maneuverings were increasing his speed downward as he plummeted toward the point where he couldn't cut loose and deploy his reserve.

Without thinking about how low I was—shit, I didn't *think* at all—I snapped free of my own main and tipped down into a delta. I intended on swooping down, grabbing Sean, deploying his reserve, and then jumping free and pulling mine.

That's a mouthful, and, even so, it's easier to say than do. By the time I got my body angled right, Sean had gained so much momentum I couldn't even see him. When I finally did spot him, I didn't think I could get him.

Then I *knew* I wasn't going to get him.

Then his twisted chute smacked the side of my face.

I hooked my arm under his like a Marine on shore patrol picking up a drunken sailor. He grabbed at me. (He swore later he thought he was rescuing *me.*) It took forever to get his chute free, and I nearly lost him when it snapped clean. But somehow I got one arm tangled in the strap at his chest and helped him deploy his backup. All this in the space of maybe a thousand feet of semi–free fall. Which translates into less time than it takes to spit, if my math is right.

Two heads may be better than one, but two parachutes aren't. I dropped free, tucked to the side, and deployed my reserve. I didn't have a chance to look at the altimeter, but given the shock to my knees when I landed, I'd say I deployed my own chute no higher than five hundred feet, and more likely half that. Steering was more a matter of praying than tugging, but since I am a pious lad, I hit square in the center of the landing zone.

On top of a trailer.

The metal roof took some of my fall, and I rolled on my side as I came down, so all in all it wouldn't have been bad if Sean hadn't landed right on top of me. His boot landed in my ribs and he thumped into my head, about as close to a controlled landing as Britney Spears is to being a virgin. As a parting shot, he dug his elbow into my ribs as he rolled to his feet.

Two hundred and something pounds worth of elbow.

"What are you homos doing?" Trace asked from the ground.

"Dancing," I told her. "So where are the guards?"

"Just the one back near the entrance. Looks like they're saving their energy for tomorrow."

"Dogs?"

"Already asleep," said Trace. She pointed down the aisle of parked trailers toward one of the mutts, who lay on his belly. Dobermans are cute when they're sleeping, especially if their nap has been induced by Demerol-laced hamburger.

The chutes we had cut away had sailed somewhere into the night, hopefully never to be seen again. We couldn't worry about them now, so Sean and I climbed down and got to work, setting our tags inside the trailer and then slapping pyrotechnic bags at the top.

In case you're wondering, the video cameras I'd spotted earlier were probably still working, and undoubtedly doing precisely what they were designed to do—keep an eye on the perimeter of the depot. There were none trained on the interior. Whoever had designed the security system didn't think there'd be many people dropping in during the middle of the night, which also accounted for the poor lighting in the vast center of the facility where we were.

Scary? Nah. You want to be scared? Go down to your kitchen and open up the food cabinets or pantry or wherever it is that you keep your eats. Jack open the refrigerator. (Grab a beer on me while you're at it.) How much of that stuff you figure travels in a tractor trailer at some point?

The answer you're looking for would be: just about all of it.

Now think of what would happen if, instead of Demo Dick and his band of Red Cell II warriors planting smoke bombs on the tops of the trailers, a group of thoroughly whacked individuals were lacing the trucks with food-borne viruses or bacteria? What if we went to the trailer that contained three hundred and twenty cases of aspirin and replaced those cases with ones of our own that included three random strychnine pills mixed in with the acetylsalicylic acid? Or injected the chickens in the refrigerated truck with botulism? Or replaced the Walkmen with ones rigged to explode in exactly one hundred forty-three hours?

I'm not Stephen King, so I'll stop with the horror stories. But the vulnerability of America's trucking industry—our lifeblood—is immense. It's not just the trucks you'd expect, the hazardous waste shipments or the chemical tankers. Sure, those things are vulnerable. But they're just icing on the cake. There were one hundred and thirty-three trailers with loads in that yard. Imagine each one with a time bomb rigged to explode three hours after the truck pulled out of the yard. Not a big bomb—just enough to blow up the trailer and the tanker and maybe the cars next to it. Imagine the traffic jams on the interstate? Imagine the downtown area at rush hour? Although airport security efforts get all the headlines, securing the nation's ports, waterways, coastline, and land assets are an important part of the Department of Transportation's mission. Some statistics to illustrate the areas of responsibility in the United States: we have 3.9 million miles of public roads, 122,000 miles of major railroads, and 2.1 million miles of pipelines, which carry combustible materials like crude oil, gasoline, and natural gas. There are 26,000 miles of commercial, navigable waters. Public transit systems account for 9.1 billion commuter trips each year. A total of 11.2 million trucks and 2.2 million railcars enter the country each year, while 7,500 foreign-flagged ships make 51,000 ports of call each year at the nation's 361 ports. There are 104 nuclear power plants, of which 63 are accessible by water. All these targets of opportunity make any SEAL giggle, especially a Red Cell–tasked SEAL.

Several of the trailers were equipped with interior electronic locks, and a couple even had fancy GPS reporting gear that could send a signal to a home base if they were tampered with. I hate electronics; they take the fun out of everything. In the past, you actually might have had a chance to get your hands dirty. Now, breaking into these trailers was a simple two-step process. First, Sean turned on a signal emulator, which could communicate with the satellite tracking system or block another GPS unit from communicating with it, depending on which way he flipped the switch. (Some locator units use cellular systems instead, but we didn't find any that night. Sean had another doodad for those.) Trace then set a pair of magnetic clips onto the wires coming from the electronic lock's keypad and attached the wires to a master unit, which sent the unlock code to the doors and brakes. The procedure took a grand total of thirty-five seconds on all but the first trailer, where Trace stopped to pet the sleeping dog. We packed little "gotcha boxes"—I'd wanted to do exploding jack-in-the-boxes but hadn't thought of it in time—into the trucks and resealed them. I suppose if we'd wanted to we could have moved the trailers around the yard for a bit of fun. Even better would have been coming across one of those new systems from an outfit called Vehicle Enhancement Systems over in South Carolina, which hooks the inside of the trailer up with an infrared camera. The idea of mooning the boss is kind of hard to resist.

Thank God there were still a few old-fashioned padlocks holding some of the trailer doors closed.

Not that they presented much more of a challenge. It just warmed the traditionalist in me to see locks I learned to pick back in junior high still in use. By the time we had everything set my watch was just notching 0530. We took a break between a pair of diesel tractors that had been set out to pasture. Trace had brought a thermos of coffee and some cups, and we shared a jolt before moving on to phase two.

The video monitors were observed at a small security shack adjacent to a metal warehouse building toward the front of the facility. There was one guard in the shack and no outside security except for the snoozing dogs. The Guardsmen were across town at a vacant college dorm. Not that I can blame the Guardsmen for preferring mattresses to macadam; if you're going to have a wet dream, best to have one on something soft. But it would have been a sneeze or two tougher to spray-paint "Gotcha" on the side of the trailer had there been a few soldiers mumbling in their sleep nearby, especially since the cans of the so-called "invisible" paint—visible only under black light once it dried—had small metal balls inside that made a hell of a racket when you shook them.

Then again, a company or two of soldiers milling around would have provoked the vandal in me, leading to all sorts of juvenile behavior. Here I was content to leave the message on the door and retreat to the parking area, waiting for the morning patrol to arrive. It was now 0600, and as our battle plan called for us to remain in place until 0900, I had a notion of finding a little hooch-away and taking a nap for a few hours. But before I could find a spot, Sean came back from his walk-around and told me there was something going on near the warehouse that I had to see. We made our way toward it just in time to see three human gorillas making their way from the back of one of the trailers, each carrying large boxes in their arms. They walked with the boxes around the side of another trailer. Unlike the first trailer, this one wasn't hooked to a tractor.

"Shrinkage?" asked Trace.

"I say we stop it," said Sean. It was the law enforcement officer in him.

I waited a minute or so, watching as they came back to the trailer. They were wearing dark clothes and working without lights, but it was at least theoretically possible that they were warehouse workers simply moving a load from one truck to another.

I'm not a big theorist myself, but it *was* possible.

Nah.

"Dickie says let's do it," I whispered finally, getting out of my crouch and trotting up to the trailer after the last of the trio disappeared around the corner. I peered in from the side, not sure if they had a companion in the back.

They didn't. They had two.

The one nearest me didn't see a thing. The other one may have, because he started to react as I grabbed the ankle of his comrade and jerked him to the left. Stooge Number One fell backward into Stooge Number Two. I leapt up and put my heel into the face of the man I'd tripped. The second guy played dead and I went along with his game, giving him a gentle love tap in the ribs with the front of my foot before collapsing his cheekbone with the instep of my right foot.

They say the instep is the hardest part of the foot. Someday I'll have to conduct some experiments and find out. I can say that I got good loft on the kick. Stooge Number Two rose a good sixteen inches off the floor of the trailer.

"You should have saved one of them for me," said Sean, pulling himself up into the back of the truck as I dragged the men back.

I put my finger to my lips, not sure whether the others would have heard the commotion. We off-loaded the two goons, dragging them around to the front of the truck, where Trace lashed their arms together and tore gags from their pants. Interestingly enough, they shared the same tailor. Their clothes weren't black but dark blue, with little pocket emblems bearing the name of the establishment.

Sean and I slipped back to the trailer just as the lead gorilla got there. I'm calling these guys gorillas for a reason—they were. Sean's a *big* boy, and I'm no shrimp, but the shortest of the trio had at least an inch on my sidekick. Not that that would have stopped Sean; he was aching to feel the smack of flesh against his knuckles. I held him back, hoping to hear the jokers talk.

But they didn't. Instead, they continued to work as before, ignoring the fact that the two men who'd been helping them before were missing. Maybe they thought the pair went to take a leak or something. Maybe simians aren't as smart as scientists say. Anyway, I waited until the trio had strung out, then sprung on the man at the end of the line. Between my chokehold and as sharp a punch to the kidneys as I'd landed in a while, he folded instantly.

Instantly wasn't quite fast enough. His two companions threw down their boxes and raced back. I looked up as they were turning the corner ten feet away.

Two on two would have been a fair enough fight. They had a weight and height advantage, but we had them on IQs at least four to one.

The MAC-10 the thug on the right held threw the odds somewhat.

Sean apparently spotted the gun before I did. Ever the gun lover, he jumped at the opportunity to take a close look at it, launching himself toward the weapon. The submachine gun went flying in the dust along with the gorilla.

Which left me and Goon Number Three to waltz together.

He must've studied Tae Kwon Do or a similar Oriental art, because he made the most god-awful yelp as he ran toward me. He made an even worse sound as I sidestepped him and gave him a nut adjuster, courtesy of my knee. Give his gonads credit, though. He didn't go down right away. He puked first. Two good thumps on the temple laid him flat. When I looked up, Sean stood triumphantly over Gorilla Number Two, holding the MAC-10 in his hands.

"This gun's illegal," he said. "We can charge him with a federal offense."

"Thank you, Mrs. Clinton. Haven't you heard of the Second Amendment?"

In the back of my mind, I'd been wondering if

these scumbags were terrorists rather than thieves. They were all wearing uniforms that indicated they worked at the depot. If I were a terrorist worried about being caught, I might don just such a disguise before clearing out a truck and loading it with goodies. Or if I were truly diligent, I might infiltrate the organization, chill there a few months, then do my dirty work.

Yes, there are diligent terrorists.

I was thinking about the railroad incident, where I and my merry band of warriors had foiled an attack through no fault of our own. Not that that kind of coincidence doesn't happen, and not that I'm not damn glad to take the bow for Lady Luck's handiwork, but to say the coincidence bothered me is to say the Grand Canyon's a ditch.

And now here was *coincidink* number two. Unfortunately, there was no way to find out who the men were. The quintet might have been terrorists; they might also have been a jazz band moonlighting for extra cash. More likely they were just run-of-the-mill asshole thieves. Interrogation would have to wait until they returned to a wakeful state and regained whatever limited use of their brains they had been blessed with. We trussed 'em and then moved them to the trailer where they had been hauling the boxes earlier. They were heavy mothers; fortunately, the fight had limbered me up or I might have pulled something.

And in the boxes?

"Baseball cards," announced Sean.

"Oh, bullshit on that," said Trace, jumping up to look for herself.

But that's what they were. Cases of baseball cards. We'd broken up a ring of desperate sports nuts.

"Bit of a switch from nuclear detonators," I told them. Sometimes all you have is your sense of humor.

We looked over the boxes and made sure that they weren't hiding anything else. They weren't. It was now nearly 0700, so we secured the truck and the twerps, then went back to our regularly scheduled operation. We scouted around the area, making sure our commotion hadn't caught anyone's attention, and then worked our way back to the clutch of older trailers across from the two Hummers.

A few minutes later, all three of us dove under one of the older trailers as a Humvee and a pair of M-809 five-ton 6x6 cargo trucks drove up and parked nearby. A dozen soldiers piled out of the back, shambling around as they took up posts and began walking in what I guess were supposed to be sentry patrols at the front of the area, about five or ten yards away.

Now came the hardest part of our mission: doing nothing for close to an hour. SpecWar is filled with long pauses, and dealing with them is the one thing that you really can't learn in training. The instructors can teach you to tread water in the ocean and count flies in the jungle, but the really hard job of sitting next to a truck tire for hours while your knee cramps, your nose fills up with snot and dust, and two armed guards are telling very bad blonde jokes a few feet away—that's something you have to learn by doing.

It would have been different if the jokes were funny.

Just when I was thinking I'd have to practice my silent takedown technique, a major came up and chewed them out for a uniform deficiency, jawboning about how the VIPs were due any minute and how the unit had better look damn good, because Washington was interested and the colonel has his eye on you, son—yes, *you!* You never heard such bullshit in your life, and I wish I could say the same for myself. But this is the kind of shit the modern fighting man has to put up with—bullshit about whether his shirt is tucked into his pants right, how important PR is to the big picture, and on and on. Meanwhile, the powers that be can't even get the right stinking oil for a soldier to clean his weapon with.

But those slobs' loss was our gain. The major ordered them into better positions fifty yards away—probably so the light would glint off their eyes just right when the TV cameras showed up—and Sean, Trace, and I got a chance to stretch our legs.

"Better make sure all your buttons are squared away," said Trace. "That major'll write us up."

We didn't have much time to laugh. The major's full-of-himself strut once more filled the air as he scraped his boots in our direction. We rolled flat against the ground just as he marched up with an entire detail in tow. I don't know what they looked like above the knee, but I can tell you they sounded impressive. The feet slapped down hard and exactly in step, and there was a double snap and a brisk *"Hoorah!"* at the end.

"Great. We got it. Thanks," yapped someone at the far end. The voice sounded suspiciously like the sort of thing that would come from the mouth of a director or a news videographer.

Tell-Me-Dick was protecting a truck depot with a set of parade ground soldiers. Nothing against the men ordered to do the marching, you understand. An order is a fucking order, asinine or not. But what was the purpose of this drill? Security? Or looking good on the six o'clock news?

Stupid question. But I had to ask.

As the squad began to leave, Sean gave me a light tap in the kidney to let me know it was time to move on to phase three. After I got my breath back—the kid's knuckles are made out of brass—I crawled out to the far end and got up, heading immediately for the Humvee near the security shack. Trace and Sean circled around.

Two Guardsmen were standing near the Hummer. Both men had rifles. It appeared that they had been belatedly posted to guard the security shack. Better late than never, I guess.

"This'll do," I said loudly. I made sure I had eye contact with one of the soldiers, then spun on my heel. My uniform had come equipped with the leafy things majors wear, but the growl in my throat was all the rank I needed. "Where the *hell* are you two, damn it? *Jeee-zuz-H-Cripe-shit!*"

With that, Trace and Sean double-timed forward. I hope my cursing sounded Army-like enough. Standards are different among the services, but I like to think we can all get together on four-letter words.

"Why the *hell* is it that *evvv-errry* time I'm ready to go somewhere, my people are somewhere else?"

"Sir, sorry, sir," said Sean, hamming it up in the fawning tone of a private with maybe six days of experience. I don't think even the Army has such smarmy soldiers, but once Sean gets into character it's hard to get him out. As he snapped to attention, he nearly popped a button. The uniform Danny had procured for him was just a tad tight around the chest.

"You, Dahlgren, you drive. Mako—in the fucking Hummer. *Now, soldier!*"

"Sir, yes, sir."

Fucker thought he was Brad Pitt.

I turned slowly to give the two nearby guards a stay-in-place glower. If either of them had any thought of challenging me, it died right there. I strutted around to the passenger side and pulled open the door, sliding into my seat.

"Why the fuck isn't the engine started, Trace?" I whispered, staring again at the guards.

"Something's screwed up. I can't get it to work."

"I thought you checked it earlier."

"I did." She started kicking something under the dashboard. "It *should* work."

We had reached the stage of the operation that warms all warriors' hearts: SNAFU, or Situation Normal—All Fucked Up.

The door to the trailer opened. Two suits and the major we'd seen earlier came out, followed by six more suits—all of them packing, if the bulges beneath their sport coats were to be believed. Three more military uniforms passed through the door, sergeants and specialists, then a full-bird colonel and two lieutenants. I can't imagine that the trailer possibly held all of those people; it must've been some sort of circus trick.

I studied the colonel's profile, but it was clear at first glance that it wasn't Telly; the man was walking and talking at the same time.

"Patrol at three o'clock," hissed Sean from the backseat. "Checking IDs against a clipboard list."

"Maybe we can borrow their car," I said.

No sooner were the words out of my mouth than the Hummer roared to life. Trace threw it into reverse so quickly it stalled.

Ah, the next stage of the operation: TARFU—Things Are Really Fucked Up. I was starting to feel right at home.

Just then, the drone of a small airplane overhead turned everyone's head. Trace got the Hummer going again and wheeled us around toward the entrance.

"Doc's got a way with timing," she said.

"Too bad," I said. "I was considering taking the colonel out for breakfast."

"He looks like he oughta lay off the donuts," said Trace.

"Good point."

"Did I tell you that you look good in an Army uniform?"

"I'll get you for that."

The guards at the gate had been augmented by a dozen soldiers and a full range of high-tech doodads. Told to be ready for someone trying to come *into* the facility, they were more than accommodating to anyone who wanted to leave. They couldn't get the gate open fast enough.

We passed through at exactly 0900:15. I like to be punctual; those fifteen seconds really hurt.

We rendezvoused with the rest of the team at a place called Alice's Diner, which served the thickest blueberry pancakes I've ever seen outside of Arkansas. I was surprised to find Doc sitting in the booth when we came in, still dressed in our borrowed BDUs.

"You got back fast," I told him.

"How's that?"

"That wasn't you in the airplane?"

"Last night?"

"This morning, back at the field. A small plane buzzed the truck depot."

"Wasn't me," said Doc.

"Next time I'll try to screw up just for them."

"I expect they'll appreciate it."

We gave Tell-Me-Dick time to run his men around and work off their excess energy before returning to the scene of the infiltration. When we arrived, Danny and Hulk were sitting on the hood of their rented car across from the front gate, staring at the business end of a 25mm cannon. The gun was mounted on a Bradley Fighting Vehicle—the tank wannabe that replaced the M113 armored troop taxi the Army used over in Vietnam. The Bradley was parked in the middle of the truck depot's driveway, and definitely had the Toyota overmatched. Fifty feet behind it, a line of trucks snaked back toward the buildings; Tell-Me-Dick had stopped all traffic out, apparently as part of the exercise.

"What the hell are you doing, Marcinko? Give up already?" he squawked when he finally ambled over with his lapdogs a few minutes after we got there.

Tell-Me-Dick lorded it over me for a while, going on and on about how tough his defenses were, how he had the whole place set, and how I was just a washed-up, never-had-been Vietnam vet who had probably lost a few zillion brain cells to Agent Orange and never saw a chain of command I didn't trip over—that sort of thing. I couldn't argue with him, though it would have been nice if he could have said it all without spitting. If you're going to brag, at least be dry about it.

When he finally stopped for a breath, a worried look came over his face, sneaking in from the side of his eyes.

"You're not saying anything," he told me.

"You pretty much said it all," I told him.

He did a screwy thing with his eyes, as if he could shift the focus somehow and look into my skull.

"Well, are your people attacking the place or not?" he said. He glanced at his watch. "It's half-past ten. The operation was supposed to start at nine."

"Did we say start at nine?"

"Nine o'clock, yes."

"*Start* at nine?"

"Well, it doesn't have to start *exactly* at nine. Let's get going."

"So it doesn't have to start at nine?" I asked, as if

Tell-Me-Dick had just provided me with the secret recipe for slicing bread. "It doesn't?"

"No."

"But it could."

"Not now, damn it!" His face had begun shading red.

"Tell me, Dick," I said. "How are we supposed to attack with a Bradley Fighting Vehicle staring us in the face?"

"We do have a Bradley, don't we?" The haughtiness returned to his voice. "You didn't *expect* a Bradley, did you?"

"I can honestly say I didn't. You're more the M1A1 type."

His smile flickered, but only for a second. "You're not planning anything now, are you?"

"My whole team's here," I said, gesturing. "Tell me, Dick, how could I do anything now?"

He turned and glanced around. "Miss Dahlgren, is something up?"

Trace gave him the innocent schoolgirl shrug. "Up?"

Tell-Me-Dick walked back to the phalanx of ass-kissers he had waiting back by the gate and gave the order to let the trucks and trailers through.

"Tell me, Dick!" I yelled to him as the trucks began clearing the gate. "You do read, right?"

I guess he might not have been able to hear what I said, because he walked all the way back over to where I was standing.

"The paper," I said. "Do you read it?"

"Of course I read the paper."

"You read it today?"

"Front to back."

"You might look at page three," I told him, handing him a copy I'd brought along.

Tell-Me-Dick opened up the paper and stared at the full-page advertisement Trace had ordered the afternoon before, right after our planning session. There wasn't much to it.

"Today's Homeland Security Operation will be conducted at or around 9 A.M.," the ad began.

That was in 72-point type, which is pretty big.

"'At or around' doesn't mean *starts,*" the ad continued.

That was in 96-point type, which is bigger.

"In fact," the ad concluded, "it means *ends,* because that's when we're going through the gate."

That was in 104-point type, which the people at the paper said was the biggest type they'd ever used since V-J Day.

I know Dick was reading the ad because his lips were moving. He seemed confused when he looked up. I might have asked which word he didn't understand, except that at that moment the first trailer was let through the gate. The firework pack we'd planted on the top ignited, set off by its proximity to the transponder in the Toyota. Bottle rockets and Roman candles began exploding all over the place. Tell-Me-Dick threw himself to the ground as the fireworks began playing a Souza tune composed entirely of *sha-bams*.

Wonderful what they can do with gunpowder these days.

I probably would have started laughing, but two

seconds after the song ended there was a loud explosion behind me. Two things occurred to me as the blast shoved me to the ground.

One was that what had just exploded was not one of our firecracker packages.

The other was that I had just been out-Marcinkoed by somebody. Which made kissing the dirt all the more humiliating.

4

Here's something you can say for bank layoffs: it lessens the number of potential victims when scumbags set off a pile of explosives at the ATM machine outside the building. In this case, if the bank hadn't been closed, the bomb would have killed the manager, whose office was right behind the machine. Whether that would have been a good thing I guess depends on your opinion of the banking industry.

I ran over to the bank with Danny and Trace to find out if anyone was hurt. We scrambled inside, sidearms drawn, mouths covered against the dust. Taped to the door of the bank manager's office was an eight-by-ten glossy of yours truly. It wasn't a bad likeness—a little grainy, maybe. It had been taken just a few days before, back in Iowa at the hospital we'd taken over during the exercise. The person who'd posted it here had even gone to the trouble of touching it up, coloring in my front teeth.

Not that I take that sort of thing personally. The fact that it was suspended by a knife, which went right through my cheekbone and ruined the perspective—that kind of pissed me off a little.

Trace was going to pull the knife out, but I stopped her.

"I doubt there are prints," I told her. "But let's give the crime scene people something to do."

"This," said Doc, holding up a piece of cloth, "is from a satchel charge. Very similar to what a frogman might have used back in the day."

"Similar or the same?"

"I doubt it's really that old," said Doc. "I don't know how long that explosive'll last, but I doubt it would be stable after thirty years. Lab might be able to figure it out. My guess is that it's the same sort of thing we found on the railroad bridge. Only this one went off."

While we poked around the bank area, Sean went with Danny to alert the locals to the lugs we'd trussed in the trailer. Danny, turning on his police-style charm, got in on the "interviews." Danny has his own personal style of persuasion which the locals could no doubt appreciate, but I doubted they had anything to do with the bomb. The person or people who did were into much more important things than baseball cards. They were playing with my head, or trying to. That part didn't bother me—I'm too fuckin' old to be psyched out by some asshole who knows how to use a camera or cook up some old-fashioned explosives. But the fact that they'd gotten close enough to take a picture without me knowing it—the fact that they had obviously piped into my operation and figured out what I was doing—that shit bothered the hell out of me.

The question was: what the fuck was I going to do about it?

The video cameras closest to the ATM couldn't see across the street to the bank. According to what Danny told me after chatting up the investigators, the police were working on the theory that the bomb had been planted by someone local with a grudge. I dismissed that outright. Someone local wouldn't have gone to Iowa to take my picture. And, while my presence in Iowa and here hadn't exactly been code-word secret, my strike on the train *had* been a surprise. We'd indicated only that we were going to strike in a hundred-mile area of the state. Much as I wanted to blame Tell-Me-Dick for a leak, it seemed more likely that the information had come from someone who worked for me.

It was possible that one of my shooters—*my* shooters—was the bad guy. I didn't want to think that. I certainly *didn't* think that about Doc or Danny or Trace. The first two had sweated with me through shit—brown, black, and purple; no way they were selling me out. I hadn't known Trace for as long as the others, but I'd known her in a way I didn't know the others, so I could rule her out as well. Ditto for Karen, who hadn't known the operational details, anyway.

Sean and the Hulk, though, had to be considered prime candidates. Both had gone through security checks and screening up the yaya, both had been SEALs, both had come highly vouched for and proven themselves under fire . . . but relying on them now would be foolish. In my judgment, neither one of them was a traitor or a fuckhead. But could I trust my judgment?

Reader, take note: here I was, Demo Dick, Rogue

fucking Warrior, *the* top SpecWarrior in the world, and I was not only doubting my own team, but I was questioning my judgment. Nobody had seen more shit than I had in the past thirty odd years—not a brag, a fact of life, boys and girls. You've seen the resumé. If anybody should have been sure of himself, it was me. But I did have doubts—not enough to run away and hide, not enough to check out the latest designer drugs for head control, but questions about who I could trust and how I was calling the shots. And *that* is the point of SpecWar. That's why you don't just blow up the depot behind the lines; you screw with the enemy's head. *That* is the point of the spear.

Whoever was doing this was good. I had to give the cocksuckers that.

Along with everything else I wanted to give them, I had to give them that.

The media's interpretation of the incident, apparently based on minutes of investigative reporting:

HOMELAND SECURITY EXERCISE FOILS WOULD-BE BANK ROBBERY.

If I thought Tell-Me-Dick could spell, I'd swear he wrote the news stories himself.

The five thugs we'd found inside the truck yard turned out to be exactly that—thugs. Two of them had an arrest record about as thick as this book—and each one had a job at the truck yard. They hadn't donned uniforms to sneak through security; they were helping provide it. All were minimum-wage workers who were supposed to "float" between security and box shuffling. They supplemented their less-than-living wage by requisitioning a few extra loads once a week. One had a real sob story about how his mom needed an operation. Really might've pulled the ol' heartstrings if the orphanage hadn't called asking when he'd be home for dinner. The mastermind apparently had a brother-in-law in Michigan who sold collectibles at shows across the country. If you added all of their IQs together the number still wouldn't top the speed limit, but the real genius was the idiot who hired them without background checks.

I'd realized pretty much from the start that they weren't involved in the bank bomb incident, nor did they play a role in any of the Rogue's further adventures, but it does tell you what sort of people are safeguarding your rice crispies and shampoo.

Danny stayed behind in hopes he might dig up a little intelligence based on the bank job. The rest of us headed back East as originally scheduled, though we mixed up our travel plans for security purposes. We left the plane reservations at O'Hare in place and rented other cars to drive to Missouri, where Trace had located a feeder airport where we could catch random connections out. Doc and I spent a little time together on the road trying to pry the situation apart.

"Who'd like to fry your ass?" he asked.

"Hell of a long list. Starts in Nam and ends with Tell-Me-Dick. Could be about a zillion people."

Realistically speaking, the list was considerably shorter. A lot of the people with reason to hate my guts were long gone or didn't even know who the hell I was, especially those in southeastern Asia. And as much as they might dislike me, very few Navy people harbored true homicidal intentions or the will to carry them out. They may have wanted to kill me, but in most cases their respect for the law would outweigh their wish for revenge. It was the story of their lives. Not mine, but theirs.

Still, if you took out all the people who were gone or lived too far away or liked to clean their fingernails first thing in the morning, there would be well over a thousand people left. I guess that's the problem with getting old. So many shitheads want to kick your ass you start to lose track.

"IRA might be likely," suggested Doc. "They like to blow up things. Satchel charges would be right up their alley. And they hold grudges."

I'd crossed M16s with the IRA in the past—check the details in *Detachment Bravo* for the whole story—but this didn't have the Irish ring to it. They would have used better explosives. They also weren't big on head games. If they wanted revenge, they just killed you.

"We used C-3 in Vietnam," suggested Doc.

"That's what they want us to think," I told him. "That's too obvious. I think it's a blind."

"You're the guy who lives by the KISS principle."

"True."

"You think we got a fink?" said Doc.

You work with people long enough and you

start to share their thoughts—or at least their paranoias. But I guess I still wanted to believe that the people close to me weren't scumbags.

"We may have made a mistake that let whoever's behind this know what we were up to during the sneak and peeks," I told him. "I don't like to admit it, but it's possible. I've been known to fuck up from time to time."

"What was the story with Sean's parachute? You think it was sabotaged?"

Honest to God, until that moment I hadn't thought that it had been sabotaged. It wasn't likely, but I should have thought about it, if only to dismiss it.

So maybe I did have reason to doubt myself. Maybe I was becoming like Pinky, aka Rear Admiral Pinckney Prescott, whose fat butt I had routinely kicked—figuratively speaking, of course—when the original Red Cell fell under his theoretical command. Sobering fucking thought. If I thought it were true, I'd have to do the honorable thing and find a ship to go down on.

I stared at the road a while, replaying the sequence of events.

"The lines got tangled," I told Doc. "It happens. If you're not a very experienced jumper, you can make it worse."

"Sean's done night jumps."

"Not in a while. Wouldn't they have gotten me?"

"Maybe they want to dangle you in front of the cat for a while."

We pack our own chutes, but anyone on the

team might have had access to them. And there were times during the past week when the gear was unattended. Locks could be gotten around. But if you were going to screw with a parachute, the most logical thing to do would be to *really* screw with it—scrape the lines so they'd break, or get vicious and muck up the cells. A line tangle by itself won't guarantee a fatality.

Besides, tangles happen. They shouldn't, but they do.

Maybe it had been a preemptive play by Sean to take suspicion off himself. If so, it had been very subtle—so subtle it might not have worked. But if he knew about it and he had the backup chute ready, it was better to be subtle, wasn't it?

"What's your opinion of Sean?" I asked Doc.

"Good kid. Still a bit of a kid, if you know what I mean. You know him better than I do, Dick. What do you think?"

I thought he was solid. "What about Hulk?" I asked.

"Bigger, a little slower. Otherwise about the same. Younger breed. They think a little longer before they pull the trigger, if you know what I mean. It's not a bad thing. It's just different from us."

I couldn't disagree. It wasn't a knock, just a statement of fact.

"I don't think they're cocksuckers, if that's what you mean," added Doc.

"Yeah."

I didn't think they were scumbags, either, and I knew that they didn't have anything personally against me, certainly not enough to want to frag me.

I can be a prick and I'm the first to admit it. I run my team hard; it's the only way to do it. But on a personal level, I'm not *that* hard to get along with, as long as you're not trying to give me orders. I still remember what it's like to be a grunt, and, to the best of my ability, I attempt to make it easier by stripping away the bullshit.

"What do you think about hanging around and seeing if there's anything new about the headless horseman we found in the water the other night?" I asked Doc. "Talk to the medical people, the coroner, see what exactly they think. I have some hand-holding back East I have to take care of before we head up to New Jersey and New York for the exercises there."

We had Red Cell II gigs planned at a container port in Jersey and a nuke plant up the Hudson River north of New York City in a week. I wanted to proceed as if I didn't think I had someone looking over my shoulder. With luck, this would prompt whoever was trying to fuck with me to keep coming. I'd nail the SOB between the eyes.

"Sure, I'll do it, Dick."

"You sure you're up for this, Doc?" I asked. "Donna'll never forgive me if you break a toenail or something."

"Fuck you, Cock Breath."

"Your terms of endearment go right to my heart."

"And the horse you rode in on, asshole."

"What the *hell* is going on?"

Those were the first words out of Karen's mouth

when she met me in the terminal of Ronald Reagan Airport back home.

"Lovely to see you, too," I told her.

Karen started to say something else, but I demonstrated that her tongue could be put to much better use. Realizing I was right but refusing to surrender on my unconditional terms, she frisked me for weapons.

"I missed you," she said after a thorough search. She slipped out of my arms and went back to work for the government. "Now, what the *hell* is going on?"

I got her to agree that an airport terminal was hardly the place to discuss security operations, past or present, and she agreed to head over to Rogue Manor for an executive session. I had Sean and Hulk ride with Karen in her car and took Trace with me in a rental. Somehow, when the time came to present the credit card, Tell-Me-Dick's plastic popped out of my wallet.

There was a time when Rogue Manor was located in the bucolic countryside. The house hasn't moved, but the countryside sure has. There are nine new traffic lights since I bought the place, and if I had a dollar for every bulldozer on a flatbed I've spotted going down the road I'd be a rich man. The worst thing about the traffic is that every eighth or ninth driver has his head up his ass and wants the world to know it. We nearly got sideswiped by a Honda Accord about a mile from the house. It was so close that Trace jumped up in the seat, Beretta ready.

"You can't shoot him," I told her. "Unsafe lane

changes are only a two-point violation in this state."

"Just getting paranoid, I guess."

"I know the feeling."

I'd already contacted a few old friends and had them en route to beef up security arrangements at Rogue Manor. I'd also asked a friend at DIA (the Defense Intelligence Agency, aka Dirtbags, Idiots & Assholes) to backtrack my two new shooters and make sure their shit didn't stink. We had planned to work out a few new recruits before heading north, and Trace wanted to know whether to proceed with those plans in light of the present situation.

"Definitely, if you're comfortable with it," I told her.

"I'd prefer working off campus," she suggested. "In case something fucks up. Can we rent that tent at Quantico?"

Quantico is a big Marine base that kinda sorta backs up to Rogue Manor, if you ignore the wilderness and housing developments in the way. The base commandant and I are acquainted—a good sod for a jarhead—and Rogue Warrior Inc. had made use of some of the facilities there before. I agreed that it was a good idea and left it with her to handle the arrangements. Trace may be young but she's old school. Give her an assignment and you don't hear about it until it's done, and even then it's a bullet summary that rarely goes beyond came-saw-conquered.

The resident canine security patrol gave us an enthusiastic welcome as we pulled up at Rogue Manor. The dogs, being dogs—and male—gave the women a good sniffing and the men wary barks.

Can't say as I blame them, though I finally did have to order them away from the ladies or we'd never have gotten into the house.

A hearty glass of Bombay Sapphire later, I had filled Karen in on all that had happened in the Midwest. She, in turn, briefed me on the still-evolving situation inside the Beltway. Colonel Dickless Telly had been telling anyone and everyone that Fucking Dick Marcinko and the Red Cell II project were a serious threat to life and limb. We had almost poisoned an entire Midwest town and blown up a bank, and if we weren't stopped soon, who knows what further horrors we would wreak.

A group of terrorists had managed to get close to two operations in two different states under his jurisdiction, but *I* was the problem.

"What's the latest on my Topless Tango?" I asked, pouring myself a refresher.

"FBI thinks it was a local dispute," she said.

"They have an ID?"

"No."

"Doc thought he might be Asian." He'd left a message to that effect on my cell phone, adding that he still had a posse of people to talk to and planned on getting more definitive information. "If that's true, then the local-dispute theory doesn't make much sense. Not that it makes much sense, anyway."

"There *are* Asian-Americans in Middle America, Dick." She was using her PC tone. "It could be some sort of Chinese gang."

"If it were California, New York, even D.C., I might be inclined to agree. But how many Asian gangs are operating in Flyover Land?" I hate stating the obvious, but somebody has to. "What about the bridge and the explosives? Anything new on that?"

"The FBI claims they're bringing people in for interrogations. They've sent out a team of experts to consult."

Bureauspeak for: *we have no fucking clue what the hell is going on.*

"Dinner is served," announced Trace, who had made herself useful in the interim, sizzling some sirloins.

Sean and Hulk were as frisky as the dogs outside and twice as hungry. The food made them positively loquacious. Sean regaled us with stories about his days on SEAL Team Two, which happens to be one of my alma maters. Even Hulk managed more than his usual grunts. Trace threw in a few stories about "the funny unit"—the sole Army Delta team that includes women (it doesn't officially exist, but then, neither does Delta). It was a regular bacchanalia of bullshit, well lubricated by meat and spirits.

Karen had expressed a proper amount of professional concern when I detailed the personal nature of my find at the bank on the last job. She expressed her concern in a less professional manner a few hours later when we held an executive session in the hot tub. There's nothing like hot water and a hotter woman to ease the aches and pains of a deployment. We did our own version of the SEAL workout to further unwind. Afterward, I had the best rest I'd had in weeks. By the time I woke in the morning, Karen was already dressed for work. She had an early breakfast meeting at the Capitol, and even my powers of persuasion couldn't get her to delay her plans in favor of some early-morning maneuvers.

After she left, I checked the email and my website, looking to see if any of the intel feelers I'd sent out the night before had brought anything back. The long and the short of it was: no. It was too early to use the phone, so after doing my reps on the weight bench outside I grabbed my H&K P7M8 and went to pop a few caps on the range out back. The pistol has been with me a while, and although I truly believe a gun is just a gun and there's nothing metaphysical or romantic about it, the pistol's familiar snap as I squeezed off caps had a reassuring feel to it. There's nothing like the smell of cordite and black coffee in your nose to get the day off to a good start.

Even the dogs seemed to appreciate the company as I jogged with them around the perimeter, inspecting the premises even more carefully than normal. I have other security arrangements—I'm not going to detail them here for obvious reasons—but I think the canines are the most dependable part of the system. They've been trained not to fall for the poisoned-meat routine, and the only way an intruder would get the better of them would be to shoot them. Even then, I'm not sure they'd give up.

Back in the house, I got the blender to work on a fresh juice combination (pineapple, pulpy orange, apple, strawberries, and banana for the ape in me), getting it all pretty in my glass before wolfing it down. Thing sounds like a New Age concoction channeled in from an Indian Yogi, but I actually learned how to make it from some of the young turks on SEAL Team Six. They've learned a few things about nutrition since my day, and I have to give them credit there. Besides being good for you, the thick juice blend sticks to your ribs.

Around eight, Trace wandered in for a little light workout action before grinding down the nuggets. "Well you're not dead," she said as she barged into the kitchen. As always, lovely in the morning.

Being away from Rogue Manor and my various business situations for more than a week left me with a lot of catching up to do. After PT and a little weight-pile moving to keep my muscles honest, I left Trace to her own devices and retired to my office, where I began working my safety net: the informal intelligence connections that not only told me what the hell was going on but kept my ass from being fried too badly by the bozos with the flamethrowers inside the Beltway.

Irish Kernan began life in Noo Yawk. Then, to show the world how tough he really was, he became a Marine. He retired as a colonel but couldn't break the government habit and found a job at the DIA, where his specialty was gathering tactical intelligence and drinking beer, not necessarily in that order. I'd met him at the Air Force Air Command and Staff College back in 1978, and we'd been friends ever since.

"Hey, Dirtbag," I told him when I finally got past the phone menu and found him not only in his office but answering the phone. Maybe he mistook it for his watch. "How about some lunch?"

"Can't stop for lunch. We'll have dinner," he

said. "Prelim word on your guys is that they're clean. I'm getting you a list of people who've worked alongside them. Some of your Christian friends say Sean saved one of their PMs in Afghanistan by running through a minefield."

"I already know my people are dumb," I told him. "I just want to make sure they're as dumb as I think."

"The proof is that they're working for you. We're going over the nugget list Trace sent, too. So what's this all about?"

I gave him some details on our operations and the fun we'd had in Missouri and Illinois, then asked if he could reciprocate. Neither state played very high in the various alerts, estimates, and briefings on threats that floated across his desk. The states didn't hit the radar with any of my other sources, either. Most of the action and attention was focused on the two coasts.

Al Qaeda came up in a lot of the conversations. It always does. Al Qaeda is the big bad wolf that you talk about when you can't come up with anything else.

"Possibly funded by al Qaeda."

"A link to a suspected al Qaeda member."

"A pattern that suggests al Qaeda."

Don't get me wrong. The raghead slimebuckets have one of the most successful terrorist organizations in the world—well-funded, well-led, extremely disciplined. Bin Laden, aka Been Ladding, is a psychopath, but he's a brilliant psychopath. And rich, which doesn't hurt. Still, it's become almost SOP to stamp the group's name on every rumor and memo that goes into the system. Maybe it helps the case officers get their vouchers approved, I don't know. But it sure doesn't provide any real intelligence.

The long and the short of the briefing: there were more than a thousand files corresponding to suspected terrorist cells in the areas where we'd staged our drills, and not one of them represented anything tangible. I found pretty much the same thing from the other sources I probed.

I was just about ready to come up for air when Doc checked in with the latest.

"Who do you know in Belgium?" he asked.

"Couple of people with Eurocorps and NATO," I told him.

You're probably familiar with NATO. Eurocorps is kind of a mini-NATO designed by the French and Germans originally to bury the hatchet over World War II thirty years after the fact, and it's evolved into a kind of rapid response force, Europe's pale version of the 101st Airborne, without parachutes. Eurocorps personnel look good in parades. The Belgians have a couple of mechanized brigades that are part of a rapid response force, and the last time I checked, the head of Eurocorps' Navy representation at headquarters was a Belgian. History hasn't been particularly kind to the Belgians, whose country was perfectly positioned to play doormat in World War I and World War II. They were ferocious fighters, but they still got the shit kicked out of them by the Krauts.

"Anybody with the Belgian customs office?" asked Doc.

"I can work on that. What's up?"

Doc explained that the body was believed to be that of a Belgian businessman—not from any positive ID, as the head and hands were still missing, but because an intrepid police officer checking area motels found that a Belgian businessman had skipped town without paying his bill or collecting his clothes. Doc had managed to talk his way into the motel room, and by his estimate, the dead body and the missing Belgian could have shared the same size 36 short sport coat. He'd convinced the motel manager to let us see the phone records—the manager was a Navy man who'd gone out as a chief petty officer some years before—and was on his way over to the local phone company to look at them.

I mentioned that he had told me earlier that he thought the man in the water was Asian.

"I'm trying to keep an open mind," Doc replied. "The motel manager said he looked a *little* Asian, but he showed him a Belgian passport."

"A *little* Asian?" I asked.

"I'm working on it," Doc said. "The manager said the guy was in his mid-thirties—maybe—but could have been younger."

Danny checked in shortly after Doc. He'd spent the last twenty-four hours talking up police task forces and investigators. The battle cry was familiar—not enough communication, no resources, little direction from Washington. We laughed over the last point: there was no such thing as too little direction from Washington.

More relevant to our situation, the crime lab had

determined that the explosive was indeed C-3. It appeared to have been homemade—though how the lab techies could know that I haven't a clue. I guess it had something to do with the impurities in the chemicals. Whoever had mixed the stuff hadn't filtered it as finely or mixed the ingredients together as well as a factory would have. It still went boom, so how bad a job could they have done? But I would have guessed a home job anyway, given the fact that C-3 was no longer in general circulation.

The police had all sorts of fingerprints. In fact, they were able to match one set to a bank customer who hadn't paid child support in a year. Doom on you, asshole. But none of the prints had shed any light on who made or planted the bomb.

Danny gave me some ideas about the Belgian connection. Between playing with some weights and reviewing Rogue Manor's security arrangements, I used Danny's intel to work the strings of my information network, like a spider testing his web. This was needle-in-the-haystack territory, but by dinnertime, I had arrived at the conclusion that a) the headless man was about as Belgian as I was, and b) America's borders are as porous as ever—in every direction.

Neither point being exactly a revelation.

However, after quite a bit of how-ya-beens with old Navy friends who now worked for a living, I managed to run down someone in Immigration who was part of a team tasked with keeping track of Belgians. I wouldn't have thought you'd need an entire team for that—hell, the damn country's smaller than Philadelphia—but it turns out that Belgium is the go-to place for passport forgery these days. Not that you actually have to go there to get one of their passports. In fact, they prefer it if you didn't. The little brown documents are readily available on half the streets of Cairo and in a third of the bars in Athens. European passports are especially valuable these days, since they arouse much less suspicion than documents from anywhere else in the world outside of the U.S., and they don't rouse half the snotty comments that American passports get. The Belgians know about this problem and promise to do something about it by the end of the twenty-second century.

The Immigration and Naturalization Service's Belgian section was headed by a sweet-sounding woman named Julie Barr. She said it would be possible to supply us with a list of people who had come to the U.S. from Belgium over the past few months, but we'd have to do our own legwork checking them out. I told her I'd take the list. She promised that printing it out would require several reams of paper.

I'd just put the phone down when it started to ring again. The caller ID told me it was Karen using her cell.

"And how are you this fine afternoon?" I asked, picking up the phone.

"Not so good, Dick. But better than you."

I laughed, then listened to Karen explain that Rich Armstead was rumored to be heading for a new slot in the Defense Department. This might have been good news for Rich (that's debatable), but it was definitely bad news for just about everyone else. To make matters worse, the rumors had popped up on the day Rich was leaving for a trip to Central and South America. He was already in the air and unavailable to address them.

The rumors had thrown the place into disarray, though admittedly that's not saying much. In the meantime, the recently appointed Deputy for Security Matters and Training had finally taken office after several weeks of "transition"—read: paid vacation from his old job—and was in the process of reviewing his realm. Apparently, the squire had decided that I was one of his vassals.

"He wants to meet you," said Karen. "At your earliest convenience."

"That's easy. It's not convenient."

"It'd be better for you to meet him, Dick. Play nice for once."

"You're the cutout," I told her. "You meet him."

"I could cut his throat," she said. "But he still wants to meet you. Technically, you work for him, not me. Your activities are paid out of a line in his budget."

Karen had a tone in her voice that women get that tells you it's senseless to argue with them.

"Set it up," I told her.

"Already have. Tomorrow afternoon, two P.M."

Rogue Manor's new computer setup includes a computer system designed by a tech-head wop dweeb named Paul Guido Falcone, a wise-ass wop who henceforth and forever shall be known as "Shunt." Shunt has shunts in his head. They're some sort of metal inserts placed into his skull because he was born with water in his skull; I think of them as brain gutters. He's barrels of laughs at airports, unless you happen to be stuck behind him with a plane to catch. Shunt tried to lie about the fact that he had metal in his head and join the Navy; somehow they figured it out, so he tried the Army instead. He had all the papers filled out and was just about to swear himself to God and country when the recruiting sergeant noticed the compass on his desk was acting very strangely. The Army ended up bouncing Shunt so far that he went to college instead. I told him one time that the Marines would have been glad to have him because they would have saved money on a helmet. The look on his face told me he thought he'd wasted the last ten years of his life. Unlike a lot of wannabe's, Shunt's basically a good goatfucker who keeps himself in decent shape and might—*might*—have completed BUD/S if the Navy had overlooked the permanent antennas in his skull and the dazed look in his eyes. Their loss was my gain; kid knows everything there is to know about computers.

The college he'd gone to, by the way, was MIT. He has three or four advanced degrees, including one he picked up while briefly under contract to No Such Agency, known to those of us who officially don't know as the NSA. (Now that I've told you that, I'll have to kill you.) I don't know what Shunt did for the agency that doesn't exist, but I'm guessing it didn't involve basket-weaving. He now runs a computer consulting business, but I wouldn't be surprised to find out that he made most of his money by hacking into commercial systems and then selling them information on how he did it. Not that he's felonious, far from it. He just seems to spend a lot of time pursuing hobbies rather than working. The hobbies include flying airplanes and picking horses. He's pretty good at the first—he can handle a two-engined jet and at one time owned a timeshare in a Cessna—and very lousy at the second, which accounts for the fact that he no longer has the timeshare. Or owns his own home.

Shunt came around dinnertime to start running some checks on my system. Before he got to work, he demanded his usual payment up front: two Rolling Rocks and a box full of Fig Newtons. He chugged the beers and went to work. After a half hour of chanting and typing—he tends to talk to himself while he works—he stood up from the machine.

"Clean, Dude." Somewhere along the way Shunt decided that computer geeks are supposed to call everyone they meet "Dude."

"Great, Shunt. We're going to keep it that way, right?"

"Oh yeah." He stuffed a few Fig Newtons into his mouth and hunched back down. "Power filter is working," he said. But with his mouth stuffed with cookies, it came out sounding more like "puwahfulakillswuksing." This led to a long lecture on the evils of power fluctuations, which had killed one of the routers in the Rogue Manor network a few months back. Small fluctuations in the current apparently fry the shit out of microchips. Shunt seemed especially attuned to this thanks to the metal in his head.

"So we're cool then?" I asked him.

"Done, Dude," said Shunt. "I put a couple of upgrades in." He started talking about adding the latest coding for wireless defibrillators or some such. My eyes glazed about midway through. "I can get to it tomorrow."

"Put it off for a while," I told him. Then I asked how his cousin was.

Sheila is a senior analytic cryptographer for the agency that doesn't exist. That means, basically, that she's a special kind of mathematician who breaks encryptions. As a point of information, they don't call the things they "break" codes anymore, because they're actually these very involved mathematical formulas that translate data bits from one form to another. Think of it this way: Sheila and her people aren't so much interested in the message the Green Hornet sent for you to decipher on your secret decoder ring; they're interested in re-creating the decoder ring. She runs one of the top decrypting teams, and in a lot of ways her job is essentially overseeing and interpreting the work of computer hackers, who spend their days eating pizza and drinking Diet Coke, wondering if there's any *there* there.

She also has unbelievable equipment fore and aft, and lips that tingle when they touch yours.

"Sheila's good," said Shunt.

"She's still handling internal analysis?"

"Dude, you should call her. I know she'd love to hear from you."

"What's her phone number these days? Better yet, could you get her on the phone for me?"

Sheila was home. She smacked her lips as soon

as she said hello, and I immediately regretted not having gone to talk to her in person.

"I need a favor," I told her after we got through the how-do-you-dos.

"I hope it doesn't involve breaking agency protocol," she said, licking her lips again.

"I'd never ask you to break agency protocol," I told her. Of course not. NSA protocol was too secret to be revealed. The agency that doesn't exist has very strict rules about what its employees can say and do, and Sheila was undoubtedly breaking one of them simply by talking to me. The NSA has its own special enforcement brigade, called the Men in Black, who enforce the protocol. They have more authority than any other legal enforcement agency in the world, and they actually train to do their job. In the Navy, about the only time you can use deadly force in peacetime is to defend nuclear weapons. Rumor has it that the Men in Black can use lethal force on anyone considered a threat to the agency, which includes anyone who wanders onto their property at Fort Meade. I once watched them blow up a car parked in the wrong lot. It was a new BMW, so it was kind of fun. They didn't see the joke. At the NSA, a sense of humor is considered immediate grounds for dismissal.

"What is it, Dickie?" said Sheila. Then she sighed. Only the fact that I had promised Irish a dinner kept me from commandeering a helicopter and rushing up to Baltimore to continue the interview in person.

"I've been doing a little job for Homeland Security," I told her, before launching into my best bureaucratese. "They're having trouble figuring out which interface to intervene with to get information about intercepts regarding the Midwest. I was hoping you could find out who the right person was for me to talk to."

"The Midwest or the Middle East?"

"Domestic. Illinois and Missouri, to be exact."

"Oh." I waited, but there was nothing with the lips. "Have you tried George Boreland?"

"I will in the morning."

"Do it the right way, Dickie."

"Oh, I will, I will." I knew Boreland. He'd never take my phone call, let alone give me information. I'd have to hand off the assignment to Karen.

"Dickie, we'll have to get together."

"You know I'd love that."

"Say good-bye to my cousin."

"Good-bye to my cousin."

Trace returned from the wilds of the Beltway in time to catch dinner with Irish and me at a roadhouse tucked away from one of the traffic lights on the main highway. I could tell something had stirred up her Apache blood by the way she bounced her shoulder-length hair around.

"Who the *fuck* is Tiffany Alexander?" she said as she sat down.

"Hello to you, too," I said.

"Tiffany Alexander," repeated Trace, giving Irish a perfunctory wave. "She's a friend of yours?"

"I've known Tiffany since she was three."

"What the fuck do we want a bellhop on the team for?"

"I'm going to go catch a cigarette," said Irish, excusing himself. "I'll be right back."

No, he doesn't smoke.

I hid my smirk behind my tumbler of Bombay. I'd known Tiffany and her sister Brandy since they were three and four respectively. Yes, Brandy Alexander. Her parents had a sense of humor. Brandy has long since gotten used to the jokes. They tend to be popular with men of a certain age, and she claims to enjoy the attention. Brandy now lives in New York City, on the Lower East Side, where she's doing whatever it is actresses do while they're looking for their big break. She's a talented young woman and has already had some roles on-stage and in commercials. Brandy had just moved to New York the week before the terrorists struck at the Twin Towers. She breathed that dust for weeks and hated every breath.

Tiffany is a very different sort, though she's definitely a beauty in her own right. She's always been a practical girl, even at three. Trace's slur about the hotel bellhop was a reference to the fact that Tiffany had just completed college and gotten a degree in hotel management. If Tiff ever did become a bellhop, she'd be the smartest damn one ever. Her resumé also includes military school and six years as a counselor in an Outward Bound–type program for disadvantaged kids. She also won a bunch of Junior Marksman contests, and I think she was a finalist for a slot on the women's Olympic archery squad.

"So Tiffany showed up, huh?" I asked.

"Don't give me that. She says you promised her

a job. You reviewed all the candidates. I know you know her."

"She said I promised her a job?"

"She implied it."

"I'd be surprised if she said anything except that she wanted a chance to make the team fair-and-square," I told Trace.

"I have to take her?"

"Of course not. Treat her like everyone else."

"That means I have to take her. She came in first in every fucking trial."

Trace *didn't* have to take Tiffany onto the team. That was the deal. Every one of the nuggets had already been screened by yours truly, as well as by Doc and Danny. They'd passed physical and mental tests and extensive security checks. But those were only the first hurdles, and Trace, as Nugget Mama, could bounce anyone she felt didn't make the grade, no questions asked.

Admittedly, Tiff lacked the military background that most of our other shooters brought to the table. She was also several years younger, and maturity *is* one of the things the War Master likes to see in a nugget, since the wisdom to stay out of shit is nearly as important as the smarts to get out of it once you're in it. But, obviously, Trace saw the same promise in Tiffany that I did.

And something else. Trace also saw her as a challenge from me: could she deal with a younger version of herself? Not that I thought of Tiffany that way—the two women were very different, though their builds were similar—but that was probably the way Trace did. And she wasn't the type to walk away from a challenge. Her ancestors had marched across the desert, kicked the shit out of Mexicans, and harassed the American Army for the better part of a hundred years. A little female competition was the *last* thing Trace Dahlgren would walk away from.

"You should've told me about her, Dick."

Trace looked up at the approaching waitress and ordered a seltzer. She keeps a strict limit on alcohol intake, mostly for reasons that have to do with her Native American beliefs, but it also helps keep her five-eight frame a trim one hundred and thirty-five pounds.

"If I told you about Tiffany, you would have thought I was ordering you to include her on the team," I said when the waitress left. "You would have kicked her off the team in spite, because you're stubborn."

"Fuck you I'm stubborn. You're not ordering me to take her on the team?"

"Of course not. I told you, you're Nugget Mama-san. You have the yea or nay. Besides, all senior members of the team have a veto. That doesn't change."

"Fuck you," said Trace. "You want her on the team. Otherwise, she wouldn't have been in the screening session."

"I think she'll be damn valuable, yes. But you can say the same thing about every one of the newbies, without exception. And if Tiffany can't hack it, or you have an objection, or Doc does, then she's gone."

"Doc's not going to object. He knows her, too."

"Or Danny."

"Fuck yourself," said Trace. "Fuck yourself backward."

And thus was Tiffany Alexander officially accepted into the fold.

Round about midnight, as I checked the last of my emails, I got a call from Doc with the latest info dump.

"How's your French?" he asked.

"Allez-vous faire voir chez les Grecs," I told him politely. It's French for "go get fucked," or "eat in a Greek restaurant." I forget which.

"There's a connection between one of the phone numbers my Belgian called and the French ministry of black holes," said Doc. "One of the subgroups under the DCPJ that doesn't exist."

"Where'd you find that?"

"I didn't," said Doc. "One of the Christians made the connection for me. I have a hunch our headless Asian is French, drawing a paycheck from the DCPJ and hiding his profession with a phony passport."

DCPJ is the Central Directorate Judicial Police, France's central police force. There really isn't an equivalent in America, but if you can imagine a cross between the Justice Department and every state police unit in the country, then throw in the CIA and Homeland Defense, you'll get the idea. The Frogs don't have quite the same taste for bureaucracy that the Krauts do, so the whole thing is arranged like the inside of one of their cathedrals—nooks and crannies all over the place. The Sub-Directorate of Criminal Businesses, which was set up to deal mostly with gangs, has at least one (and maybe more) national brigades specializing in antiterrorism. That's the unit Doc was referring to.

"You're telling me this guy was a French spook?" I asked.

"I'm not telling you anything, Dick. But it does look like a possibility."

"One worth pursuing?"

"I hope so. I have an appointment in Paris day after tomorrow to talk about it."

"Good."

"There's only one thing. I don't speak Frog. And I'd like somebody we can completely trust, Dick," Doc added. "I don't like the smell of this. Nobody's cooperating out here, and I can't tell if it's because they're a bunch of ignorant shits who don't know anything or because they've gotten the word to clam up."

More likely the former, but I sympathized. "What about Tiffany Alexander? She speaks French."

"Tiffany'd be great, if she's available," said Doc. He, too, had known her since she was knee-high to a grasshopper. Doc and Donna briefly had taken care of her and her sister when their parents divorced, and he'd kept close tabs on her as an honorary uncle and extracurricular guidance counselor.

"Trace gave her a passing grade," I told him. "She's in."

"Sparks flew, I bet."

"As you predicted."

"She had to take her, because not passing her on

the team would be like admitting she'd had her butt whooped. Just like you said."

"I'm not always right," I told him. "Just often enough for government work."

Danny called a little later. He'd been working the police bar circuit and had finally managed to sift a few kernels of truth from the amber waves of grain waving in the fields nearby. Or at least they seemed like kernels after a long day and a few beers.

"Homegrown terrorists," he told me. "Like McVeigh. Only bigger."

"Bigger organizations, or bigger people, Dan?"

"Both. A guy out here thinks there's a militia connection, with people getting money from persons unknown. The persons unknown would be related to our Colonel Blanchard."

Max Blanchard was not a particularly patriotic American. You can read all about him in *Violence of Action,* but the short version is this: he had his paws on a nuke that he wanted to use to make his particular view of eternity fulfill itself. I put him out of action; eternity keeps ticking on its own timetable, far as I know.

At the end of that particular nightmare, we believed—but could not prove—that Blanchard had received aid from other groups and was possibly even taking orders from someone else. The latter was particularly hard to prove, because he was tied up with some religious beliefs you don't find explicated in your typical Sunday sermon. Danny had liked him even less than I did, if that's possible, and was sold on the conspiracy theory. He just couldn't decide who the conspiracy was with.

"So how would Blanchard fit into this?" I asked him.

"I don't know that yet."

"Did they bring up Blanchard's name?"

"Nobody did," said Danny. "That's just a working theory."

"Why do they think it's homegrown?"

"Because they think foreign Tangos would stick out."

"They have any wetbacks working in the bar there?"

"Who doesn't?"

"You think they're all Mexicans, with maybe a Guatemalan thrown in?" I asked.

"Uh, you could have a Guatemalan."

"How about someone from Yugoslavia. Doesn't speak English, on the dark side."

"I get your point," said Danny.

"If the people were well-funded, why would they use C-3?"

"That I have a theory on. They're just fucking with your head, Dick. They're trying to get you to think it's Vietnam all over again."

"Could be." Obviously, they were fucking with my head. Beyond that, though, there were no conclusions to be drawn—yet.

"One of the guys has been checking around for the chemicals used to make C-3," added Danny. "We may have it narrowed down."

"Good."

"Say, Dick, you mind if I ask you a question?"

"Fire with both barrels."

"What would you do if out of the blue you got an email from someone claiming to be your daughter?"

"I'd wait for the subpoena."

"Seriously, what would you do?"

If Danny had been sitting next to me at the bar, I would have prescribed him some Bombay and filled two glasses with the world's best medicine. I settled for one myself, then I listened as Danny told me a story about the 1970s and his days immediately after making captain in the Marine Corps. The Marines had a program to give their up-and-comers a bit more polish in the civilian world, so they shopped Danny to a college out West to study engineering. It was more like a paid humpfest; he ended up sharing a bed with a girl named SueLi for most of the semester. After the final exams, they shook hands and never heard from each other again.

Sometime after that, she got a surprise. Roughly nine months later, the surprise opened her eyes, didn't like what she saw, and wailed. Her name was Melanie.

"How'd she track you down?"

"Through the police department where they live in Washington State. Her stepfather is an assistant DA."

He practically winced as he said the word "stepfather."

"Sounds a little suspicious to me, to be honest," I told him, even though I knew he wouldn't want to hear it.

"She's the right age. Why else would she try to

get hold of me? She doesn't want money, and I don't have any. She's been sending me emails. The other day she sent me a picture. I'll send you a copy."

"Great."

"Wants to meet me," he said.

"Where does she live?"

"In Richmond."

"Grew up in Washington State and now lives back East?"

"Is that a crime?"

It might be, or at least some sort of moral transgression. "Not trying to get out of a traffic ticket or something like that, is she?" I asked.

Danny laughed. But it was a forced kind of laugh.

"I'd hold off until I felt real comfortable about it," I told him.

"She's my daughter, Dick."

"I don't argue about family matters," I told him. "I'm just saying, if you want my advice, I'd hold off."

"Yeah," he said, hanging up.

Well, at least the gin was good.

5

My sit-down with a new Homeland Security deputy honcho went every bit as well as you'd think it did. He started spitting the second I walked into his office, and things went steadily to shit after that.

I didn't mind being growled at. Hell, if I'm not yapped at by some asshole or another every few weeks, I head down to the local DMV and stand in the wrong line just to soak up some abuse. But Junior—his name was Relaford Cartwheel Horsesass Jr., or something similar—hadn't called me in to abuse me. He was pulling the plug on Red Cell II.

"What the fuck do you mean?" I said.

Actually, I doubt I was so polite, but I can't recall the exact words I used.

"You are no longer under the employ of the Homeland Security Agency," squawked Junior.

"I'm not an employee. I have a contract."

"Don't pull that legal shit with me," he said.

"I'm not pulling any legal shit," I said. "I'm pointing out that I can't be fired. If you want to end our agreement, there's a provision in the contract."

Said provision provided for full payment, anyway. The woman who negotiates my contracts is one tough hombre. But rather than going to the file and pulling my contract, Junior told me to get the hell out of his office.

"Rich Armstead approved this?"

"Mr. Armstead is not going to be with this agency for very much longer," said Junior. "He's moving on."

"Well, I'd like to hear about this from him."

"You will when he comes back two weeks from now," said Junior. "In any event, I'm in charge."

Karen was waiting for me in her office.

"How did it go?"

"Asshole fired me."

"He fired you? He can't do that."

"No shit. Where's Armstead?"

"He's at a conference on terrorism in Buenos Aires. I told you that yesterday. Then he goes to Brazil and Costa Rica and Mexico. He won't be back until the end of next week."

"So the mice play while the cat's away, huh?"

"Did you read the *Post* this morning?"

"No. Why?" I try not to admit I do anything with a newspaper but use it to wrap coffee grounds in, but in this case, I didn't have to lie; I hadn't had a chance.

"A3. Top of the page."

The story there said that an ongoing exercise testing Homeland Security's internal command and coordination infrastructure—basically, Tell-Me-Dick and the people above him, including the newly appointed Junior—was proving to be a fiasco, because the department didn't know its elbow from the standard male equipment somewhat farther south. The reporter also accurately blasted the local agencies, but most of her venom was aimed squarely at Homeland Security. The gist of the piece was that deadwood like Tell-Me-Dick ought to do their logging somewhere else.

I will say one thing: for the daughter of a SEAL, that girl can sure write.

"You wouldn't be the source in that story, would you Dick?" asked Karen.

"Source?"

"The unnamed source close to the agency."

"Clearly can't be me, because I'm not close to the agency."

"Three congressmen have already called to complain, and those are only the ones I know about. If I didn't know any better, I'd swear you wanted the contract to be canceled."

"Hell no." I didn't, but I could tell Karen didn't believe me. Sometimes your reputation for going against the grain precedes you. The reporter had called. I returned her call, and because I knew her father, I trusted her when she said she wouldn't use my name. The fact that my answers to her questions hurt Tell-Me-Dick was purely coincidental. That I thought the story might help flush out anyone with a homicidal grudge against Homeland Insecurity was not.

"They will can you. Rich can only do so much," said Karen.

"They still have to pay me," I told her. "Besides, I was getting bored. And the way it looks to me, they weren't all that interested in me doing a good job for them, anyway."

"You have to play by the rules."

"I play by the rules."

She gave me a face. "Your rules."

"They're the same rules the bastards who killed all those people in the Towers and at the Pentagon play by. They're the only rules that count."

"No, they're not, Dick. And we're not talking about war here."

"Sure we are, Karen. People are dying. Innocent people. My job is to help prevent that. Training has to be as realistic as possible. Even peewee soccer teams know that."

"The training can be realistic without embarrassing people."

I love Karen; no use denying it. She was wrong on this—way, way wrong—but I love her, anyway.

"Well, you're not getting paid. They'll freeze your check."

"That's where you're wrong, Karen. Money was wired into the account yesterday." Old service rule: it pays to befriend the paymaster's clerk.

"Don't make me go to the bank and get it debited."

I shrugged. I had foreseen that possibility and had the cash transferred to a different account in a different bank in a different country. Not even my accountant could have found it.

Easy come, easy go. Typical sailor.

"You're supposed to be straight with me," she said.

As a rule, I love double entendres, but I let that one be. She was genuinely pissed. I like that in a woman.

"I need you to do me a favor before you throw me out of your office," I told her. "There's a guy over at the NSA I need some information from. It's a long shot, but if anyone knows anything, it'll be him, and he won't talk to me."

"No, Dick, no."

"George Boreland. He's the head of the analytic team on one of the terrorism task force intercepts. You could talk to the FBI, too, but I don't think they'll be very helpful."

"It's not my department, Dick." She hesitated. "You should talk to Cox at Tadpole."

"Great. Dinner tonight?"

"No."

"Hot tub afterward?"

"No."

"I'll see you around eleven, then."

Karen looked at me, then frowned. "If I come for dinner, what would you make?"

Tadpole Captain Cox's secretary told me that he wasn't in, but before I had a chance to barge through the door and prove her wrong, he appeared behind me from the hallway.

"Dick Marcinko, what the hell are you doing here?" he said, thrusting a hand out at me. "Come on inside and rest your bones. How the hell are you?"

Now I'd met Cox *maybe* three times before, and even by the crazy timers cell phone companies use, our previous conversations wouldn't have totaled more than five minutes. But in the Coast Guard as in the Navy, ship drivers are bred to be part-politician, part–human resources managers, and Cox had clearly gone back for a second helping of those genes. His inner office revealed his ambitions clearly. There was a "look-at-me" wall behind his desk featuring photos of Cox and just about every member of Congress and the Administration above the G-9 level. The wall to the right was covered with certificates praising his ability as a Coast Guarder. He seemed to have gotten a piece of paper for every day he spent in the service. This inadvertently hinted at a shortcoming Homeland Insecurity was designed to help him address: a narrow band of experience. The only non–Coast Guard certificates were a proclamation lauding his contributions to the Americans Against Casino Gambling and a thank-you note for giving to Jerry's Kids. (An odd couple, it occurs to me, but never mind.) He didn't even have so much as a Rotary pin to broaden his resumé.

The bookcase on the left was stacked high with management books, ranging from *The Idiot's Guide to Management* (there's an apropos title) to yours truly's *Leadership Secrets of the Rogue Warrior.*

I was flattered. The spine of the book was even creased, so maybe he'd read a page or two. Then again, he could have bought it used.

Cox asked me what was going on, and I let him have it with both barrels, putting his hail-fellow-well-met routine to my advantage.

"That's disappointing," he said when I finished detailing what Junior had told me.

Let's translate. To a career bureaucrat, "disappointing" means: "sucks shit through a vacuum cleaner." It also usually means: "better you than me" and "sayonara, sucker!" But Cox followed it up not only with the expected, "I'll back you if you go to the mat on this"—a generally hollow promise, in English as well as bureaucratese—but also, "What can I do in a tangible way to help you?"

"Tangible" is a code word for career government employees. It means: I think there's a pony here I can ride to get ahead in this rat race. I have nothing against mixed metaphors, or helping someone else succeed in some obscure way if they help me accomplish my mission. So I charged straight ahead. Cox didn't blink when I told him about Boreland at the NSA. He admitted that he didn't know many people at the agency that doesn't exist—who does?—but he would use all the powers of Tadpole to get "meaningful data" for me. I somehow managed to thank him without making a crack about his becoming a toad someday.

Fair warning: if you don't have a strong stomach, you may want to skip ahead.

Just because I'd parked in a supposedly secure parking lot didn't mean my car hadn't been screwed with. Before boarding, I took out yet another handy doodad from the buckaroos at Law Enforcement Technologies and scanned for wireless transmitters and receivers. It looks like a very slim flip cell phone, except that it doesn't flip and you'll always get a wrong number if you try to call out on it. The really advanced models can be used to track wireless signals, but they're a little bulky to carry conveniently in your pocket if you have keys and any amount of change. The thing to remember is to stand back if you're using it to detect detonators. The device does this by pulsing a signal across the radio spectrum. If it finds one, the detonator goes boom.

No boom, no problem, which was the case now. And there weren't any bugs, either, at least none that were using radio waves.

High-tech gadgets can make you lazy and dead if you rely on them too much, so I followed up with a visual inspection of the vehicle, dropping to my knees and holding a little foldout mirror to check for wires and bombs. The underside of my GMC Yukon was just as dirty as ever. That's by design—I want the top of the car spotless and the bottom caked with fresh grease, in both cases making it easy to see if someone's been messing with my vehicle.

Assured that no one had, I fired up the Rogue-mobile and headed home. I had made the highway and started in the direction of Rogue Manor when the phone vibrated. I reached to my belt and hit the talk button.

"Yo, Dirtbag, you got a Honda bike tracking you about a quarter mile back."

It was Dan Capel. Capel is a plank owner from SEAL Six and had been on the original Red Cell. You dedicated readers also know him as Nicky Grundle. (Check out *The Real Team* for a full rundown of his resumé.) He tells stories about how he saved my ass more than once, and it would be impolitic of me to contradict him. He went out of the Navy on a medical retirement, but retirement is a relative term, especially in Dan's case. He heads a VIP protection firm, bought an advertising firm as a lark to exercise his artistic side, and owns a commercial database company that does work for one of the credit-check companies, as well as the government.

But forget all that. His left fist could stop a charging elephant. I don't want to talk about his right. If I had to pick one guy to be on my back—and I did—it was Dan Capel.

He'd flown into town the day before with six of his best ops from the protection service to set up a net around yours truly. The idea was that if, as seemed likely from my adventures in the wild Midwest, I was being trailed, Capel and crew would find the trailers and put a few twelve-penny nails into their skulls. Assuming there was anything left for them when I was through. He'd been on my back at the airport when I met Karen, staying in the shadows the whole way home. As a nod toward paranoia, he had recommended that I not introduce him to anyone else on the team and not bring him and his people into Rogue Manor until he was ready.

Capel was riding with one of his ops in a Toyota behind the motorcycle. Two of the other ops were directly behind me in a van equipped with enough firepower to subdue two M1A1 tanks and take down a squadron of A-10A attack planes at the same time.

A good shadowing operation will use several cars, moving up and falling back at intervals, shuffling around so that the subject can't see that he's being followed. It'll also vary the types of vehicles as much as is practical, making them more difficult to spot. Our job now was to ID all of the vehicles in the operation.

Actually, *my* job was just to drive. I took out the P7 and put it on the seat next to me, ready for use. I also checked my Glock 26s, which I carried as concealed or "hideaway" weapons. The Glock is a small but powerful gun, and like everything the manufacturer puts out, it's a very well-conceived, well-made shooter's tool. Mine are almost stock, the main improvements being titanium drive rods and enhanced recoil springs. The 26 is a small gun, easily hidden but very accurate; it fires a 9mm round. I was carrying one in a special shoulder holster below my jacket. I nudged the holster slightly to make sure I could grab it without blowing my tit off.

I stayed on the highway for another five miles, then took one of the exits Capel and I had lined up earlier. I wanted to be followed, so I slowed down at the light, then pulled into a McDonald's. My trail van pulled in as well. The motorcyclist passed by while I was inside grabbing a coffee. As I walked back to the Yukon, I pulled out my phone and studied the keypad, as if selecting a number out of the phonebook.

"Hey, Dirtbag," I said to Capel.

"Just the motorcycle so far."

"You're not looking hard enough."

"You're not making yourself enough of a patsy."

"Hard to fight biology."

"Leave the phone on."

I got in the SUV and made my way back to the highway, driving lackadaisically. I figured there had to be somebody else trailing me, but even Capel and his polished pros couldn't find him or them as I approached the intersection for the interstate. I took it, and so did the motorcyclist.

"Could be just the one keeping tabs on you,

Dick," said Capel. "Low-budget operation. More than you're worth."

"What do you think about picking him off?" I suggested.

"All right. Train station or ball field?"

"Train station."

We had already worked out two different spots nearby where we could launch an ambush. Both locations featured isolated roads without through roads or outlets. Someone unfamiliar with the area would quickly find themselves cut off. I took the next exit, swung through a town filled with antique stores and art galleries, then headed down a nearly trafficless county road.

"Still looks like it's just him," said Capel.

"Let's take him," I said, spotting the turn.

I felt the adrenaline starting to pump. We'd named the spot the train station, but it was really a large sewer treatment plant in front of an abandoned train siding and some dilapidated factory buildings. Amtrak ran through every hour or so, but otherwise the stench kept everyone but the seagulls away.

"Here we go," said Capel.

I slowed as I passed the sewer building. As soon as I heard Capel say "he's in," I jammed the brakes, throwing the Yukon into a skid. The motorcyclist, belatedly realizing what was up, sped by, pursued by Capel, the van, and one of the other cars, which had run ahead and stationed itself in the sewage plant lot. At roughly the same time, another of Capel's men put a 7.62mm slug into the back wheel of the motorcycle from his Remington. The bike skidded right and the motorcyclist tumbled off.

And then tumbled up. He bolted right, with all of us in hot pursuit. Just as he came close to the foundation of an old railroad building, the last of Capel's men sprang up. He might have made his move a breath too soon. In any event, the motorcyclist saw him and cut right.

I run every day; I do eight-minute miles and throw in some sprints. That fucker was fast. Capel and the van turned onto the access road along the track, and I swear the SOB pulled away from them.

Somewhere around there, I realized there was a train coming. And it *was* coming—the Metroliner plugs through here at about ninety miles an hour. Huffing, I crossed over to the left, figuring that the motorcyclist would do the same. He started to—but then he spotted me and tried to go back.

Bad move.

The nose of the train hit him dead on, tossing him straight up in the air. He came down right behind the engine, and seemed to disappear. From where I was standing, it looked as if he had gone right through the roof. What he had done was somehow manage to fall into the narrow slot behind the engine and the lead passenger car. He was flicked to the side, batted toward the back of the locomotive, and then pushed down to the track. Then he slipped downward. The first wheel that hit him took off his arm.

The second got his neck, decapitating him.

Part Two

STAND BY ME

"The analysts write about the war as if it's a ballet . . . like it's choreographed ahead of time, and when the orchestra strikes up and starts playing, everyone goes out and plays a set piece.

"What I always say to the folks is, 'Yes, it's choreographed, and what happens is the orchestra starts playing and some son of a bitch climbs out of the orchestra pit with a bayonet and starts chasing you around the stage.' And the choreography goes right out the window."

—General H. Norman Schwarzkopf,
5 February 1991, interview in the *Washington Post*

6

Maybe it happened a little differently. Maybe the motorcyclist took a weird bounce in there somewhere and rebounded crazily, had his head chopped off first and then his arm. All I saw was the blood splashing from the underside of the train, already more than a quarter of a mile away. By the time I got there, the torso lay on the ground; the right leg had been chopped up and a few fingers were missing from the other hand. The head lay upside down at the foot of the ballast pile a few yards away.

Capel pried the shield off the helmet and held out the decapitated head toward me.

"Know him?"

The eyes stared at me, the lid on the right eye drooping slightly. He looked European, on the darker side. He had brown eyes. His face had a sleek and empty look to it—but maybe we all would if we'd left the rest of our body somewhere else.

"Never saw him before," I said.

Topless Tango number two. I was beginning to discern a pattern. There was bound to be another down the road; good things come in threes. I thought seriously of bringing the dead son of a bitch's head back home and putting it on a fence post the way they used to do during the Middle Ages. Think of it as the ultimate DO NOT DISTURB sign. (As many of you know, the signs posted around the compound at Rogue Manor read: "Trespassers shot; survivors shot again." And I mean the neighbors *know* it!)

Capel pried the head out of the helmet, then set down the skull. He pulled out a digital camera and snapped some pictures we could use to try to ID the dead man. No, it didn't seem gruesome at the time. Even now, telling you about it in retrospect, it doesn't seem gruesome. It was a nasty part of the job (which is why we call Capel Nasty Nicky Grundle in the novels), but the job *is* nasty—the whole job, that is. I don't want to sugarcoat it for you. The people we're up against—and you're up against them, too, whether or not you want to admit it—want to kill you, and they want it to be nasty. They want the people left behind to breathe it in their lungs for weeks. They want it playing over and over on TV. I don't say you should get used to it; it should turn your stomach. But when it does, use it to do something about it. Someone punches you in the gut, nail him in the balls. Someone chops off your hand, take off his head. Be ten times the bastard he is. As my sea daddy Roy Boehm said: "Don't get even. Get ahead."

If you don't, it may be your head lying by the side of the track next time, frowning for the camera.

"No ID, chief," said one of Capel's men back by the body.

"Didn't think there would be. Anything?"

"Got a cell phone."

The cell phone was something, at least. Capel's boys began scouring the path the now-headless motorcyclist had taken to arrive at his rendezvous with the Amtrak, checking to see if he'd dumped an ID or radio or even a weapon, anything that could be used to get information about him.

I walked back and took a look at the bike. Undoubtedly it would turn out to be stolen or its ownership disguised somehow, but I made sure to copy the license plate, anyway. We left before the police arrived. Hanging around wasn't going to help them any and—with due respect to my friends in the crime-stomping profession—only waste our time.

Capel didn't take any chances. We resumed our surveillance pattern and headed to Rogue Manor. By the time we were there, the fingerprints had been checked against the FBI registry and the plate had been run. There was no hit in either the FBI registry or with motor vehicles—the license plate supposedly was unissued.

"He was working alone," Capel said. "He had to report wherever you went would be my guess, but not get too close."

"Was he a pro?"

"He had some connections if he could get a blank plate, but I wouldn't make any call on his expertise level yet. We *did* catch him."

"You think a pro would have escaped?"

"A pro would have made it a little harder."

Frankly, I thought he'd done a decent job; if the

train hadn't picked that moment to blow through, we might still be eating his dust.

"He knew I was meeting with Junior at Homeland Security," I said. "Unless he followed me from here."

"He didn't follow you from here," said Capel. "Who knew where you were going?"

No one on my team. I hadn't told Sean or Hulk—or Trace, for that matter. Danny, who had emailed some advice on who else might approach Boreland—that was it. Except for Karen. And the people at Homeland Security. Junior. Anyone who had access to his schedule. Tell-Me-Dick.

It would please me no end to find out that either scumbag was a traitor, but I just didn't think they were smart enough.

"Plenty of people could have guessed that I'd go there," I told Capel. We discussed a few theories and ideas on what to do with the cell phone. Capel has extensive contacts and promised that he'd have a full list of the calls made on the cell phone—as well as all the information that had been used to set up the account—by the next morning. He would also have the phone dusted for prints and scanned for any organic material that would yield DNA. He already had samples of both from the dead man; he was hoping to ID an accomplice or superior.

"About one chance in a zillion we'll find anything useful," Capel admitted. "Unless he loaned the phone to someone with greasy fingers who spit into it."

As unlikely as that was, I understood that Capel was pulling out all the stops on my behalf. I told him I appreciated that, along with the fact that he had dropped everything to come down and watch my butt.

"As hairy as ever," he pointed out.

"You can shave it any time you want."

"That's where I draw the line," said Capel. "Even friendship has its limits. Besides, this is going to cost you next week in New York. I expect a smile on your face and calluses on your fingers."

I'd agreed to do a meet and greet with him at a business conference. Capel is based in the city and runs a lot of seminars on executive security there. When I agreed, I figured I'd be up near the city anyway. The container port facility was across the Hudson in New Jersey, and the nuke plant was about forty miles upriver.

Great place for a nuke plant, by the way.

I reached Rogue Manor no happier and certainly no wiser. For all the excitement, I was still no closer to figuring out who was dogging me than I had been earlier. Taking the scumbag had been the right move. If it hadn't been for the damn train, we'd be squeezing him for information by now. But that's life: sometimes you can do everything right and still get screwed.

Among the first phone calls I made was one to the people up at Wappino* nuclear plant in New York, telling them that the exercise was off.

"Shit," said the security administrator, an amiable fellow named Jack Furness.

* The publisher's asshole lawyers made me use a pseudonym. What a bunch of dork shits.

I explained the situation, promising that we would make it up to him in a few months. Furness fretted that that would be too late and went on to explain that he'd been hoping to use the exercise to his advantage. A new corporation had recently taken over management of the power plant. The people who ran the corporation knew what they were doing, but as in any corporation, there was always competition for resources. Furness had hoped the exercise would help him politically at corporate headquarters.

"I have to be honest with you, we'll kick your butts," I told him. I haven't seen a nuclear power plant in this country that couldn't be compromised by a determined group of Boy Scouts with an attitude, let alone the Rogue Warrior's band of committed mayhem doers.

"That's not a problem," said Furness, and he explained where he was coming from. During the review of security arrangements at the plant, he'd come up with a plan A, plan B, and plan C for improving security. Think of the plans as a Chevy, Buick, and Cadillac—or, if you're into foreign cars, a Mercedes C, E, and S class. Plan A took security to the standard maintained by the company. This was better than the security levels at national facilities, though I won't call that a ringing endorsement. Plan B was even better, making Wappino more secure than any plant in the world—again, not a ringing endorsement. Plan C, the Cadillac version, would make it more secure than any nuclear missile facility in the country. At this level, the Boy Scouts would probably opt to earn their Environmental Catastrophe merit badges elsewhere.

The company execs knew that the location of the power plant near New York City meant a massive population would be exposed to a potential threat if anything went wrong. Just as important, they knew that *they* were exposed to the biggest collection of obnoxious and clueless reporters in the world. Even *seeming* to fuck up could send their stock price tumbling and mess up their options bonanza. So they referred the matter to their PR department, which decided that press releases and advertisements dubbing Wappino as "the most secure plant in the world" would double their own stock options. The bean counters in accounting, who didn't have quite as many of their own stock options at stake, argued for A and a half, but in the end, corporate sided with the PR boys. Expecting Furness to be out-of-his-mind overjoyed—his name would be featured in all the press releases, and even spelled correctly—they flew up to New York to tell him, between private tours of the Statue of Liberty and a night out at Yankee Stadium in George Steinbrenner's private box. They couldn't understand why Furness wouldn't go along. Didn't he have stock options, too?

Furness did the worst thing a corporate geek could do in that situation: he told them the truth. He'd spent the past few weeks reviewing the situation and decided he had been far too optimistic in his original assessment. If anything, even plan C was too basic. Fortunately, he told them this during a big rally in the bottom of the ninth inning at the baseball game, and none of the execs heard a word.

They patted him on the back, clapped and cheered, and ordered another round of George's champagne.

Being a particularly masochistic sort, Furness had not yet given up. He had decided that he would get corporate backing for plan C by using a political ploy even Machiavelli would have been proud of: the politics of embarrassment. If we kicked butt during the exercise, he'd go to his bosses and use it as an argument for what could happen in the future. He was even working on a chart showing the effect on stock options.

His story made me like him—but then I like many naive young idealists before they have stuck their pointy heads into the real world's meat grinder.

"You sure you want us to make you look bad?" I asked.

"I don't want you to make us look bad. But if it happens, it happens. If it doesn't, hell, then I'll go along with corporate."

"You're not thinking of making your guys take a fall, are you?"

"They're too good for that," he said. "They'd call me out on it right away. Just the opposite: we'll get ready for you like it's the Super Bowl. If you kick our butts fair and square, that's fine. If we kick yours—well, then I have serious bragging rights and probably get a promotion. I win either way."

"You won't kick our butts," I told him. "But we'll have to wait until we're back on the payroll. Taking the team north involves a lot of expenses."

"I have a training budget," said Furness. "How much money do you need?"

Ah, an idealist with an expense account. Nothing is more dangerous in the world.

We talked about it a bit, and I ended up holding him off. I needed to go over the situation with my people first, but more important, I was concerned about the asshole who had been tailing my operations. I didn't want to take a chance that I'd be showing these jerks how to irradiate half the New York metro area.

"Let me think about it and get back to you," I told Furness. "I'll call no later than tomorrow night."

"I'll be waiting."

I held an impromptu meeting of the Red Cell II team out back after the sun went down, setting the mood with a monster spread. I had everything going: T-bones and chickens on two large Weber grills, along with a pot of lobsters and clams, all the vegetables Trace could find at the local vegetable stand, and enough beer to fill three large coolers. It was a little like some of the barbecues we used to have back in my SEAL days; the big difference now is that I pay for my eats rather than scrounging them. Scrounging does add a bit of spice to the meal, I admit—an admiral's steak always tastes better than what you find in the supermarket, no matter how it's marinated. Around 2200, I brought out one of the speaker phones and got Doc and Danny on the line for an impromptu conference call. With the gang all here, I laid out the situation: at least for the moment, Red Cell II had been furloughed. I told them flat out they were out of jobs and free to go, get rich, get laid, get bent, get off, whatever particular definition they wished to attach to that four-letter word: F-R-E-E.

Free.

"And you're free to fuck yourself," they told me. No one wanted to abandon me, especially not while some psycho loony had me at the top of his shopping list. Which made for a real touchy-feely moment, them cursing and bragging about how no whacko asshole was going to deprive them of the pleasure of plugging yours truly themselves. They mustered all the four-letter terms of endearment I'd ever used and then some. I just stood there smiling to myself, thinking of the hangovers they were going to have in the morning.

With that out of the way, I outlined an agenda for the next two weeks that included an operation at the nuke cooker. By my timetable, we'd arrive in New York on Wednesday morning, set up a temporary command post and initiate an intel operation. From there, I'd work the actual game plan, but most likely we'd give them their money's worth starting Thursday and running through Saturday. The meet and greet I owed Capel was set for the following Monday, and I'd decided I'd throw in a seminar for the security folks at the nuke plant on Tuesday. That would justify keeping my people in New York over the weekend with two free days to kill beers and seduce tourists—a little well-earned R&R for the Rogue Warrior's favorite slimeballs—just a traditional work hard–play hard evolution from days gone by, before the world was forced to be politically correct.

"Pack your swimmies," I told them. "And the live ammo. We'll work out a special plan to deal with Shadow if we flush him."

"I think he was the creep that got run over by the train," said Hulk.

"Probably not," I told him. "But it's possible."

"We're going to visit the Big Apple?" asked Sean. His eyes were about the size of silver dollars.

That or he was trying to take in Tiffany's many assets.

"We'll see how it plays," I told him. "But that would be the general idea."

"I hope it does," said Tiffany. "I'd like to see my sister."

"I'm afraid you're not on the Event Team," I told her.

You'd've thought I kicked her in the stomach. Sean didn't look all that happy, either.

"Paris is nicer than New York this time of year, Tiffany," said Doc over the speaker phone. "Besides, not knowing what half the people are saying when they're cursing you to hell can be a real bonus."

Tiffany looked at me. "Paris?"

I felt like a dirty old sugar daddy at Christmas. I could get used to that.

"Doc needs somebody to change his diapers for him," I told her. "Nappies, or whatever the French call them."

Tiffany just about jumped up and down, rattling off something in French about diapers. Trace gave Tiffany dagger eyes from the corner. Sean—poor Sean looked like he'd just lost his best friend.

"Your flight to Boston leaves at five A.M.," I told Tiffany. "Doc'll meet you up there."

"Five?"

"Gives you just enough time for your mandatory morning PT," said Trace.

"Sure, if I get up at midnight," Tiffany shot back. "It'll take at least an hour to clear security at the airport, and between packing and getting ready—"

"You weren't planning on sleeping, were you?" said Trace.

I heard Karen's car coming up the driveway and slipped away. Knowing what I did about Trace and Tiffany, I expected that bit of back and forth would go on for quite a while. Besides, as much as I love female mud wrestling, there'd be plenty of other opportunities to watch catfights in the future.

I spent the next day and a half seeing to some business and working my way down the various honey-do lists. Trace worked the new recruits, making them sweat from places where they didn't know they had pores. Trace's ancestors were Chiricahua Apaches and she counts one of the last great chiefs of the tribe, Chihuahua, as her direct ancestor. Chihuahua's clan saw great hardship and were *tough* mothers. They lived in the desert and were practicing guerilla tactics on their enemies long before whites came to America. Trace would have fit right in. The old chief must be smiling in the afterlife.

Capel headed back to New York, arranging for more clean ops to spread a net behind us when we hit the power plant. He and I had worked out a plan to keep the team under surveillance, hoping that whoever had sent the mangled motorcyclist would have more fresh bodies to toss into the fray. The cell phone we'd recovered had proved less than helpful. It had been used to receive two calls, both from telephone booths. The phones were in Alexandria and Reston, suburbs of Washington in Virginia. In both cases, the booths were convenient to highways but were not located anywhere near the route I had taken. The account had been opened up with a credit card that ostensibly belonged to a seventy-three-year-old woman in Portland, Oregon, who, until Capel called her, had no idea that her identity had been pinched. He ruined her night and probably the rest of her month by informing her that the thieves had gotten hold of her Social Security number as well. The credit card he'd traced had only been used to buy the cell phone, and Capel suspected that it had been purchased from a cell phone number broker specifically for that purpose. But according to the credit report in front of him, her information had been used to open several other accounts, all of which had large balances in arrears. He offered to help the victim tag her accounts so that they could be watched for any other illegal activity. She readily agreed—a good thing, since Capel had already gone ahead and started the process, checking on the accounts and setting up a net to tell him whether the woman's Social Security number or even her address was used to establish a new account anywhere over the next month or so.

The phone calls had been made while I was in the Homeland Insecurity building. Capel concluded that there had been a much larger team keeping tabs on me that his people had somehow missed. He seriously doubted that the kid who had died was the only person who had been shadowing us. I usually take what Dan Capel says as Bible, but in this particular case, I disagreed. Certainly someone had been running this kid, but as far as trailing me, it seemed obvious that he had been working alone. If he'd been part of a team, he would have been more careful when I stopped at the McDonald's. If he had had backup, he either would have handed me off right away or toughed it out and gone right into the restaurant. He'd gone down the road and hid rather than taking the easier play and parking across the street in the Burger King lot. To me, that meant he was worried that he had been spotted—or would be. If he had had a team at that point, he would have zipped off.

I also thought it meant he was an amateur, or, if a pro, operating in very constrained circumstances.

If I was right, that suggested several things. For one thing, it meant my shadow had only a small group at his command; he couldn't afford to run even two cars. It also probably meant that, at this stage, Shadow was still roughing out my routine. A single tail following at a distance was useful for getting an overall notion of a subject's habits without committing all your resources to the project.

Losing the motorcyclist was the first hit Shadow had taken. How he would react would be interesting.

How would I have reacted? By not changing a thing—or at least not appearing to.

"You know why they blew up that ATM in Illinois?" Capel asked when I drove him to the airport the day after the party.

"I'm guessing it wasn't because they were mad at being charged a buck and a half to take their own money out of their accounts."

"Probably not," Capel said. "They wanted to get your attention. It's totally personal."

"I realize that. The question is: why didn't they shoot me then when they had their chance? It's only going to get harder."

"Maybe they couldn't."

"If they could get close enough in Iowa to take the picture of me, then they could have shot me as well."

"Not necessarily. It's easier to move around with a camera, even one with a long-range lens, than with a sniper rifle."

"Maybe. But I think the goal isn't to kill me—not yet. They want to play with me a bit. Then they'll take me down."

"Like a cat with a mouse or a mole he catches in the yard," said Capel.

I've never been compared to a mouse before. Unfortunately, the comparison seemed appropriate.

7

The bartender gave me one of those scowls usually reserved for politicians trying to grab money from your wallet.

"You look familiar," he said, plopping his Popeye arms down on the bar top.

"Maybe I arrested you," I told him.

He hesitated long enough to show that might indeed be a possibility, then gave me a hockey-player grin—one of the incisors on the top right of his mouth was gone—and retrieved my Bud Light. The Squat & Stomp wasn't the sort of place where you ordered Bombay Sapphire without being noticed. In fact, they didn't seem to have anything in the small pyramid of finer beverages near the cash register that one might call top shelf—or bottom shelf, either. It didn't matter. I hadn't come to drink.

I laid out a ten-dollar bill and got real change back. I hid my surprise behind the beer and slid around on the barstool, taking stock of the place. A TV tuned to ESPN sat over the door at the end of the serving area. The smell of a small Shih Tzu being fried wafted in from beyond, though no one in the place looked as if they'd come to eat.

Three guys in their late twenties worked a puck-bowl machine near the door. They blew reverently on the puck before tossing it, as if their spit had magical properties. A trio of men in their early seventies held down the far end of the bar to my right, each gaunter and whiter than the other. They took their drinking very seriously, meticulously raising their half-filled glass steins to their lips, frowning slightly at the bitterness, and then bringing the glasses down in slow motion. The men didn't say anything, and all three stared straight ahead.

About a dozen guys and three women were scattered around the rest of the bar. They wore jeans and T-shirts. Not a tie in the place. My immediate neighbor was a tall, buxom redhead who played with a box of cigarettes as she sipped from a whiskey neat, alternately twirling the box and then a cigarette around in her fingers. Smoking is outlawed in bars in New York, one of those Daddy Knows Best laws that makes it a crime to do something you might actually enjoy without official state sanction. The governor, allegedly a conservative Republican, signed the bill with huge enthusiasm. I guess I'll never understand why someone who claims to be a conservative thinks it's fine to stick the government's nose into other people's business, but then I don't claim to understand politics. And, for the record, I'm a nonsmoker. (I only smoke after sex but I don't look.)

I was about two very slow sips into my beer when the door slammed and in walked a woman with a tank top wrapped tighter around her chest than an Ace bandage. It not only accentuated her breasts but gave nice play to her midsection, where it stopped above a tattoo of a coyote snapping at its prey. Her jeans were low enough to give you a good view of the animal's claws, and from the way she filled the denim it looked like her hips had been hermetically sealed inside. Even the guys at the puck bowl stopped their game as she walked over to the bar.

She held a twenty-dollar bill out toward the bartender, but she'd already gotten his attention.

"Bud with a whiskey shooter," she said.

Popeye Arms had to pick his tongue up off the floor before he could answer her. The woman leaned forward. "You know a guy named Jimmy Ferro?"

The bartender stared at her cleavage as he responded. "No, ma'am."

"He works over at Wappino."

"Lot of people do," said the bartender.

She frowned at him. "Can I have my drink?"

"Yes, ma'am."

"That pool table over there work?"

"Uh—" Popeye Arms's brain had become detached from his mouth, and it took a great deal of effort for him to restore the connection. "Think so," he managed finally. "You'll, uh, need quarters."

"So give me some, handsome. With my drink."

You'd have thought she asked him if he was free after work. The poor slob couldn't hit the keys on the cash register fast enough and then gave her way too much change. She made a point of settling up properly, then slugged the beer and swallowed the shooter. She slammed the whiskey glass down and pushed the beer mug forward.

"Just the beer this time," she said, taking the quarters over to the pool table.

Seemed to me slamming the glass was a *bit* much, but I don't like to critique my minions in the middle of an operation.

Trace—you knew it was her, right? The coyote's some sort of tribal thing—racked the balls on the table as well as just about every other set of cajones in the place, including those of the three old men. She broke and ran the table with thirteen shots before the bartender finished pouring her the beer.

"Anyone want to play?" she asked, chalking the cue as she walked over for her draft. "Just for fun. No bets."

Everyone wanted to play, though not necessarily with the bar's cue sticks. Several guys sauntered over, and eventually two were culled from the pack. One stood about five-four and if he weighed one-ten then I'm touching five hundred pounds. The other wore a mustache that looked like something you'd use to clean the streets. Shorty and Brush Face actually seemed to know what they were doing; each man beat Trace at least once, and even when she ran the table, they seemed in the game until the end.

They were on their fourth beers when Trace asked if they happened to know her friend Ferro. This segued into a long discussion about Wappino. The two men worked there as maintenance people. Trace expressed surprise, though of course she'd already spotted their tags. It would have been difficult to miss Shorty's, since it was around his neck. Brush Face's was clipped to his pants pocket.

I'd tell you exactly how she stole them, except that she was so quick I didn't actually see. I would have guessed a paw-and-grope diversion, but Trace was very subtle in her teasing and had the IDs off by the time Brush Face and Shorty realized they were an hour late for dinner and staring at rather frigid evenings with their wives. Had they realized they were missing their badges at that point, they wouldn't have found them on Trace. She'd already slipped them to me while getting some refills. We made the handoff as I was on my way to the restroom. Before I relieved my bladder I relieved my fingers, putting the badges in a small bag and then tossing them out the window to Sean, waiting outside for the relay. The bar could have been searched for days and the IDs would never have been found.

It wasn't searched though, and I'd be willing to bet that in Brush Face's case, at least, he didn't notice he'd lost his ID until the next morning when he went to go into the plant, if then. Odds were that neither man reported losing his badge, probably making do with temps for the day and planning to tear up the house and car when they went home. They may even have had spares. They had a good incentive not to report that their IDs were gone: losing your ID meant you were docked two hours of pay and charged for the cost of a new one. If you were only making two dollars an hour over minimum wage, that represented a decent hunk of take-home.

Trace's sip and rip wasn't the only ID operation, though it was by far the most fun. Hulk and two of the new ops hit a health club about a mile down the highway from Wappino, prowling the locker rooms while some of the power plant workers were turning the treadmills and pushing the weights around. They came up with two IDs. Rather than simply stealing and using those as is, Hulk ripped off the laminate and pasted our pictures over the originals. Then he zipped them through the small laminator tucked into his gym bag. Hulk's fingers were a little too thick to make the operation a smooth one, but he got the originals resealed and back before being discovered.

This gave us four legitimate magnetic cards allowing access to the entire plant. We ran them through a reader and discovered that the patterns were all the same, making it easy to make counterfeits. This was extra work since we would almost certainly not need the additional tags, but the company was paying for the "event," and doing it this way would leave them with some souvenirs at the end of our visit. ("Rogue Warrior Blew Up My Nuke Plant And All I Got Was This Lousy ID. And Leukemia.") Most times that we steal IDs, we simply use the original and thumb over the tiny photo when flashing to a sentry or anyone else who cares to be flashed. You'd think guards would have caught onto the ploy by now, but it still works as easily today as it did ten years ago.

Now, if you're a careful reader, you're probably wondering how we knew what the blanks looked like. The blanks were the backs of the tag that included the metal part, and while there wasn't much artwork involved, we had to know the general design going in. After all, Hulk had blanks with him when he went to the health club, which he left with the two workers.

If you're well-read, you may know that security IDs only come in a few configurations and generally don't employ high-tech anticounterfeiting techniques. That's true, but it still would have meant going in with about a half-dozen cards, and we like to travel light whenever we can. (Never mind the weight of the laminator.) We knew what the tags looked like because we had very detailed photos of them long before we arrived in the area to check out Wappino—photos good enough, in fact, that we could have made IDs from them.

We also had pictures of the plant. Really good pictures of the plant—aerial photos from every angle, along with shots from the river and the land, with enough detail to show not only where the fences and security posts were but also where the vehicles were kept and even where the security cameras were. We had pictures of the insides of all of the important buildings, and enough snaps of guards to tell us who two of the three shift lieutenants were.

No, I hadn't sent Trace in with a video cam in her navel. I let my fingers do the walking on the Internet at the local library. The plant was extremely controversial. A lot of people don't want a pile of plutonium in their backyards, and in this case a lot of the people raising the fuss were doctors and lawyers and astrophysicists who lived in the affluent surrounding towns, so their screams carried clout. This clout in turn led the corporation running Wappino to launch a PR campaign that did everything but put a smiley face on the containment vessels.

Actually, a smiley face on the containment vessels would have been a smarter idea. Because, in the course of their PR campaign, they invited one of the local news hounds in to do a feature story. The story made the plant sound like Shangri-La; I have no doubt that a large blowup of the story is hanging on the paneled walls of the corporate dining room. But it also provided us with intelligence that would have taken considerable legwork to obtain. I'm not saying we wouldn't have gotten it, anyway, but it did allow us to put our resources to better use elsewhere.

Put that one down to corporate stupidity, and the unconsidered dangers of living in a media-saturated world. But the people opposing the plant did their bit to make our intel gathering a snap, too. There were several groups against the plant, each vying with the other to be *the* voice of the people. One of the loudest managed to obtain a copy of an internal security study completed at the plant just a month before. Almost surely the source was a disgruntled worker, pissed off about a decision to limit overtime at the plant, but I digress. The voice of the people quoted from the report to make its point that the plant was not safe. And then these geniuses scanned a copy of the report into their computers and posted a link on the Internet.

I guess they figured that if some slimebags blew up the plant, it would prove their point.

The report did not give a step-by-step plan for taking down the facility. But it told us how big the force was, what weapons they had, how often they trained, and yada-yada-yada, as the folks in New York say. Reading between the lines, anyone with a brain would know how many people to expect on any given shift, how the force would leapfrog back for ammo, and the like. It took slightly more experience and skill to deduce the way the security people had been trained, how they were organized, and how they were likely to respond to an emergency—these things were not outlined specifically. Still, even someone with limited mental capacity could have figured out what they were up against.

Or not up against, depending on your perspective.

I will say this one thing: the Hudson River is a *beautiful* fucking river. Full moon out, nice spring breeze going, few things are going to top the scene. It's so idyllic you just want to take a sailboat out and cruise gently downriver, rocking along like you have not a care in the world. It's a river made for sailboats, harmless throwbacks to another era.

Did I say harmless? Well, *almost* harmless. Harmless except for the three SpecWarriors in black Rogue attire easing into the water just north of the plant. It was a good night for a swim, and the half mile to the power plant dock got us loose. The photos had shown that there was no fence and no video cameras in front of the northern turbine building.

The only difficulty, if you could call it that, was getting past the dock area, which was patrolled by two men with dogs. We'd watched them earlier in the evening, however; the paths they took were confined to the spot-lit area back off the water, and unless you climbed directly over one of the two formal docks and stood directly in the light, they'd never see you. Both men could also have been picked off by a sniper from the peaceful little sailboat or even the two sexed-up speedboats backing us up in the shadows, but the idea here was to sneak in and out. And, unlike terrorists, we weren't supposed to actually hurt anyone.

Video cameras covered the ramps just off the dock, but they were easy to avoid. A large discharge pipe, cooling unit, and what looked to be some sort of internal plant sewer treatment facility obscured their view both of the water directly in front of them and the northern side of the dock and ramps leading to the rest of the plant. Which was where Sean, Trace, and I chose to come ashore.

The wind blew in our direction (making it harder for the dogs to pick up our scents if we messed up the timing), and, as an added bonus, it cut down on the distance to the turbine building. The perimeter fence ran down to the water just to our left; it was anchored there by a sentry station about thirty yards from the water. The post hadn't appeared occupied earlier in the day but now proved to have not one but two guards in it.

One was female and not entirely in uniform. I wish I could say I'd thought of setting that up myself, but t'ain't so.

We tiptoed across the shadows, taking advantage of some trailers parked in the lot for cover. We reached the corner of the building and went up, one at a time, to the roof. We hadn't brought a ladder, but the climb couldn't have been easier if we had; the bricks had been set in a decorative pattern at the corner, providing handy footholds. The second roof was harder to reach. There was no decorative pattern, and it had to be scaled quickly, since it was in the sightline of one of the guards patrolling the dock area. Trace went to work on it, making her way up with a special set of climbing gloves and footgear. She found a spot to anchor a rope at the top, and after the guard passed out of sight, Sean and I climbed up and joined her, aided by a rope she'd tossed down.

At this point, the facility was basically ours. We were not in a position to do maximum damage yet—the reactor building was several hundred yards away—but from a public relations point of view, an explosion of ten pounds of C-4 here, or even a few grenades tossed around the nearby area, would have been a disaster nearly as devastating as an unplanned release of radioactive water vapor.

Trace and I scooted to the edges of the roof to get a look at the rest of the plant, Sean began placing IEDs at various points around the roof. I had a digicam with me, recording the plant from a new angle. After I finished taking my pictures, I went back and saw that Sean was ready to go.

Trace, on the other hand, was nowhere to be found.

"Where's Ms. Apache?" I asked him.

"I thought she was with you."

A quick scan of the rooftop failed to turn her up.

Halfway between being angry and concerned, I went to the east side of the building, where I'd last seen her. There was a large vent stack about ten yards away, part of a large cooling complex. Thinking she had gone down the side in her climbing moccasins to look at the buildings there, which we had little information on, I crawled to the edge and looked over. I didn't see her. As I raised my head, though, I spotted a dark shadow near the top of the cooling pipe.

Trace Dahlgren, human fly.

We had radios with us, but we wanted to keep their use to a minimum. Our scan of press stories about the plant showed that the company had recently won a grant from the state for advanced radio equipment, which might have been code—which *should* have been code—for high-tech frequency detectors. It probably wasn't, but I didn't want to take a chance and blow the operation just because I was pissed at Trace.

Kicking Trace's butt a mile—well, that was a different story. Lucky for her there were other things for us to do.

We'd made it down to the lower roof when Sean caught my attention. One of the security vehicles was coming down the perimeter road a few yards away. We slipped to our bellies and watched as it proceeded up the road, then stopped right near the bend in the fence that had been our next destination.

There's one thing about this exercise that I haven't had a chance to mention until now. And that is that, because we didn't want the plant to be unarmed if my shadow made an appearance, the guards at the site had not been told that a security operation was underway. Furness knew, his chief of security knew (actually, he was Furness's deputy, but the title substituted for a raise), and the watch commanders knew, but they were under strict instructions not to tell their men.

Which meant that the guards were carrying live ammo. Granted, most of them hadn't chambered a round in the Glocks they were wearing, nor were there shells in the few shotguns that the guards were assigned. That may not have made much of a difference, since for the most part the men only used the weapons once a year, firing at paper in well-lit, air-conditioned rooms. But bullets are bullets, and just because someone aims at your chest doesn't mean he won't hit your head.

So that's why when one of the guards flicked on the search beam on the side of his SUV and swung it toward the stack, I felt a jolt of concern. I was worried about Trace.

"Skipper, we moving?" asked Sean.

I held my hand up a second longer. The guard played the beam in the direction of the tower, then swung it around. Sean and I ducked as it played over the edge of the building. The guard swung it around a few times, then got back in the truck and resumed his patrol.

"If she gets her ass caught, I'm going to kick it into next week," I told Sean as we headed for the perimeter fence. "And then I'm going to kick it into next month."

"Me, too," he said.

There were sensors along the fence line, a whole suite of high-tech infrared and motion detectors. The thing was, they were designed to deal with the likely threat—which meant they were all located on the other side of the fence. We planted a series of IEDs along the fence area, then worked our way up through the complex. The fence itself was a standard chain-link job topped by four-strand barbed wire. There were runs on either side of an asphalt road.

Hard to climb? No. Hard to cut through? No. A psychological barrier that will lull the security force into thinking they have a secure situation when in reality it's a sieve? You got it.

With the devices planted, I took a look at the containment vessel of Reactor Four, which sat beyond a large water holding tank to my right.* Air pressure inside the vessel is kept lower than the external pressure, so that in the case of a leak, any radioactive vapors will remain inside.

Theoretically. And only if it's a small leak. But we'll leave the quibbles to the engineers.

The vessels themselves are thick concrete. They were originally engineered to protect against earthquakes, and if you do any sort of research at all you'll find that they can withstand a good amount of shaking before failing. That same research will show you where the weakest point of the containment containers tends to be. I'm not going to do

* There were only two reactors, each with its own building. They were, however, called Reactor Three and Reactor Four, apparently because the original plans had called for four reactors to be built.

your homework for you, but I will give you a hint: it's not where you think it is, and it's vulnerable to a surprisingly low amount of explosives, if you use a very targeted weapon.

If you're a diligent terrorist and you do your homework, you'll also find any number of reassuring points about how the containment vessels will withstand crashes by private airplanes and even fully loaded jetliners. There's a reason for that. The front of an airplane is not a particularly hard point, and even in a 747, it's as much the momentum of the object rather than its mass at rest that does most of the damage.

We should also remember that we're speaking theoretically here. To my knowledge, there has only been one real-world test that even attempted to simulate severe trauma on the concrete shell of a containment vessel, and that was on a scale model in Japan a few years back. In real life—who knows?

I digress. Sean and I went to the fence line and planted the rest of our IEDs. They were a mix of timer and radio controlled smoke bombs, with a few flash-bangs thrown in. Then we retreated to the rendezvous point.

Where Trace stood waiting for us.

"What took you so long?" she asked.

"I ought to put you over my knee and spank you," I told her. "What the hell was the idea deviating from the game plan?"

"If you hit me, you better slug Sean, too, or I'll file for sex discrimination," she said.

"Cut the shit, Trace. Why'd you go off like that?"

"You tell us if we see an opportunity, take it," she

said. "I planted my camera up there with the wireless transmitter. We'll be able to see everything that happens. Valuable intelligence."

"It wasn't worth the risk. Next time you do that, I'll kick your ass, little girl."

"Why wait?"

She reminds me of the daughter I never had. We slipped out into the water, stroking toward one of the speedboats, which had anchored itself upstream after we made land.

Not that the night's work was done, not by any means. While Trace, Sean, and I were rummaging around the northwestern side of the plant, a team led by Hulk had scouted the perimeter fence on the southwest. Their primary mission was peeking. That part of the campus lay outside of the reactor perimeter and was heavily forested. The pictures we had were taken in the summer, and we weren't entirely sure what lay beneath the foliage.

To the north of the security fence—outside of the nuclear zone but still on the campus grounds—sat a large administrative area that was as easy to get through as Central Park in New York forty miles away. The buildings themselves were lightly guarded and the large parking lots were unlit, as were the nearby holding areas for trailers and supplies. I thought the area might be useful for the actual assault, and it was up to Hulk to find out.

As they were proceeding, he spotted an area we hadn't mapped. It was a set of trailers where, at least according to the signs, low-level waste was stored. These were barrels with various items, no more radioactive than the medical chest at your local hospital, but still necessitating special handling. The area was covered by video cameras, but there was a gaping hole in the defenses at one end. Hulk took the opportunity to plant some IEDs there. Then he and the team worked their way to the perimeter fence and called me on the sailboat.

"The bird is primed for plucking," Hulk said, handling the tongue twister better than I thought he would. It was perfect timing. An old-fashioned seaplane was just skimming down on the glassy water a hundred yards away.

"Vulture is on its way," I told him. "Ten minutes."

The aircraft heading toward us was a genuine old-timer, a PBY Catalina borrowed from one of Dan Capel's clients. Most of the airplane's flight time was spent at air shows, where its gooselike hull and fuselage blisters filled some of the crowd with nostalgia and the others with curiosity. I'm not a nostalgic type and I really don't give a hoot for airplanes, except as tools to get the job done. In this case, the job was to provide a real-time thermal scan of the facility, showing us how the security force reacted to the probes Hulk was about to launch.

It was also helping us watch our backs. If Shadow was watching me, he'd see me go aboard the PBY and presumably take an interest in it or some other element of the operation, like the sailboat.

While the showy seaplane did its thing, a much more mundane two-engined Fokker borrowed from the DEA was flying farther above watching us. One of Capel's partners, Jeff Storey, supervised the sensor reads and had at his disposal three two-man rapid response teams made up of my new shooters. If Shadow started following me or one of the boats, we'd follow him.

Trace and I left Sean to kick back with a brewski and paddled out to the flying boat. The plane's owner welcomed us aboard. One of the conditions of allowing us to use the aircraft was that he be with it at all times. Since Capel vouched for him, I had no trouble with that.

Originally intended as crew member observation posts back in the days when the flying boat was used for long-range patrols, with slight modifications the blisters in the rear fuselage were excellent posts for infrared and radar pods. The Coast Guard has similar gear in its HU-25 Guardians that allow it to watch ground objects from a good distance away. The DEA has slightly different gear but with the same basic capabilities.

Capel's client had upgraded the PBY's engines to improve their efficiency and range. The mods, coincidentally, made the engines much quieter than the originals, and the aircraft could fly relatively low without being heard from the ground.

The nuclear power plant was in a special restricted flight zone, with two F-16 fighters from an air base in nearby New Jersey assigned to enforce it. But Capel had flown around the area yesterday and discovered that he wouldn't be challenged as long as he stayed just outside the bubble. He'd also taken the precaution of alerting the area controllers that he would be practicing night flights and water landings in preparation for an air show planned at Atlantic City later that month. The air show was being heavily promoted, and the PBY was well-known in the air community, which made the cover a natural—so much so that one of the tower people at Westchester called over to see why Capel was flying instead of the owner, whose voice he would have recognized. That was easily handled: the owner chimed in from the copilot's seat, assuring the controller that he wasn't going to let his friend dent his million-dollar toy.

The infrared gear was so good and Capel timed his first cut over land so perfectly that I could see Hulk set up the small wind sock devices on the security perimeter to start the next phase of the operation. The idea was to set off the sensors and test the security force's response. We already knew how big the force was and roughly how they were deployed, but "roughly" is a sure way of guaranteeing that an operation will hit FUBAR—Fucked Up Beyond All Repair—well ahead of schedule. The devices set off the detectors on the fence. This meant the response team had to come and check them out, giving us the plant's MO for handling problems. It also got them used to being annoyed, subtly lowering their attention level.

One truck, two guys. That was the entire response "team." They left their shotgun—assuming they had one—in the vehicle. That might be a moot point. The fence was easily monitored from the cover of the woods, and anyone with a decent rifle and nightscope—hell, anyone with a bow and arrow—could have taken out both men before they found the sock.

Actually, they seem not to have spotted it at all.

The guards stared for a while, then called back on their radios to HQ that there was nothing there. We got the whole communication on the scanner, recording it for further analysis and possible use.

Hulk's team continued the probing operation several more times, varying their approach. In one case, a team member went to the fence, pried the bottom up and then rolled a warm soda can across the sensor track. This set off all sorts of alarms, but the response was pretty pathetic. One of the guards found the soda can resting against the fence and kicked it. Hulk told me later that the guard laughed as the warm soda exploded against a fence post. I wonder what he would have done if the can had been filled with something other than agitated carbon dioxide and sugar.

Rather than thinking they were being screwed with—and perhaps initiating a lockdown and calling in reinforcements, or at least contacting their boss—the guards wrote it all off to a series of flakeouts and, maybe, ghosts. I'm sure if there had been a full moon they would have blamed that.

Earlier I mentioned that security isn't just a matter of money, it's a mindset, and this was the perfect example of that. There was a perfectly logical explanation for everything that they saw, everything that happened. Forgetting their other errors for a second, if one guard had taken a step back and said, "Gee, there have been a lot of weird things going on tonight, I wonder why," the outcome of the exercise might have been much different.

Or at least we would have been forced to be more creative.

Capel practiced a pair of touch and go's on the river—part of the cover story. Then we did two more circuits and prepared to call it a night. Hulk's team was already rendezvousing with their transport, a nondescript Dodge Caravan about a mile south of the plant entrance.

To keep our tail operation secure from Shadow, I didn't communicate directly with Storey in the DEA plane. But I was monitoring the frequency he would have used to send the coded transmission to the backup teams. The line had been quiet all night. Below, the river was empty except for our sailboat and the two speedboats we'd borrowed for the operation.

I picked up the radio and broadcast a message on the frequency we'd been using from the sailboat. "Let's pack it in and get some rest," I said. "We dance at high noon."

A decoy, yes. If Shadow didn't fall for the subtle, maybe he'd go for the obvious. But he didn't show the next day, and I was starting to think maybe he had been the mad motorcyclist after all.

The car that pulled up to the gate of the Wappingers Falls Volunteer Ambulance Company around five A.M. Saturday morning looked like your typical soccer-mom mobile. A Dodge Caravan with a dented fender and plenty of sticky fingerprints on the windows, it might easily have taken a wrong turn while looking for the town soccer field, which happened to be just down the hill. A ditzy-looking soccer-mom type got out of the van, pulled the zipper up all the way on the jacket of her matching sweatsuit outfit, adjusted her kitten-face head band, and checked her RedveryRed lipstick in the van window. After a few moments of dazed introspection, she went to the door and began ringing the bell at the side of the ambulance company building. This woke the person upstairs. (Though traditionally staffed by volunteers, the company had faced the realities of an era where civic responsibility was no longer a given and hired full-time paramedic drivers to stay with the ambulance, ensuring quick response no matter what the day or hour.) The paramedic on duty, a thirty-year-old chain smoker whose gut and unshaven mug made him look about fifty, plodded down the steps somewhat haphazardly.

"You're an hour early," he said, pulling open the door.

"It's never too early to have fun," said the ditzy soccer mom, who had reached beneath her sweats and produced a Kimber Compact .45. You don't see that weapon very often around town, especially in the hand of someone who favors RedveryRed lipstick, so I don't blame the ambulance attendant for being surprised. The Kimber looks a bit like a Colt .45 that's gone through a serious aerobics program. As pretty as it is, the serious work is on the inside, where the craftsmen have worked hard to make the weapon durable and dependable.

The paramedic was no doubt thinking of all of this when he saw the gun. Overwhelmed, he did the only rational thing possible—he fainted.

Which actually made Trace's job more difficult.

She had to toss the poor lug over her shoulder and carry him back up to his bedroom. By the time she came down Hulk had the company's backup ambulance out of the bay and was already playing with the light switches to see what cool patterns he could make in the night.

We're considerate Tangos, aren't we? We left the main ambulance, took only the backup, and tarried not to slit the paramedic's throat. That's terrorism in the twenty-first century, for you.

Roughly a half hour later, precisely as the shifts were changing at the power plant, a rented twenty-two-foot Chris Craft 22 Launch plowed into the Wappino plant's dock area. The air cracked with the sharp reports of explosions. Light flashed. Smoke spewed forth.

Sean used too many flash-bangs for the pyrotechnical display, in my opinion, but you can't argue with the results. As that was happening, the ambulance Trace and Hulk had borrowed barreled off the highway and sped toward the main security gate, lights and sirens flashing. They were prepared to crash the gate, but for some inexplicable reason, the guard there flung it open without even challenging them. Trace leaned out the window and yelled, "We're here for the heart attack victim. Heart attack, heart attack!" she repeated as the ambulance rolled through the security perimeter and turned toward Containment Building Four.

As Trace shouted, several items dropped from her hands. These were soon revealed to be a flash-bang and two smoke grenades. By the time the ambulance turned onto the perimeter road a hundred or so yards away, the sentry area looked like a volcano.

These nearly simultaneous explosions—we were off by about thirty seconds—signaled the "indoor team" to move along with the main event. Hulk and I, along with four of our newest and brightest, had slipped inside the campus almost an hour earlier, coming through the woods where the previous night's excursions had shown infiltration would be child's play.

We hadn't been twiddling our thumbs all that time. We'd arranged a few oil drum smokers to provide additional busywork and confusion for the security team. These are about as low-tech as you can get. They consisted of a) one oil drum, b) some oil and an accelerant to make it burn (the possibilities are endless), and c) matches. We set four alight, then headed out. By the time we cleared the inside perimeter, thick smoke furled out near the edge of the parking lot, and we could hear not only the plant fire alarms but the city's fire siren going off by the time we reached Containment Building Four.

Give credit where credit is due—as Hulk burst through the door, two guards pulled their pistols and leveled them at him.

By the time he ducked away, the guards had lost their pistols and were rolling to the floor, covered by netting from a special shell in my M209 grenade launcher. The shell scattered them with pepper spray as it exploded. It's intended to be a fine mist, but it comes out more like a spluttering splat than a sustained shower. That's not particularly important unless you happen to get one of the splats in your eyes, in which case you scream like a motherfucker. (Another toy I snookered off the shelves of Law Enforcement Technologies; it pays to be a board member to make sure you are a winner.)

Poor bastards. I had to cover my ears as I ran down the corridor with the rest of the team.

We were now inside the reactor building, which lay wide open and empty before us. What would you do with a nuclear reactor? Fire an antitank missile at it? Steal the control rods? Break the machinery? Whip out the Duracells and recharge for free?

We could certainly have done all of that, though the truth is that such mischief would have only amounted to vandalism and very bad PR for the company. The reactors are designed to withstand stresses like those I've mentioned without catastrophe. I'm not saying that we wouldn't have caused damage, just that none of those scenarios—the kind you're always reading about in doomsday stories—would have had the same impact as blowing up the cooling system and neutralizing the air pressure system in the containment building, which could be accomplished with a mere daub of explosive.* We put happy face stickers in the appropriate spots to demonstrate that we could have done all of those things. Oversize coffee cans filled with cement were strapped on the most vulnerable point of the building—no, I'm still not telling you where it is—to show where plastic explosives would

* Actually, you could kick the machinery for the air pressure system apart with your foot. But with my flair for the dramatic, I always favor the option that includes blowing something up.

have been located to crack the containment vessel. They weren't enough to bring down the building, but that wasn't the goal; all we were looking for was a hole wide enough for the radioactive material to plume out through.

Meanwhile, Trace and the ambulance had gone to the building where the control room was located. A security officer trotted over as Trace and Sean, dressed in what looked like ambulance uniforms, jumped out. He was yelling at them that the plant was in an emergency situation. Talk about your understatements.

"We know, we know!" said Trace.

"Your gun loaded?" Sean asked, pointing to the holstered Glock.

"Uh—"

"Mine is," said Sean, producing an H&K MP5 from behind his hip.

The ex-SEAL told me later that he'd never seen hands shoot up so fast. Or that much piss stream down a leg.

Around this time, my team left the containment building and headed for the other entrance to the control area. It was at this point that the video camera Trace had planted proved its worth. Capel, monitoring the device from the seaplane, spotted a security SUV heading in our direction. He warned me, and we were able to take cover before it passed by, rushing to the oil fires we'd set a few minutes earlier.

The plant had certain sensible procedures the people inside the control room were supposed to follow in case of an unspecified emergency, which this one was. They'd gotten as far as locating the black spiral books where the procedures were recorded when we swept in. The four people in the room stared in disbelief as four black-clad ninjas with shotguns and submachine guns vaulted the pipe railings and spread out around the room.

All of the security people assigned to guard the control room were doing just that—guarding the control room from its two entrances at the far side. We came in through the restroom hallway, having noticed from the photos that the windows were not barred and were large enough even for Hulk's bulky frame. There were no security people inside the control room. Not that they would have made much difference, I suppose, but it is something to note.

The plant operators remained dumbstruck for a few moments, unable to react or speak. The reactors are controlled by a very large panel of switches that look like something out of an early *Star Trek* episode. There are a number of pull buttons and levers. We'd had a chance to study up on the controls in advance, thanks to that news story and photo spread we'd found on the Internet. This made tagging the proper switches pretty quick.

"What the *fuck* are you doing?" said one of the operators as I hung my last *Oops!* sign. "What the *hell* is this?"

"Armageddon," I muttered. When I turned around I found a middle-aged Greek woman, five-four and all *koutsomoures tiganites*—a strong fried fish—staring at my kneecap.

"We're blowing up your reactor," I told her. "Sorry if it's a bad time."

"Like fucking hell you are."

I like cursing in a woman, especially a woman past fifty. So when she marched up to slap me, I merely grabbed her arm.

"Careful now," I told her. "Unlike your security force, our weapons are loaded."

With plastic bullets, but still . . .

"Fuck yourself. No one told us there'd be a drill today." She snapped her hand back and put it on her hips. I felt as if I were back in elementary school and getting ragged out by the vice principal, Mrs. Sit-on-Your-Face.

"Terrorists usually don't announce themselves in advance," I said. "You're the supervisor?"

"I'm the fucking President of the United States as far as you're concerned, asshole."

Which is how I came to carry the fucking "President of the United States" out of a nuclear power plant, screaming until I gagged her. I lashed her hands and feet as well, but she squirmed like a shark on a line.

Trace and Sean had stolen two of the workers' vehicles from the back parking lot and were waiting for us as we emerged. The "President" was placed in the trunk of one of the cars. I slipped into the driver's seat and drove to the gate. I had to turn the music up loud to drown out my passenger's thumping in the truck.

By now, the security force had realized that something deep and dirty was going down and belatedly began to respond with the serious intent a goatfuck requires. (Their goatfuck, not ours.) The guard at the gate seemed to recognize the car as I came up but was unsure about stopping me. We'd caught them in the middle of the shift change, when people were always coming and going.

I made the decision for him, pausing to chat.

"What the hell is going on?" I asked. "What's all this smoke? What's with the alarms?"

"Some sort of fire on the south side," he said. He glanced at the ID I was holding out, though I doubt he actually stopped to read it. If he had, he might have asked precisely how my first name was pronounced.

The tag read: "Phck U. Dickhead." Even Tangos like to have fun.

"Are we under attack?" I wondered aloud.

"Attack?" he repeated.

It was at that moment that I pushed the transponder to set off the IEDs we'd planted the night before.

8

Were the explosions on Turbine Building Three the coup de grace? Or was it the chain on the main gate applied by one of our sleepers on a bike as the last escape vehicle cleared the facility? Hard to say, really. By the time we rendezvoused back at Peekskill's Squat and Stomp for lunch, a five-county region was under a nuclear cloud. The local bridges and highways were jammed; the air above was filled with helicopters and fighter aircraft. The sirens had stopped sounding, but I had a feeling that Furness wasn't going to be smiling the next time he saw me.

I'd taken the precaution of getting the fee up front and using his company credit card to cover our expenses. I *think* he said that was the way I was supposed to do it. Though as I look back on our conversation now, I can't seem to recall how the card number came up in conversation, or why it would have included the extra security code on the back. I'd say that he lent it to me when I stopped by the day we arrived just to say hello, except that he wasn't around his condo at the time to let me in.

Our luncheon's guest of honor turned out to be

half Greek and half Sicilian, which accounted for her fury. When I picked her up out of the trunk, she tried running down the street, which wasn't ideal with bound feet. I let her work off some of her energy, then when she'd calmed down a bit I explained who I was and what we had been doing. This didn't mollify her, either, a fact she made clear when I undid the gag on her mouth. A torrent of abuse streamed out.

"You don't have to impress me," I told her. "I already like you."

She screamed even louder. I folded my arms and waited for the storm to subside. When she ran out of breath, I told her the situation and the plan. "We're going to pretend that you've been kidnapped. You can set whatever terms you want. A raise, maybe?"

"*Pretend* that I've been kidnapped?"

"Look, you can go if you want," I said. "But then you'll miss lunch. Whatever you want, it's on the house. Well, your boss is paying for it. Come on. Have a drink."

I took out my long combat knife and hacked through the restraint at her feet. I was surprised that she didn't kick me.

"Don't patronize me, Mr. Mar-chink-o," she said, drawing it out as if she were one of my Navy instructors back in the golden days of yore. "Don't fuck with me, either."

"I may yet give it a shot."

"Screw yourself."

"Where would the human race be if we could?" I started to laugh, and she did, too.

"Well, all right, if I'm being kidnapped," she said finally. "I guess I might as well get something to eat. And have a beer."

The Squat and Stomp won't find itself listed in any haute cuisine guides, but the fried clam fritters weren't half bad. I let the kids enjoy themselves a bit, then gave Furness a call on his cell phone.

"Well, you kicked our butt, I'll give you that," he said, a sadder but wiser man than the last time we'd talked. "My phone lines are jammed, I have a stack of messages from the local media, and every elected official this side of Syracuse wants to slit my throat, after they tar and feather me. What do you think I should tell them?"

"The truth—that you wanted to find security deficiencies and you called in the best in the business to find the flaws."

"Yeah."

"You didn't notify the local police and emergency agencies because that wouldn't have allowed you to do a realistic drill."

"Yeah."

"For obvious reasons, you can't discuss the results, but they will be implemented in a comprehensive plan to make Wappino the safest nuclear toaster on the planet."

Sometimes I think I should go into PR.

I can't say his mood lightened, but we did set up an appointment for Tuesday. Then I turned the phone over to our hostage, who managed to squeeze a week's worth of paid vacation from Furness for her trouble. I have no doubt she could have gotten more if she had wanted to.

I'd just racked up a set of balls on the pool table to see how good Trace was when she wasn't wearing camouflage when my cell phone rang. It was Capel, who was running our Shadow-watch team from the DEA aircraft.

"Dick, we found your Caravan out on Route 9 a few miles from where Trace and Sean left it," he told me. "Back near the plant. You want to go down there and take a look."

That's Capel—short and to the point, especially with bad news.

9

Sean had parked the Caravan, which had been rented from a local Rent-A-Wreck the day before, in the lot behind the ambulance company building. We might have been tempted to think that the paramedic had followed the team to the plant, except for the fact that he was still back at the company building.

That and the fact that there was a high-powered rifle with a sniper scope in the front seat of the van.

"They weren't close enough to penetrate the building," said Trace.

"That wasn't what they were trying to do," I told her. "They could've gotten anyone coming in and out of that road there."

Anyone including me.

I hate getting sucker-punched.

The van's engine was warm but not hot. Capel suggested getting a thermometer to figure out how long it had been sitting there, but I didn't see the point. Nor was there any sense in scouring the car for DNA or fingerprints; it hadn't been particularly clean when it was picked up.

Of more interest and value was the sniper weapon: a Russian-made Mosin-Nagant.

The weapon used by Charlie's snipers in Nam.

The Mosin-Nagant 7.62 x 55mm M1891/1930 sniper's rifle was antiquated by the time the Vietcong and NVM army got hold of it. As I understand it, most of the guns were hand-selected from standard stock, originally issued to the Soviet Red Army in the 1930s. Their sights were small stubby things, especially when compared to the scopes Americans used. In the hands of a good marksman—and despite what you've heard, not every commie with a gun was a great shot—the Mosin-Nagant was accurate to about a thousand yards. If you gave me my choice of weapon from the period, I'd much prefer the modified or hand-built Remington 700s that Marine snipers favored. But, as any sniper will tell you, the finger on the trigger is more important than the trigger itself.

"Well, they're going to an awful lot of trouble to tell you they remember you from the old days," said Trace.

I put on a pair of gloves and took the gun from the car. It was loaded. I turned in the direction of the power plant entrance, back about a mile and a half, trying to see what the sniper could have hit. I'd driven down this way. Had I seen this motherfucker along the road?

No, I didn't think so. Admittedly, I hadn't been looking for him; I was paying far too much attention to the ruckus in the truck. Still, I think I would have noticed him sitting in the van. I think I would have noticed the van, even if I didn't recognize it as ours.

Most likely he'd parked the van there after I'd passed, continuing his little campaign of head games. He knew he couldn't get to me, or the nuke plant for that matter, but he could make me think he could.

"Charlie, or us?" asked Capel over the phone. He couldn't see the gun from the sky, but we'd told him what we'd found.

Capel's question threw me back thirty-something years to Phong Dinh, where I'd spent some of my shortest days and longest nights in the South Asian Theme Park. We'd fuck the VC by bringing along two sets of footwear—GI issue and native—leaving different tracks in the muck. We left our M16s at home, preferring AK-47s, which didn't shout "SEAL Team Round Eyes!" every time we used them. We'd switch their cached ammo with doctored versions so it would boom when they fired at us. We'd put on French Foreign Legion togas every so often, sending the walking ghosts out to spook the gooks in the middle of the night. It was all about head games, blowing their minds before they blew ours.

"Not Charlie," I told Capel.

"He work with you there?"

"Maybe."

It hurt to admit that. The pain was more than I could say.

•

We kept Capel's team in place watching the nuclear plant, then dispersed to new hotels across the river. Our gear would be picked up by a separate team later on. We used a buddy system, two to a cell; no cell knew where the other was staying. Trace and I buddied up, sharing a room with two beds in a Super 8 Motel about five miles off Route 17 in northern Noo Joisey. We rendezvoused at a fancy restaurant called Xavier's in Piermont, New York, around nine, our last big splurge on Furness's credit card. By that time, I'd spoken to Karen and told her to stay at Rogue Manor for the foreseeable future. A few trusted friends would sleep outside her door for the duration. She argued and she complained and she claimed that I was being overprotective, and I told her what she could do with that. Karen can certainly take care of herself, but I wasn't in the mood to take any chances. Until I found Shadow, the people close to me were vulnerable, too.

I thought about Capel's question for most of the afternoon and evening. I didn't think this was being done by any of the guys I'd served with in Vietnam, certainly none of the SEALs. You live with people in that sort of situation and you end up knowing a hell of a lot about them. Even the guys I hadn't kept in touch with weren't going to be screwing with me like this. Hell, they had a lot easier chances to gun me down thirty years ago.

Ruling out a gook who nursed a grudge wasn't quite as easy. But it seemed unlikely. Even supposing one of them had sufficient reason to remember me and information about who I was, an awful lot of bicycles had rolled down the Ho Chi Minh Trail since I'd been in Southeast Asia. As dedicated as Charlie was, I just couldn't see a fifty-year-old former guerilla coming to America to mess with my head. Kill me outright, maybe. But then why didn't they try to get me when I went back to South Vietnam with a group of Vietnam vets and wives years ago with a film crew to visit old ambush sites and get the lay of the land for future investment potential for clients? I had no warriors with me other than Jim "Patches" Watson, my old point man.

No. It seemed to me the best theory was that someone wanted me to think I was being screwed by someone close to me. They were using that as a misdirection play, with their actual goal as yet unknown.

Which basically left the entire world under suspicion. Nothing like being too fucking paranoid.

Doc's call that night backed up my theory. With a little help from French intelligence—yes, a contradiction in terms no matter what language you speak—he had backtracked the French phone number to a small apartment in a residential area on the outskirts of Paris, near the end of the number 4 métro line. The landlord had turned out to be an eighty-year-old Frenchman with an appreciation for fine legs. He volunteered to Tiffany that his tenant hadn't been in the apartment for several weeks. The tenant was an Asian male in his thirties, which would have been about the right age to be our Topless Tango.

"His apartment frig-fuckin' wall was covered with your pictures," said Doc after he told me how they'd charmed their way inside.

"What do you mean, my pictures?"

"You. Eight by ten glossies, magazine shit, author pictures from your books, little diddly out-of-focus things that ran in the newspapers, even that *National Enquirer* piece on you last year."

Doc has a habit of speaking loudly over the phone. I think he doesn't trust the wires and electronic gadgets and figures his voice has to carry all that way on its own. (You know the picture: two tin cans and a long wire.) I had to hold the phone away from my ear so my eardrum wouldn't shatter.

"The *National Enquirer*? Well, that was a good picture, at least," I said.

"Of your hairy tush," smirked Trace, sitting nearby on the bed.

Her usual exaggeration. Said photo had been of yours truly sunbathing while on vacation. No tush was involved.

"He had all your books," Doc told me. "And a bunch of things on SEALs, all sorts of material. A lot of it. Very weird."

"Hero worship," said Trace.

"Studying the enemy," I said.

"The enemy's enemy," answered Doc. "The guy at the DGSE who helped me figure out the phone number was a little too cooperative. I have a meeting with his boss tomorrow, which I take as absolute confirmation that the headless horseman was one of theirs," said Doc. "And his landlord gave us a tip about where he thought the kid worked in the city. Happens to be on the same block as one of the DGSE offices. In fact, that's all that's there, except for the bakery on the corner. Which has great cookies, but never heard of him."

DGSE stands for *"Direction Générale de la Sécurité*

Extérieure." Imagine the CIA with croissants and half of the FBI's responsibilities as well as its own and you have the general translation. Doc's acquaintances among the Christians In Action had given him an entrée among the French.

"Landlord give you anything else?"

"Got some sort of a girlfriend or maybe a sister, hasn't seen her since the tenant went on a trip. My guess from the description is she's a girlfriend who has her own place. We're trying to run her down. Otherwise, quiet, not too many friends. Low profile. Stuff you'd expect if he were a spy."

"So he infiltrates the operation somehow, then gets his head taken off as a reward," I said, figuring out how it must've gone down. "They killed him because they figured out he was an agent."

"Poor dumb fuck probably tried to stop them," agreed Doc. "And he got himself nailed for it. Didn't watch his back."

"Didn't retain what he read," I told him.

I played target that night, trying to be obvious about my movements while different members of the team and Capel's unit watched for Shadow. But even doing all the obviously predictable things didn't draw Shadow out. I even went down to Asbury Park and walked along the boardwalk.

No Shadow. Maybe he observed the Sabbath.

While I was making myself easy prey, Danny Barrett was humping out in the Midwest, trying to pick up information on possible terrorist cells in the heartland. Danny had managed to gather and sift enough rumors to decide that there were at least two cells of Muslim terrorists operating in the area where we had been. The FBI, in fact, had information on one, which had an alleged Bosnian connection. The connection was tenuous—an M16 that had been stolen from an American peacekeeper there some years before had been found in a raid of an apartment rented by a former resident of Yugoslavia, who had not been heard from since some light-headed judge granted him bail at a hearing after the raid. (The man had become a nationalized citizen two years before and could not be held on any immigration charges.) The local Bureau rats were still trying to track the seller, who'd had a table at a gun show; they thought maybe he'd sold the box of grenades that had been found in the Yugo's place as well.

Tenuous as that all was, it intersected in an interesting way with what the French DGSE told Doc when he met with them: the dead man, whose name was Pierre Diem D'luc, had been assigned to penetrate a smuggling operation with ties to an organization with roots in Bosnia—part of the former Yugoslavia, remember.

The group's name was Shitheads for Allah. Something may have been lost in translation. In any event, Pierre's investigation had led him to America and possibly a terrorist group there, though the DGSE briefer had been "artfully vague"—Doc has a way with words—when it came to describing what he was up to. The Christians In Action supplied a few tantalizing hints: in France, the group Pierre had snuck into specialized in smuggling humans in from the Middle East. They also turned a quick profit on cheap handguns and possibly—only "possibly," a big word in the CIA's vocabulary—had ties with former Yugo military people, who were now auctioning off old weapons as quickly as they could rub the dust and cobwebs off them.

Doc thought he could get more information on the French operation, specifically why the Frenchies would let their agent go to America. Clearly that was something we wanted to pursue. He also wanted to find out more about Pierre's background. The obsession with me certainly would have made him a candidate for the role of Shadow, and if he hadn't been killed, he'd certainly be the number one suspect.

Just my luck. The prime suspect turns up dead. Where's fucking Sherlock Holmes when you need him?

"We're only assuming that was him under the bridge," I told Doc. "That's one thing we have to clear up."

"True. Weight and height are right, though."

"We still can't be definitive."

"Right, Dick." Doc gave me one of his walrus sighs. It's a bit like a subdued bark. "I think if we could put some pressure on, I might be able to get to his case officer here, or someone who was familiar with his mission. They were pretty grateful that we came to them, because they had no clue what was going on. Just a little push from the top."

We decided that Cox at Homeland Insecurity Intelligence could help us—the French tend to be overly impressed by official credentials and long titles—and I told Doc I'd have Cox call him. I also told Doc that I would help Danny Barrett get hold of him and offer to help the French with the ID of the body, maybe through DNA or some other means.

Trace and I took a breather with a light workout—light by her standards, that is. She warmed us up with a nice little five-mile run—"trot," she called it, though by my watch those were seven-minute miles. Then we started doing calisthenics from the SEAL handbook. My big mistake was letting her count them off; I swear she missed every other rep. She grinned the whole time, daring me to mention it.

Her cell phone rang about two-thirds of the way through and she stopped to answer it. No way I was breaking; I wouldn't give her the satisfaction, even if my piles were dragging on the floor.

She glanced at the number before she answered and greeted the caller with the words, *"Hon dah."* It wasn't about her car; the words were Apache for "hello," and they meant that she was talking to one of the "old people," relatives of her mother's. I didn't listen to what she was saying—not enough blood in my ears as I grunted through sit-ups—but when she clicked off and resumed the workout her smile was gone. We finished up in silence, found our respective ways to the shower, and recouped. Trace seemed damn contemplative as we sipped a little mineral water.

"Something up?" I asked her.

"How so?"

"Well, either something's bothering you or that bottle of aqua vita has some great significance I can't fathom. You've been staring at it for a good five minutes."

"Very pure water," she said, taking a sip. She smiled kind of wryly, then added, "They want me to be a godmother."

"Great. Who had a kid?"

"That's not exactly it. Not exactly."

Trace explained that traditional Apache girls go through a ritual called, in English, "The Sunrise Ceremony." It's a coming of age deal that's spiritually more like a bar mitzvah or confirmation than a baptism, and physically closer to the qualification course you take to join special operations. A pubescent girl proceeds through a long ceremony assisted by a godmother or sponsor, as well as a medicine man. Proper preparation takes months and involves a wide range of tasks, including quite a bit of physical training and deprivation. To be chosen as the godmother was a great honor, but also an awesome responsibility; the woman became the girl's role model, defender, and spiritual guide. Trace had not yet been formally asked; that in itself involved an elaborate ceremony. The girl's mother did not want to risk being rejected—it could be interpreted as a great shame—and so Trace had to give her informal yea or nay within a week or so.

"Sounds pretty cool," I told her.

"I don't know if I want to do it."

Her remark floored me. Trace doesn't hit people over the head with her Apache heritage, but if you hang around her at all you understand it's pretty important to her. And from what I know of the Apaches, she truly has their genes. These were tough people, used to scratching a living out of the desert. Trace's family line goes back to a line of great chiefs named Chihuahua who struck fear into the hearts of Mexicans and Americans, as well as rival Indian groups. One of the chiefs was the next-to-last holdout against the whites in the Southwest, surpassed only by Geronimo, a great medicine man and also a distant relative of Trace's. Women played an important role in Apache culture. The society was matrilineal. When a couple married, they lived with the girl's mother, and women had an important say in all community matters. Most of the truly great and powerful healers or shamans in the tribe were women.

For Trace, deciding to act as godmother in the ceremony would mean tapping into something more than just her personal history.

"You can't tell them no?" I asked.

You'd've thought that was the dumbest question in the world from the way she rolled her eyes.

I'd been planning to call the king of Tadpoles, but he beat me to the punch Sunday around noon.

"I, um, uh, need to talk to you in a secure manner," said Cox. "The sooner the better. Face-to-face. Tonight, if possible."

Cox suggested we meet halfway, which by his calculation was Baltimore. I countered with a McDonald's in Delaware, just south of the Jersey line.

"Be there at eight P.M.," I told him.

He was, but I wasn't. Instead, I stopped at a gas station the next exit off the interstate and called the McDonald's. I had the staff call him to the phone—

probably a first for McDonald's—then told him to get back on the highway and meet me at a Burger King in a mall two exits away.

Which gave me plenty of time to make sure Cox wasn't followed. I watched him from a pizza parlor across the road, then had Trace call over. Burger King employees don't pick up their phone as quickly as they do at Mickey D's; I almost had to have Sean retrieve him.

"You don't fuck around," Cox said when he finally walked into the pizza parlor.

"I fuck around as much as I possibly can. What's up?"

"That NSA contact you gave me—that Boreland fellow? We struck pay dirt."

Pay dirt being a series of encrypted messages that were being transmitted to parties unknown from parties unknown, though later said parties were believed to be located in the former Yugoslavia, more specifically in the region of Bosnia.

Which, of course, got my attention. Not that I let on.

"You and I define pay dirt differently," I told him. "Pay dirt means something useful. This is just—I don't know what it is. Nothing."

"No, no, it's something. It's definitely something."

I'd seen the funny look Cox had on his face before. For lack of anything better, I'll call it the "gung-ho vice admiral look," after the place where I saw it most memorably.

This was back a few years, when I was in the service. A vice admiral I knew fairly well wanted a package delivered to a city in the Middle East. The city happened to be on the water, and the admiral had come up with a plan all by himself to get it there. A very daring plan. He came to me with it, because he knew me well and knew I did that sort of thing. We were on a first-name basis at the time: he called me Dick, I called him Admiral.

"Dick, here's what you do. C-5A out of Stewart gets you there around 0400. You execute a HALO jump off the front deck of the aircraft and parachute onto the beach, where a CIA op will be waiting. I have the code words and authentification all worked out for you."

He said all that without taking a breath. Then he gave me that look Cox had just given me.

Where do you start? With the fact that no one jumps off the "front deck" of a C-5A? That a C-5A would not be the best choice for that mission? That even if it were, what would the point be? The usual means of delivering a package—which for all I knew was a ham sandwich—involved carrying said sandwich in a diplomatic pouch and whisking it over to the embassy. It almost surely would have sufficed in this case—and in fact it did, because that's what I did. But I digress.

"This is going to be big, Dick," said Cox. "We're not there yet. But we will be. Which is where you come in. I hope." His face changed. Now his expression wasn't gung ho vice admiral. It was more wide-eyed, as if he were practicing to become a golden retriever.

"How am I involved?" I asked.

"You know what a server is?"

He wasn't referring to our waitress, who

couldn't manage to get the drink order right. He meant a computer used in a network, in this case as a host for the site where the encrypted messages were being passed along. The NSA had managed to partially trace the route the messages took but could not get all the way back. They believed, however, that if they could plant a mole in the server they had identified, they'd be able to.

"A mole?" I asked.

"A worm, I mean," said the Tadpole King. "Whatever. They have some technical geek name. It's something that will let them trace the information route back and find the source. I can get one of the computer guys to explain it to you if you think it's important. I don't really know it that well."

"What does this have to do with me?"

"Someone has to plant the mole. I mean worm. Which is one thing you're good at, right?"

"Why don't we just ask them to put it on their computer?"

"Because we don't know if they know. They might. Or maybe they'll do something to tip them off inadvertently."

"Like?"

"Maybe you better ask the tech guys. I'm over my head on the technical end of this stuff." He shifted around in his seat, eyes as big as ever. "There's a hard drive ready to go, you slip in, take out the old one, put in the new one—bing-bang-boing, it's done."

"You think it's going to be that easy, huh?"

"Well not for anyone else. For anyone else, it would be hard. But for you, it'll be easy."

If I had been in a better mood, I would have opened my shirt to show him that I don't wear a Superman uniform. I had to do it, of course, because it represented a potential connection with Shadow, even if Cox didn't realize it. But I wasn't going to make a commitment to him without getting a lot more information and control over the operation. I had leverage and I was going to use it.

Cox readily agreed to let me run the mission any way I saw fit. He even said something along the lines of "Isn't that the way it's supposed to work?" and wasn't just trying to jerk me off. He also agreed to cut me in directly on any intelligence he received. I got the impression that the NSA was using him. Boreland or someone else there had probably hoped to run this gig for some time, and they saw Cox—and by extension, me—as a ripe mark, easy to use.

That wasn't an argument *not* to do it, assuming it could be done easily.

"Where is it?" I asked him finally, after we'd more or less sketched out an agreement.

"Very convenient for you in New York," he told me. "It's right in the city. Queens."

In a bank. Across from a police station.

A real snap.

10

Dan Capel's New York City office had been designed by a world-class architect and design team with one goal in mind: to impress the piss out of corporate clients. It must work, because if it didn't, he would never be able to pay the mortgage.

I stepped off the elevator onto a marble floor. A receptionist sat behind a teak throne far enough across the area that I would have needed binoculars to read her facial expressions. As I walked toward her, my progress was recorded by two different optical cameras and a video system. A biometric laser system took my measurements carefully enough to prepare a suit that would have required no alterations, not even in the notoriously difficult to master crotch. Panels below the marble recorded my weight. They weren't contemplating my coffin. All of this information was compared to the data that had already been collected downstairs to make sure I hadn't somehow outfoxed the preliminary security system as well as the two guards who screened anyone using the private elevator. (There were also security people in the main lobby, employed by the landlord, but they were about on par with most security people in building lobbies, even New York's. It might have taken twenty seconds' worth of thought and effort to get past them, assuming they were in suspicious moods. The bank off the lobby had a rent-a-cop as well, though he looked to be about seventy.)

The secretary at the desk had black belts in karate and Krav Maga, an Israeli self-defense method that teaches practitioners to kill without using weapons other than their hands. It's doubtful she would have had a chance to use either art if attacked, however. The metal strips that line the walls, floors, and ceilings aren't meant to be decorative, though they do give the place a high-tech flash. They're arranged to send enough current flying across the room to stop a bull at the push of a button. Anyone who flirts with the secretary risks setting off the system, because, in addition to the hot button on her desk and the two hidden nearby, the system is tied to a computer that constantly monitors her vital signs; shoot her or even get her to breathe hard and it goes off.

And that's just in the front room.

Capel was waiting for me in his office down the hall, a nice fresh pot of coffee and a tray of fruit on his desk. Rubbing shoulders with the corporate elite hasn't changed him personally, but it sure has taught him how to treat guests. He put his hand to the mouthpiece of his phone as I came in, giving me a "Hey, Skip, how's it hangin'?" smile.

"Have to make a few phone calls to do a little hand-holding, Dick," he explained a few minutes later. "Then we'll hit the road. No more than ten more minutes, if that. Amuse yourself."

A dangerous invitation, surely, but rather than playing with some of Capel's high-tech toys or the weight bench in the corner, I went over to the glass and admired New York City. Capel had the good taste to locate his office near midtown, and on a nice sunny spring morning, the view was fantastic. I'm not talking of the skyline or the river, which you could see if you used the telescope he had set up near the corner. Much better was the view of the young ladies walking to work, and no telescope was necessary. New York has some of the greatest museums in the world, but the best art is free on the streets.

We did the meet-and-greet thing for a few hours. I enjoy it, though being in a sea of suits can be a little disorienting. Capel moved so smoothly among them I swear someday he's going to run for office as mayor or President—nothing in between.

The Queens Savings Association is a small savings bank where you can get a holiday club account and maybe a mortgage. They give Tootsie Roll Pops out to kids, and there's at least a fifty-fifty chance the bank clerks will say hello cheerfully when you come in. If you've had an account for any length of time, the bank manager will probably know your name.

Yup. Prime takeover target for a heartless conglomerate. Don't know how they missed it for this long.

The interior was protected by infrared and motion detectors; the doors and windows were wired as well. The windows on the second floor were grated, but the ones on the three stories above that weren't. It would be rather risky to climb in that way, however; the bank sat across from a police station.

Capel posed as a small businessman interested in finding out what kind of services the bank offered. The information he wanted took all of five minutes to obtain, but the bank was sparsely staffed, which meant Capel had to wait for the manager for nearly a half hour before he got a chance to ask his questions. This was just fine with him; it not only gave him a chance to observe the routine but also gave him an easy excuse to inquire about the restroom, which turned out to be on the second floor.

Capel wandered up there and quickly discovered the computer area, which sat directly off the hall. He went through the open door, ostensibly to ask which way it was to the restroom, but of course getting a feel for the layout. A bored looking techie sat in the corner, playing the latest version of interactive Doom on a PC connected to the Internet via a T1 line. The geek seemed somewhat annoyed to have to look up from his game, and Capel had an easy time snapping pictures of the room with his digital camera. He noted that, like the downstairs area, it was protected by motion detectors, but otherwise it was not under surveillance. The bank had only the first and second floors of the building. There was no direct access to the upper offices, which had belonged to a clothing manufacturer that had sent its subsistence-level wages overseas a decade before.

I looked things over outside. Unlike many buildings in the area, the bank and the others nearby didn't have backyards. A narrow alley ran behind them, just wide enough for a car to get through. The alley ran from the street to the back of an apartment complex. Past a certain point, a vehicle would get snagged against a cement sidewalk that jutted out on the left. Someone on foot, however, could get inside the apartment through one of the open passages, run through the basement area, and then out onto the main street or one of two other side streets, since the building spanned an entire block and the basement doors were not locked.

Another alley, this one wide enough to be a street, flanked the north side of the bank. A three-bay garage that must have dated from the Thirties sat on the far side. A spotless BMW M5 was parked in one of the bays. A telephone pole sat at the head of the alley; there was a transformer on it.

The sweatshop had once had a fire escape but now only the rust spots remained. From the outside, it looked deserted, and the separate entrance at the side of the bank storefront was locked shut. It looked possible to get in by getting onto the roof of the building next door and simply going through one of the upper windows; I decided to find out.

I got into the building with no problem, but the layout of the apartments prevented easy access to the roof or the building next door. If at first you don't succeed, try, try again. The building next to the one with the hardware store was also three stories, and this one had a fire escape on the back side that connected to the roof. I pulled myself up and was just starting to climb when I heard a voice below.

"Hey, mister, what are you doing?"

A six- or seven-year-old squirt squinted up at me from the ground.

"Lost my baseball on the roof over there," I said, trying to come up with a story that would seem plausible to a kid. "I'm going to get it."

"Want some help?"

In fifteen years or so, sure. I told him he could look around in the yard and let me know if he found anything. Then I scampered up and made my way across to the sweatshop. I didn't have to break the windows; someone had done that long ago.

More pigeon shit than you can imagine. Otherwise, bare floors and a lot of dust.

The sweatshop hadn't left one thread of material behind. There was a large service elevator on the top floor, which stopped on the other floors and went directly to the bottom landing, next to the stairs. I walked down the stairs. There was no way into the bank from the shuttered area. I went back the way I came. The kid must have been called in to do his homework or something, because he was gone when I jumped from the ladder.

I went back around the alley, went through the apartment building out onto the main drag, then walked down the block to the local deli and bought myself a water—two and a half bucks for a glass of something that used to be free. Sipping slowly—

every mouthful was worth about fifteen cents, by my reckoning—I sauntered back down the street, watching the comings and goings of the block. It was a little past four; the police station was quieter than the bank.

Capel emerged from the building with an armful of brochures. "If their security were any good, I think I'd open an account," he told me. "Not only are the interest rates good, but some of the tellers are real lookers. And they're open five, six days a week."

"So maybe you should open an account. Say Wednesday around noon."

"I think one o'clock will be better, maybe a little later," he said. "New York banks do a lot of business around lunchtime, and the ones that actually care about customers delay their employees' lunch hour until the rush slacks off."

Banks that care about customers—you can find *anything* in New York.

Capel explained the layout and personnel setup. The upstairs geek was the only difficulty, and there were several ways of dealing with him once we were inside. We discussed the possibilities of how the bank's computer system had come to be used by scumbags. It doesn't take much to surreptitiously get something onto a computer hooked into the Internet—run Spybot some time on your home machine and you'll see. Capel thought the fact that the geek was playing a networked computer game meant he didn't bother spending all that much time on security, though I didn't jump to that conclusion myself.

"You have an idea for getting in?" Capel asked as we walked toward his car.

I turned and pointed toward the telephone.

"Ah yes, Con Ed. Always a handy villain," he said. "You're picking on power companies a hell of a lot lately."

"It's the least I can do. They upped my rates last fall."

Since finding the rifle and the van we'd continued to shuffle our lodging arrangements, keeping things fluid. We also adjusted the trail system. Shadow was eventually going to make another mistake; in the meantime my best strategy was to make things hard for him.

I decided I could use a "clean" operative in the bank, someone to play customer and keep the manager occupied besides Capel. Since we were in New York, Brandy Alexander sprang to mind.

There's no way I can describe Brandy with words. Anything I say will sound clichéd and overwrought, and still it'll fail by a mile to capture how beautiful she is. You may have seen her on a few commercials by now; a print ad in some of the big mags featured her hawking Chivas Regal. Dark, raven hair, five-eight, penetrating eyes, and a presence—she just walks in a way that dominates a room. The air around her begins to catch fire, and you find yourself staring even if you didn't intend to.

It even happens to me. I met her in a small Greenwich Village restaurant Monday night, and when she walked into the place every eye in the room glued itself on her, mine included. I rose up gallantly. I may be a rogue, but I can muster a bit of Polish polish when necessary, especially in the presence of a BYT, aka "Beautiful Young Thing."

Brandy had spent the afternoon at a theater tryout, vying for a part in an off-off-off-Broadway play. I've forgotten what the name of the show was, but I remember the part she wanted: a Catholic nun. I knew when she mentioned it there was no way Brandy would get the part; she might be able to act it, but I doubt she would look chaste and repressed in sackcloth. Even if she would have, it would have taken more imagination than any human being could possess to translate her image into that of a nun.

She ordered a chardonnay and took sips a bird would have thought scant. She told me about the audition and then we talked about the city, which by then had returned to normal after the terrorist attacks on the World Trade Center downtown. Normal on the surface, I should say; tension lurked just below. A councilman had been shot at City Hall a few weeks earlier; the news reports had made sure to include the bulletin that it was not a terrorist attack, which Brandy said showed how jumpy everyone still was.

"It was on everyone's mind, that it'll happen again," she said. She took one of her tiny sips—my own glass of Bombay was nearly drained—then put her hand on mine. "Do you think it will, Dick?"

I wanted to lie. I wanted to reassure her more than anything, take her in my arms and say everything was going to be okay. But I couldn't. I see massive security holes everywhere I look. The nuclear power plant was just one example. More has to be done; we're simply not serious about the threat we face, and too many of the people calling the shots are unwilling to do what it takes to get real about the world and its problems. But I'd given that lecture earlier in the day at Capel's bash. Now I told her I hoped so and turned the conversation back to her acting, listening to some of her stories about commercials.

"Have you ever played a bank customer?" I asked finally.

"No," she said. "Is it a speaking part or a walk-on?"

"A little of both," I said, ordering another drink.

About midnight, there was a knock on my hotel door. I got up from the bed where I'd been watching CNN and walked over, pistol in hand.

"Yeah?" I whispered.

"It's me, Trace. I don't have my key."

We all had code words to use in case we had been taken hostage, different ways of alerting someone in a situation like this that there was a person or persons with weapons behind us. Trace hadn't used hers.

On the other hand, I knew that she hadn't forgotten her key, since I'd made a point of reminding her about it earlier in the day. I slipped my cell phone out and dialed Rogue Manor, where I'd posted an on-duty op as a kind of safety net. Worst case, he'd hear what was going on and send the cavalry.

Or at least the guys with the body bags.

I slipped the chain away and pulled open the door, gun ready.

"You're going to shoot us just because the champagne is the cheap Spanish stuff?" asked Trace, holding up two bottles and some glasses.

Even better, Karen stood behind her.

Karen had brought news that our status at Homeland Insecurity had been restored, but she could have told me that the universe had just been nuked and I would have been just as happy to see her. It turned out that Trace had checked in with Rogue Manor earlier and found that Karen had left a message; she had arranged to meet Karen and take her to our cell's lair. It was a nice, sisterly gesture on Trace's part, looking after me like that; it was also a signal that she accepted the platonic turn our relationship had taken and wanted it to continue. She stayed for a drink, then pretended she was tired and headed for a room she'd just reserved down the hall.

I'd adopt her as my daughter but she'd make me pay for her wedding someday.

The hotel room came with a double-size bathtub.

'Nuf said.

Considering we had kicked the security team's butt all over the two-hundred-something acres at Wappino, they were pretty gracious at the debrief. Furness especially. He organized the afternoon session as a clambake, trying to keep it on the free and easy side. The highlight was the race to retrieve Trace's remote video cam, won by a slip of a kid who bolted up the tower so fast I had Trace get his name in case we ever needed someone for human monkey work. He was undoubtedly motivated by first prize—a kiss from the Apache princess herself. She put so much lip action into it I'm sure the kid had wet dreams for a month.

Did Wappino get the Cadillac security system?

I haven't checked. They did pay our bills without a whimper, however.

Wednesday morning around eight A.M., Queens Savings experienced a minor power surge. It wasn't anything much, just enough of a boost to register on one of the logs kept by the system administrator and annoy the manager, who was just starting the coffee machine in the back.

At ten-twenty-two, there was a similar event, strong enough to set off the audible alarms.

At twelve-thirty power went out. Con Edison, which just happened to be in the area, responded almost immediately with a truck, and power was restored in less than twenty minutes.

Fixing the problem and finding out exactly what had caused it, however, were two different things. Around one-fifteen a unit supervisor arrived on the scene, talked over the situation with the lineman, and—after considerable head-shaking—took one of his techies around the neighborhood on a power-usage survey.

What did that have to do with the blackout? And what did the survey involve?

Nothing and a whole lot of nothing respectively, but it sure opened doors. I was the supervisor, having borrowed the creds of a Con Ed worker who'd been at a local gym that morning. I also had a very official-looking hard hat and an equally impressive clipboard. I also had an ID that I flashed, thumb over the picture.

We took our time getting to the Queens Saving Association. I thought I'd have to get physical with Sean when he saw the BMW in the garage; he was still talking about it as we found the manager. I tried explaining what we were up to but the manager had little time for me; he needed, *really* needed, to get back to a customer who had just come in and was crossing her miniskirted legs in his glassed-in office.

Not that I could blame him. Brandy had mentioned she might want to deposit a considerable amount of money, but somehow I think he was the one who was interested in making a deposit. We were handed off to the computer tech geek, since he handled all things technical. While we were waiting for him, my beeper went off and I asked to use the phone. My party picked up on the second ring. Our conversation lasted only a few minutes before I agreed very loudly that our tech guy ought to get his lunch finished and meet me here before I kicked his butt over to LILCO.

"You're ten minutes away? You better be here in five," I growled, loud enough for the women behind the teller windows to jump. "And don't give me any more crap about union *rules!*"

The computer dweeb happened to walk in as I

slammed down the phone. He quaked a bit, then offered Sean a tour of the building.

"Say, boss, should I wait for Jankolunitz?" Sean asked.

"I'll take care of Jankolunitz," I told him. "Get the job done, would you? I don't want these poor people to go without power again. This is a business they're running here. And if I hear one more word out of your mouth about that BMW piece of shit, I'm going to glue your car locks with Superglue."

Sean went off with the dweeb, who by now was shaking like a birch tree in a hurricane. Jankolunitz came running in a few moments later. I raised my finger at him accusingly, caught the manager frowning at me from inside the office, and then told my errant Con Ed specialist to wait for a second.

"Can I borrow a room upstairs to, uh, chat, with my employee?" I asked the manager, forcing a smile on my face.

"Go, go right ahead," said the manager, eager to avoid an explosion in the lobby.

"I knew you'd understand. Managing people these days."

I shook my head sadly. The manager gave me a knowing and relieved nod, then went back to ogling his prospective customer.

Jankolunitz followed me up the steps, tool kit in hand.

Jankolunitz is such a long name, especially when it's an alias. Why don't we use the one I know him and love him by: *Shunt*.

Cox had suggested we use an NSA techie, but under the best circumstances, I didn't want anyone coming onto my team whom I didn't trust 100 percent. And these weren't the best circumstances.

Shunt, of course, loved it. He figured he was finally living out his dream of being a SpecWarrior, and I did nothing to dissuade him of that, even if my mock anger downstairs was maybe one-tenth as intense as everyday commands issued by some of the chiefs who had put me through my paces when I was knee-high to a bootlace. You call it flattery, I call it ego management, but Shunt was ready for anything.

"IBM shop, Dude," he said, shaking his head as we walked into the computer room.

"That make it harder?"

"Hell, no. Easier." He stooped down and looked at the workstation the techie had been using. "Doom. *Duuuude!*"

I played lookout while Shunt went to work. He had to somehow bypass the system before he swapped the drives, arranging it so the computer wouldn't realize it was having its gonads snipped off. I don't know the proper terms, let alone exactly what he did, except that when I put my head back in he had the computer in several pieces spread out on the floor.

"We're on a timeline here, Shunt," I told him. "This isn't Rogue Manor."

"On it, Dude."

I put my head back out the door. Not a minute had passed before I heard footsteps trotting up the stairs.

The Doom *Duuuude* was heading back to check on his game.

I stepped back into the doorway, turned around, and let Shunt have it with both barrels.

"And another fucking thing. When I tell you to use 12-gauge wire, damn it, I mean 12-gauge wire. Who the hell do you think you are using 10-gauge? This is a commercial operation. I have a budget I have to live with. And if—"

I heard a sound suspiciously like a gasp behind me. I spun around. Doom *Duuuude* looked like he was about to faint.

"Yes?" I asked, leaning over him.

"I, uh—just going to the bathroom," he said, spinning and sprinting across the hall.

I heard the sound of a case being clicked behind me.

"Ready and wilco, Dude," said Shunt, pushing the computer back into place. The game on the screen appeared not to have been disturbed.

"Ready and wilco, Shunt?"

"I'm trying to, like, do the SEAL thing."

Mission accomplished, we trotted down the steps.

"They had a mirror RAID system and it was nothing to slip it right in," explained Shunt. "NSA guys are good. By the way, Dude, 12-gauge wire—that's the sort of thing, like, a homeowner might use, not a power company. I don't think you'd find it even in a commercial installation, like."

"Next time I'll run the script by you," I told Shunt, gesturing to Sean to follow us out.

"Cool. When's next time?"

"Soon," I told Shunt, waving to the bank manager, who had spread out a brochure in front of

Brandy and was leaning over the desk trying to explain it.

We got out of the bank just as an empty cab drove down the street. We hailed it and headed over to Steinway, one of the main drags a few blocks away.

Anyone familiar with New York City knows that cabs never magically appear like that, certainly not in Queens. The driver was Hulk, who'd been waiting up the block with another of our shooters. For a number of reasons, taxis are good covers in the city not the least of which is the fact that the driver can be as obnoxious as he wants and still stay in perfect cover.

As we were pulling up in front of a Greek coffee shop near the Astoria side of Queens, I heard a police siren in the distance. Five minutes later, my beeper went off. It gave a number that I recognized as a code from Trace to get in touch with her. I tossed a twenty on the table to cover our coffees, and we got back in the cab and headed over to her post, which was in a Laundromat just up the street from the bank. She was supposed to wait there and then escort Brandy away.

It took five minutes to get to the Laundromat, and it was a very tense five minutes. We actually didn't make it—the area was in the process of being cordoned off by the police.

Trace met me near the police barricade when I returned on foot a few minutes later.

"Some bozos tried to rob the bank a few minutes after you left," she said. "The alarm went off and they panicked. The police have the place surrounded. Brandy's still in there."

"Shit."

"Yeah. And one of the robbers yelled out that they're going to start killing people in a half hour if NYPD doesn't bring a bus down to take them to the airport."

11

I don't know if you've seen *Dog Day Afternoon*, but if you have, you'll recognize the situation. It's an old Al Pacino movie without too much of a point that I can see, except that it's based on a real incident that happened in New York City a number of years ago, when some punk bank robbers got caught trying to rob a bank and decided to take everyone inside hostage. It turns out New York City deals with this sort of situation all the time. They had a very similar hostage situation in 1983 or something, and yet another one in 1995. Probably correlates with sunspot activity.

Whatever. Mr. Murphy sure picked a hell of a time to stick it to us.

New York calls its tactical squad or SWAT team an "Emergency Response Unit." It sounds almost benign, doesn't it? The city is, after all, the capital of PC government. Whatever they're called, though, the city's team is actually pretty damn good. They train regularly, and even better, have enough situations to get on-the-job experience easily. Not that that's better if you're on the wrong end of the emergency, but you get my point.

Besides the sharpshooters, their hostage-negotiating team literally wrote the book on how to deal with these sorts of situations. The negotiators are more than good; they've given their spiel to SEAL Team Six and not been laughed out of the joint. It's their track record that counts, and they have a long list of saves, everything from little old ladies to psychos whacked out because they forgot to take their little green pills. The negotiators' philosophy is more than a little different than the typical SpecWar attitude—they'd rather talk than fight—but they've proven their worth in a number of situations. You need a lot of tools in your kit when things get tough, and sometimes a blunt object is not the way to go.

It should be, but it's not.

Capel joined us near the police barricade as Trace finished giving me her situation report. "Building's locked down," he said, adding a few more details to Trace's report. He'd come out of the building right after us, looking for Shadow or one of his minions. He'd passed the two robbers going in, or at least thought he had. He told me later he thought they looked a bit suspicious and wished he'd turned around and gone in after them. He might have stopped the robbery. Or maybe he would have been killed. Hard to say.

"What kind of assholes rob a bank across from a police station?" asked Trace.

"Maybe they're with the NSA and they want to check our work," I said. But actually I was thinking something very different—I wondered if these jackasses had been sent by Shadow.

Capel knows half the police department, including most of the Emergency Response officers and just about all the area commanders and the deputy police chief. He got us past the barricade and down the street, where two officers with a bullhorn were trying to communicate with the people inside. That in itself wasn't a good sign; negotiators almost always prefer to work with phones.

"Can't get them to answer the phone," said one of the detectives on the negotiating team, whom Capel knew. He referred Capel to the local commander, who had set up a command post in the police station—which was, after all, across the street.

"What do you think about going in through the abandoned sweatshop?" I asked Capel as we crossed the street. "Climb up from the hardware store building."

"Only if they let us."

"I'm not asking Mommy-may-I when one of my people is in shit. I'm getting her out."

Capel didn't argue. He did, however, have a point. There were already SWAT people covering the back alley and the nearby roofs, so there was no question of sneaking in *that* way without some sort of official sanction.

When we found the assistant chief, he'd just been faxed a set of plans on the building from the bank's central office. On the plus side, the bank did well finding and hustling them over. On the minus side, the plans were pretty clearly out of date, something I was able to point out to the chief as I looked at them upside down on his desk.

"Besides being a friend of Big Dan's," said the

chief, "which is a recommendation—who the fuck are you?"

"Dick Marcinko." I shoved out my hand. "I was supposed to meet a friend of mine down the street and I saw all the commotion and then saw Dan."

I didn't tell him that I had an op inside the building for two reasons. One, that would make it clear that we'd just conducted an operation there, which would scotch a mission we'd just completed, apparently successfully, at least as far as the objective was concerned. And two, I was afraid that they'd think I was emotionally involved or something and not let me help.

Because I was going to help. One way or another.

"Dick Marcinko sounds familiar," said the chief. "But I can't quite place it."

Capel played PR agent, talking me up as a security expert, former SEAL, all around hard-ass. He didn't lie about any of it, but I had to smile when he was done.

"I do some work for Homeland Security these days," I added. "Don't hold that against me."

"You have someone in the bank?" asked the chief.

I looked at him eyeball to eyeball. Give him this: he wasn't stupid. And he didn't blink.

Should I lie, or let it all hang out?

Gut call. And the gut says: when in doubt, fall back on the truth.

"Yeah, I do," I told him.

"And you want to help get him out."

"Yeah, I do."

The chief could have told me to fuck myself. At that moment, I expected he would. But maybe Capel's speech had softened him up, or maybe he knew exactly what I was feeling. I had the sense from looking at him that he'd bust his own belly to help one of his guys.

"If you can help us, we'd appreciate it. But you're under my command," he said.

"Fair enough."

A customer had managed to escape after the robbers pulled their weapons, which helped NYPD blueprint the situation. Two men had gone into the bank for a robbery. Having more bullets than brains, they'd panicked when one of the tellers didn't understand them at first, drawn their weapons, and plugged the security guard near the door. Alarms started going off; people started screaming. The punks had herded a half-dozen people back behind the tellers' windows.

"There were two, but they had a backpack with them," said one of the detectives who was coordinating intelligence. "We can't see inside the building well enough to get a good feel for what's going on, let alone figure out what they brought in with them."

The possibilities ranged from dinner to enough dynamite to take out the block. The layout of the building made storming the offices difficult at best; there were only two ways in or out—the front door and an alarmed exit at the back. Screwing with the power sounded an alarm on the door—a fact I already knew.

The negotiators, meanwhile, still had been unable to make contact.

"Assholes won't pick up the phone," said the police chief.

"What you need is another door in the place," I said. "Fortunately, you have one."

Everybody looked at me as if I had two heads. I jabbed my finger down at the plans. "It's right there in the women's restroom. You go through there and come right up this corridor and get them from the back."

The expressions changed. Now I had *three* heads.

"Go through the elevator shaft that runs from the old lobby back here up to the sweatshop," I explained. "The elevator's parked on the top floor."

"How do you know that?" asked the chief.

I shrugged. "I just do."

I took his diagram and showed him how the shaft—marked on the plan as a utility area—bordered the restroom. Come across the roof, get into the building, pry open the door, rappel down and cut in.

"We could do it inside of twenty minutes."

"We?" said the chief.

"In the interests of interagency cooperation," I told him, "we'll let you help."

Capel frowned and the chief shook his head. I'm not sure what I would have done if the chief had held his ground—slugged him, grabbed a gun, and gone off by myself, I guess.

And if I were in the chief's position? I'd've kicked my butt and told me to take a hike. In the end, the chief proved smarter than me.

"All right. Let's try it your way," he said.

Part of the reason he did that may have been the fact that they had the security guard lying on the floor inside the bank bleeding. Another part was probably the failure of the bad guys to pick up the phone. That's not a good sign in a hostage situation, especially one that sets up like this, where the bad guys ought to be looking for a way to cut their losses and get out.

And on the other hand, they were sure moving around a lot inside—possibly setting explosives.

We knew they were moving around because NYPD brought up a special radar unit they'd been using on a trial basis. Nicknamed "Soldiervision," it's basically a personal-size radar that can be used to look inside buildings without cutting a hole through the wall. It's not as powerful as Superman's X-ray eyes, but it does a reasonably good job of looking through walls and about forty or fifty feet beyond, depending on the thickness and composition of the wall. The technology is still being worked on, but it represents the next quantum leap in dealing with combat and law enforcement in an urban environment.

At that point, the only leap I was concerned with was the one down the elevator shaft. Rather than risking any odd noise by prying the doors open, Capel and I—with six ninjas from Emergency Response tagging along—went to the sixth floor and the elevator. As we had hoped, there was a trap-door in the bottom of the cab; the hinges were a little rusty, but the squeaks were faint.

"Still not answering their phone," said the policeman handling communications, as Capel and I started downward.

I went first, easing my way down with the help of a rope. When I reached the first floor, I made myself as comfortable as I could on a brace at the side, then took out a razor and worked it into the plasterboard, pulling down quietly but forcefully. It took a few minutes to score a Rogue-sized passage, and even longer to get something wide enough for Capel's frame. The bathroom wall was made of ceramic, and the mastic that held the tiles in place made it hard to get the second layer of plasterboard off. I had infrared glasses on, but it was hard to see precisely how deep I was making the hole. The metal studs were placed at odd intervals—I'm not sure why, maybe to provide a brace for something on the other side—and in order to make the largest possible hole, I worked right up to their edges. That gave me a good guide for the horizontal cuts, but I kept jamming my hand against the stud and cursing as silently as possible.

Capel was perched a floor above me, whispering with the Emergency Response team and commander through the comm system we'd borrowed from the NYPD. We'd chosen to use NYPD gear rather than ours. While the range and security on Capel's was light-years ahead of the police versions, being able to communicate with everyone involved in the situation was a hell of a lot more important than showing off the latest and greatest.

"See daylight?" he asked me.

"Not yet." Cutting the plasterboard was harder than I'd thought it would be. I couldn't go fast and be quiet at the same time, so I opted for quiet. The Emergency Response people were shifting above us, ready to swing down on their ropes like a troop of monkeys. Two teams were waiting near the front of the bank. If things went to shit, they could blow the window and get inside in a hurry—probably just in time to ID the dead bodies on the floor.

The temperature in the elevator shaft had to be close to a hundred. Sweat poured out of me, even my eyeballs.

"I hope the scumbags don't decide to use the ladies' room instead of the men's," I said.

"What kind of perverts do you think we have in New York?" Capel asked as I knifed pieces of the wall away. "Our scumbags are high class."

Obviously bank robber/hostage takers had one union, Peeping Toms another.

Finally, I got some daylight through the wall. I made a peephole and stuck a small, telescoping cam through and had a look-see. I worked it through, then connected the viewer.

Things had been far too easy to this point, so I wasn't surprised when the layout of the restroom turned out to be different than what we'd seen in the one upstairs before scoping the plan. Rather than being at the back end of the room, hidden from view by a stall, the opening I had just cut sat exactly opposite the door to the room. Something had been moved during construction, and anyone opening the door would have an unobstructed view of yours truly pulling tiles out of the way.

I pulled the scope out and told Capel I was just about ready. He signaled the scene commander, and in a few seconds I could hear the rattle of a jackhammer starting up across the street. It was meant more as a diversion than to cover the noise I was making. I continued as quietly and carefully as I could, scoring and pulling off the tiles one by one. Capel slid down beside me—a tight fit; you couldn't have gotten a fart between us. He hunched over as I pulled a large section of wallboard back like a folding closet door.

As I slipped inside the room I heard footsteps in the hall. Three quick strides got me across to the door. I pushed back against the wall as the door opened. At this point, I wasn't thinking about anything, I was just reacting. I grabbed the person who walked through the door, hand clamped as hard as I could on her mouth, and pulled her back against the wall with me. We stayed frozen there for a second. I expected one or more of the hostage takers to be right behind her, which would have meant Capel would have blown his head off. All hell would have broken loose next, our carefully laid plans blown to hell by an untimely need to pee.

But the door swung closed and nothing happened. Capel came up, finger on his lips. I felt the woman nodding. As gently as I could, I turned her sideways, my hand still on her mouth.

"We need you to be very quiet. We're with the police," I said.

She nodded.

I took my hand away. Her face was as white as a skeleton.

"Go to the bathroom," I told her. "Go ahead."

Hey, everything in its place.

Capel took the door. I went back to the wall and pulled enough away to make it easier for the ninja boys, who were still slipping through. Our hostage had a full audience when she came out to wash her hands.

"How many kidnappers?" I asked, my voice in a whisper.

"Two."

"Describe them."

"Unshaven. Jeans. One's about your height but real skinny. Other is around five-eight, five-ten." She told me that they were in the room at the front of the bank with six employees and three customers. The customers would be easy to ID—they were all older women. The male employees were better-dressed than the bad guys, but all were about the second guy's height.

Of course, there was one easy way to tell them apart—the bad guys had guns. She'd seen three pistols.

"They came in with a backpack," I said. "Are there explosives?"

"They put money in there."

"They mess around with the computers?"

"Not that I saw. They've been in that front area there the whole time."

That eliminated the possibility that it was anyone involved with the computer. Whether it was my friend Shadow remained to be seen.

"All right," I told her. "I think we can work with this. Come on." I turned her toward the door.

"You want me to go back out there?"

"If you don't, they're going to know something's

up," I explained. "We need to get the full SWAT team into the hallway so we can get them. If one of them catches us in the hall, the other will shoot the hostages."

"You want me to go back out there?" she repeated.

"It's the safest way for your friends."

"Not for me."

"No, not for you."

I could see her thinking about it. It was a tough choice. Here she was safe. Out there, who the fuck knew?

"All right," she said. Her jaw quivered a little bit, but she clenched her teeth and set it. "Be careful," she added, starting for the door. I grabbed her arm.

"Hold on just a second. We're coming with you," I told her. I worked out a little routine with her: she'd open the door, scan the hall to make sure it was clear, then give us a yea or nay. Yea meant we'd come up after her, moving to the edge of the hall, where a pair of copy machines would provide some cover. She'd continue into the bank area, which was to the right. Nay meant we'd wait for her to get up to the front. Then we'd go back to our original plan, snaking the scope out from under the door and waiting until the hall was clear. We'd make our move from the top of the hall one way or the other.

Of course, she wasn't going to say "yea" or "nay." She'd cough for yea and do nothing for nay.

We gave the ninjas the setup and went for it.

I was pushing out the door for her when the

commander started screaming in my ear about letting the hostage back out there. He had a real hang-up with that; it was apparently against department procedure or some other fucking piece of paper. I just ignored him, listening for Mary's "yea."

She gave a nice polite cough. Capel and I slipped out, guns ready. The emergency response boys were right behind us as we moved up to the edge of the hall, slipping behind the copy machines.

I slipped behind the copy machines. Capel slipped *against* the copy machines. And somehow when he slipped, the dork managed to hit the copy buttons on both machines. Both started spitting out paper.

Doom on you, Capel. What a time to become a spaz.

Doom on us, I mean.

I could hear someone cursing down the hall. Mary yelped. Footsteps.

"Go!" I hissed as Mary turned the corner. Then I shouted "Down!" real loud. As I did that I was extending my arm and firing the P7 point-blank into the soft spot right above the medium-size hostage taker's ear.

One shot. Fuck me if I need more at that range.

By the time the blood began splattering I was charging down the corridor. A flash-bang—two flash-bangs, three—whapped at the front of the bank. A big hulk appeared in front of me, thick Glock in his hand, screaming girl shielding his chest.

Then in the blink of an eye, he threw down the gun and surrendered, begging me to send him to prison, where he would mend the error of his ways, find Jesus Christ as his personal savior, and go forth and change the world with his unselfish acts of kindness and contrition.

Yeah, right. In my dreams, maybe.

Or his.

12

Goon and I looked at each other for maybe one one-hundredth of a second. Neither one of us liked what he saw.

The bad guy took the first shot. I took the one that killed him.

Note to hostage takers: if you're going to use a human shield, pick one that's as tall as you are. My bullet took Goon square in the forehead. The slime flew backward, pulling the woman with him. By the time he hit the ground, ninjas were all around. I think they were pissed that I'd taken all their fun, but they had the manners not to show it. They scurried forward to get the hostages.

Brandy wasn't with them. Something clutched at my throat, and the scumbag Angel of Death screamed that he'd won another round.

"There," said Capel, pointing toward the manager's office.

I spun, gun ready.

Brandy stood up slowly; the manager followed. They'd hidden there the whole time, miraculously undiscovered by the slimebags. We had a quick reunion.

"I'm okay, Dick," she whispered. "Really, I'm okay."

"I know you are," I told her.

"Stick to the script?" she asked. Two of the ninjas came in behind me.

"Absolutely."

Capel, meanwhile, had gone over to the men I'd shot.

"Just punks, I think," said Capel. "We'll know soon, though."

They had driver's licenses; he snapped pictures of the IDs as well as their faces with his tiny digital camera, then pulled out his cell phone and called a police contact who was deep in debt to his favorite bank. We knew that both men were native New Yorkers with good-size rap sheets before the investigators had even been let into the building.

I made it outside just in time to see Trace land a kick in the crotch of a swarthy fellow across the street. The next kick was better—a running roundhouse to the head that sent him ricocheting against the side of a nearby building. I was enjoying myself too much, I guess; it took me a second to realize that the cops running up to her weren't there to assist her but to stop her. Bad move. Before I could get off the sidewalk both policemen were reeling on the pavement, and Trace had finished His Swarthiness off with a heel at the top of the head.

I yelled and waved my hands, trying to get Trace's attention, as well as that of the three officers who'd pulled their pistols out and were running to the assistance of their comrades on the ground. Fortunately, Capel was right behind me, and one of the cops recognized him. We managed to calm things down without anyone else getting hurt. The police wanted an explanation; I trotted out the words "national security matter," but that didn't mollify them much. However, some of the SWAT team boys were just emerging from the bank, and when they started loudly congratulating us, the wariness of their NYPD brethren dissipated.

His Swarthiness was sleeping rather peacefully, and thus had no objection to a thorough search. When said search produced a weapon in his waistband—a Walther P5 Compact, which, as the name implies, is a very small gun—the cops were positively joyous. The weapon made His Swarthiness a criminal suspect in their eyes, as New York's gun laws make it extremely difficult for anyone to legally carry a weapon unless they're sworn law officers or federal officials such as *moi* and the rest of my Homeland Insecurity team. But charging His Swarthiness with a crime complicated things for us; the reason Trace had attacked him was that she believed he was one of Shadow's minions.

Trace had noticed him and two other similarly shady fellows lurking about when Capel and I went into the police station, and, in her opinion, they were much more interested in us than in the hostage situation—so much so that they had used a small set of opera glasses still in His Swarthiness's pocket. They had surged forward with the crowd, turning around immediately when I came out and glancing back surreptitiously.

I wanted a chance to talk with His Swarthiness ourselves, perhaps employing techniques of persuasiveness beyond those permitted our blue-coated brethren. I ended up playing public defender with the police, arguing that he shouldn't be charged and that there were dozens of possible reasons that he might have a gun. I even suggested that he be released to my custody.

I'd have made a lousy lawyer. They packed him in and scooted him away to be booked while he was still unconscious. I called over to Sean, who, besides Capel, was the member of the team most likely to speak police-eze. "Stay with him," I told Sean. "Tell them you think he's Bosnian. Suggest they talk to Immigration. I'll call you with more information as soon as I can."

I called Cox to tell him we'd made the switch—and that we needed some leverage with NYPD.

"Already? Shit. Great!"

That's what I like in a superior: confusion, followed by wild enthusiasm.

Cox agreed to hop on the phone and see what he could do about getting the thug released into our custody, or at least get Homeland Insecurity allowed into the interrogations. In the meantime, Capel began pulling strings of his own. It was, however, the last favor I could ask of him. He had a business to run, and had already been more than generous with me. I told him that straight out, and while he protested that he'd give me another twenty years if I needed it, we both knew that he really needed to get back to his office before his presence was missed in a big way. He let me keep some of the Shadow watch team on the job, another favor I'll never be able to repay at Christmas.

Sometime that afternoon, Doc checked in with more information from the French security service. The Frenchies had been pretty forthcoming, partly because Cox had made nice with their honchos, mostly because Danny Barrett had cut through some red tape for them and come up with a DNA sample on the dead man. Their labs hadn't had a chance to cinch the ID and wouldn't for a while. French bureaucracy is several times worse than ours, and there was no way they would get solid information for at least three months, even on a rush job. They weren't even sure they had a sample from Pierre. But everything else about the body matched.

The French information had to be translated and decoded, and not just with the help of Tiffany's masterful French. The thing to understand about Frenchmen is that they think the Eiffel Tower is the center of the universe, and that everybody loves their wine. I once had a few hours to kill in Paris and stopped in at a war museum there. Wandering around among the displays, I came across a giant map of D-Day, which showed pretty definitively how the French had saved the invasion and set the stage for the liberation of Europe. Pretty much told me all I needed to know about the French.

Foreign filters removed, the basic information came down to this: Shitheads for Allah smuggled people into France from a variety of locations in the Middle East. There were several routes, but all involved the successor republics to the former Yugoslavia. The people would be brought into the country—usually Bosnia—and then given fake identity papers. These usually claimed that they were contract workers for NATO sent on a relief mission by France. The papers were decent forgeries, but the relief missions had pretty good local identity procedures, and the odds were that the phony papers would have been spotted as such by anyone in-country. They also didn't substitute for passports or travel documents, which were checked pretty carefully (or at least might be) at the borders of Bosnia, et al. Shitheads for Allah therefore packed the people into trucks and got them out of the country, depositing them by a circuitous route—as yet unknown to the French—in France itself. There the people would stay with relatives or friends for a while until they were deemed ready to go "above ground." At that point, they would begin to gather legitimate documents, usually starting with a driver's license, based on the work documents. The usual spiel was that they had lost all of their official documents somewhere, but had managed to find the papers from their last job. The key was getting the first real piece of paper, be it a license or job certificate or whatever. From there, they could build an identity trail much as one would do in America. The papers were a bit different, but once you had one you could get the rest.

See why giving away photo ID licenses to any immigrant who wants one without a system of checking is less than intelligent? Not to mention that some states include automatic voter registration in the packet. Just remember to vote before you blow us up.

Shitheads for Allah had other sidelines in

France, including selling cheap guns and other weapons to their former clients. A very vertical and enterprising organization, which, at least from the way the French described it, was more interested in lucre than the word of the Prophet. The source of the cheap guns, used in at least two murders in Paris over the past year, and countless robberies, was *not* the former Yugoslavia; those weapons were not dependable or reliable enough to be used by dedicated criminals. American and German weapons were greatly preferred. Makes sense to me. On the other hand, surplus war matériel—the French specifically suspected Semtex, the plastique explosive originally manufactured in the Czech Republic—*might* be heading out in the other direction, perhaps to terrorists or others of that ilk.

But why send a Frenchman who looked Asian as an undercover agent into the organization?

A reasonable question, and one that Doc asked. The answer was that they hadn't, at least not at first. Pierre had been working on a different smuggling case the year before involving the importation of cut flowers. Apparently there are a lot of euros in daffodils, as long as you don't have to fill out the paperwork. Doc figured the French weren't telling him the whole truth about this. It seemed likely that the flowers were a cover for a drug operation from Asia, since, on a pound for pound basis, heroin brings a better profit margin than unprocessed flora. I agreed, but that was all irrelevant to us. At some point, Pierre found himself dealing with Shitheads for Allah and just went with the flow. Within a few months he was in pretty deep. After aborting several business deals, he and his handlers decided he better let one go through or the rest of the group would become suspicious, so he went to America to set up one.

"A very big risk," the official had told Doc in heavily accented English. He shook his head ominously.

"So why the hell did they let him go?" I asked Doc.

"I got the impression they had no choice. They left him on a pretty loose leash, basically for his own protection. Makes sense."

"Yeah."

"He's also a contract guy. Had some military experience, supposedly, though I haven't been able to pick that up. Unit on his resumé was disbanded."

A lot of intelligence agencies these days use contract agents for special jobs for a variety of reasons. One is that they simply don't have the manpower to do the job their governments want them to do, and for some reason the bean counters find it easier to justify hiring temp workers than putting on full-timers. It can also be easier to accommodate people with a wide range of skills. And most important, your conscience doesn't pang quite as badly if they get popped.

"They think Shitheads for Allah was trying to buy M16s to be used in a variety of places," continued Doc. "They trotted out al Qaeda as a possibility, like these guys are trying to step up into the big time by becoming Guns 'R' Us. They have a number of company names that do at least some legitimate business. The pipeline is what it's all about. Once they have a system set up, they can use it to transport anything, from guns to flowers to people. But I think the deal Pierre was involved in had something to do with mustard gas."

"Gulden's?"

"No, the shit they used in World War I. There was a stock of it in Yugoslavia before the breakup of the country, and it's gone now. The Frenchies swear Pierre had nothing to do with that, but it makes sense that they might be lying. The gas is missing and may be over in the States. They told the CIA about it a month or two ago."

And what did the CIA do? Filed the information under "F" for "forget about it." When we tried tracking the information down later, we got nowhere.

The gas had been stored in shell-like containers designed to be launched by artillery. As near as Doc could figure out, the shells dated to World War II or just afterward, which meant there was some question about how potent the gas would be. It had been found by NATO and stockpiled at an old prison waiting for disposal by a French company. When the company got there they found half the containers were missing. If the records could be trusted, there were something like ten to twelve full tractor trailer loads gone.

"It gets better," said Doc.

I couldn't imagine how.

"The reason I think it's related to Pierre's deal is that right around the time that this stuff had to have been taken—there's like a six- or seven-day window—the French tracked a shipment of M16s into their country. That was the deal Pierre tried to abort. The guns, by the way, got lost, even though the French were tracking them. But they got the names of the shipping companies they think carried them. They're still watching them. They split the load, see, over a couple of different firms. The companies may have taken turns, and there's a shell game covering the ownership arrangements, which leads back to radical, money-grubbing Islamic ragheads."

"Can we get the names of the companies?"

"FBI's had them for a month," said Doc. "A copy was hand-delivered to the New York office as well as Washington."

What was the FBI's nickname again? Fucked-up Bureau of Incompetents?

I played nice and put on a smile when I walked into the head of the FBI counterterrorism office in New York. I laid out the information we had obtained about the French operation. I explained that I believed it possibly tied in to an active terrorist cell or cells that were targeting me as well as different sites across the country. I admitted that I didn't know everything, but I put the dots together for the local FBI boss man so he couldn't miss the significance of the situation. I wanted to make it obvious why he ought to share whatever intel they had gotten in the weeks since they'd been investigating the companies.

Presumably investigating.

We already had the list, but as a gesture of humility I didn't include that piece of information up front.

"I'm not sure why I'm the target," I told the FBI boss. His experience in terrorism before coming to the job consisted of reading Danny O. Coulson's book *No Heroes,* about the FBI's Hostage Rescue Team or HRT (among other things). Great unit, great book, but reading it is not the same thing as living it. "It may be something personal. But more likely they're trying to get me out of the way of something. I don't know what."

"With an ego like that, I'm surprised your head fit through the door," he told me.

All right, I'm not ego-challenged, but that was a fairly inappropriate remark completely beside the point. Whatever he thought of me, I was at the intersection of serious shit and nasty assholes. If he truly didn't like me, he should have helped me and hoped Shitheads for Allah blew my head off.

"So can we get an info dump from someone?" I asked, still playing Mr. Sunshine. "We may be in a position to help you as well."

"We can't share details of an ongoing investigation."

The conversation degenerated rapidly from there. I'll spare you the blow by blow. The bottom line is that my puffed-up head and I somehow managed to squeeze out the door and head back uptown to the hotel, where I got a message from Sean that our prisoner had been IDed as an illegal immigrant. This gave Homeland Security more muscle, and Cox used it to remove him from NYPD custody. He was being held at a specially constructed unit at the federal prison in Danbury, Connecticut, about an hour and a half away.

Twenty minutes by helicopter, which is what we took.

Danbury has a reputation as something of a country club, though no prison is really that. The special facilities they had built there were not luxurious at all—a single set of cement cell blocks down the hill from the main buildings, with three rows of razor wire and a full cordon of guards, augmented by electronic sensors. Two vehicles with men in full riot gear patrolled the perimeter. Credentials were checked at a post just outside of the perimeter, where a full search was mandatory for all. If you weren't a bad guy, the search didn't include the rubber glove routine—but that was only because they used a special magnetic resonance imaging machine to do the work for them. They also had a retina ID machine and a tracking system that kept tabs on the inmates *and* the guards at all times, with a double backup. The guards were armed with a variety of lethal and nonlethal weapons. They practiced on animatronics dummies every other day. If you failed to qualify you had one chance to redeem yourself before being rotated to another assignment. I'm sure I could have figured out a way in, but it would have taken more than a few minutes of diddling around and wasn't worth the effort.

There were twelve prisoners in the block, including His Swarthiness. He'd been tentatively IDed as a Bosnian—ah, very *inter-est-tink*—who'd entered the country on a student visa three months earlier.

Looked a bit old for kindergarten, if you asked me.

There was a serious downside to all this security: advanced interrogation techniques, such as those Trace and Danny had employed on earlier operations (see *Violence of Action*), were not possible. Shame, that. Each prisoner had an interrogation officer assigned to him, who, despite the title, functioned as a commander and stayed aloof from the interviews. Homeland Insecurity had studied the operation at Guantánamo, figuring out its downsides as well as its successes, and tried to improve the system. One of the biggest problems at Gitmo was the tendency of a few people who dealt with the prisoners regularly to begin to identify with them, or at least feel sorry for their families. It's hard for the average American to understand it—it's hard for me to understand it—but under stress and over time people start identifying with those around them, even when the people are killers and their sworn enemies. That's what the Stockholm Syndrome is all about—victims starting to see themselves as friends of their kidnappers. While the phenomenon can be overplayed to excuse things that shouldn't be excused, it does exist, and steps were taken here to prevent it. The bad guys' backgrounds were emphasized every day, translators and interrogators were constantly monitored and rotated, and all contact was carefully regulated.

As far as the inmates went, a conscious program of building relations and "managing the interrogation script" was followed, with personnel assigned very specific roles. The unit used a variety of techniques—the simplest being sleep deprivation—to encourage cooperation. In my opinion, knuckle persuasion would have been much faster, but they hadn't put me in charge of the cell block.

The man who *was* in charge greeted us inside with a suspicious glare. I liked that. He stood about six feet and had been a Marine. He didn't volunteer this, but few people get their arm tattooed Semper Fi unless they're jarheads. He also looked like a Marine, with a squat haircut, crisp khaki pants, and a white short-sleeved shirt that showed off his thick biceps as well as his tattoo.

"Marcinko?"

"That's right."

"Don't fuck around with my people."

"Gotcha, Gunny."

He frowned at me. "I went out as a master sergeant," he snapped, before handing me off to his assistant. This man was a less-muscled, even grouchier version of his boss, and if he was supposed to play Mr. Friendly to Master Sergeant's Gruff, he hadn't gotten the memo. Mr. Friendly in turn handed us off to a person I'll call Twenty Questions, who headed the interrogation team. Twenty Questions was much closer to being a member of the human race.

"Uncooperative. It's early days," he told Trace and me, leading us to the interrogation area. We watched from an observation room while His Swarthiness was put through the paces by a pair of interrogators, who spoke to him in both Serbian and English. He grunted a few times and said something nice about New York.

"Wow, what a bullshit artist," said Trace.

Twenty Questions smiled. "He's different from

our usual guests," said the interrogation supervisor.

"Because he's Bosnian?" I asked.

"Yes, but that's not the whole thing," said Twenty Questions. "He's not obviously religious, unlike most if not all of the other guests we've had. He also hasn't tried to send a message to his family or anything like that."

Twenty Questions explained that most of the prisoners would typically protest their innocence and give a list of people who could vouch for them, at least if they had been apprehended in circumstances such as His Swarthiness. Or, alternatively, they attempted to establish a rapport with their captors, convinced that they would win them over or influence them somehow. Al Qaeda leaders were like that; for the most part, they wanted to talk, because they wanted everyone to understand how righteous they were. Some also had an agenda to mislead their interrogators by giving them false information. His Swarthiness simply kept his mouth shut.

"You think he's just some numbskull off the street?" I asked. It was a dumb question, but the answer needed to be on the record.

"No way," said Twenty Questions. "He'd act completely differently. Even if he were a common criminal. Say he was involved in the bank robbery that went bad when you picked him up. Well, again, in that case, he'd be acting very differently. He's hooked into something; we just don't quite know what yet. We'll wear him down after a few weeks. But it's also possible he doesn't know much."

"It's also possible he's been in worse places," I said.

"That, too."

I gave Twenty Questions as much background on what I thought was going on as I could. Then Trace and I waited a bit, watching and reviewing a briefing log, before Twenty Questions decided it was a good time for us to go in.

His Swarthiness jerked back when he saw Trace enter. I came in a half-minute afterward and didn't get any sort of reaction.

"Why were you so interested in me?" I asked.

Blank look.

"Your name is George, right? You're in big trouble, George. We may be able to help."

Blank look.

"Do you believe in God, George?"

Blank look.

The pros took over, asking him to describe why he had been in Queens yesterday. But George, who hadn't exactly been loquacious before, was positively mum now. Finally, Trace got up and left the room while I stayed behind. He watched her go, then turned back to us.

"She's a bit of a bitch, huh, George?" I said.

A faint—very faint—smile came to his lips. "A real devil. I'd like to get her alone."

"Maybe I can arrange that."

He frowned. Clearly that was something he did not want to happen. The negotiators tried a few more questions, then they announced that they had nothing more to ask.

"I do," I said.

"Fine with us. We'll be outside." Both men got up and left, following the script Twenty Questions had given them before they started.

I waited until they were gone, then leaned across the table. His Swarthiness had cuffs on his hands locked to the table; the chains on his feet were bolted to the floor. He couldn't have blown his nose if he sneezed.

"We can work out a deal," I told him, my voice barely over a whisper. "But you have to answer my questions. Or you'll rot here."

He scowled. I sat back upright.

"Who are you working with?" I asked.

Back to the blank look. I slammed my hand on the table—not an act—and told him I wasn't fucking around. Either he helped and we were friends or there would be consequences.

Another frown, another scowl, and then words:

"I don't know."

We boxed, we danced, we sang—verbally, unfortunately, because my anger was growing and it would have felt damn good to release it. I couldn't, of course. I'd promised not to get physical, and besides, the response team in the hallway would have been inside with their pepper spray and billy clubs in the tick of a clock. But I was frustrated, and I laid it out for him:

"I can be your best friend or your worst enemy. Somebody is trying to fuck with me, and I'm going to get them. You can help, or you can be fucked along with them."

If he knew something, he was very good at concealing it. After twenty minutes, the two interrogators returned and resumed their questioning, following up on the very scant information he had given them earlier. I listened for a while, then got up.

"If you want to save your butt, you ask for Dick. They'll know how to get me."

Trace grumbled that it had been a waste of time as we headed for the airport where the helo had landed, a small burp of a place located near a shopping center a few miles away.

"It wasn't a waste at all," I told her. "We know that he's working in a very small cell with very specific instructions. He's on the low end of the food chain, just keeping tabs on us. And he was chosen for this sort of job because he does well under interrogation."

"Those are all guesses," said Trace.

"Educated guesses."

"So who does he work for?"

"Ten-million-dollar question," I told her. "Though right now I'd like to know how the hell he figured out where we were."

Shunt supplied a possible answer to that question.

"Dude, who's been using their cell phone?"

"No one," I told him. We were having a quick reassessment in Manhattan before breaking camp and heading home. "We switched to the beepers and pay phones."

"Could they have tracked the beepers?" asked Trace.

"Harder," Shunt said. "Like, you're sure there was no GPS mode?"

On cell phones, GPS—the abbreviation stands for "global positioning system" but it's become a generic term for any positioning system, in this case one using cell towers—allows 911 operators to locate you. Shunt explained that the cell phones were essentially small computers and could be hacked.

"I called a cell phone that morning," said Trace. "Danny Barrett. He'd called Rogue Manor and wanted an update. Would that count?"

"Well, like, if they had hacked into his phone and could figure out the number, they could backtrack and find out where it was."

"How can we find out?" I asked. "Without them knowing that we know?"

"I don't know, Dude. I'll have to talk to some of my gearhead friends at Verizon. Maybe we could, like, program a Trojan horse to go after their virus or whatever it is they got in there, if they got it in. We'd have to, uh, figure it out at the company level maybe. Might have to hack into their system."

"Could you?"

"Dude."

I got hold of Danny on a landline and had him go to a pay phone and call a number at a randomly selected restaurant (their cooperation was assured by a hundred-dollar bill and a promise of a signed copy of the next book—hope you're enjoying it, Max!). Danny nearly broke the telephone when I told him Shunt's theory.

"We want to look at the program in the phone. But we don't want them to know we know, if that's what's going on. Make another call later, then power it down and bring it back with you."

"Call who?"

"The weather. Nobody important."

"I'm sorry, Dick."

"It's not your fault, Danny, and it may not even be your phone. I think this is a wild goose chase. But we need to find out."

"I'm done here, anyway," Danny said. He gave me a quick update. It didn't come to much—except for the name of a company that some of the locals on a combined Homeland Security–state police–FBI task force believed might be connected with the three cells they'd been trying to track down in the Midwest.

Brod Prevoz.

Roughly translated, "Ship Transport," in Serbo-Croatian. And, more important, one of the firms connected to the Shitheads for Allah.

"Why are they interested?" I asked.

"The explanation is very convoluted. Remember the gun dealer I was telling you about? Well, at some point one of the suspects in the cell that bought weapons from him used their address on an immigration paper. Computer kicked it for some other reason, and one of the new Homeland Security overseas investigators actually went to check. They listed it as a phony address, but then someone on the task force recognized the company as a shipper that transports in and out of Europe. The Bosnia connection was what interested them."

Was this the Department of Insecurity we were talking about? The same people who had placed Tell-Me-Dick in a position of mistaken authority?

There *is* hope for this government organization yet.

"So what was the upshot?" I asked.

"Nada so far. The company checked out as a legitimate shipper. They ran a credit check, that sort of thing. They stopped one of their transports at some point and inspected it; it checked out completely. The company's on a watch list that's as long as the phone book. The guys working on the gun dealer and the Bosnian cells went back to square one, figuring it was just a screwup. They think the slimer probably reversed the digits on a legitimate address he knew of, or even made a mistake."

"Did the guy with the papers have any dealings with the company or any other company?"

"We haven't been able to check that."

"Let's ask."

"He was deported. They only developed some of this in the last week or so. And even with everything I've told you, there'd be no reason to hold on to him."

In movies and books and on television, terrorist networks snap into full view with a single sentence or intercepted message. In real life, nothing is ever smooth or in full view. Was this guy related to a company that was a cover that shipped weapons all across the world? Was the address just a bizarre coincidence? Remember the story of the blindfolded scientists placed in a room with an elephant and allowed to touch only once? That's what a real-life investigation is like—except, instead of an elephant, you're in the room with a ticking bomb.

Or an alarm clock. Up to you to figure out which.

"I did more checking on the trucking company," Danny said. "They do a lot of business with a trucking company out here every so often. That company took a shipment of surplus Army gear two months ago and delivered it to them."

"M16s?"

Danny rifled through his papers. "Blankets."

"Did the shipment go to France?" I asked.

"How'd you know?"

"Find out when the last shipment is going out."

"I already did," said Danny. "It's due the day after tomorrow in the container port near Hoboken. Caught my eye because it was the same place where we were going to drill."

"Danny, pack up and drive to the airport. Call us and tell us what flight you're on."

"Where am I going?"

"New York. Just tell us what airport and we'll meet you. Let me give you a number."

Container ports are basically very large parking lots with giant Erector set contraptions near a dock area. Containers come in on one side and go out on the other, hoisted from and aboard ships by special cranes. In the fall of 2002, the feds unveiled a program to improve security at the ports of New York under the jurisdiction of the Port Authority of New York and New Jersey that included electronic tags tracking each container. They also increased reporting standards, mandated more "manual" inspections, and announced plans to buy one hundred portable X-ray scanners that make random inspections somewhat quicker. Money was even set aside for detectors to track radiation through the ports. Senator Chuck Schumer and some other big shots gathered round and proclaimed this "pilot program" the greatest thing since sliced bread was packaged in plastic bags.

That stuff looks great on the press release and probably made a kick-ass spot on the nightly news. I'm sure it'll be part of Schumer's reelection ads. No strike against the senator; he's at least *trying* to do something to protect his constituents. But think about this: it's a *pilot* program, children. It hasn't been done before. Until the fall of 2002, there wasn't even a plan to beef up security at the ports.

And how secure do you think those electronic tags are?

"Might take a few minutes to break in if you didn't have an EPROM reader handy," said Shunt, checking out the tag on one of the Brod Prevoz containers.

An EPROM reader is a fancy electronic tool that reads data on memory chips; if you look around, you can get one for under five bucks, though a really good one may set you back a bit more. We didn't need to hunt around for one, though. We'd borrowed a real tag reader from a state police truck stop on the turnpike a few hours before. They had two. I doubt they missed it until we FedExed it back to them the next day.

Four of us infiltrated the cargo container's outbound holding yard while Hulk and Danny Barrett, newly returned from the Midwest, played lookout beyond the fences. We had some of Capel's people watching for Shadow's net. Inside the yard,

Trace and Sean took up covering positions, while Shunt and I did the work. Not that getting past the locks and seals of a shipping trailer is real work.

The fact that we had originally been scheduled to hit the container port made our unauthorized foray a little easier than it might have been, but I doubt it would have taken more than a few hours of advance work on the scene to figure out how to get in and out. To be honest, we could've probably called ahead and told the site security, the state police, or the Feds that we were tiptoeing and they wouldn't have caught us. But we saved our quarters.

Anyone who would have checked the electronic tag on the container would have seen where it had been. They would have had no trouble (assuming all the computers were working) discovering what it contained and whether the shippers had dotted their t's and crossed their i's. And they would have felt very confident and secure, assured by modern technology that they were keeping a close eye on the world around them. But they'd have been wrong.

Remember the old saying, "Garbage in, garbage out"?

The data on the shipment indicated that the trucks contained industrial drills. And there *were* industrial drills aboard—the first two rows of crates at the back, and at least some on the side. But the first crate we checked in the middle of the third row had M16s in it.

Early models, probably U.S. Army surplus. We didn't bother checking them closely; we kept the box open long enough to slip a tracking device inside and then resealed it. My idea was that Doc would stay in France and help the French authorities there as they tracked the guns. When they captured their bad guys, we presumably would have information on Shadow as well.

As we repacked the crate Sean spotted a port security car headed our way. Everything was snugged and buttoned up by the time the beat-up white Taurus passed down the lane where we'd been. It had searchlights on both windows but the beams hit the cargo containers around chest high; we could have sat down next to the roadway and probably not been seen. We waited for the car to pass, and then went on to the second part of the job on the other side of the lot.

Danny's information had led me to wonder what else the company might be hauling. As it turned out, the company didn't seem to have any more business in the metropolitan area, or at least none Cox's records hound could find. Naturally, this made me suspicious, so I had Shunt fire up his laptop to see what he could come up with. He also drew a blank, and then I knew we were onto something. Danny called on some old police contacts, and we began running back registrations and license plates, getting nowhere—until we found that Brod Prevoz and another company, this one called American Furniture Hauling, had sold each other the same truck twice over the past two years.

And, as it happened, American Furniture Hauling was supposed to make a pickup on the other side of the yard in the morning. The container had supposedly come from Albania—which isn't all that far from the former Yugoslavia, is it?

By truck it is, and even with porous borders, this was a long-shot play. But since I was already in the container port, I figured I might as well have a look-see. You never know where you're going to find mustard gas or other more interesting items these days.

Security in the incoming area was a bit tighter than over in the outbound lot. Dogs and more than a dozen teams checked containers in a dedicated area directly off the highway. Once a container passed through customs and whatever dockside inspections had been ordered for it, it was stored in a fenced-off no-man's-land just beyond the inspection station. I wouldn't say getting into that part of the compound was easy, but I wouldn't say it was particularly hard. Trace had probed the situation the day before, testing responses at the gate. I had originally thought we'd come in posing as truckers making a pickup. But that turned out not to be necessary. Once past the customs area, trailers generally didn't stay very long in the holding paddock. All of the security was concentrated in two places—on the preinspection side of the fence, where the idea was to keep something from slipping over to the cleared spot before inspection, and on the exit ramp, which was really a double-lane highway winding around the perimeter of the complex. This was supposed to be an emergency exit for the holding area and had a chained gate with two guards posted at all times. But if you came in from the side of the lot, all you had to deal with was some razor wire and a chain-link fence. It was at least a hundred yards long and only one corner was lit. Of course, to get in from the side you had to be in the incoming section of the plant—where, by golly, we just happened to be.

We worked our way inside and located the trailer in question. But before Shunt and I could examine the locks, Hulk sounded an alert from outside. A pair of Crown Vics had driven up to the entrance of the yard and were being quickly waved through security.

"Feds or state people. All suits. In a hurry."

My interest piqued, we slipped back to watch as the cars cruised down the access road toward the emergency exit. But then they passed right by, continuing around on the road behind the lot. I was disappointed at first—then I realized where they were going.

"Move toward the outgoing lot area," I told the rest of the team. "Be careful, because they've got a good view of the outgoing lot from the row where the M16 containers are. Keep plenty of distance between you and them."

The rear of the trailer was exposed to the other lot and getting inside it would be risky with the Feds stumbling around; besides, I wanted to see what the hell they were up to. Shunt and I slipped tracking sensors on the trailer we'd located, just in case someone came for it before we got a chance to get inside. We went back over the wire, using a Teflon blanket to avoid an unnecessarily close shave, and moved around the last row of the trailers. The trucks hid us from the automated lifting area, where the claws pick up the containers and ramp them across to the ships. A low chain-link fence—no clue what the hell that was supposed to do beyond routing traffic—separated the parking area from the railroad tracks. Beyond the fence, it was an open run to the water.

I kept Shunt next to me the whole way. I trusted the kid's computer skills, but he was more Boy Scout than shooter. Though his heart was in the right place.

"We could pick them off from here, Dude, bam-bam-bam," said the techie as we crawled up to two rows from the trailers.

Somehow, the words "bam-bam-bam" don't sound right coming from a guy who's six-one and weighs a hundred and thirty pounds, even if he had exchanged his glasses for sports goggles and tucked his long frizzy black hair under a cap.

The suits did a circuit of the yard. As they came back to the security gate, an HRT unit—the FBI counter-terror SWAT people—drove up in three plain blue vans. ("HRT" stands for "Hostage Rescue Team." They're like a super SWAT team, trained in techniques SEAL Team Six and Delta pioneered.)

"Skip? This looks like a big show," said Hulk. He was sitting in a car not far from the sentry box. It was one thing to avoid being noticed by bored security types and quite another to slip under the HRT radar screen; they actually know what they're doing.

"Go over to phase two," I told Hulk. "Grab a boat and play backstop."

"On it."

"What the fuck are these assholes doing?" asked Trace. The HRT team filtered through the yard, setting up lines of fire around the M16 containers.

"Shunt, are you sure there was no bug on that container?" I asked.

"I used the scanner, Dude. You think they're looking for us?"

"I'd say they're looking for somebody else. You sure we didn't trip anything?"

"Can't rule it out."

"Danny, can you hear me?"

"Gotcha, Skipper."

"What do you think about getting to a pay phone and seeing if you can find out what HRT is up to? Call the New York Terrorism Czar on his cell phone. If that doesn't work, go through Karen."

"What about Cox?"

"Or Cox. Or anyone else you can think of."

"You think they're going after our boxes?"

"Don't you?"

"Well, maybe, but, these containers are on the way out, not in. If somebody wanted to grab something they wouldn't have put it in, right?"

A very logical mind. But not every situation called for logic.

"I can't argue with you, Danny. But I can't argue with twelve shooters, either."

That's how many were piling out of the vans and taking up positions around the yard. Things remained quiet for a half hour or so. I considered sneaking back to the other container and opening it, but decided against it—not only because I thought we might be seen, but because I thought there might be a possibility the FBI or someone else had planted some sort of device on it we couldn't pick up. Our sensor would allow us to track the trailer; we'd just have to wait to get it open.

Danny made his phone calls, but probably because of the time—it was now past one A.M.—found nobody to talk to. We were trying to come up with some other possibilities when Sean saw two figures come in off the water. We watched in dark clothes as they snuck through the yard toward the containers that were staked out. As soon as one of them put a hand on the seal, a portable searchlight flipped on behind them.

"Shit!" I said—but not loud enough or soon enough to prevent the slaughter.

In the FBI's view, they were completely justified in taking down the two men. Both spun around, pistols in firing positions. One of the men took a shot, probably at the searchlight that had blinded them, though if so he missed. The HRT people had legitimate orders to fire if fired upon, and they did so.

They did not miss. So, rather than having two potential—emphasis on *potential*—sources of information about a clandestine smuggling operation, we had two more dead illegal immigrants, sprawled in front of the trailers. I waited until the Crown Vics drove up, then slipped through the shadows and appeared right behind them so quickly the HRT people thought I'd gotten out of the car. Among the suits was my friend, the local FBI counterterrorism wannabe expert, who proceeded to strut and frut as he congratulated himself on snatching a full load of rifles destined for America's overseas enemies. I guess he thought they were headed for the French army or something.

"Why the fuck did you kill these assholes?" I told him. Fortunately for him, I was in a diplomatic mood. "You just screwed up everything."

"I screwed up everything? What the hell are you doing here, Marcinko? How the hell did you get in here? What the hell are you doing?"

"I'm involved in an investigation. What the hell are *you* doing here?"

Members of the Fucked-Up-Beyond-Imagination Bureau don't like to hear the word "investigation" coming from someone who doesn't have a government-issue BuCar; they think you're trying to hone in on their pension plan. Wannabe started sputtering and stuttering about how he had just apprehended a major terrorist organization and saved America from another 9/11.

It's hard to argue with logic like that, let alone try to understand it. I waited for him to mention the other container, but he didn't. And if he wasn't going to bring it up, I wasn't going to, either.

The dead men had carried backpacks filled with electric circuit boards. This seemed very interesting to the FBI honcho, who started spouting something about secret coded information.

Shunt rolled his eyes off on the side.

"First of all, Dude, the word is encrypted," he said. "Second of all, if they were shipping data, they wouldn't do it on boards like these." He held them up to the light. "More likely they're just beating some sort of export restriction or maybe, like, a weird tax. These look like, uh, Pentium III chips. Old ones. Not worth much. Too bad, like, you don't know who stole them and who was getting them and like that."

Smoke started coming out of Wannabe's ears. He started yelling about having his own people "handle the technical aspects, thank you very much."

"Doom on you, Dude," snapped Shunt.

We all cracked up, even the nearby HRT shooters. Wannabe turned so red his face glowed in the searchlights.

"Armstead is going to hear from me," he said.

"You want his home number?"

"Fuck you, Marcinko. Fuck you."

A dollar for every time somebody says that and I'm on a beach in Antigua.

With the full weight of the FBI thrown into the investigation, I had no doubt that what had been a promising lead was now completely shot to shit. Even so, we set up to track the inbound container. Wannabe made it impossible to get into without being noticed, so we planted a small video cam on an old signal bridge on the rail line nearby to keep an eye on it in case the tracking transponder screwed up; then we broke into shifts, waiting down the road. Danny got hold of some friends in the Bureau of Alcohol, Tobacco, Firearms and Explosives, and they agreed to detail a strike team of Treasury agents trained in HAZMAT situations as a backup strike force. The agents needed an hour's notice to assemble; this wasn't optimum, but I figured it would beat having the FBI blow the last chance we had of developing the lead. Danny also worked out a plan so that Jersey state troopers would be able to cut off the container truck if it went off the highway and into an area we didn't think we could control safely.

In the meantime, I called Doc and got him just before he was to start his morning rounds—sightseeing with Tiffany at Versailles.

"I've never been to the Sun King's palace, Dick," said Doc cheerfully. "I'm really looking forward to it."

If he'd lived back then, Doc would have been one of the people Marie Antoinette told to eat cake. But I guess there's some sort of poetic justice in rabble like us trooping through the marble halls and snorting at how the king and queen pissed through their loot.

"The Sun King's going to have to wait for another day," I told him. "Maybe even another trip." I filled him in and told him he'd better head over to his French friends and fill them in *tout de suite.* They might want to roll up anyone likely to hear the news from America.

"Why the hell did the FBI close in?" Doc asked.

"Besides inbred stupidity? They got some sort of tip. Wannabe claimed they'd been watching the containers for weeks, but you know that's bullshit. I'll have Danny Barrett check his contacts out West to see if they were the source. It's possible that they did alert New York, but I doubt it."

"Maybe they have an agent inside the cell and

they don't want to tell us. Or the French," suggested Doc. He's a kind soul. He gives people far more credit than they deserve.

"If they did, raiding the containers wouldn't make any sense. It'd make people suspicious of the agent."

"Unless they arrested him with the others."

"They killed both guys."

"Killed them?" said Doc. "Why the hell would they do that? You sure those guys weren't set up?"

If you were there watching it happen, it looked like a bad dream unfolding in front of you—but it also seemed to make some sense, at least according to the crazy logic of real life. But standing where Doc was—in his skivvies across the ocean, probably badly in need of a shave and coffee—it looked and felt like a setup.

"You send two guys out on a bullshit mission, then call the FBI to kill them for you," he said. "Make sure they have guns. No muss, no fuss."

Two immigrants, thus far without IDs. But what if they were friends of His Swarthiness? The only connections between His Swarthiness and Shadow?

Which would explain why they'd been assigned to sneak worthless chips into the truck. Or would merely be the latest blind alley in a tangled mess of blind alleys. Maybe His Swarthiness knew which one it was. But if so, he wasn't telling it to me, at least not at Danbury. He wasn't talking to anyone there, as I discovered the next morning when I showed up at the compound around eleven. The Tango had been taken to twist elsewhere.

"To where?" I asked Twenty Questions.

"Part of the protocol is that they don't tell us," said the interrogator apologetically, shrugging and frowning. "If I had to guess, I'd say Gitmo, but it might also have been to Texas. There's some new place there. One of ours."

"Why'd they move him?" I asked.

More shrugs and citings of protocol. Even when I got Twenty Questions to stop reading from his script, he seemed honestly not to know why the prisoner had been moved. But I thought my new best friend in the department might.

"Dick, I've been trying to track you down for hours," said Cox when I called him a short while later. "Where the hell are you?"

"In a McDonald's in Brewster, New York," I told him. I was actually in a Burger King in Connecticut, but it was close enough for government work—and for anyone who might have been listening in and really trying to track me.

"That hard drive you guys planted worked like a charm. We've got great information. I want—I mean, if you're interested, if you'd consider it, I have a possible mission. Can you get to D.C.?"

"Possibly."

"Do you want to hear about it?"

"Not now. I'll meet you in your office tomorrow to talk about it."

"When?"

"When I get there," I said.

Whether or not he had his promotion wagon hitched to me, Cox wasn't used to being talked to that way, so there was a pause before he told me that would be fine. He'd be around all day. I then proceeded to grill him about His Swarthiness. He did know about the transfer; in fact, he had requested it.

"There's this new facility down at Lackland, Texas, that we're running with the CIA. People are supposed to be A1," he said. He went on, sounding like he was recommending a resort rather than an interrogation facility. Some sort of psychological expert had designed a state of the art interrogation system supposed to unlock a prisoner's "inner soul." Those were the words Cox used, and they were completely in context. If he had told me they gave the prisoners massages, I wouldn't have been surprised.

I know what kind of massage I would have recommended.

"I want to talk to him," I told Cox.

"Any time, Dick. Not a problem. As soon as he's settled."

"Settled? What the fuck, settled?"

"Settled is what they call it. They condition him for a response. Takes a couple of days."

Maybe we were talking in code about torture; there's always hope.

"I'm going to send somebody down there. They'll be there tomorrow."

"Fine," said Cox. "I'll clear the way."

"Have you heard about the container port?" I asked.

"Oh yes, the FBI called us about that this morning. From what I heard, they claimed you were interfering. I covered for you, though. The liaison called me directly and I told them you don't work for me."

"Who'd you say I worked for?"

"I didn't, but, um, I did say, uh, that if they had a beef they should talk to Karen."

He tossed out some bullshit about how thorough I was, ass-kissing for the inevitable question: "So you will help out on that other matter, right?"

"We'll talk about it tomorrow," I said.

I made it back to Jersey in time to take a watch with Trace. I'd given some thought to turning the operation over to customs or maybe having the ATF people do more than simply stand by, but for the time being I held off. As tenuous as it might be, this remained my best link to Shadow. I'd also been racking my brain trying to remember if I'd come up against anyone in Yugoslavia or its successor madhouses who might hold a grudge. The answer remained negative, but the world's a small place; it was certainly possible that I'd axed someone in a previous lifetime who was now out to do me in—and cause serious mayhem in the meantime.

Or not. I couldn't quite see the elephant yet.

Trace and I were watching the video monitor we'd placed from a Chevy SUV a short distance from the facility. When my stomach started growling, she surprised me by revealing a secret hankering for a Big Mac.

"And large fries," she said. "With a strawberry shake."

"You eat that?"

"Once a month. Helps keep me regular."

Sometimes you can have a little too much information about people. She grabbed lunch and brought it to the car while I checked in with each member of the team.

"You like Texas?" I asked Trace.

"Not particularly."

"Good. That'll put you in the right mood. They moved His Swarthiness down there so he can be conditioned."

"Conditioned? What the fuck does that mean?"

"I haven't a clue. Maybe they ran out of shampoo. Should I send Danny with you?"

"To chaperone?"

"To apply more conditioner."

Trace looked at me. Secret sauce leaked out on her chin: very attractive.

"I can handle it."

"Should be set up by tomorrow," I told her.

"What's up with Danny and his kid?" Trace asked.

"What's up what?"

"He's pining after some long-lost daughter or something. He wants to meet her."

"It sounded to me like he wasn't even sure it was his daughter."

"Well, he's sure now."

I chewed on that as well as the burger I'd ordered. Neither was very well-cooked, but then I always prefer my meat raw and bloody. After I finished, I got out of the car and went to the phone booth. I managed to get hold of Doc, who stopped grousing about his postponed trip to Versailles long enough to tell me that the French were not particularly grateful that the Bureau Without a Clue had made the bust before the weapons got to France.

"They think it's a racket to protect some American," said Doc.

"Or someone involved with the smuggling operation," I told him. "Did that DNA sample Danny arranged to send ever arrive? Maybe he thought they were after him and went on the lam. That would make sense if they had these guys axed."

"It turns out they don't have a sample to compare it to. I can't tell if they slipped up or they just don't routinely take one. I've heard it both ways."

The Frenchies were looking for Pierre's sister, though they weren't sure exactly where she lived. If they could get a sample from her, they should be able to use Danny's to get a close enough match for an ID. And, yes, the package had arrived.

Doc had more news: the FBI had decided to throw some of its muscle into the case. A "high-level delegation" was en route to Paris to compare notes on the M16 case and ooh and aah at the Eiffel Tower.

"If they're obnoxious enough, the French may toss them off the top," he said hopefully.

"What do you think they traded for the guns?"

"Dunno. The mustard gas is still missing."

"Could be. What if it's not?"

"Just about anything. The French keep bringing up flowers as if there's money in that. And speaking of euros, there's a network of bank accounts that they've been trying to track. They keep getting lost in Austria. Banking laws there make the Swiss look like big mouths. The Frenchies think the money gets smuggled in as cash or gets distributed somehow through credit cards or lines of credit. It's supposedly pretty tangled."

Pretty tangled was the order of the day. While I'd been gone, the two men the FBI men had killed were IDed as Bosnian immigrants in America on tourist visas—which had expired six months before. Obviously they were having so much fun that they just lost track of time. The Jersey State Police and the Bureau of Alcohol, Tobacco, Firearms and Explosives had thrown themselves into the investigation, which allowed Danny to learn from them that the FBI's tipster had called Wannabe directly. We thought that might be significant until we found out that his office, home, and cell phone numbers were listed on an official website. Guess he wanted terrorists to know how to get hold of him if they decided to surrender.

Danny's sources also opined that the FBI had no idea what was going on with these Bosnian and French connections.

Unfortunately, they weren't the only ones. And so we waited. Nothing happened that afternoon. Or that night. Or the next morning. I left the team around ten to head for D.C., planning to be back in time for my next shift at eight.

13

The NSA's virus—Shunt said it was more like a Trojan horse with a Pony Express messenger service attached—that we had planted in the bank had tipped the NSA to a string of coded messages concerning a mission being bankrolled by an outside group. The messages gave Web addresses for information about different ports, and gave a credit card number along with security information. The credit card had been used for three days only, making five-hundred-dollar withdrawals each day, the card's limit. The withdrawals had been made in Baltimore. The account owner lived in Wyoming and was a retired teacher. He was almost certainly the victim of identity theft but just in case was under surveillance. The account was also being watched.

"The long and the short of it is, we think they're aiming for a natural gas port," explained Cox, laying the situation out for me in his office with his usual obsequiousness.

"I'd like to hear the long and the short," I told him. "And everything in between."

Cox glanced at Shunt, whom I'd brought along

as a technical consultant, and then asked about his clearance.

"Code-word level," I said. "And I can vouch for him personally."

"This is very need to know, Dick. Very need to know."

"And Shunt needs to know."

There was some fretting and sweating, but in the end Cox anted up with apparently everything he knew, which frankly wasn't all that much. The NSA had identified a ship called the Methane Duke—honest to God, the real name—which had shipped out of Algeria and was due at Cove Point, Maryland, in three days. There was also a website featuring Japanese dragons; the intel boys thought it was some sort of code for a fire strike.

They were all obviously thirty or younger. Dragon was the nickname for the M-47, an antitank guided missile used by the Army in the early 1970s and still around in an improved version. The latest version has a range out around fifteen hundred meters; it's wire-guided and can puncture armor up to 500mm thick. It's not particularly known for its accuracy—but liquid natural gas tankers are pretty big.

"Could it take out an LNG tanker?" asked Cox after I explained it.

"I don't know. The missile would have to go through an outer tank or the hull before it got to the cargo tank. There's a vacuum and insulation, sometimes as much as two feet of it. The arrangement is a little like a thermos bottle. The LNG would be pretty cold so it might be that if you hit it right, the whole tank would blow up. Coast Guard might know."

Cox frowned, then seemed to remember that the Coast Guard was part of his department. He grabbed at the phone and began jabbing madly at the keypad. Within a few minutes, two lieutenant commanders emerged from somewhere deep in the bowels of the bureaucracy, blinking their eyes like molemen suddenly summoned to the surface world. I gave them a general rundown of what the situation might be, then sat back and listened as they discussed the matter between themselves. The sum total of their knowledge and expertise could be summarized in a single sentence, which, when stripped of its bureaucratese and translated into standard English, amounted to:

Dunno.

Neither man was an expert on LNG tankers or weapons or hazardous situations—even though, according to Cox's flowchart on the bureaucracy, they were supposed to be all three. I was eventually able to reach a real expert, however. The Coast Guard has done considerable thinking about the problem of the tankers in general, but most of their studies were concerned with structural failure and collisions. They had been complaining for years that they needed more inspectors just to handle these concerns.

Fire a missile at it? No one had actually studied that.

"I think, given the amount of insulation, the way the tanks are structured—I don't think a small shell like the one you describe would rupture the tank, at least not with one shot," said my expert. "They're made to withstand pretty strong collisions."

"Would you bet on it with your life?" I asked.

He didn't say anything. Which was all the response I needed.

I know a little bit about LNG carriers and ports and had the good fortune to lend a few of my thoughts on security at Cove Point, Maryland, the largest liquid natural gas port in the country. If you remember your high school chemistry, you know that gas becomes a liquid when it's cooled. That's true of H_2O, and it's true of natural gas. One of the tricks in transporting natural gas is to keep the tank cool; as long as you can do that the fuel is about as easy to deal with as oil. The guys who work on these big boats have busted a lot of pencils and worn down a lot of erasers, but they've come up with a pretty efficient system, and one that's surprisingly safe.

Of course, we *are* talking about natural gas, and if it's not dealt with correctly things can get ugly. Spill a whole bunch out on the water and you're likely to create a cloud of gas. A *big* cloud—anywhere from a mile to fifty miles wide, depending on the leak. The scientists say that such a cloud is less likely to explode than a similar cloud of liquid petroleum gas, which really helps me sleep at night. The Coast Guard has conducted a variety of tests that show a small explosion *probably* can't be used to trigger the gas cloud to explode. All that will happen will be a massive fireball.

Like I say, very reassuring. Especially since the scientists have recently developed a new theory that shows the gas could explode after all if the conditions are right.

Even if the LNG cloud didn't go boom or torch a fifty-mile radius of earth and sky, the psychological damage of an LNG "event" would be immense. You probably don't give much thought right now to that black pipe routing through your basement to the clothes dryer. Watch a video of a floating birthday candle torching the night sky five or six hundred times over a weekend, though, and your attitude is going to change. And when the experts come on to tell you how "lucky" we were that the fire cloud was fueled by natural gas rather than petroleum gas, that white tank of propane you've got out on your deck beneath the Sunbeam grill is going to look awful suspicious.

LNG ships are massive. There are a couple of different ways to construct them, but basically they look like oil tankers with a wedge or a row of fat Christmas ornaments on the front deck. The wedge covers a series of double-lined and -insulated tanks; the ornaments represent a slightly different approach but do the same thing: keep the LNG contained, cold, and at the right pressure so it doesn't decide to evaporate into gas.

Armed with his intelligence, Cox did what bureaucrats do when they sense a problem. He formed a committee, officially called a "task group," which was supposed to coordinate protection efforts. The Coast Guard, Navy, and port and local police authorities were all players in the task group, which had already met twice and was planning a video conference later that afternoon. They'd made fantastic progress so far. Their agenda included an agenda to make an agenda, and to take steps toward forming several subcommittees.

Even though he'd developed the intelligence and gotten the disparate authorities together, the law of bureaucratic pecking orders made Cox a bit player on the Ad Hoc Emergency LNG Protection Task Force Team/Provisional. Rare for a bureaucrat, he actually seemed to realize this and suggested that my ideas about beefing up the security operation ought to be directed to the lead Coast Guard official on the project, a vice admiral from the Fifth District. He also wanted me and my merry band to play the role of roaming patrollers, darting across the harbor area in Zodiacs.

I avoided making a commitment on what role, if any, I'd play, but I did agree to talk to the admiral. Cox put the call through himself and then handed me the phone. I found myself speaking to the admiral's chief of staff in Portsmouth, a captain who had the annoying habit of saying "of course" after every sentence I uttered. They had already realized that the crews on the ships were a potential weak link, and besides assigning cutters and possibly Navy vessels as escorts to every LNG tanker approaching the harbor, they would put boarding parties with technical experts on every ship. It sounded good, though the real test would be the execution. I told him a few things about the onshore arrangements. He didn't ask if I wanted to sit in on the teleconference and I didn't volunteer.

After I hung up, I prodded and poked Cox for more information about the operation he and the

NSA boys had unearthed, trying to see if I could find a real connection with Shadow. Even though I was sure there was something there, nothing Cox told me confirmed it, let alone gave me any tangible information about what the NSA had actually figured out. The agency that doesn't exist casts a certain black aura over everything they do. They've never been caught up in public scandals like the Christians In Action, and pulling intelligence out of thin air gives them a certain mystique that's hard to penetrate. That mystique is one of their main products, and they work hard to maintain it.

I'd tried getting hold of George Boreland several times, and gave it another shot once Shunt and I got out of the office. I borrowed an encrypted phone—actually, the office holding it—and called into a work number I'd obtained from another NSA staffer. A gruff voice answered—not with "Hello" or "Yeah?" but with the words "How'd you get this number?" Whoever was on the other side—I don't know for a fact that it was Boreland, just someone who worked in that section of the Agency—slammed the phone down before I even had a chance to open my mouth. The number no longer worked when I called back.

I was just hanging up when my cell phone rang.

"They're moving," said Trace.

"On my way."

Shunt and I had come down to D.C. aboard a Coast Guard HH-60 Jayhawk. The aircraft had been generously detailed to me by the air commander of the First District, who apparently was under the misimpression that Rich Armstead himself had ordered the aircraft made available. I don't know how he might have gotten that idea; maybe it was the email that went out, or seemed to go out, from his office. The HH-60 is the Coast Guard's version of the Blackhawk, which is about as ubiquitous today as the Huey was back in Vietnam. They're great, versatile aircraft—but at one hundred ninety-three knots top speed, an HH-60 wasn't going to get me up to New York as quickly as I wanted.

I did, however, have a backup plan.

The two guards snapped to attention on the tarmac as Shunt and I approached. Behind them sat an HU-25A, one of the few French nondrinkable exports that's worth anything. Officially dubbed the Guardian, the HU-25 is actually a modified version of a Dassault Falcon 20G. The Falcon can go more than twice as fast as the Jayhawk and more than twice as far.

This one was waiting for a Coast Guard VIP. The guards snapped to as Shunt and I trotted to the aircraft. We hopped aboard and made our way to the flight cabin.

"No pilot," said Shunt.

"Yeah. Real shame," I said.

"I don't think we should wait, do you?"

"I don't think he'd want us to."

Shunt took the stick and we rocked off the ground after the world's quickest preflight, humping toward New York. The HU-25A lacked a SatCom connection, and after hunting around trying to get a frequency that would connect with Danny, I gave up and pulled out my cell phone. If the phone screwed up the cockpit gear, Shunt never mentioned it. Danny picked up on the second ring.

"We're on the turnpike, coming north," he told me.

There was only one driver in the truck, and as far as Danny could tell, there were no bodyguards or a trail team nearby. We had three cars in the operation, not counting Capel's crew, which was trailing my guys. The ATF strike team was assembling at Teterboro Airport, a small airport in northern New Jersey that had been selected because it was easier to deal with than the majors nearby. Their helicopter had been fueled and would take off within five minutes.

"We're about twenty minutes from Teterboro," said Shunt, leaning against the throttle. "We could land and get on the helicopter if the timing goes right."

I pulled out a paper map to get an idea of the area. The Jersey Turnpike, also known as I-95, runs the length of the state, crossing over the Hudson River at the George Washington Bridge. As I-95, it continues across the city into Westchester and then over into Connecticut. There were hundreds if not thousands of possible permutations.

"Shit," said Danny. "He's heading for the Lincoln Tunnel."

"Shut down the tunnel," I told him, ruining the afternoon and a good hunk of the night for thousands of people about to be caught in the resulting traffic jam. Ten minutes later—after Danny had confirmed with the state police that the tunnel had, in fact, been closed—the container truck turned off the highway, heading back to the west. The next time Danny checked in, he was headed north on Route 17 in northern New Jersey. The truck had bypassed the main arteries into New York City, though it was still headed through a well-populated area. It looked no different than thousands of other tractor trailers that head up that busy highway every day.

"Stewart Airport might be a better place to land," suggested Shunt, looking at my map. "The helo with the SWAT team could meet us there."

He made the necessary course adjustments, and I went back to the map. Stewart was thirty or forty miles north of the Jersey border, near the Hudson River in the town of Newburgh, New York. The ATF helo checked in and it looked like we were set for a good rendezvous at the airport.

Too bad the guy driving the cargo container hadn't been briefed on the mission.

"He's going east on I-87, the New York Thruway," said Danny a few minutes later. "Heading for the Tappan Zee Bridge."

I went back to the map. I-87 ran across the river at the Tappan Zee and then back south into New York City. But it also connected via 287 with Connecticut and from there to the rest of New England and Canada. We could land at Westchester County Airport and meet the helicopter there. But before I managed to set up the rendezvous, Danny called back with yet another change of direction. The truck had gotten off on local roads, gotten back onto the thruway, and was now coming off a ramp at a large shopping mall in Rockland County called Palisades Center.

"I'm three cars behind him," said Danny. "He's going *into* Palisades Center."

Palisades Center is a large enclosed mall in Rockland County. If you get there at three o'clock on a Thursday in July, you can't get a parking spot.

"Dick, if he's got canisters of mustard gas in there, the mall would be a perfect target," said Danny. "He's going around the back."

"Detail somebody to pick me up if he starts moving again," I told Danny. "I'll be there in five minutes."

"Time for Plan B," I told Shunt.

When the Coast Guard bought the Falcons, they made a few million dollars' worth of changes to the aircraft. Among these were trapdoors that allow equipment and supplies to be parachuted to ships in distress. The openings are only twenty by thirty inches wide. To give you a better idea of how small they are, they fit in the aisle at the middle of the plane, which is squeeze city, especially if you happen to be wearing a parachute. I got stuck as I squeezed out, and anyone with a camera would have had a hell of a picture, since it probably looked like the airplane had a pair of legs. I managed to push a little left, and as I got unstuck the aircraft lurched hard to the right. The side of the hatchway or maybe the bottom of the plane slapped the side of my helmet pretty hard, and it took a few seconds for me to get myself oriented as I plummeted in what may best be described as a free fall. By the time I opened my chute, Danny had the truck surrounded at the far end of the mall near the entrance to the movie theaters. I could see a flood of people streaming from the other sides, and it's probable that if I weren't wearing a helmet, I'd even have been able to hear their screams.

A black bug appeared on the horizon to my left. I decided it must be the SWAT team in its helicopter. Below my feet I could see that Danny and one of the shooters with him were near the corner of the building, but the others weren't obvious. It could be that they were stuck in the traffic that was snaking back to the thruway.

I steered my chute around, legging into an approach so I could drop onto the roof near the truck. As I did that, the door to the cab opened and I watched the driver get out. He had something in his hands.

No, it wasn't an umbrella.

The rifle—it turned out to be an AR-15—jumped as the driver shot in Danny's direction. By that time, I was maybe fifty feet from the ground. It's possible that if I had had more time to think about it, I would have stayed exactly on the course I was on and landed safely on the other side of the truck. But I've always leaned more toward action than contemplation. I pulled hard on the steering togs, changing course.

The driver started to turn toward me when I was about ten feet away, which made it easier for me to kick him in the face. He fell backward and the rifle went flying. By the time I had the harness on my chute unsnapped, Danny had appeared and was standing over the man with his rifle.

Danny grinned. "Nice of you to drop in." Then he went to the cab. "I saw him screwing with this," he said, reaching in. "That's why we moved in."

He held up a gas mask.

The ATF SWAT team had fanned out behind us. Between their helicopter and my arrival, we'd attracted a bit of attention. I told Sean to try to find the mall security people to keep the scene under control, but by then word had spread that there were armed men at the rear entrance of the mall. The crowd gave us plenty of room all right—they panicked and began flooding away from the place. I found out later that even the security people had taken a hike. Ten bucks an hour and Tuesdays off wasn't enough to risk your neck for when the shit hit the fan.

We didn't see much of the panic up close. We were at the rear end of the mall, with the helo in a gravel lot and the truck near the door. We couldn't see the people streaming for the exits on the other side. We knew the state and local police were responding, along with a HAZMAT team from the county. Danny and I decided we'd interview the driver while we waited.

First we had to wake him. There being no water handy, Danny decided that any liquid would do. While on stakeout, he'd taken the precaution of filling two five-gallon jugs with extra gasoline, just in case it became inconvenient to find a gas station while tracking the truck. Odds are the American Medical Association wouldn't have approved of his method, but it did wake the truck driver up.

"Now start talking," said Danny, holding up a lighter.

The man started crying instead. His tears didn't elicit much sympathy.

"Who the hell are you?" I asked.

He said something in a language I didn't recognize.

"Who are you?" I asked again.

"English," added Danny.

"Seriv Dogglebash."

"What are you doing with the truck?" I asked.

"I drive it here."

"No shit, Sherlock. Why did you try to shoot Danny?"

Seriv didn't answer. Danny flicked his thumb, lighting the flame on the lighter. Given the stench coming off Seriv, I'm surprised he didn't spontaneously combust.

"You were going to shoot me," he blubbered, really bawling now. His accent made his words difficult to understand, but he pointed to the side of the building.

"What were you doing with the gas mask?" I asked.

He shook his head. Danny raised the lighter. Seriv screamed.

"What were you doing with the truck?" I asked.

He started speaking his native tongue again, the words rolling out quickly. To this day I have no idea what he was saying or what language it was in, though I guessed then that it was Serbo-Croatian. He looked as if he were from that part of the world—pudgy and dark-featured. Neither well-dressed nor clean shaven, smelling of gasoline, he tried to move backward from Danny's flame but found his path cut off by the curb.

Sean returned and told us what was going on inside the mall. "Pandemonium" wasn't in his vocabulary, but that's what he was describing. I told him to take some of the ATF people and try to get things settled down at the front, at least enough for the police to get through the traffic. At that moment, I truly regretted sending Trace down to Texas and Tiffany over to France. Either one of them would have stopped traffic in an instant.

Danny continued to wave the lighter in front of the driver, but all he got out of him were uncontrollable sobs.

"He's pretty scared of getting fried," said Danny. "You think he's telling us something in Serb or whatever the hell it is he's talking?"

I pulled out the phone, thinking I would call Karen and get her to run down a translator. But she wasn't at her desk or answering her cell.

"Maybe we ought to tape what he's saying," suggested Danny. "While we've still got him scared."

I made Danny promise not to have a pig roast before I got back, then trotted inside. A large electronics store sat about four slots down on the right. I'd just picked it out when something flashed at the far end of the hallway.

Call it a knee-jerk reaction, but even before my eyes and brain began processing the spark, I'd launched myself toward the floor.

Gunfire tends to have that effect on me, especially when it's coming from an MP5 submachine gun.

14

Fortunately, whoever was firing the MP5 was not a particularly good shot. Otherwise, the fact that my dive ended well short of the store and anything remotely capable of providing protection would have been more than just disappointing. I managed to push myself forward and roll into the store, knocking over a display of Jap robots, which scattered over the floor and began writhing as if they were the ones that had been shot at.

Here's a smart shopper tip you won't hear anywhere else: if you have to be shot at in a shopping mall, try to pick one that has a gun store. Even better, try to be in front of the gun store when you get shot at.

Two or three of the robots began making their way out toward the hall, chirping and beeping as my friend in the hall emptied his magazine. The little things had sensors in them that were attracted to noise, and being Japanese they didn't know any better, marching toward the gunfire like brave samurai. The appearance of the miniature army annoyed the gunman, who kept up his fury until he burned clear through the magazine.

Mistake.

I pivoted from my crouch by the doorway, firing three slugs down the hall from my P7. None of them hit the gunman, who dove into one of the stores down the aisle. I started to sidle toward him, closing down the angle of fire, when I caught a shadow moving on the opposite wall. I ducked back into the electronics place just as a second submachine gun opened up from the direction of a Victoria's Secret four doors down. Nothing like a Tango with a panty fetish to make the day interesting.

A video camera had been mounted on a tripod near the front of the store, and when I looked up at the wall of TVs on the right I saw my face on half the sets. I've looked better. I thought about using the camera to spy down the hallway and even got up and started to push it toward the door. But the cord had already been stretched to the max. As I hunted around behind the unit I got another idea, more out of desperation than anything else. The camera was a small digital job that had a still mode as well as replay. I fiddled with the knobs—fortunately, it was similar to a unit I'd bought myself a few months back—and got myself to reappear on the screens. I hit freeze and voilà—is it live . . . or Memorex?

I pushed the cam around so that it looked like it was aimed at the spot near the wall. Then I retreated toward the back of the store. The robots were still writhing around on the floor at the front, jabbering away. I heard, or thought I heard, one of the gunmen kick one and curse. Then I saw the top of a short shadow at the side of the entrance. From where he was standing, he would have just barely seen the television. A second later, the two men spun into the front of the store, fingers pressed hard on the triggers of their pretty submachine guns, barrels aimed in the direction of the camera.

My first bullet took the man on the right in the temple. I got a second bullet into the back of his head. My third shot caught gunman number two in the throat—maybe I was tired—but my third and fourth rounds put two more openings in his face. As I got up, I noticed a small minirecorder in a plastic display card on the right. I hesitated just for a second—which turned out to be the second that saved my life. For as I turned back to the front of the store, the hallway exploded.

No matter how many explosions you've witnessed up close and personal, the next one is always the scariest.

Unless you set it off, of course.

There had been a third man with the other two. He'd strapped plastic explosives to his body, and detonated them as soon as he got the nerve after seeing his comrades die. The force of the explosion blew out the glass in all of the stores along the hall on that side of the mall and took down several of the thin plasterboard walls nearby. It knocked me off my feet and showered dust, dirt, and debris everywhere. Half of the TVs exploded.

Danny and some of the SWAT people were inside the mall by the time I made it to the hallway. Bits and pieces of the suicide bomber now decorated the hall, along with debris. The force of the explosion had shattered much of the plasterboard and glass lining the hallway, and a fine mist of plaster filled the air.

"Here's the tape recorder," I told Danny, handing him the package. "Batteries and everything."

The driver was an American citizen of Serbian descent. He was a Muslim, which is not against the law. He was a real truck driver with a commercial license, which was also not against the law. He lived in a rented apartment in a small city upriver called Beacon, the sort of place rats go when they want to slum. Also not against the law. But the M16 he'd had was. As were the five cases of mustard gas containers in the cargo container and the Semtex in the crate behind the seat of the tractor.

The stooges in the mall were not quite as easy to identify. One was now confetti, strewn across the hall. The other two gunmen had no IDs, and an extensive check of their fingerprints and faces—badly mauled by the explosion of their comrade—would eventually lead nowhere. They wore new Levi's, Nikes, and T-shirts with NYPD logos; whoever dressed them had a sense of humor.

Was it Shadow? I sensed that he was in the distance somewhere, even though my guys weren't able to spot him. Every passing helicopter, every screech of tires, even a motorcycle in the distance—had my head turning. Tickle someone by the short hairs until sweat starts pouring from his pores and he can't calm down enough to take a leak—that was Charlie's tactic in the jungles. For something like thirty years now, it had been mine, too. Shadow was trying to turn it back around and screw with my head.

Doom on you, asshole.

"I really thought he was the guy Trace caught down in the city," said Danny as we made way for the state police's crime scene people. "But if these guys were still taking orders—"

"We haven't gotten Shadow. He's too good. As good as I am."

"Never heard you admit that before."

"Lot of people have been as good as I am. They just haven't worked with as good a bunch of people around them."

"Maybe he was the jerk who blew himself up," said Danny.

I knew that wasn't true—not Shadow's style, unless I was right there in his face—but I didn't bother saying anything. My cell phone—a new one, certified clean by Shunt and his consultants—rang after I finished looking over the container trailer about a half hour later.

"Thank God you're okay," said Karen as soon as I clicked the phone on.

"I'm okay. How did you hear what happened?"

"I didn't," she said. "But I just got a fax. It's a picture of you shot through a gun sight. You look like you're inside a mall or something, on TV."

In case you're wondering, I peed just fine when I hit the head a short time later.

The state troopers, with the help of the ATF strike force and the local security people, searched the entire mall and surrounding property without finding anyone or anything they could tie to the terrorists. Still, the live trucker and the dead bodies represented a potential treasure trove of information. Everyone wanted custody of the trucker—ATF, the state police, customs, Treasury, the FBI, CIA, and us. Hell, the DAR and IBM probably wanted a piece of him, too. The troopers had a barracks not that far away where he could be held and questioned. Even better, they had access to some professors in New York City who could help translate Serbo-Croatian, if that's what he was talking. But what really clinched it for me was the late arrival of the FBI, Wannabe himself in the lead. The troopers, with help from Danny, whisked out of exit number one as the *Federales Who Believe in Insanity* whisked through entrance number two. Wannabe and I were getting to be old friends, and he was so happy to see me he started yelling and screaming even before his car stopped.

"What the hell are you doing here, Marcinko? Is that a container truck? What the hell is going on?"

"They're having a special on suicide bombers inside the mall today," I said. "My guess is they planned to lock some of the doors and set off gas near the others so everyone would panic. Then the suicide bomber was going to ignite himself in the middle of the place. Just a guess. They didn't seem all that bright, so they may have figured on doing it the other way around."

Wannabe said something to himself that included a lot of four-letter words and stalked away. J. Edgar Hoover would have been very proud to fire his ass on the spot.

Knowing that Shadow was around somewhere nearby, I told my people to make their own way to Rogue Manor, where we'd rendezvous the next afternoon for PT and planning. Shunt had landed at Stewart Airport and had to return the airplane to D.C.; I told him to do it on his own. Then, after checking with Danny at the trooper barracks—the driver wasn't saying much, and what he was saying remained indecipherable, even to the alleged translators—I began making my way home alone. I made it as obvious as I could that I had no bodyguards or companions. I drove my rental so slowly that even old ladies in Buicks passed me. Around seven, I stopped for dinner at a Denny's. I took a booth at the far end of the restaurant, surrounded by nothing but empty tables. At ten o'clock, somewhere in Pennsylvania, I pulled into a cheap motel, got a room, and left on the light.

Anybody who wanted to could have shot me through the curtains. If they'd aimed well, their bullet would have gone right through my shirt into the pillow I'd stuffed it with. And I'd've seen them from the opposite roof where I was hiding.

No one came.

Rogue Manor looked comfortably inviting when I arrived the next afternoon. The house itself looked comfortable. Karen, dressed in a silky shirt and business skirt, was even more inviting. She pulled me to her, folding her arms around my shoulders. We retreated to my private quarters to reacquaint ourselves with each other's contours. When we emerged two hours later, the house was already filled with team members. Doc and Tiffany had returned from

France the night before and came armed with souvenirs of red wine and eyes irritated by jet lag. Danny's police frown creased his brow. Sean looked like he'd spent the night studying Danny's expressions and perfecting his own version. Hulk was Hulk, quietly sipping a beer. Shunt sat on the couch talking to himself in geekese, and the newer shooters were quiet and watchful, as nuggets should be. The only person missing was Trace, who was still down in Texas trying to get information out of His Swarthiness. After everyone was brought up to date on yesterday's adventure, I outlined the situation at the LNG port.

"I've been asked to roam the area as a human watchdog," I told them. "As a security measure, I'm not sure how much value it'll be. But it will give me a better chance to find my friend Shadow. He's been pretty close to me lately."

I dropped the faxed picture on the table in front of me where everyone could see it. Shadow had taken a shot of one of the TVs. I could tell now where he must have been standing. If he'd been there when the bomb went off, he would have been splattered almost as badly as the suicide bomber himself. He'd missed it by no more than a minute, if that.

"I think it was the suicide bomber," said Danny.

"Probably someone he knew," I told him. "But I don't think that was Shadow. He would have run up and made sure I was in his face."

"No one got out of that mall," said Sean.

I pointed out that there were plenty of people around the scene immediately after the explosion: security people, volunteer firemen, customers who hadn't been able to get out of the traffic jam and then came back in out of curiosity or a sincere desire to help out. We had the names of some, but not of anyone who looked like he might have belonged there—as Shadow undoubtedly would have.

The phone rang as I finished. With his impeccable timing, it should have been Shadow. But it turned out to be Trace.

"They're not getting anything out of him down here, Dick," she complained. "And it's hotter than hell. A hundred and ten in the shade."

I let her bitch for a few minutes, then told her she could come home if she wanted.

"Good," she said. "Because I'm calling from the airport."

Typical Trace. What wasn't typical, though, was what she said next: "I want you to watch your ass the next few days, Dick. I had this weird dream about you involving coyotes."

"Since when do you dream?"

"This is serious. The coyotes walked on two legs and they were right behind you, waiting for you to fall."

"Well if I see any coyotes like that, I'll be sure to let you know."

Back inside, Doc and Danny began lining up a plan to patrol the harbor around the natural gas port and watch for Shadow at the same time, basically setting up a bear trap with me as the bait. The idea was for me to take a boat out near the LNG carrier, sail parallel to it for a while, and then go back toward an isolated part of the port area where it would be easy for someone to ambush me. The trick was finding a spot where it would be easy to ambush the ambusher.

"The thing that's not clear to me," said Doc, "is whether Shadow is just on your butt or calling the shots on the other operations as well."

"Has to be calling the shots. He was in the mall," said Danny.

"Not necessarily. He could have had someone else take the picture."

"Yeah, I don't mean him personally," said Danny. "But he would have gotten the picture from someone in the mall. That means he's the one calling the shots."

"Not really."

I agreed that didn't mean Shadow was in charge—but that was certainly a reasonable conclusion. But it seemed to me the attempted strike on the mall was different than Shadow's earlier adventures. Those seemed designed to tweak me rather than create an actual incident. But Danny pointed out that the train and bridge incident would have been similar had we not happened on it.

"Maybe Shadow was pissed that we screwed up his party," said Danny. "He taunts us in Illinois, but otherwise he's sticking with his own game plan. The mall had to be targeted quite a while ago. First he had to find it—a place close enough to New York City to get major media coverage but far enough away so they didn't have the infrastructure to deal with it. You saw how long it took the police to get over there. It'd be different in the city. Then he had to work out the plan, get things in place—months of work, at least."

"I don't disagree that this must have been in place for a long time," said Doc. "I just don't want to jump to conclusions about where Shadow fits. It could be two different operations. Or parallel operations that intersect every so often."

Or that happened to intersect with me. Doc's French sources saw the terrorist network as a series of isolated beehives whose inhabitants came together very rarely but had the same aim—a general war against the West. One or two might have their own separate agendas—like making my life miserable—but still be part of the overall game plan.

Tiffany added more details from the French, describing a pair of cells they had broken up in Tours several months back. The cells didn't know each other or details of other missions, but both had been trained to strike at the same elementary school on the same day from different directions. Only at the last minute were they alerted to the fact that another cell was involved. The French had managed to round them up bare minutes before the plot was supposed to be launched.

The setup was not particularly unique, but Tiffany wasn't old enough to know that. The most important ingredient in such a decentralized organization wasn't communications—as the French had claimed when explaining their theories to her, no doubt over several bottles of wine—or even money or manpower. Having a few very bright if twisted people of the caliber of an Osama bin Laden was helpful, though not critical, either. The most important thing was faith. You had to follow the orders you received without doubt or hesitation, even if—

especially if—those orders were for you to kill yourself. That's why religion was such an important part of the equation.

It's not politically correct to talk about the connection between religion and terrorism these days, but you can't understand how a lot of the fanatical Islamic cells operate without understanding it. That isn't the same thing as saying that all Muslims are terrorists or that the religion breeds terrorism. If you want to call me a bigot, go right ahead, but you're not paying attention. During the Vietnam War, every so often Buddhist monks would immolate themselves with gasoline to prove their point, not to mention pollute the air. Saying that their religion had a role in that helps you start to understand what the fuck they're about and up to; it makes no comment on the religion itself. Same way with Islam. God forbid you talk about it, though.

The dangerous terrorists weren't poor fucks stuck in poverty so deeply they couldn't afford to eat. Poverty's bad, but it's not the reason for terrorism, despite what the papers and TV commentators usually claim. The really dangerous terrorists—and the people involved in 9/11 are a good example—are the kids who tasted something they thought was an alternative to God, got lost, then refound Him as the Answer. Most of the people who share the assholes' religion know that the "Him" they found wasn't the real Him, but that's who they found. And "He" helped them figure out the way the universe was supposed to work. In return, they were willing to do whatever "He" wanted, including blowing everything up.

But why come after me? Was Shadow pissed off because we screwed up his fun, as Danny suggested? Or was it some psychological mumbo jumbo bullshit reason—Big Daddy who has to be killed by Baby? The representative of all that is good in the world taken down by the representative of all that is evil?

Fuck you very much.

Personally, I like simple and obvious. Shadow and I had probably tangled before, and he wanted me now. Throwing the Vietnam crap in my face was either a signal or a misdirection play; take your pick. Either way, he could fuck himself if he thought it was going to give me the creepy crawlers. I'd play along with him until I found a way to put it back on him. Then there'd be payback. Which everyone knows is a bitch.

We worked out an agenda for the next five days, beginning with a scoping session at the port and surrounding waters on Friday, which was tomorrow. Then we scattered, a few to bed, a few to R&R at some of the local R&R venues, a few to their nearby homes.

And me to work. The vice admiral's staff working on the LNG task force had called several times now, apparently thinking that I was going to give them a written report on my findings. It may have been that they just wanted something that was easy to throw in the trash can, but I ended up sitting down at the computer, and, with the help of some all-purpose Bombay lubricant, smashed out a coherent memo on what they should watch out for. I was hunched over the keyboard when Karen found me.

She began kneading my neck and shoulders, which were knotted from working the keyboard. It was a good thing that I had already finished the memo, because her therapy demanded my full and proper attention.

"Las Vegas?" she murmured later, after we'd had an opportunity to fully relax.

"What Las Vegas?"

"You're supposed to go to Las Vegas for the parade Monday."

I looked up at her. My head was not exactly in Las Vegas.

"The Independence Day parade in Las Vegas," she repeated. "You said I could come."

"I totally forgot about it. Shit."

She frowned. I hate frowns on a pretty face, but there was nothing I could do about this one.

"We'll still be on the port. I'm going to have to cancel."

"Oh."

"Well, you go."

"Not without you. They don't want to see me in the parade."

I love Vegas; it's one huge adult amusement park. Even better, the people out there have a real friendly, live-and-let-live attitude, which fits perfectly with my own philosophy of life. You want to rebuild the Egyptian pyramids a stone's throw from a super highway and fill it with gambling machines? Hey, go to town. You want gondolas and guys in striped shirts singing "Mamma Mia" for tourists in the middle of a desert? Why the hell not? You can get just about anything you want in

Vegas, and plenty of things you didn't know you wanted until you got there, too. The nice folks in town had invited me to come out and be one of the guests of honor in the grand Independence Day Parade they were planning, the Strip's first ever. It was a typical Las Vegas extravaganza, set to happen near some of the newest hotels, including Vegas Starship, which supposedly looked a bit like a UFO that had plopped down between the Venetian and the Wynn. Very big, very brash, very Vegas. The parade committee planned a giant fete, and little ol' *moi* was supposed to be one of the guests of honor.

Duty, alas, took precedence over pleasure. Story of my fucking life.

I picked up the phone and called up the event organizer, who picked up on the second ring. It was one of the few times I'd used the phone that I actually wished I'd gotten voice mail. Telling him I had to cancel was not the highlight of my day. He accepted graciously, as Vegas people always do, and even offered a rain check.

"They offered to send a plane just for me," I told Karen when I hung up. "They're really great people."

"Did they want you to jump out of it?"

"As a matter of fact, they did."

They'd originally suggested that I parachute from an aircraft and skydive into a moving car after the parade began. Had to turn that one down—the "S" in SEAL does not stand for stupid.

"They even offered me a rain check," I told her. "Said come to town anytime."

"I hope you said yes."

"Well . . ."

She slugged me on the shoulder. "You better. And take me, too."

"We'll see."

"We'll see?"

"All right, I will."

"Promise?"

"I promise," I told her. We proceeded to seal the promise. The last few days had left me drained and, given the circumstances, an early bedtime seemed in order. I was drifting off to sleep a while later when the phone rang. I let the answering machine pick up, but Shunt's voice carried a tone I'd never heard before, at least not from him—alarm.

"Dick, Dick, Dick! Pick up! Pick up! Pick up!"

"Shunt, what?" I asked, grabbing the receiver.

"Danny! He has a virus on his laptop."

"I thought you ran an antivirus program this afternoon," I told him, instantly annoyed that he was so hysterical and that I'd picked up the phone.

"No, this is really good. *Really* good. It came in through the cell phone when he used the Bluetooth modem. That's why my friends couldn't find it on the phone. Dick, you have to find him and tell him. He's not at his house."

I glanced at the clock. It was now nearly eleven. The last I'd seen Danny was downstairs a few hours ago. He was probably on his way home by now via a random route sure to include a police bar or two. There was no sense tracking him down; Shunt had both the laptop and the phone. This was one time bad news could wait until morning.

"I'll tell him as soon as I can. If he got it on a call, can you figure out from which call?" I asked.

"I don't think it'll be easy." I could hear the metal grind in his head. "Yeah, wait, I have an idea—look for a data transmission associated with something. Oh shit, that's how they got it in! I figured it out, Dick! I figured it out!"

Shunt actually didn't explain it then, and I'm not sure I was awake enough that night to understand it even if he had. Basically, what had happened was this: Danny's spiffy new phone and lightweight laptop could connect to each other using something called Bluetooth. Bluetooth is a type of short-range wireless connection involving hardware and software that, among other things, allows you to use a cell phone to connect to the Internet. (It does other stuff, too, but that's not relevant here.) On one of those connections, the cell phone transmitted a virus to the laptop. Calling it a virus is really an insult, because according to Shunt the program was extremely sophisticated. It replaced part of the code in the laptop's Windows XP Pro operating system without drawing any attention to itself or adding anything extraneous to the computer. It was as if the hacker were a surgeon, reaching into someone's body, pulling out his heart and replacing it with one exactly the same size and weight. The new heart beat exactly the same—except that every time it made a connection through the cell phone, it activated an outside program on another computer to run a series of its own programs. That program gave the hacker a view of everything on Danny's computer and information on all the calls the phone had made—location and time. The technical aspects were pretty impressive, Shunt said, at least on par with the work the agency that doesn't exist had done on the hard drive we had replaced. The techie said the hacker deserved a spot in the hacker hall of fame.

I said he deserved a spot in Danny's woodshed.

According to Shunt, the virus could only have affected Danny's computer, not any of ours, but just in case, I got up to shut everything down. On my way to the office, I crossed through the living room, where Doc was leaning against one end of the couch reading a book. He's a committed computerphobe and won't go near a computer except at the point of a gun. I didn't bother telling him about the virus. All that would have done was invite a hearty "I told you so."

"Danny's not around, right?" I asked.

"Left for home an hour ago."

"No. He's meeting his daughter in a bar over in Richmond at midnight," said Tiffany, opening up an eye in the oversize leather chair in the corner. "He was all excited about it."

"Which bar?"

"SciClub," she said. "It's right near her place in Richmond."

I'd never heard of it. Apparently it was a very happening place if you happened to be twenty-two.

Family reunions aren't my thing, and Shunt's virus, as high-tech as it might be, didn't seem reason enough to break this one up. Until a half hour later.

I was back in bed, just about dozing off, when the phone rang and the dream that had begun percolating in my brain was replaced by Shunt's fervid screech on the answering machine.

"Dick! Dick! Dick!"

"What the fuck, Shunt?"

"I know where Danny got the virus!"

"Uh-huh."

"Who does he know in Richmond, Virginia?"

"I don't know, Shunt. Has to be a million people. You have his phone, right?"

"The number is unlisted, new. Can we, like, tap into some police connections to get the details? Or should I just say 'fuck it' and hack into the phone company."

"Uh-huh." I was about to tell him we'd deal with it in the morning when I finally realized what the hell was going on.

Doom on me for taking so long.

15

Doc Tremblay had known me so long that his handlebar mustache jumped to attention just from the snap in my voice. Tiff jumped up as well, and within a minute of Shunt's phone call all three of us were running out to the Yukon. Sean, who'd been dozing in one of the spare guest rooms, came out as I turned over the engine. I told him to crank up his motorcycle and follow.

SciClub was located on an alley off North 14th near Route 360 and the railroad tracks. Aesthetically, the area was less than optimum for a club, which apparently made it perfect for a club. The thing I didn't like about it was the easy access to the highway; Danny could be miles away by now, trussed and squeezed into somebody's trunk.

"We oughta check the address where the phone call was made first," suggested Doc. "That's where he'll be."

I tended to agree, but Shunt hadn't called back with it yet; he was still hacking away at the phone company computers, which he warned might take a while. We settled for the club. Doc and I would stick out like the old farts we were, so sending Tiffany and Sean in first to sneak a peek was a no-brainer. Both were packing. Sean had two Berettas, one from the service and the other from his police work. Tiffany had a smallish Walther P99 in her purse and a smaller P5 Compact hidden—well, *somewhere* on her body, though I defy anyone to find it. The P5 Compact is smaller than a lot of pistols, but not *that* small, and how Tiff got it under her clothes without producing a telltale bulge—well, all women have some secrets, and that's one of hers.

We swung off the ramp, took a right, and looked for the block. I figured Shadow was behind all of this, and in that case, it was very possible that I was the real target and this was a trap to set me up for a sucker punch. We'd peek first, strike next.

Though if it *was* Shadow, it made sense to be ready for anything. That's why Doc had pulled the M249 SAW machine gun out from under the seat in the back. It also accounted for the MP5 in my lap. Overkill? Only if I had to explain it to a traffic cop.

"Should be the next turn."

I backed off the gas as I turned the wheel onto 14th, not quite knowing what to expect. Sean was a few cars behind us. Doc had reached Hulk by cell phone; he was heading over with two of my new shooters as cavalry. They were at least another ten minutes off. A police car passed me as I turned; I pushed the submachine gun lower, even though it was already out of view.

"Nice and slow, children," I said. "Alley is right over there on the right, and there's the front door of the club."

The words were barely out of my mouth when the door burst open. A body flew to the ground. I hit the brakes and jumped out, leaving the car in the middle of the street. Tiff and Doc followed, crouching in firing position, heads rotating in a quick sweep. The figure on the ground rolled just enough for me to realize it wasn't Danny. As I took a step toward him, the door opened again. Another large body tumbled out, did a half turn, and then flipped onto the hood of a parked car to the left. His arms flailed, but Tiff cut short his effort to get up by pulling him off the hood and gently placing the heel of her boot on his throat.

Perhaps it wasn't quite that gentle. A mash of words spewed from his mouth; none of them were "Have a nice day." A second kick, and instead of words, he began spewing vomit. Tiff took a step back and applied a soccer-style coup de grace to his side, wedging him into the gutter next to the car.

"Something I learned in France," she said.

The club door opened again. This time, Danny Barrett stepped through the frame. He did not look like a happy camper, but he was intact and moving under his own power.

"Danny!" I shouted.

"Yeah, I know. I'm a fucking asshole. A fucking asshole."

Actually, I'd been trying to warn him about the gorilla about to tackle him from behind. It was unnecessary, however. Just as he finished his personal assessment, he ducked, timing it perfectly. The man flew out over him so quickly that he couldn't get his hands out to break his fall. His headfirst splash on the pavement was as convincing an advertisement for helmets as I've ever seen.

"They're just fucking bouncers. Assholes," added Danny. "Let's get the hell out of here. I'm parked a couple of blocks over."

He explained what had happened as we drove to his car. For weeks, Danny had been trying to set up some sort of meeting with the young woman named Melanie who claimed to be his daughter. He'd been frustrated at first by the fact that she wouldn't give him a phone number or anything besides an email address to contact her with, and he had some police department friends check around to see what they could come up with. He was also interested in finding the girl's mother, SueLi. Call it nostalgia or misplaced romanticism, but he had a crazy notion of talking to her and maybe doing something to pay her back for all the years she'd raised their daughter by herself. Danny's "daughter" Melanie eventually gave him SueLi's phone number, and with everything else that was going on, he more or less forgot about contacting her mother—until he set up the meeting with his daughter. He was en route when he called his friend, thinking he might take a long shot on calling her mother. The friend had written down the number a week ago, while Danny was out in the Midwest. He had it on a Post-it right near the phone.

"So I called," said Danny. "And I said, 'SueLi?' And she said, 'No, this is Melanie.' Melanie."

"She was visiting her mom?"

"Well, yeah, except that her mom lives in Oregon. That was the area code I called. Melanie wasn't supposed to be there but was checking on her mother's place. The mother and stepfather were away on a vacation in Europe."

Danny had called from down the street, using a pay phone. Aware that he was being set up but unsure for what, he snuck inside the bar through a back door, checked over the place, and spotted the girl pretending to be Melanie getting ready for the meet.

"Cute little Asian number. Thirties but definitely hot. SueLi's mother was Korean and she looked a bit like her," Danny added. "My guess is that she was going to drug me."

Danny called the police, claiming that the girl had a gun in her purse; he figured it would be easier to deal with her once they approached her. He thought it was likely that she was armed, but even if she wasn't, he could swear out some sort of bullshit and use his influence to have her run into the station. Two uniforms arrived but as they came in she beelined for the ladies' room. Danny tried to follow. He rattled the door, realized it was locked, then started to back off when the bodyguards began hassling him. He yelled at the police officers that the girl was getting away and explained that she had gone out the rear window in the restroom. The cops didn't know him, but after a squint or two, they decided better safe than sorry and pounded on the door. Then they broke down the door, whereupon a cute but drunk blonde began screaming. It wasn't the same girl, not even close, and she didn't have a handbag, let alone a gun. But the worst thing was, the only window in the place had very thick bars. A fire violation, to be sure, but also an effective way of limiting egress.

"She wasn't in one of the other stalls," said Danny. "It took me quite a while to figure it out. She'd cased the place pretty well. To get out, she went into the last stall, stood on the toilet, took off one of the ceiling panels, and pulled herself up into the gridwork above, which was heavy steel because the place had been a warehouse before being converted. Then she crawled up across the grid of the drop ceiling to the second story. It was too narrow for me to follow, and by the time I figured it out, she'd been gone for more than forty minutes. The cops didn't even hang around."

"What was the discussion with the bouncers about?" asked Doc.

"They had a problem with me being in the ladies' room."

Shunt called back in the middle of Danny's story with the address. We figured it was unlikely we'd find Danny's pseudo-daughter there, but we decided searching the place would be educational, and so we all proceeded in that general direction. Interestingly, the address was similar to but slightly different than the one Danny had gotten from her—a reversal of integers that, had Danny tried to drop in on her, would have led him to the park down the street.

We rendezvoused with our reinforcements and broke out some surveillance gear from the goodie bags in the SUV, courtesy of Law Enforcement Technologies, with a few smaller items purchased at the No Such Agency Annex, aka Radio Shack. With the apartments under and above the target occupied, we played it safe and quiet, setting up a microwave scan device on the flat, two-story roof directly across the parking lot.

Originally developed for eavesdropping, the MSD reads vibrations off a window's glass. The sensitivity can be adjusted to such a degree that you can hear a mouse running across the floor or scampering through a wall. *Hear* is a figure of speech; you see a bouncing line on a screen and have to be able to interpret it, but you get the idea. These devices have been used since at least the Cold War, and they've gotten smaller and more sensitive as time has gone on. Ours was not quite the superdeluxe model, but within sixty seconds of climbing to the top of the roof we knew that the apartment was empty.

That or whoever was inside had a way to stop his heart from beating.

Danny and Sean took the front door, while Doc and the newbies watched the stairs and the street. Meanwhile, Tiff and I played Spiderman, climbing up a fire escape on the side and working our way around the side of the building. The ledge was nearly six inches wide, so don't hold your breath.

Except for the part near the window, where a black shadow jumped across the night about three inches from Tiffany's shoulder. She jerked back off the edge. I grabbed her, barely keeping my own balance.

It felt like it took a half hour for me to get my breath back. I love holding beautiful women in my arms, but I certainly prefer to do so under better circumstances.

We crouched on the ledge, staring at the shadow. It seemed too square to belong to a person, but it took a while to figure out that it was being cast by a large piece of cardboard or something that could spin around somehow. The light inside was dim, coming from somewhere beyond the room, possibly a hallway. I squeezed down at the corner and gave a peek around the edge, easing upward slowly when I didn't see anything. The room appeared empty. The window was single-pane, easy to break and large enough to duck through, the sort of thing they used to put on buildings around 1940 or so when heat was cheap.

"How are we?" asked Doc over the commo set.

"Good, I think. Back room looks empty."

"Sean's using that SoldierVision thing, and he swears the front two rooms are empty, too. I don't know if we should trust that thing. I think your high-tech shit is bullshit."

"We can trust it," said Sean. "And the microwave said the same thing."

"All fucking bullshit," insisted Doc. "Jetsons stuff."

"Hey, Dick, I think the door's unlocked," said Danny.

An unlocked door to an empty apartment spells "booby trap" in my dictionary, so we took a collective breath while Sean used the sniffer to see if there were explosives rigged to the front door.

Nothing. So either it was a *really* clever booby trap—likely, given what we knew about Shadow—or not a booby trap at all. There was an easy way to find out, and a slightly harder one. We put a daub of

C-4 on the door, got a fistful of flash-bangs ready, and . . .

Boom.

More like: *Boom KA-BOOM KA-KA-KA-KA-FUCKING BOOM!!!!*

The flash-bangs illuminated the apartment and set off enough of a shock that any explosive rigged to a light or motion detector system would have ignited. Half the car alarms in the neighborhood went off, and every dog within a twenty-block radius began howling ferociously.

Doc, being the kind and caring soul he is, had evacuated the people from the downstairs apartments, clearing the building. The people—all old folk—assumed that the kindly gentleman in body armor, trailed by two black-clad ninjas, was a cop, and he did nothing to correct that misimpression.

Flash-bangs are basically big-ass Fourth of July firecrackers designed to sound loud and blind anyone dumb enough to keep their eyes open when they go off; they're called stun grenades for that reason. The charges aren't powerful enough to kill anyone, though I wouldn't want one in my teeth when it exploded.

C-4 is a somewhat different story. There's an art to using just enough to get a door down, especially an old wooden one; too much and the door and surrounding hallway turn into sawdust and cinders. Let it be said: Sean is not an artist. He blew a big enough hole at the front of the apartment to drive a pickup through.

Dear Landlord: Hope the security deposit covers it. But those are the hazards of renting to scumbags.

I smashed the glass and pulled up the window, stepping into the apartment with Tiffany just behind me. We rolled our eyeballs around the place—the light had survived the blast—and got to the hall just as Danny and the others came in from the front. We had the place secure in twenty seconds—not hard to do when it's empty. The only surprise came in the far room. There was no furniture, no nothing, except for hundreds of pieces of paper pasted to the walls. Let me be more specific: hundreds of pieces of photos and newspaper articles and printouts and maps, all of which had to do with me. The maps were torn from a Rand McNally atlas and traced my recent progress across the country.

"Someone has a real fucking hard-on for you," said Danny.

"This is exactly what we saw in France." Tiffany went close to one of the photos and frowned at it. It happened to be the same one from the mall, printed out from a computer printer in black and white. "Not a very good picture. You ought to try smiling some more."

"It *is* a lot like what we saw in France," said Doc. "Except for the maps and such." He knelt down on the floor examining them. "You were in Las Vegas?"

"Not in two years," I said. I went over to Doc and bent down to look at them. The parade route was marked in red.

"You planning on going there?" he asked.

"Maybe."

Besides the boarding parties and cutter escorts for each ship going into Cove Point, a Navy antisubmarine patrol had been set up outside the harbor. Helicopters patrolled overhead. The normal exclusion zone had been extended, and it would have been hard for an unauthorized boat to get within three miles of the shipping lanes. Three companies of Marines—bad haircuts and all—were in the port itself, giving cross-eyed stares at the odd scraps of paper that crossed along their path. A pair of LAV-25s—light armored vehicles that look like miniature tanks with wheels—provided muscle near the entrance, though they were more for show than of practical value. If you want to talk about shows of strength, the Marine Corps "Whiskey" versions of the Cobra gunships were downright nasty-looking buggers, beating the air with the heavy whomp-whomp of their blades. Between the Coast Guard, Navy, Marines, local police agencies, native security teams, and your various and sundry official hangers on, there had to be upward of fifteen-hundred people casting a net over the harbor. And that's not even counting the hundred and forty or so in the SSN.

Secure, right?

Well, no.

There are a thousand different ways to skin a cat, and a million ways to eat it. One way: join the party. And if you can't BYOB, then steal one. That is, if you can't bring your own boat, take one that's already invited to the party. Or looks like it is: for example, the WPB 82' Coast Guard Point Class patrol boat Point Ricardo, tied up as a working museum piece across the harbor only a month or so before. Beginning in the 1960s, the WPB 82's were built as all-around offshore search and rescue, etc., craft. Most of the boats were completely overhauled at least once during their lifetimes, and, with only a couple of exceptions, have been retired now for the slightly larger eighty-seven-foot Coastal Patrol Boats.

The Point Class is nowhere near as sexy as, say, the Mark V Special Operations Craft, which is your basic speedboat on steroids adapted to a SpecOps mission; the Mark V is one slick raft and definitely my chariot of choice for waterskiing.

But the Mark V would have stood out in that harbor. A bright-orange old sailor flying the American Flag and proudly wearing the Coast Guard insignia did not. The baby cutter required only a small crew—its normal complement is ten—which meant not only that I could handle it with a dozen guys or less but that it would have been relatively easy to take over even had it been manned.

The Point Ricardo's security detail consisted of three eighteen-year-olds considerably more interested in playing craps on the bridge than watching for pirates. Not that I blame them; the bridge is definitely the place to be throwing dice. We advised them that their game had been moved to a nearby storeroom in an abandoned warehouse. They were happy to relocate, as that appeared to be a better option than being shot and fed to the sharks.

Point Ricardo's two Caterpillar D3412s groaned a bit as we turned up the steam, but after a minute or so they warmed to the task, and we managed close to twenty knots before swinging around into the channel. Speed wasn't what we were about, though; looking like we belonged was. I guess we must have, since we weren't challenged once, not when we came up near one of the eighty-seven-foot cutters, not when we sailed within ten feet of the command ship, not when we did a drive-by on the Navy destroyer, not even when we wallowed in the middle of the channel next to an outgoing (and empty) LNG tanker.

Next, we moved into the docking area, again unchallenged. Here, we disgorged a couple of petty officers and one nodding civilian—Doc, whose mustache is about as civilian as you can get. The party proceeded with clipboards, recording fire hazards near the unloading area. There is something about talking about fire hazards that gets people's attention—and opens doors. Doc had his unsupervised hands on one of the control units for the gas-pumping and pipe mechanism inside five minutes. He left a couple of smiley faces as calling cards and backed out.

The baby cutter displaced something like sixty-six tons over its nearly eighty-three feet; it wasn't particularly wide, and anything you put on the deck near the bow would stand out. Still, I figure we could have packed several tons worth of explosives onto the ship without slowing it down appreciably or putting us so low in the water that someone nearby would toss a line. The American guided-missile destroyer USS *Cole* was nearly sunk by a speedboat packed with only a few hundred pounds*

* Estimates vary between four hundred and seven hundred pounds and are based on the size of the hole the explosion punched in the armored hull. The bastards who actually know were pulverized beyond the powers of DNA reconstruction, a fate too good for them, in my humble opinion.

of explosive, probably C-4. Then again, maybe it was the fact that the suicide bombers stood at attention at the very end that made the strike so devastating.

The vice admiral took the news of our misdeeds rather calmly when I told him what we'd done. He had to be calm, though—we had him aboard Point Ricardo, sailing out to sea.

"We'll fix this, definitely we'll fix this," he said, shaking his head next to me on the bridge. Doc had spotted him when he was just finishing his review and figured, "What the hey?" I offered him a shot at driving for a while, but he declined. Nor did he want a drink of anything stronger than Pepsi. Which was probably just as well; he had a long afternoon and night ahead of him. He did share the barbecued chicken from the Marines' temporary "mess." Those ol' gunny sergeants sure know how to take care of their troops.

After dropping the admiral off and returning the cutter to its rightful berth, the team dispersed. We were still on the watch for Shadow, and I decided on a random shuffle of routes to our rendezvous point, which wasn't our real rendezvous point but a dummy destination staked out to see what turned up. But Shadow had obviously had his fill of fun for a while and remained his elusive self, appearing only in the periphery of my mind. Trace met us at our newest home away from home—a watering hole known poetically as "Watering Hole" and located in a stand-alone building off a county highway in Calvert County. It had been chosen for its location as well as the two large pool tables in the backroom.

I could practically smell the ozone frying in the air as Trace eyed Tiffany. Sean undertook to separate them, or at least I think that's what he was doing when he asked Tiff if she wanted to dance. In the meantime, Trace and I consulted on the Texas situation. Her basic take was that the interrogation routine was overkill; the Bosnian maniac was being held in security so tight it took two hours to get him into the talking room. The change of scenery hadn't made him any more loquacious. If anything, it had had the opposite effect.

"I think he's told them everything he knows, such as it is. Which is squat."

Trace leaned back in the chair, arms furled at her chest. When she stretched her legs, I noticed she'd taken the opportunity to do a little shopping in Texas. A pair of brand-new snakeskin boots peeked out from under her tight black jeans.

"Real rattlesnake," she said, pulling up the pant legs to show them off.

"Purr-ty. You had time to go shopping, huh?"

"There's always time for shopping."

"New necklace?" I asked, pointing at the stone around her neck.

Trace's face tinged slightly. She touched the stone, which was bright red and highly polished. A simple piece of leather through it. "Kinda new. For me. But it's been around for a long time."

"Apache?" I was guessing, but it wasn't much of a guess.

"More or less." Trace's tone said, *No more on this.*

I returned us to the matter at hand. "You don't think they're *trying* to keep this guy quiet, do you?"

"Trying to keep him quiet? By putting him in an interrogation center?"

"Best place in the world to keep somebody quiet," I said, jumping up. I had just realized something I should have realized long before—long, long before.

"Where are you going?" Trace asked.

"Kidnap an NSA official. Want to come?"

16

For an organization that obsesses about security, the agency that does not exist doesn't do a very good job protecting its employees. In fact, it could be argued that they don't do any job, or at least they didn't in the case of Boreland. Not that it would have mattered if they had.

We ran it like a nighttime snatch circa 1969 or so, an oldie but goodie and a nod and a wink at our friend Shadow. In quietly, out even quieter. We slid into the condo complex in onesies and twosies. I appropriated a mountain bike from the next complex over. Cheap chain locks should be outlawed in this day and age. This allowed me to get into the targeted area via a path at the rear of the apartment cluster. It also made me look like a wingnut yuppie getting his predawn exercise, always a good cover for a snatch operation. I was just coming up the path when Sean signaled from the lookout area on one of the roofs.

"Out of his unit, heading for his Nova," said Sean, who was lookout. "Got coffee, paper, briefcase. Asshole's going to work this early?"

Sean's amazement was understandable, given that Boreland was a government employee and it was barely five A.M. Nonetheless, there are a few dedicated souls left in the Washington, D.C., area. Boreland had thrown us a curve, but it was a hanging pitch.

"We'll take him here," I said. "How's the lot?"

"No guards. We're clean," said Sean.

"Do it."

Boreland, juggling a travel mug with coffee and a newspaper in one hand as he reached into his pocket for his keys, was about eight feet from his car when another vehicle sped into the lot, wheels squealing. He stopped, terrified for a moment as he realized the auto was heading straight for him. But the car swerved sideways, stopping about twelve inches from the frozen NSA honcho. As he winced, a young woman strolled up behind him and placed the cold end of a pistol in his back.

The cold end probably wasn't that cold, considering where it had been carried, but a Rogue is allowed some poetic license. The car's rear door flew open and Boreland was pushed inside by the girl with the gun. The yuppie on bicycle jumped off his bike and ran to the other door, sliding in just as the car left the scene somewhat more sedately than it had arrived.

Being a polite sort, and like all NSA employees rather intelligent, Boreland didn't curse or demand to know what the hell was going on. He just blinked twice as Hulk drove us out of the lot at a leisurely pace and headed for the highway. I glanced toward the mirror and saw a look of pain on Hulk's face; obviously, driving at the legally posted speed took more out of him than I thought.

"Mr. Boreland, I'm Dick Marcinko. I'm sorry we have to meet this way. I'm a friend of your cousin."

"Sheila," he said, as if he were filling in a blank on a test.

"I need to talk to you about that intelligence you gathered from our little switch operation in New York."

"I haven't a clue what you're talking about."

"I know. And officially you don't exist, either. But I've been having some second thoughts about some of the people at Homeland Security we're working with."

"I haven't a clue what you're talking about."

"Don't make me hit you," said Tiffany. She might have been a new member of the team, but she had picked up the basics real quick. Trace, who was sitting in the front seat next to Hulk, grinned in spite of herself.

Boreland's face pinched in at the cheeks. I think he lost his breath for a second. He tried to say something but ended up only shaking his head.

"Spit it out, Boreland," I told him, though I already knew exactly what he was going to say.

"I haven't a clue what you're talking about. I haven't run operations with Homeland Security."

"You know a guy named Cox? He's with Tadpole. Or he *is* Tadpole."

"Cox. Yeah, I guess. Talky little twerp who's always pestering me for intelligence and claims he has scoops. I tell him to work through channels. I have to keep changing my contact information because of him."

"You didn't run a job through him?"

"I haven't a clue what you're talking about."

He didn't, either. It took a few orbits of the block to make sure we were all talking about the same thing, but in the end it was pretty damn clear: there was no cooperative effort between Homeland Security Intelligence and the NSA. We had planted a bogus hard drive up in Queens, or at least one that did something different than what we were told it did. That was not necessarily a bad thing. The SpecWarrior is often the last one to be told the actual truth. But it meant Cox and I had to have a very serious talk.

After I rearranged his dental work.

Unlike our NSA friend, Cox believed in security, or at least in muscular types roaming the bushes around his Maryland yard. One of them was actually an ex-SEAL, but I wasn't in a particularly friendly mood. He and another bodybuilder closed ranks at the front door in what was probably intended as an intimidating stance as I approached.

"No," I told him, pointing. I used about the same voice I would use on one of my dogs when I was in a good mood. "And you"—I pointed to the right, where one of the security team members thought he was hiding in the bushes. "Don't even think about using that Taser, or Pepco is going to be plugging you into their circuit to draw off extra current for a week."

"Who the fuck are you?" asked one of the security people.

"Dick Marcinko."

"Not Demo Dick?" said the former SEAL. "*The* Demo Dick? Like, the guy who wrote all those books? I'm a SEAL. I used to be."

I told him I was heartened to hear that they were still taking guys who could read, and joy for him aside, I was in a pissy mood and wanted to talk to Cox, posthaste and immediately.

"Can't do it, sir. He's out."

"Look, don't bullshit me. I have an NSA guy in the car who I have to deliver up to Fort Meade by nine A.M. or he's going to turn into a pumpkin. And besides, my backup people get awful cranky."

The SEAL didn't fall for that old gag and turn his head to check for my backup team. He stayed focused on me with very admirable discipline. This made it easier for Hulk to get closer. Not that it mattered at this point. What's another two inches when you're just a foot away? Especially if the weapon you're holding is a SAW. Overkill maybe, but I wasn't lying about being pissed.

"Geez, I'm not shitting you, Dick," said the SEAL when Hulk made his presence known. "Can I call you Dick? I mean, it's Dick, right?"

I'll skip the rest of the starstruck crap. The shift supervisor, who'd been watching the whole thing unfold from inside a post in the garage, came out stage left, demanding to know what the hell was going on.

Let it be said that Homeland Security is an equal opportunity employer. The supervisor in question was a thirty-something blonde with a very snug waist, nicely sculpted biceps, and even better breasts. Perfect teeth, too. She insisted that Cox had gone away. My bullshit detector told me she wasn't lying. I think it was my bullshit detector. It was so close to the pussy detector in my brain that I wasn't entirely sure. I asked to be shown inside. She frowned, but the way she frowned told me she was going to make the suggestion herself.

What's twenty minutes when the day is young?

Cox had, in fact, left. According to his office calendar, he had an appointment in Los Angeles on Tuesday, the day after Independence Day. He'd arranged to take off yesterday afternoon and all of Friday, arrive early, and spend the weekend. He was so anal or maybe so worried about GSA auditors that he had even arranged to separate out the billing on his travel so the government would only be dunned for the business time. There was absolutely no reason to doubt his integrity, and far be it for Dickie to impugn the integrity of a U.S. government employee.

I did, however, have one question that no one—not the security commander, not Cox's secretary, not even Karen—could answer.

Why did a person who was a charter member of Americans Against Casino Gambling include a stop in Las Vegas on his itinerary?

Part Three

GAMBLIN' MAN

"It is bad to lack good fortune, but it is a misfortune to lack talent. . . . The fortune of war is on the side of the soldier of talent."

—Field Marshal Aleksandr V. Suvorov (1729–1800), quoted in Ossipov, *Suvorov*, 1945

17

Some people say that Las Vegas could only exist in America. I say, Las Vegas could only exist in Nevada. It's the one place in the U.S. where people will *really* let you alone to do whatever the hell it is you want to do. And the fact that they do that defies all sorts of logic or formulas or theories about behavior or whatever you want to throw at people. If there is a scam, has been a scam, will be a scam, it is, was, or will be tried out in Las Vegas. Las Vegas remains a test bed for anything that can make money.

Factoid 1: A lot of the land that the major casinos are built on is owned by Mormons, whose teachings may not necessarily be considered the most hospitable to gambling. Or some of the other things that take place in those hotels.

Factoid 2: The massive casinos that dominate the Strip cost over a billion dollars to build. They are the most lavish monuments to entertainment ever constructed by mankind. Next to them, the Colosseum in Rome looks like one of those carnivals that sets up every year in the next town over to help raise a few bucks for the local fire department.

Factoid 3: Las Vegas can be a real shitty place to die.

Ask Luke Cox.

Not that he's likely to tell you much. Nine-millimeter bullets have a tendency to shut up even the most loquacious among us, especially when they're fired point-blank into your skull. Four of them, especially. Has a serious impact on the sheets as well.

"He was shot right here," said Danny, as we waited in the hotel room for the Vegas PD to arrive early Saturday morning. Danny stood by the side of the bed and showed roughly where Cox would have been when the first bullet hit. "He started to spin back. Must've realized there was a person there on the side in that chair whom he'd missed when he came in. First shot probably killed him; the rest were to make sure. I've seen pumpkins in better shape than that skull."

"Wrong season for trick or treat." We took a quick peek around the hotel room. Cox's suitcase sat near the end of the bed; it had been rifled through and the clothes strewn nearby. The cop in Danny wouldn't let him touch anything, but I had no such qualms. Cox's license and credit cards were still in his wallet, which was in his back pocket. Otherwise, his pockets were empty.

"So I guess he wasn't the mastermind," said Danny. "Not Shadow, either."

"You're still thinking like a policeman, Danny. Jumping to conclusions."

"Just interpreting the evidence."

"That's what I'm saying. Jumping to conclusions."

The body was cold. We'd have to check with the maid to find out when the room had been made up last, but it was a good bet that the DO NOT DISTURB sign had kept her out the day before. The room had a certain stuffy smell to it.

"Police on the way, Dick," said Sean over the commo system. He was downstairs in the lobby.

"You all right with handling this on your own?" I asked Danny.

He nodded. Danny had been the one to call the cops. He had a straight rap for them, which hinged on his official position in Homeland Security. The local police wouldn't know the organization well enough to realize that the Office of Internal Security Affairs (Danny) and Threat Data, Polling and Logging/Intelligence (Cox) barely existed on the same planet together, let alone had any real dealings. Danny wasn't likely to have to get all that exact, anyway. As for myself, while there are only a few things I like better than talking for hours to cops, I generally prefer that such interviews take place in the company of a good bottle of Bombay Sapphire, or perhaps a few cold Buds at a lobster bake. I had a hell of a lot of work to do, beginning with some phone calls to make back East. I was about to ruin the holiday weekend for a whole slew of people.

I began with Karen, who'd already told me her weekend was ruined, anyway, since I wasn't around to share it.

"What do you know about Cox?" I asked when she picked up the phone.

"I'd hang up if it were anyone but you, Dick," she said.

We traded a bit of that back and forth, and then I told her what we'd found. She didn't think Cox could be a scumbag—a dupe, maybe, but not an active member of any sort of terrorist network or cell. I trust her judgment of people, but trust wasn't the issue, nor was judgment. I left it to her to start hitting the phones at the agency, alerting the different pooh-bahs to the problem. She promised to get back to me with as much intel on Cox as she could by the end of the day.

I called Rich Armstead myself. I hate being the bearer of bad news but it is one of the unshirkable duties of a commander, and even if I hadn't felt it was my job, on a personal level I owed it to him. Rich, who was still in Argentina, took it about as well as you'd expect, with a few "all rights" and clipped sentences, and maybe one or two four-letter words thrown in. The sailor in him had not died, and Annapolis had never purged those four-letter descriptive adjectives from his vocabulary, especially when he got a little emotional.

I met with Mayor Oscar Goodman later that day. By then, the local news people had found out about Cox's death, and he'd been bombarded with questions. He'd already gone on record saying that it had nothing to do with the Independence Day Parade. I can't blame him. For one thing, no one, including me, knew that it did. More important, one of his jobs as mayor is to reassure people, and that's what he was doing.

Oscar is the consummate politician, and Las Vegas is his baby. I had been the grand marshal for the Veterans' Day Parade in 2003. Oscar held the parade in downtown Las Vegas to give the area a "rebirth" economically. The major casinos on the strip bitched a little, and Independence Day was the payback. Oscar was in the "I will not fail" mode, which I admire, since I have been placed there myself more than once.

At the same time Oscar was playing easygoing papa for the media, he was kicking butt behind the scenes to make sure he was right. He even gave me a tenacious bulldog grilling when I saw him later that morning, as if I were responsible for Cox's demise. Oscar can get downright vicious when it comes to protecting Vegas; he's a homer in the best sense of the word, and I wouldn't want to cross swords with him—at least not in a fair fight. I had to be honest with him. I had no idea why Cox had been killed or whether it was related to a terrorist operation targeting the city. He asked me point-blank if I thought he ought to call off the parade, and I told him no. There's a fine line between security and paranoia. You can't completely screw up your life just because someone's determined to mess with it; if you do, you've let the assholes win. Oscar asked if I'd lend a hand reviewing the security arrangements. I told him it went without saying.

"Well thanks for coming out," he said. "When I heard you canceled, I was thinking of sending a few police officers out to arrest you and drag you here." The mayor smiled, and so did I.

"That would have beeen interesting."

We walked downstairs to a command center to meet the police chief and some of his security directors. I made a few small suggestions over the next hour and a half, but overall their plan was a solid one. The majority of the security directors are old street warriors who have been there, done that. Their experience allows a certain amount of common sense to flourish beyond the gadgets and glimmer of the strip.

The parade was taking place up on the strip near the large casinos, ending right near the newest extravaganza, Starship Vegas. All of the major casinos had gotten together and worked with the local authorities on a specific security plan for the event. Vegas is pretty unique when it comes to security. It's always been a major concern for the gambling industry, and there's not a technology or method that they haven't tried. Some of the casinos use pretty sophisticated methods to track individuals considered personae non grata, and I'd venture to say that Vegas is ten times as secure as any other city in the world. That doesn't mean that bad things can't happen there. The security people and police will tell you that right out. But they start from a much more effective base when they gear up to protect their family jewels. They spared neither expense nor effort in this case. Besides thousands of private security people, police officers, and National Guardsmen, the Air Force had supplied a JSTARS surveillance aircraft and its attendant sensors to help keep track of the area. The airplane had been equipped with some new systems designed to work in an urban warfare environment, and they had Army Delta threat specialists aboard and hooked into the network. A full-scale fighter patrol covered the sky, with rapid response helicopters to hit trouble areas. The casinos donated their own helicopters to the cause for additonal surveillance and response assets. These birds are normally reserved to transfer the high rollers from the airport and their private jets to their suites without the aggravation of the limo ride through all the daily traffic in Las Vegas. There were undercover security people in the crowd and enough video and high-tech sensors to keep Motorola in business for another twelve months.

I rendezvoused with Danny and Shunt late Saturday afternoon at a little shooting gallery off East Tropicana, where we took turns puncturing paper with vintage tommy guns. Nothing like the loud rip of an ancient submachine gun to calm your nerves. Shunt had never fired a Thompson before, and between that and the women walking around underwear-optional, I think the poor boy was about to overload. Put a dweeb in the City of Sin and powerful things start to happen. Appetites whetted with gunpowder, we crossed over the Strip to West Tropicana and a little Italian restaurant near Dunville. You won't see the place written up in any gourmet magazines, but that's their loss.

"Police have been watching the railroads for the past few weeks," said Danny. "Cox sent some intelligence their way that indicated that something was up. Which must mean that the action's somewhere else."

For just a second I had a paranoia attack: maybe the LNG port really *was* the main show. But I couldn't see how that would fit with Cox's murder. Nobody arranges their own demise to divert attention from a terrorist attack.

According to Danny, the detectives investigating Cox's murder theorized that he had been killed by another hotel guest who'd managed to hack the computerized card key and gotten into his room. Danny thought it was more likely to have been an employee or someone posing as an employee, since it would have been easier for him or her to grab a master key. All of the employees' whereabouts, however, were accounted for, as were their cards. The police had interviewed most, though not all, of the employees with no results.

The way Danny reconstructed it, Cox had arrived sometime around three P.M. Friday, gone into his room, then left, possibly to get some dinner. When he came back—around twelve, though until the autopsy it would be impossible to say—he was murdered by someone already in the room, or by someone he let in.

"They have surveillance cameras near the elevators. No one came or went around that time," Danny added. "He didn't use the steps, at least not all the way down to the lobby, because there's a camera in the lobby that covers that door, and no one came out around then."

"Down or up the steps to another floor, where he caught the elevator?"

"Maybe. If he did that, once they have the time of death, they'll be able to check better."

Or maybe not. My guess was that the stairs opened into at least one place not covered by a video camera—the basement, say.

"Where'd he go after he checked in?" I asked.

"The ten-million-dollar question. He didn't use

a credit card, and he didn't charge anything to his room. He's on the elevator-area video at eleven fifty-four. Alone."

We had some dinner and then checked in with Trace, who'd taken charge of settling the rest of the team into their various hotels and getting them to bed so they'd be fresh in the morning. She told me she was going to bed—and that I ought to check in early myself.

"Early to bed, early to rise makes a man healthy, wealthy, and wise," she mocked.

"Words to live by," I shot back. "Especially in Vegas. Pleasant dreams."

"My ass."

"Maybe you'll see those walking coyotes again."

I expected her to say something sarcastic, but instead she nodded very seriously. "I already have," she said, touching the stone on the necklace around her neck.

"They come from that thing?" I asked.

"This?" She hadn't realized she'd pawed it, I guess. She glanced down and then laughed at herself. "No, this is just a rock."

"You see your relatives when you were away?"

"They're out in Oregon, Dick."

"Just asking."

"I decided to accept."

"The godmother thing?"

"Yeah. It's more than that." She reached into her pocket and took out a small rock about the size of a very large jawbreaker. It looked similar to the stone around her neck, except that it was bigger and neither as polished nor as symmetrical. It also didn't have a hole in it. "You see anything in the stone, Dick?" she asked, handing it to me.

Gray veins slanted through the red glint of the rock in an odd starburst pattern. If it was supposed to be a crystal ball, the reception was particularly cloudy tonight.

"Can't say that I do."

"Feel warm or cold?" she asked.

"Warm. Because it's been in your pocket."

She smiled at me, as if that weren't so. "Certain members of the nation are chosen to feel the power," she said. "It's not up to them—it just comes. They can choose to go with it, to accept it or not. Geronimo—he's probably the most famous Apache to people outside the tribe, him and Cochise, maybe. The power was very strong in him, and he accepted it. He was a great medicine man. That's how he could lead the people."

"Into a big slaughter with the U.S. Army."

"No. The Army fought him but never could defeat him. The general who tracked him made a deal, but the President reneged later on. Geronimo lived as a prisoner, but only because he was tricked. He was never defeated. He couldn't be."

"Okay." I didn't know what else to say; it sounded pretty New Agey to me. Not that I don't have great respect for Indians; on the contrary. But when some of their spiritual beliefs get translated, something gets a little screwy in the translation. "So, you still have those dreams then, huh?"

"I want you to be very careful."

"You believe in talking coyotes, Trace?" I was

half-kidding, half-serious. We'd never had this deep a talk about her beliefs.

She explained that, according to Apache legend, coyotes had once been a tribe of people who'd been transformed into animal shapes. They were important omens, but their meanings could be mysterious. She didn't understand everything that was involved in the dream, except for the most obvious part—that I was in danger.

"The battle between good and evil continues every day. The forces are stark in the desert," she added. "Apache warriors understood this. Show no mercy."

"Pretty much the story of my life," I told her, bidding her a good night.

Danny, Shunt, and I hit a bar where the girls worked with G-strings and nightsticks. Shunt's eyes rolled back into his head and we took him back to his hotel, hosed him off, and put him to bed. With the night still young and nubile, Danny and I found our way over to Caesars on the Strip. While Danny threw away some of his money at the blackjack table, I slipped back to the security office, where I made contact with an old friend. I was interested in seeing whether I was being tailed. I'd decided to dispense with Capel's shooters since that hadn't brought any results. Danny and I double-backed several times en route to the hotel and even split up but didn't come up with anything. The video cameras covering the game rooms didn't reveal any noticeable trail team. Maybe Shadow had taken the night off.

My cell phone rang as I was leaving. It was Karen burning the midnight oil back East.

"Can you get to an Internet connection?" she asked.

"Shouldn't be too hard."

"Check your email. I'll forward you a URL."

A few minutes later, I logged onto my email server from the office of the casino's security director. The URL Karen had sent had slashes and backslashes, question marks, and numbers. I had no idea where the hell I was going until I ended up there: the electronic morgue of a newspaper in Port Hammond, Delaware. A story popped on the screen of a murder-suicide that had taken place in 1972. A man had killed his wife and three kids, apparently because of financial problems. The weapon was a .38 revolver; everyone had been shot at very close range.

According to the story, one of the kids had survived, though he was reported in critical condition.

His name was Luke J. Cox.

18

There were a half-dozen other articles about the Cox family in the newspaper morgue. The longest ran several screens and had been written about a month after the murder-suicide. The crime had been the most shocking thing that had happened in Port Hammond since the town had been incorporated in 1710, and the local newspaper had assigned two reporters to try to figure out what had happened and why. According to the story they wrote, the Coxes had been pretty much your typical American family at the time. Mr. Cox, whose first name was Harold, had been in the U.S. Navy during the Korean War; he'd spent a lot of his time on the aircraft carrier *Coral Sea* and had gone out as a petty officer at the end of his hitch. After the usual period of post-service adjustment, he'd found his way to commercial fishing. There was a gap there, but somehow he'd become a mate on a tugboat, soon managed to get a post as a captain, and eventually bought his own tug. He'd spent perhaps a decade building up the business, and according to the stories had become pretty successful.

Along the way, though, he'd developed a taste for gambling. He'd indulge in his hobby by taking trips to Las Vegas once a year, then more often as his business grew. Vegas was a different place in those days, but human nature wasn't. The reporters couldn't say how well he'd done in the early years—they seemed to believe he'd gotten his first tugboat after a trip to the old Caesars Palace—but if Lady Luck had been a particularly good friend at first, she'd soon turned fickle. Two weeks before he killed his family, he'd filed for commercial and personal bankruptcy.

Back in those days, bankruptcy was a pretty shameful thing, but there seemed more to it than that. The reporters found that Mr. Cox had been visited by "unnamed employees" of a small casino after he'd filed for bankruptcy.

"More likely they weren't connected with the casinos at all," said Danny, who by this time had found me and was reading over my shoulder. "They're probably connected to debt that's not covered by bankruptcy laws."

The reporters carefully quoted from the police report, which said there was no sign of forced entry, and they were pretty conclusive that Mr. Cox had done the shooting. But anyone reading the story might wonder whether those "unnamed employees"—who'd been seen around town the day before the homicide—might have helped him out a little. Mr. Cox was not known to own a .38, and there were no records indicating where the gun had come from.

Another very small news item reported young

Cox getting out of the hospital three months later. The bullet that had been meant to kill him had merely grazed the side of his head. The police theorized that he had been the second one shot, sleeping in the room with his other brothers, and that perhaps the noise had woken the third boy, who was shot near the door. Perhaps that accounted for the miss, they told the reporters; between the haste and the trauma of killing his own kid, Cox senior had botched the job.

"The hand of God pulling the gun away," said one of the detectives.

I tried some more search terms in the database but didn't come up with anything else. Danny had me go over to Google and see if the courts or police departments had anything online, though we figured it would be pretty useless. It was now after two Vegas time, which meant five A.M. back East, still too early to call the local police and see if there were any old-timers who might remember something.

"So now we know why Cox hated gambling," said Danny. "And probably Vegas. That accounts for the certificate you saw and then some. He blamed them for killing his family. But why would somebody kill him?"

"Because he knew something that they don't want known, or he wanted to do something they didn't want done," I said. I went back to the email program and wrote a little thank-you note for Karen, attaching an IOU for a more personal show of my appreciation.

"Maybe he already did it," said Danny.

What had Cox done? He'd kept me on the East Coast, away from Vegas.

Shadow—assuming he was tied to the apartment we'd seen—wanted me here.

"It might be that they wanted me out of the picture. He helped, but he knew too much and he was killed," I said.

"Or maybe this has nothing to do with you or even Vegas," said Danny. "Maybe his murder is about his father's death thirty years ago. Maybe he figured out who did it, went to the police or threatened to, and they bumped him off."

"Danny, you're not jumping to conclusions anymore."

"Didn't you tell me to stop thinking like a cop?"

"Yeah, but since when did you start doing what I told you to?"

Danny laughed, then got serious again. "I don't know. Some of the guys I've talked to said Cox's information occasionally was decent. He was certainly not a rocket scientist, but I don't know how crocked he was. And I don't think he'd be so dumb that he would try to take you out."

"Come on. I think we ought to see if they're still serving decent drinks in this town," I told Danny. "And then I heard about a place back in the city that's supposed to be haunted by the ghost of Dean Martin."

If Dean Martin does haunt Las Vegas, I didn't find him that night. I did manage to get a few hours of sleep before driving up to Nellis Air Force Base, where an AH-6 had been placed at my disposal for an aerial inspection of the parade area. Nellis is a U.S. Air Farce facility, a humungous collection of runways and hangars and test ranges. Besides the "official" sections of the base, Nellis is the doorway to some of the USAF's "black projects." The infamous Area 51 is located a short hop away; when UFO enthusiasts gather on the nearby ridges with high-powered binoculars and telescopes to look for flying saucers, what they're actually seeing are high-tech Air Force projects being put through their paces.

At least that's what the Air Force says. They may just not want to admit that they believe in little green men like the rest of us.

My helo ride lasted about forty-five minutes. Security checkpoints had already been set up around the Strip, and teams had begun implementing random searches of traffic.

How do you keep one car bomb out of the center of a city? You can't, not dependably, not forever. Maybe you can shut down Las Vegas, but can you shut down Sacramento the same day? You close down Des Moines—what about Urbandale up the road? Or Pleasant Hill? Or West Des Moines? That's why dealing with terrorists at the source is so important.

In one sense, the fact that these assholes like to go for really big targets makes the job a *little* easier. They want to take down symbols, and in their minds, Urbandale—and with respect, even Des Moines—just don't cut it as symbols. The Palisades Shopping Mall would have qualified only because it was so close to New York City that the media would have come running. Vegas, on the other hand, was a supersize target, the capital of sin and decadence in their eyes, probably even more potent than D.C. or New York.

The trip up and down the Strip convinced me of one thing: whatever they were planning, it was already there. Las Vegas Boulevard—the official name for the Strip—runs roughly parallel to I-15. Las Vegas Boulevard runs through downtown Las Vegas, but the Strip is actually to the south of the city proper. Huge hotels line both sides. Each hotel is its own world, with literally thousands of guest rooms. The gaming rooms are massive and are connected to small shopping malls filled with boutiques and different stores.

The hotels have different themes; you've probably heard of the most famous: Luxor, which has a pyramid and a sphinx; Circus Circus, which is a circus; and the Venetian, which comes complete with gondolas and hallways that look like they were ripped right out of the Doge's Palace. Not every big hotel is on the Strip, and not all of the interesting things that happen or can happen in Vegas take place in the hotels, but if I took the time to describe the whole place to you, this book would be as long as the *Encyclopaedia Britannica.* My best advice is to plan a trip at some point. Tell 'em Dick sent you, and I'm sure they'll lead you to what they claim is my favorite video poker machine.

"You're welcome," said Karen when I called her that afternoon. "And I will take you up on that IOU."

"I hope so. The women out here are nice, but they lack a certain sophistication."

"Don't make me come out there and scratch their eyes out."

"I'd like to watch that."

"I'll bet you would." Karen sighed, signaling she was turning back to work. "The intelligence alerts that went out about Las Vegas have very little behind them. They were all about trains. I followed your suggestion and looked for some intersection with the Bosnians, but I couldn't make any connection."

"There may not be a direct connection. What we may have is a series of very small isolated cells. If so, they probably won't connect with each other until the very last moment, when they're called into action. Has anything new come of the check for the poison gas?"

"We've been tracking all of the shipments of the companies that Danny gave us," said Karen. "We have a total of ten trucks going into Illinois at some point over the last month that aren't accounted for after that. It doesn't mean they were involved in anything, just that we can't trace them beyond that state."

In Tell-Me-Dick's territory. A coincidence?

Probably. But I didn't mind turning the tables on that asshole. I told Karen she ought to sic the dogs on him and see if he came up with better information. In the meantime, we were going to have to assume that whatever the terrorists were going to use had already been delivered and was in place. The hotel security teams had already begun searching for anything that might be used to store or hide poison gas. Doc and Tiffany were checking on that angle and making sure that the hotels and casinos knew what they were looking for. Danny was liaising with the police. Trace and Sean were out beating the sand looking for intelligence. The rest of my team were out rattling doors and checking windows, seeing what the holes were in the net.

Around five my time, I checked with the LNG port command. The day had gone smoothly, without any attempts on the port. They had detained two people in a small boat who'd been acting suspiciously. The men had been put in jail on a disorderly conduct charge, so the locals had a chance to check them out. The thinking was that they'd been on a sneak and peek. I didn't disagree, though by then I'd concluded that the port had been a blind manufactured by Cox.

I had dinner up at the Rio, which has a tall tower and is located opposite the Strip on the other side of Interstate 15. Shadow had not visited yours truly yet in Las Vegas, but I was sure he was out there, watching and planning. Maybe he was putting the finishing touches on tomorrow's operation. Maybe he was just a foot soldier in that operation, with little to do.

Maybe he was in bed already, getting a good night's sleep. Maybe he'd found one of the women in the short rayon dresses who hung out near the edges of the bars. Or maybe he was the slim guy at the table across the room, sitting by himself, sipping Perrier and looking bored.

Actually, probably not. The guy at the table across the room was Pete Simms, and he was from Wyoming. I had taken the liberty of borrowing his credit card and then running a credit check on him.

Pete, if you're reading this, you really should try to pay down some of those cards, my friend; they're killing you with the interest.

I had dinner by myself, then went out onto the terrace and looked back over at the stream of lights.

"Penny for your thoughts," yelled Trace from the upper level.

"They're worth at least ten bucks," I told her.

Never one to use the stairs when she can drop twenty feet or so, Trace swung over the railing and dropped down.

"You're getting careless in your old age," she said.

"I knew you were there. And Sean's up behind that post. And Doc is just inside that window there."

"You didn't see Hulk?"

"He's downstairs by the steps watching the elevator." It was kind of touching that the Rogue team felt they ought to watch out for me. It also told me I ought to sit on their asses a little harder. Scumbags even charged dinner to the company.

"If Shadow's going to show, it'll be tomorrow," I told Trace. "But I appreciate your watching my back. I'm touched."

"I've been thinking that maybe it was Cox all along," she said. "He had access to a lot of intelligence. He knew where you were."

"Cox was definitely involved, no doubt. But I think his game was to try to throw me off so I wouldn't be here. He didn't want us screwing up his plans."

It was also possible the asshole didn't want me

getting killed and was trying to save my butt, but I didn't want to think too charitably of a known asshole. Doc walked over with a pair of drinks. I took mine and turned out toward the city, staring at the laser shining up from the Luxor pyramid.

"Go for it, Shadow," I thought to myself. "Take your best shot, asshole."

19

Monday started off with a boom and went downhill from there.

I jumped out of bed at five A.M., a few minutes before the alarm went off. I hit the head and started some light stretching to get ready for morning PT when the television timer woke up and snapped onto *Fox News.* I caught the broadcast in midsentence.

". . . not much is known at this hour, except that the aircraft was a small plane that did not answer hails by either the ground controllers or the two F-16 fighter jets sent to intercept it. Cove Point authorities assure Fox that the situation is under control."

Cove Point?

Son of a bitch.

Son of a fuck-me bitch.

I grabbed for the cell phone and hit the quick dial for Karen's cell.

"What's going on?" I asked as soon as she picked up.

"Dick?"

"The LNG port? What the hell's going on?"

"An aircraft failed to respond to hails and was shot down," she said. "There's a recovery operation underway right now."

I could see that. The network had a live feed from a helicopter circling in the distance. Several boats were rushing toward what looked like empty water, though I assumed that there was some sort of floating debris field.

"Get those boats out of there," I told her. "Clear the helicopters. Get everything the hell out. Now!"

"What?"

"It's a cover for them to slip in. Tell the commander to stick with his protocol on the ships and boats that are allowed in the area. They used the aircraft to get themselves in."

"OK."

"Call me back. Go!"

I hit the end button and then immediately called Capel, who'd come down to sit in for me at the port. I told him what I was seeing. Already there were two boats in the area that I knew hadn't been vetted; they were speedboats. "Get them," I told him.

I spent the next few minutes pacing around the room, watching helplessly a couple of thousand miles away as the nightmare scenario unfolded on the television screen. The news helicopters should have been shunted away from the area immediately. They were just at the edge of the exclusion zone, but the local authorities could have kicked them out if there was an emergency, and this qualified. Hell, if I'd been there, I would have grabbed a SAM and shot the suckers down myself.

But I was glad they didn't. The truth was, I

wanted to watch. No, the truth was, I wanted to be there myself, taking aim with one of the Whiskey Cobras and firing a TOW missile up the ass of the second speedboat as it made a beeline for the harbor area. I saw the smoke from the missile as it zigged toward the boat, which was on a collision course with one of the docking areas. It hit, but nothing happened. I kicked at the side of the bed, pissed that some jackass munitions vendor had screwed up the fuse or something. Then the boat blossomed into a mushroom. The small warhead of the missile had exploded below the deck, igniting the explosives packed there. The geyser obliterated the boat, engulfing it in a massive cloud of steam, smoke, and fire. The shock was so violent that the television station's helicopter supplying the feed stuttered in the air.

Fortunately, the speedboat had been far enough away from the dock that the explosion did no damage to the facilities. By now the other boat had also come under fire. The video caught a closeup of an F-16's wing passing at very close range, then the feed went crazy and died. The on-air announcers started freaking, wondering if their helicopter had just been shot down. A good guess under the circumstances, though it eventually proved not to be true.

Danny, Trace, and Doc arrived while I channel-surfed for more details. Within a minute or so I found a station that was offering a live feed off a Coast Guard vessel, and it helped us analyze the situation. The two boats had been the main attack, with the aircraft a diversion to allow them onto the scene; it had almost worked. Between Capel and Karen and the security people on the scene, the boats had been spotted and targeted at nearly the last possible second. Now the Coast Guard, Navy, and Marines were throwing everything they had across the harbor, and it looked like they had the situation under control. I left a message for Capel reminding him to look for a second wave of attackers, sleepers who would be waiting to take advantage of the first wave of attacks and their confusion. I'm sure he probably thought of it himself. I can't take too much credit for the warnings I gave, but I did give them. I only wished I'd been there to give them in person.

"I hope to hell they're watching the water for swimmers," muttered Trace.

"Capel'll take care of it," said Doc. "He knows a goatfuck when he sees one."

"We better hope that wasn't the opening event for a daylong celebration," I said dryly. "Better yet, we'd better make sure it wasn't."

We watched for a while longer. When it seemed obvious that the situation was under control, we left to grab the rest of the team. We shook some oxygen into our brain cells with a five-mile run before breakfast, breaking into two-man teams fanning out from the three hotels where we'd stayed. I set a leisurely eight-minute pace; I knew I had hit the right stride as Danny groaned and moaned alongside me. The idea wasn't just to get our motors running. I wanted a street-level view of the area, and jogging suits and sneakers let us do a much better job than driving around in SUVs would have.

Danny and I swung down Flamingo, running down Charlotte and then back through the lots over to Lara Ave. We skirted some of the side streets up there, slowing our pace to take a look at what was coming before heading over on East Harmon and coming back. We were the most suspicious characters out and about, and we drew a squad car and an unmarked detective vehicle.

When we hit the Strip, two security officers on their mountain bikes rode up alongside us and asked how we were doing. Danny grunted something unintelligible, the sweat pouring off his skin. Our escorts laughed, and I did, too. They rode with us a while, then backed off.

The squad car we'd seen earlier had set up near the side of the road not too far away. Another set of security people eyed us as we hustled past the Venetian. I tried to pick up the pace to push Danny down the homestretch as we headed toward our rendezvous at Starbucks up near the Riviera, but he fell behind steadily. Finally I turned and jogged a bit in place, eyeing the nearby road as I waited.

"Time to call a taxi," he joked as one passed.

"That one wouldn't have done us much good," I told him. "It's a security patrol."

The rest of the team had had similar experiences, being spotted by police or security patrols and then handed off for close surveillance. If the Tangos decided to attack Las Vegas with an army of joggers, the defenses were ready.

Since I was one of the guests of honor, the Las Vegas Parade committee had arranged for me to have the use of a Caddy Escalade around town. The Escalade is a great SUV, though, because of my line of work, I ordinarily stick to plain-Jane vehicles, the plainer the better. People regularly tag me as a Hummer kind of guy, and, as a matter of fact, the parade people had offered me one of those, too. Again, a great vehicle, but one that sticks out pretty obviously wherever you are. You can't be a Rogue Warrior *and* be a movie star, even though people think you ought to be.

With the rest of the team dispersing to their posts and my presence at the marshalling point requested, I hopped into the Escalade for the drive over to Duke Ellington Way, where the marchers and floats were being lined up. Sean came with me, double-checking our weapons and the communications system while I drove. (I've seen his driving. No way I was letting him behind the wheel.) He stashed my MP5 in an innocuous-looking gym bag, along with a parcel of extra clips and a backup communications unit. The heat made wearing a coat a bit ridiculous, so I angled the P7M8 in my belt and untucked my shirt. I didn't have quite enough fat to carry it off—there are some downsides to being a fitness fanatic, I guess. I had two Glock 26s with me, one at my ankle—and you can come find the other one if you've got the balls for it.

Dancers, a lion tamer, all sorts of veterans groups, a dozen fire departments, actors and actresses—this was Independence Day Vegas-style. Everything was larger than life, the costumes, the routines, the floats—even for boring acts like myself. Since I'd begged off the parachute-jump-into-the-open-car routine, they arranged for something almost as showy—a touchdown via helicopter on a large float made up to look like a next-generation SEAL fast boat called the "Very Slender Vessel." I was supposed to meet the helicopter near the staging area, which gave me a chance to familiarize myself with the float before trying to land on it—always a wise idea.

Despite the asinine name, VSVs are very cool follow-ons for the Mark V. They look like what you'd get if you crossed an F-117 Stealth Fighter with a speedboat. The superstructure rises no more than six feet off the surface of the water. I've had a tour but not the chance to use one, not because I'm an old fart (true enough) but because no one's used them yet. The Navy being the Navy, they're still screwing with the suckers. Maybe by the time my grandchildren's grandchildren are meeting with the recruiters they'll put them into service. Of course, by that time, the people they'd be useful to use against will have figured out how to detect them.

Whoever built the float had a good set of photos or plans to work with, because the float looked exactly like the one I'd seen at DARPA, the Defense Advanced Research Projects Agency. Except for the platform—and the neon blue and gold paint job. But they spelled my name right on the side, so who am I to bitch?

The float was controlled from the cockpit of the boat. I spent a few minutes talking to the driver, a forty-something type named Jimmy who thought it was pretty funny that he'd been in the Army and was now driving a boat on land. I didn't think it was quite as funny as he did, but then I hadn't spent the past hour strapped into the little compartment with nothing to do but stare straight ahead. The drivers, once vetted, had been instructed to stay in their vehicles, and Jimmy believed in following instructions to the letter. Not a bad idea, I guess, if your ambition in life is to be a boat driver on land.

Security teams were inspecting all of the floats, and even after security ticked the floats off on their handheld computers, they were still subject to random checks. The flow-through point from the staging area to the marching line included another last-minute search and inspection.

By now, everyone involved in security, and most of the participants in the parade, had heard of the LNG port incident. Whether or not it made them more focused than they would have been, I can't say. The place boiled with adrenaline and nervous energy. If NASA could figure out how to bottle the frenzy, they'd have had enough fuel here to send a rocket to Saturn every day of the week.

The communications system we were using, adapted from the military's Joint Tactical Radio System program (known as "Jitters"), worked off a black box about as wide as the book in your hands and maybe half as thick. It could connect through satellites and just about any radio frequency known to man. It had onboard encryption and waveform generation, and I wouldn't have been surprised if it could make popcorn, too. It fit into the back of a special bulletproof vest as if it were a ceramic plate, and supposedly it provided the same level of extra protection.

I linked into the system through what looked

like a set of wraparound sunglasses. Besides a high-tech speaker that worked by vibrating the bone behind my ear and a miniature microphone hidden in the nose bridge, the glasses had a small screen in the right eyepiece controlled by voice commands. The commands were enabled by touching the top corner of the frame, and the system was trained to work only with my voice, so that ambient noise or nearby conversation couldn't screw it up.

As you can imagine, the glasses took a little getting used to. I felt like I was looking at the world through a floating cloud with a television show projected onto it. But the system also allowed me not only to talk with the rest of my team but to get live video feeds from the JSTARS and the various command posts scattered around the city. I felt like one of those creatures in Hindu mythology that have a thousand eyes, including one in each palm of their hands.

The helicopter was en route by the time I finished checking out the float and getting updates from my team. As I made my way toward the LZ, I saw that the security people had corralled a bunch of clowns—literally. The clowns, dressed in colorful outfits, big shoes, and red plastic noses, were not in the databank that was used to check IDs and biometric information, though they swore that they had registered and already cleared security. They were sent to the "Penalty Box"—a grandstand area several blocks from the marshalling point and the parade route—for the duration of the event, which left them none too happy.

The Army had detailed a number of Blackhawks in for the event. Naturally I got one of the special operations models, an MH-60L DAP* outfitted with a couple of 30mm chainguns, a 2.75-inch rocket pod, and a 40mm grenade tosser. The guns were all loaded in case of trouble, but the rocket pods had custom-built flares that would ignite as I touched down, adding a little fizz to my arrival.

I pulled on a headset and stood by the open door as we did a circuit of the parade route. Just above us, a pair of Predator unmanned aerial vehicles flew a slow track up and down the strip, their video cams supplying a detailed view of the action. Two Air Force fighters orbited much higher overhead. A squadron of AH-64 Apache helicopters were warming up at McLaren Airport. A flight advisory had been posted to keep all unauthorized helicopter traffic out of the area, and officials were enforcing it rather vigorously. There would be no repeat of the private plane incident at Cove Point; anything in the air that didn't belong there would be shot down long before it got close to the parade.

If it all sounds impressive on paper, it was three times that at the scene, with the hardware rushing around and people shouting over the comm gear. So why didn't I feel secure?

We took a circuit of the area, then buzzed in from the direction of the Outlet Center, the Black-

* Officially DAP stands for Direct Action Penetrator. I'll let you develop the unofficial meanings on your own.

hawk's rotors doing a heavy whomp against the street below. As we drew even with the Excalibur Hotel and Casino, I assumed the position—swinging out the door and hanging by my harness. I extended my arms and started to windsurf below the helo, but because of the way the harness had been rigged or the air currents that whipped around me—or both—I quickly found myself swinging from side to side. Within a few seconds, I'd started spinning like a top. The flares in the rocket pod started going off. I'm sure the whole thing was one hell of a show for the people on the ground, but if it weren't for the fact that I had no time to think, I would have seriously questioned my sanity. The fireworks kicked up a thick cloud of smoke, which collected around me as the wash from the helicopter blades concentrated it beneath the chopper.

Finally, either because the helicopter had slowed or just dumb luck, I stopped gyrating. The green-faced replica of Lady Liberty winked at me as I passed, and I spotted the target float ahead. I got my feet on the deck right at the Banly's, which was as planned. I don't think anyone in the world has ever snapped off a quick release harness *that* quickly. A good thing, too: the MH-60 lingered for all of a tenth of a millisecond before tearing away.

I'd like to think that the roar of the crowd nearby was for me. But just at the moment I made my entrance, a dozen beauties popped out of the cake on the float directly behind me. Wearing little more than their birthday suits, they were the prettiest cake decorations I've ever seen, and I added my applause to the crowd's.

"Hell of an arrival, Dick," said a female voice in my headset as I turned back around.

It wasn't Trace and it wasn't Tiffany.

"Where are you?" I said.

"We'll meet soon enough," she said.

The line went clear.

I didn't give Shadow the satisfaction of hearing me say anything else.

20

The military people had assured us that the commo system could not be cracked. Believing that about as much as I'd believe anything the Army ever told me, we'd worked out a backup system to communicate. I initiated it now, sliding open the cell phone and keying in a preset. It was possible that Shadow was watching, and even that she had some way of compromising the backup system, but I couldn't worry about that.

The preset initiated a series of calls to the rest of the team. They didn't bother answering the calls. Instead, they switched over to the backup radio system, which were civilian jobs that used chips and downloaded codes that changed every day. They didn't interface with the military system, but at this point that wasn't a negative. I didn't realize it then, but most of my people had already heard the voice; it had come through a shared channel.

Even after Danny's adventure, I hadn't seriously considered the possibility that Shadow was a woman. Blind spot on my part.

I still had the glasses on. The video feed was

working and I could hear the comm channels fine. Danny had been tasked to alert the event supervisors if the comm system was breached; either that hadn't happened yet or they had decided it would be easier to proceed. In any event, they were still using the Jitters units.

"Traffic's backing up on Twains," said one of the ops on the common channel. "Bunch of trucks coming from one of the construction sites. Should I send them around on Paradise Road?"

The request bounced up the line to the traffic coordinator, who approved it; it was part of the overflow plan directing traffic away from the Strip. The trucks they were talking from were coming from a construction site across from the closed Desert Inn Golf Club.

I pushed the control on my glasses and dialed into the feed from the Predator. The trucks kicked up a cloud of sand getting off the work site. With no breeze to speak of, the cloud hung in the air like a veil covering the site and the roadway nearby. The trucks were filthy; they'd been on the site for a while.

Ten of them, snaking into the line of cars parallel to the Strip and heading in the direction of the Chamber of Commerce building. They were the only trucks in the line.

"Get the trucks!" I said over the compromised Jitters circuit, realizing what was going on. "Get them."

Or I should say, realizing *half* of what was going on.

If you go straight down Paradise Road, you can get over to the Hilton, or you could take a left onto

Sahara and from there get back onto Las Vegas Boulevard heading toward the city. Or you could turn down the service road to the Riviera, jump the curb and run through the strip mall parking lot a few hundred yards from the Strip. If you didn't particularly care about the people who'd be in front of you, you'd have a clear shot at the heart of the parade—and the Strip.

Ten trucks, packed with explosives and poison gas—a very big boom. I pulled the MP5 from the bag—anyone who saw it probably thought it was just part of the show—grabbed the extra mags and started to the side of the float, intending to jump down and run over toward the Riviera and the service road, which was a few blocks away on my right. Just as I got to the street, two Blackhawk helicopters swooped down on the block and headed for the vehicles. The command circuit was flooded and even ours was jammed as everyone tried to talk at once. I could see the feed from the Predator. One of the trucks was just pulling out, pushing to get up on the sidewalk and get around the traffic. Sean yelled to me; I yelled back. Just as I started to follow him I saw something out of the corner of my eye, not through the glasses, not with the high-tech crap I'd outfitted myself with, but with my trusty Mark-1A1 Eyeballs (original equipment).

Two men were darting from the sidewalk across the street, running toward the new Vegas Starship.

Instinct made me follow them. I'd caught nothing more than the quick glimpse, but one of the outlines didn't look quite right. Both were wearing long jackets on a day when the temperature was eighty degrees, and they were running the wrong way if they were on the security team.

A few of the people who lined the side of the street started to applaud, thinking that it was part of a show or something. I yelled at them to get out of the way, but my shouts had very little effect.

The submachine guns the thugs pulled out from beneath their jackets—MP5s similar to mine—did a much better job. People started diving for the ground, and by the time I reached the low wall separating Starship Vegas from the walk, most of the crowd had either taken cover or was sprawled on the ground.

The newest, latest, and greatest hotel on the Strip, Starship Vegas looked like a saucer from one of the *Star Wars* movies that had been plopped down in the middle of the city. A large space needle towered over it at the side; from the distance, the pair looked like two spaceships competing in an intergalactic race. Up close, the area in front of the hotel was a cement garden of textured concrete with a series of pools and futuristic metal sculptures. If you stood near the entrance, you had a free shot at anything coming up toward you. Including me.

I tucked and rolled back behind the shallow wall at the edge of the property as the ground exploded with bullets and concrete chips. The parade had stopped moving forward and for a wild second I thought I might hop in the VSV and christen it as a SEAL vehicle. I might even have tried that—probably without managing to get over the curb—had I not seen a Hummer two floats behind it. This was a civilian H2 model made by General Motors, a slightly downsized version of the real thing, but I wasn't in the position of sending out a Request For Proposals. I leapt back toward the truck, yanked open the door, and threw the driver to the ground. The passenger, a local real estate pooh-bah and big shot political donor, started to object, but I told him it was a matter of national security for him to get the fuck out of *my* vehicle.

I believe he complied, though truthfully, I didn't notice at the time.

I got the vehicle into reverse and pulled around the back of the fire engine that had been following it in line, flooring the mini-Hummer and hanging on tight. The truck bolted up the walk and then across one of the shallow ponds, picking up speed. The two cretins who'd retreated to the front of the casino began unloading their weapons on the boxy front of the truck, blowing out the windshield and perforating much of the front end, including the radiator and the right tire. I set a general course and ducked down, pushing the gas to the floor and bracing as best I could as the 9mm bullets sprayed against the front of the Hummer.

The vehicle took the first of the steps up to the casino pretty well, and if there'd been only two or even three steps, I might have made it straight into the front of the reception area. But there were five steps, and by the time I hit the last one I was moving mostly sideways. The truck tumbled over and rolled into the glass doors and wall. Glass shattered and metal flew all over the place. I twirled inside the truck as the Hummer rolled at least twice more before stopping in the middle of the sloping floor that led down toward the main reception hall maybe two dozen feet inside the casino and right next to the reception desks. The laser lighting threw such a wild pattern of red around the interior of the Hummer as I scrambled up toward the window, gun in hand, that I thought the vehicle had caught fire. Fortunately, I was wrong. That didn't happen until I'd managed to pull myself about halfway out.

There was some gunfire to my left, and as I turned to return it, the vehicle shook with a kind of low rumble. I thought to myself, "Oh shit," and tried as best I could to dive away. I think I may have gotten about a quarter of the way to the floor when the gas tank exploded. Demo Dick became Rocket Man, hurtling into space where no man had gone before. I sailed into the registration area, rolling into a row of computers and then falling onto a stack of cardboard boxes where they'd placed some files. The boxes probably kept me from breaking my neck. My knee got banged to shit, but somehow I managed to hold onto my MP5. Between the fire and the laser light show, though, I had no idea where the two apes had gone.

Somewhere in the vast bowels of the hotel, security people may have been ushering guests to safety. Somewhere inside, an Emergency Response team might have been racing to deal with the situation. But if any of this was happening, I never saw it. The only thing I knew was that the front end of the casino was on fire, the automated sprinkler alarms were going off, and a Klaxon that could have woken up half of San Diego was rattling the floor.

I crawled to the side of the registration desk,

jumped up, and threw myself behind a shallow platform at the left, which housed some of the lights that played across the vast open floor that greeted people as they came into the hotel. Holograms floated across the top of the room, meteors and spaceships that ran across the room in a completely random pattern beneath a rotating sky of stars. A planet appeared at about nine o'clock midway across the room; it looked as if someone had taken a bite out of it. It was a clue to where my quarry had gone—he was blocking one of the projectors, distorting the image—but by the time I realized what that meant, the gunfire had stoked up again.

As I lay on the ground, I heard a familiar voice calling to me from somewhere around my stomach. It was Trace on the backup radio. The earbud had dropped from my ear but the device was still working somehow—definitive proof this model hadn't been made by the Chinks in one of China's prisons. As I started to pull the set up so I could hear and talk, the room exploded with gunfire from something bigger than the MP5, something at least on the order of a light squad-level machine gun. I rolled back behind the platform, keeping my head and butt at low altitude.

"Where the hell are you, Dick?" asked Trace.

"I'm in Starship, bound for fucking Mars. Where the hell are you?"

"The place is on fire."

"Yeah, no shit. I got two guys in here. Got to be a lot more. Heavy fucking weapons. They look Middle Eastern, but I didn't have a chance to ask for passports."

Danny cut in before Trace could respond. "Dick, the security coordinator is saying they've lost the entire Starship security team off the circuit. They have to be in on it. Some of them at least."

"Find out where the truck entrance is," I told him.

"They're getting schematics."

"Find out," I said as another burst from the machine gun perforated the lasers. I waited until the gun stopped firing, then gave them three very short bursts. As I fired the last one I hopped forward, took three good long strides, and leapt down onto the gaming floor, which began just off the entrance space. At that point, the machine gun began firing again. It must have murdered a dozen of the video gambling machines, which responded to the onslaught with a succession of high-pitched shouts and screams, their electronic tumblers freaking. I didn't check to see if any had paid off—I had a good idea now where the bastard was firing from.

The left side of the casino beyond the registration area was suited up to look like an alien landscape. There were craters and fake rocks that seemed to careen off the side of a volcano. Projections of alien spacemen floated through the area; the shtick was that they could lead you to a table and even take an order. My friend with the machine gun had set up at the edge of the crater, behind one of the boulders and obscured by the parade of foreign creatures. He was using the fake rock to help brace the weapon, which was a Belgian Minimi, the same weapon as an M249 SAW.

Using the fake rock was a fatal mistake. Rocks are good cover because they're solid. Plastic and papier-mâché are not.

And as for holograms . . .

I took him out with a burst from the MP5, the first shots axing into his left cheekbone and the rest popping the top of his skull like a can opener. I moved down the row of the slot machines, not entirely sure what the hell lay beyond where I was, except for machines.

"Danny, you get that schematic yet?"

"Working on it, Dick. Listen, you were right about those trucks. They were rigged to go off. But listen—one of the Delta people thinks there was a similar truck parked behind the casino a few days ago. Maybe a couple of them. They're looking around to see if they can find pictures from the earlier tests or surveys."

"Screw the fucking pictures. Where were the trucks?"

"Back loading area."

"Direct me there," I told him, trotting across to a third row of the machines. I stopped short—two figures were hunched over something down the row all the way across the room, maybe a hundred yards away.

"Dick?"

I emptied the rest of the MP5, the tracer rounds I packed at the end of the magazine warning me I'd shot my wad. Both figures crumpled, but as I ducked back, bullets once more began crashing into the machines around me. Glass and bits of plastic and metal showered across my back as I crawled to the right, trying to put something solid between me and whoever was using the weapon.

"Dick, we can't get in the front of the place," said Trace over the radio. "They put the crash doors down after you blew through."

"What crash doors?"

"It's an emergency lockdown system. We're going to try to get a team into the loading dock area. There are two trucks there. They'll have to be secured first."

"Get the fuck going," I told her.

You'd have thought—I certainly thought—that when I blew through the front end of the hotel, I left a huge gap. But what Danny, with schematics in hand, was trying to explain to me was this: the Starship had been rigged with a double set of doors designed to provide a barrier against suicide car bombers. The system had been activated by someone in the security offices, though admittedly too late to keep me out. Where once there was easily penetrable glass, there was now a metal shock shield blocking the way. A similar shield had been lowered over all street-level entrances.

I told you they're up on their security out here.

"We're coming for you, Dick, don't worry," said Trace.

"Well, do it."

"We're working on it. But—"

"I don't want to hear *but*."

"The security people think the attackers were rigging the loading dock area for an explosion. It's possible the explosives were built right in when they planned the building."

"I hope to hell you're shitting me, Trace."

"I would never shit you, Dick. You're my favorite turd."

On the page, that looks like a joke.

In real life, her voice gulped a bit when she said it.

Not the gulp you want to hear while some asshole is chewing up the room around you with a machine gun, either.

I suppose I might have been able to find my way out if I'd turned around and ran like hell toward the reservation area. Probably there were more offices behind the desk area that had windows or some sort of exit. If the way was barred by more of their magic shields, I might have been able to go up to the second floor, break a window, and leave that way. But retreat is not the Rogue Warrior's lot in life.

Besides, I didn't think of it at the time. I was somewhere between kicking ass and surviving.

The machine gun that was making my life so interesting was being fired from the top of a blackjack table a good two hundred feet or more across the room. This one wasn't a Minimi. I didn't have any trouble picking out what it was even with all the machines popping and screaming around me. I'd heard this *fucking* sound in my dreams. It was a Degtyarev RPD, a golden oldie no doubt bought on eBay from some asshole's gun closet just for me. The Degtyarev dated to the 1950s and was fed, usually, by a round drum like a tommy gun's, though the weapon has a much larger snout and a longer stock. Simple and dependable, it was standard issue for the Red Army during the opening days of the Cold War, and a common squad-level weapon in client states for a few decades after that. I'd heard those motherfuckers chewing up the foliage in Vietnam. Shadow had gotten the gun just for old times' sake, the sentimental bitch.

"Yo, Shadow, you're not going to claim you're a jilted lover, right?" I yelled as the gunfire stopped.

I thought I heard a click as if the weapon were being reloaded, but before I could raise my MP5, the room started exploding again. The RPD's 7.62mm slugs tore out a row of video bandits behind me and then started grinding down the ones just in front. Fortunately the person firing the weapon couldn't lower it quite enough to give me more than a haircut. As the bullets began moving to my right, I started to the left, rolling across the open aisle just quickly enough to escape his attention or at least his aim. I started crawling up in the direction of the game tables. I got no more than five feet when the gun began firing in my direction. Flat on my back, I realized that the bastard was taking direction from the eye in the sky cameras in the black hubs at the top of the room.

That I could deal with. I laced two on the lower ceiling near the RPD, rolling back as the gunner began trashing the nearby machines. I made a feint to the right and cut back to the left, crossing where I'd been. There was a pause, but when the gunfire began it was back in my direction again, chuttering up the remains of the machines.

At some point crawling through the glass I heard Trace yell something in my ear. It didn't sound like "Kiss your ass good-bye" so I figured it wasn't meant for me. I reached the end of the video slot machines and started to lean out; the gun spit and then made what sounded like a hollow pop.

I leapt up and laced the table. I scored a direct hit on the gun, but whoever had been at the trigger had already abandoned it. I barreled forward, charging down the aisle, eyes and head rolling left and right but not seeing anyone. I reached the area of the tables and threw myself forward, rolling under one but still not drawing fire.

As pleasant as my sojourn in the gaming room had been, to this point it had been less than profitable—a typical visit to Vegas for me.

If the place really was rigged to explode—and at that precise moment I had no reason to doubt that it was—I needed to figure out where the hell the person with the plunger was. With Danny still trying to find a map, I reasoned that some of the people I'd creased earlier might provide a clue, so I headed back over to the wall where they'd been.

The dead men had what looked like a computer cable in their hands. It was thick and round, the sort of thing we used at Rogue Manor to set up a router network for the broadband Internet connection. A metal panel sat at the base of the wall, its cover half removed. I pried it off the rest of the way; a row of what looked like oversize telephone jacks sat beneath it.

Now this was what I called on-site tech service. But the only geek who made house calls with a submachine gun was Shunt, and these guys were carrying better hardware than he usually had in his toolbox: MP9s, a kind of improved Uzi built by Ruger mostly for the police market.

"Shunt!" I said over the radio. "Where the fuck are you, Shunt?"

"Yo, Dick, I'm in the JSTARS, man. How are you, Dude?"

"Real sucky, Shunt. What do you call that wire that you used to connect the computers up back home with?"

"Ethernet 5E, Dude."

"Could you use it to blow up a bomb?"

"Only if it were, like, on the network."

"Well, let's say you had that. What else would you need?"

"Like, a computer to hook into it."

I checked Heckle and Jeckle. Neither had a laptop or handheld.

"Dick, we have that schematic," said Danny finally.

I dropped the wire and started back toward the area where the stairway was. "Tell me how to get to the computer room," I told Danny. "No, tell me how to get to the backup power generators. And in the meantime, can you get a power surge into the building, and then cut their power?"

"Why?"

"I want to fry as much of their gear as possible, and then take their power out."

"Yeah, okay. Where are you, exactly?"

"Near the blackjack tables. I think there are elevators at the far end here, and the stairs have to be near them."

"There's one closer—a stairway at the far end of

the room near the Martian Lounge. Go down two flights, then take a right, and you'll find a whole bunch of utility rooms down there. They have a backup power generator there."

"Can you work out the electricity angle?"

"I'll try."

"Where's Trace?"

"Didn't you hear her? She and Hulk are going in with the emergency response team at the back of the building."

"Didn't one of you just tell me they think it may be rigged to explode?"

"I think that's the reason they went in. That's just a theory, Dick, because they can't get hold of the security people and whatnot. And something else: the managing architect and two of the foremen on the project died of accidents, and, uh, there was also one unsolved murder during the construction."

And they didn't figure something was suspicious then? But this was Las Vegas.

"Doc, Tiffany, and Sean are coming over from the cargo trailers," said Danny. "As soon they get here we'll be in to back you up."

"I love you, Danny, but don't bother. That's an order."

"Fuck yourself, Dick."

"You're an insubordinate son of a bitch."

I heard some muffled explosions in the distance; I imagined they were flash-bangs or maybe some improved C-4 on a back doorway, wherever the hell that was. Las Vegas hotels aren't just big; they're cities unto themselves. I wouldn't have been surprised to find that the back entrance they were blowing into was a mile away.

I wouldn't have minded a few grenades myself when I reached the stairway, but the best I could come up with was a chair. I threw it ahead of me down the stairway after opening the door, hoping the clatter would provoke a response from anyone hiding below.

Nothing happened. I slipped through the door. An electric eye had been set up near the side, and I smashed it, figuring that if I had to come back this way, it would be handy to do so without letting Shadow or whoever was watching know.

I made my way down to the first level, stepped around the chair and then continued downward. I'd just reached the last two or three steps when I heard a sound above. My first impulse was to duck back, expecting gunfire. Something clinked down the steps instead. I fired the MP5 at the lock on the door in front of me, then leapt to the door. By the time I got it open, a second grenade had begun to sizzle. I pulled the door open and threw myself inside the room as the lights in the place blinked out.

"Danny, I hope that was you."

"Me and the electric company. They say they sent a pretty massive jolt through the system, but there's no telling what sort of damage it would have done. These big casinos have all sorts of safeguards."

"I wouldn't count on it, Dude," said Shunt. I think he was trying to be reassuring—he is, after all, the God of Power Surges—but with the backup systems flickering, I didn't take it that way. I started making my way toward the generators Danny had told me about when I realized there was a wire running along the floor similar to the Ethernet cable I'd seen upstairs.

"Shunt, I see some more cable. What happens if I cut it?"

"You lose your connection, Dude."

Was that good or bad for a bomb? Was it even connected to a bomb? I decided it was bad for the bomb and the hell with everything else. I snapped through it with my knife.

Either the bomb wasn't rigged to go off when this connection was broken, or the first people you see in the afterlife are two greasy-haired bozos looking to sear their names into your backside with MP5s. In any event, the latter appeared in the hallway thirty yards ahead and immediately began competing to see who could empty his magazine faster.

21

I was still on the floor and their first shots missed a little too high.

Mine didn't.

I rose slowly, feeling a shot of pain in the knee I'd whacked earlier. I limped down the hall to the two men, checking not for ID but additional magazines. As a rule, I hate using ammunition I haven't packed myself. Call me a perfectionist, but I like to know the weapon in my hand has been properly prepared, and besides, using tracer rounds to start and finish a box is the sort of habit that's tough to break, especially when your life's on the line.

But if Shadow was going to be generous and give me additional rounds, who was I to refuse? Meenie and Minie had three extra thirty-round boxes apiece; I slipped them into my rucksack and turned back to find the auxiliary power room Danny had been steering me to.

At some point, I realized I could just follow my nose—the auxiliary generators ran off diesel fuel, and a light odor of oil hung in the air. Danny's directions and the scent led me to a corridor blocked off by a steel door. The door had been locked by the remote control system. A little C-4 would have taken care of it—but I was suffering from an acute lack of C-4.

Danny led me around to a second room that connected to the area. I used the knife to hack through the plasterboard, only to find that the wall had been reinforced with blocks. The ventilation system was too small for my shoulders. I pounded the wall in frustration with the side of my fist. The sting didn't help me think, so I pounded it again even harder.

While all of this was going on, Trace and some of her old Delta friends, along with Hulk and members of the local SWAT team, were upstairs in the hotel, working to secure potential hostages. I didn't have the details at the time, but the terrorists had used the security system to lock down much of the guest areas, turning them into a prison. They'd killed about thirty of the security force. Their bodies were found in two rooms on the first subbasement level and over in the residential tower. A dozen other members of the security team were actually members of the terrorist cells; most of them didn't know each other until that day.

Trace punched a hole into one of the glass walls on the observation deck at the top and helped lead the Delta assault. After they secured the area, a pair of fire department ladder trucks were brought in and hotel guests were evacuated down the ladders. After a few minutes, they decided the process would take too long and brought in one of those inflatable beanbags for people to jump onto. But there were something like three thousand rooms in the complex. Most were empty because of the parade, but they all had to be checked and secured. The explosions I'd heard were from C-4, which had been used not just on the windows but to create mouse holes into some of the rooms for the teams to get through.

"The SWAT team is going to try to get down to you," Danny said as I pounded the walls, trying to figure a way into the auxiliary power room. "We're going for the loading area right now. Some trucks are there. We have some Tangos, too."

I heard gunfire in the background as he handed off to Doc, who became my only link with the outside forces.

"Hey, Dick, you still got the Jitters unit with you?" asked Shunt.

"I'm using it as an expensive bullet stop," I told him.

"I got an idea. You think you could take that cable you found and connect one end into the commo unit and one end into a computer socket? You said there was one by the wall, right?"

"I think there were two. But they were shot to shit by machine guns, including mine."

"I'll tell you how to hardwire it," said Shunt. "It's not hard. If it's, like, connected to a bomb or something, I could disarm it, maybe."

Or set it off. Shunt didn't think about the downsides of his operations—maybe the geek *was* SEAL material after all.

"It'll take me a while to get it," I told him.

"I ain't going anywhere."

I trotted back through the maze of hallways, retracing my route. As I reached the stairwell door I realized I hadn't had to step over the two Tangos I'd killed earlier. I knew they hadn't crawled away; a slice of imported Swiss has fewer holes than they had. But I wasn't sure if I'd taken a different way back—or if someone had pulled the bodies out of the hallway.

I had almost reached the hall near the stairs when I remembered the gas. It took another ten minutes to back out and go around to the stairwell near the elevators, and then to climb back up to the main casino level. I heard a quick series of explosions in the distance and figured it was Danny and the rest of the boys trying to get into the dock area.

I was wrong, but I had no way of knowing that at the time.

As I reached the flight of stairs leading back to the main casino level, I heard footsteps above. Thinking it was Trace, Hulk, and the Delta team coming down, I yelled up that I was there. Three or four light bursts answered me. The gunfire had been unaimed and probably reckless, but it did a lot to accelerate my progress. I paused for a second at the door, pausing to listen. I wouldn't have heard anything softer than a jet engine inside. Not only was the door fairly thick, but the machines inside were still blazing away on backup power, filling the air with a kind of manic moan. I rolled out quickly and jumped to my feet, running back toward the two men and the Ethernet cable.

These corpses were where I'd left them. And as I'd told Shunt, the wall where the plugs were supposed to go was shot to shit. I hunted around for a few seconds on my hands and knees, looking to see if there was another access panel nearby. Finally I got Shunt back on the radio and told him it was time to turn Dickie into an honorary computer dweeb.

"I have a theory, Dude. Wanna hear it?"

"If it's relevant."

"I think that's, like, a bridge to connect one part of the network with another. Like, one side maybe has a bomb and the other side has the, like, control for it."

"Which is which?"

"We have to, like, find out."

"Cool, Shunt. Let's just fucking go for it, all right?"

"First make sure we can connect the line into the Jitters," he said.

"How do I do that?"

"Stick it in, Dude."

Excellent advice, applicable to all sorts of situations. In this case, the RJ-45 male connector snapped right into the female connection with a nice sharp click. Shunt then had me amputate the head off the other end and pry the cable into its component parts. I was left with eight thin wires that looked a lot like you'd find connecting telephones together. I'd done such a good job splattering the Ethernet connection that I had to rip up the wall above it to find the wires. While I hacked at it with my knife, the doorway to the nearest stairwell smacked open.

If the stairs hadn't been around a corner from me, the coroner would have tied a small tag on my toe that read "acute lead poisoning" and sent my organs over to the Betty Ford Clinic to be dried out before being sold for scientific experiments. By the time I had grabbed my gun and rolled into a defensive position, the bastard who'd come out of the stairwell had gotten enough of an angle through the room to fire. He had some sort of shotgun; now I know how Bambi's mother felt. He was also wearing a gas mask and wasn't that good a shot, though he was quick; it couldn't have taken me more than a millisecond to squeeze the trigger and return fire but he'd already managed to duck out of the way.

"Dick?" asked Shunt in the earpiece.

"Gotta take care of something first," I told him. I'd taken off the bulletproof vest to get the radio out and left it on the floor. There was no going back for it.

Bambi Killer pumped another wad in my general direction, just to let me know he still cared. I tracked to my left, trying to be quiet and circle around to get at him from behind. But the glass and debris on the floor made it difficult to be completely quiet, and before I got very far he sent another shell in my direction. I held up my MP5 and squeezed off a few rounds. As I fired, I threw myself across the open aisle, rolling across the thick red band of carpet that the Vegas casinos use to designate the area where kids have to stay when they move through the gambling areas. Bambi Killer didn't care for rug rats, so he sent another shell in my general direction—and I mean general, because none of the pellets came within six or seven feet, at least.

His aim might have been getting worse rather than better, but you have to respect a shotgun at close range or the undertaker'll be pulling pellets from your pimples for weeks to get you ready for the casket. So I made a circuit around the room on my hands and knees, staying as well-covered as I could. It must've taken me a good ninety seconds to get around to a spot behind him and work my way forward. In the meantime, he'd taken two more shots, both in the direction of the dead men. I guess he figured they were targets he could actually see; why waste bullets on one he couldn't?

I eased forward on my belly, waiting for him to stand or move out from behind the machines so I'd have a shot. As I did, I saw the door to the stairwell creeping open. I pushed back, swinging my gun around, my finger edgy on the trigger. A foot appeared, then the barrel of a gun; I brought mine to bear and nearly wiped out Hulk, who'd come down with Trace.

"Duck!" I yelled.

I think he did, though I was too busy swiveling around and tattooing my name on Bambi Killer's forehead to watch. The gun dropped from his hand without him getting another shot off.

"You almost missed him," said Trace, catching up with us after I kicked the shotgun away. It was a Remington 11-87, the tactical gun with a fourteen-inch barrel used by a lot of police departments. Maybe he'd had such bad luck aiming it because of the kick, which can be a tad heavier than other shotguns. Bambi Killer was a sawed-off runt of a pipsqueak, barely five-three. If you'd caught him fishing you wouldn't have thrown him back—you'd have brought him home, fattened him up in the bathtub for a few weeks, then thrown him back.

"How are five bullet holes in his forehead almost missing him?" I asked Trace, running back to my wiring project.

"If he'd've ducked, you would have just given him a haircut."

"He did duck," I told her. "It's not my fault he's a runt."

She filled me in on the progress upstairs and in the stairwell, where the Delta shooters had taken out two Tangos dressed in hotel livery. Two other bad guys had surrendered—one had blown himself up as he did.

"They used gas down there," I said.

"Tear gas. We haven't found any mustard gas here. It was all across the way in the container trucks."

"You haven't found it *yet,*" I told her. "Don't get cocky."

"Listen to who the fuck is talking."

"They're going to try to get into the power room downstairs," said Hulk. "Then they'll come reinforce us."

I told Trace to warn the Delta team that there was someone else roaming in the basement. While she talked to them and Hulk went on a recon, I fished out the wire I'd been hunting for earlier. Shunt talked me through the operation, which consisted of matching up the wires color for color. Finally, something I'd learned in high school paid off.

I had to hit a combination of keys on the Jitters

unit. When nothing happened on Shunt's end, I applied the other lesson I'd learned in high school—I gave the unit a good sharp smack on the side.

"Kick ass," yelped Shunt.

"Now what?"

"Now I rock, Dude."

Before I could quiz Shunt on the technical details, Hulk came back and told me he'd heard somebody pounding on the walls or door at the far end of the hallway. Trace joined us and we moved across the room quickly, covering each other as we ran up a flight of shallow steps through an interior garden flanked by pools. The hallway on the other side led to a mall of small shops selling overpriced goods that no one really needs. I'm surprised Trace's Y chromosome hadn't kicked in with all the fancy store windows nearby.

The hall where Hulk had heard the noises from the offices sat to the right; the mall branched to the left and then divided again. I was about to suggest we split up when something flitted around the corner at the far end of the hall with the offices.

Something small and round. Curiously shaped like a grenade.

We threw ourselves into reverse, managing to turn the corner as the grenade exploded.

As we made our way back up the corridor, I sent Trace on a flanking maneuver while Hulk and I took the direct approach. Three-quarters of the way down the hall Hulk pointed to a door with a sign marked EMPLOYEES ONLY. We could hear the sound of someone pounding on the wall inside with a frantic voice half sobbing as it asked to be rescued. Dickie wasn't born yesterday; there was no way I was going into that room, given that we had no way of knowing who was what. Not that leaving them here was a particularly safe move. I passed the location on to Doc, so he could send a Delta team to check it. Then Hulk and I continued forward.

At the end of the hall we faced a right-left decision. The area to the right held more offices; there were shops on the left as the hallway led back toward the mall area. I let Hulk go toward the mall while I checked the offices. These were empty, their doors open on the hall. All four offices were quiet, without even the hum of computers to break the silence.

By the time I caught up with Hulk, he'd cornered a clerk in the smoke shop where the clerk had been hiding under the Partagas cigars. The kid—he looked like he'd been shaving for maybe a month—had an employee tag and a wet spot in his pants. Of the two, the latter was considerably more convincing.

"Did they go to the security room?" Hulk asked him.

The kid stuttered something and shook his head.

"Where did they go?" Hulk asked.

More stutters and a whole lot of shakin', but the kid could have been talking in Martian for all we could decipher. Hulk's cheeks bulged out and he blew a long sigh from his mouth. Patience and understanding were clearly not in his character, but he took his best shot, reassuring the kid that we meant him no harm and wanted to help him. His face tinged red with the effort, and I'm not sure that it didn't make the kid even more scared. But finally the youth's stutters smoothed out and he said he'd seen the store employees and some of the guests herded through the mall around the time the parade started. The direction led to one of the auditoriums.

"Show us," I told him. I took his arm and tugged as gently as I could manage, which probably wasn't very. He shook like an outhouse in a windstorm, but he managed to lead us out into the hallway and down past some of the shops. Gunfire and explosions were rocking other parts of the hotel. Doc told us that the Delta teams had run into some terrorists downstairs and up in the hotel proper. The evacuation effort had stalled.

"Shunt, how are you doing with your hack job?" I asked as we made our way down the hallway.

"It's not really hacking, Dick."

"Shunt, is that computer system rigged into the bomb or not?"

"Yes and no."

We'd reached the box office area in front of the auditorium. There were definitely people inside; we could hear them banging and yelling.

"Straight answers, Shunt."

"They're not networked into the bomb, but they have some code for, like, uh, I'd call it a 'dashboard' to control it."

"Can you hack it?"

"I told you, it's not online. I think you might have stopped them before they got it connected. You got me connected to the control side. I don't have the bomb. But I think I can disable the control."

"So the bomb'll be defused if you do that?"

"Just, like, the control," said Shunt. "I think, like, I got it! Yeah."

"Hey, Dick, I wouldn't trust this computer shit," said Doc, breaking in. "They'd have a backup."

I didn't disagree. The problem was, without knowing where the bomb was physically located, we had no idea where the backup was likely to be located or how it would be rigged, let alone how to defuse it. Shunt threw out some ideas about looking for computer terminals and more wires; those weren't horrible ideas, except for the fact that there had to be hundreds of computers scattered through the place.

"Maybe the wire is the key," I said. "Shunt, where would it go?"

"Could go anywhere, Dude."

"Doc, look on your schematic and see if you can figure out where it might be," I told him.

In the meantime, it occurred to me that at least one of the bad actors would be sitting at a computer someplace in the building, ready to press the doom-on-us key when the connection was made. Presumably, he'd have the backup or know how to get it. So the next logical thing to do was find him.

"Shunt, can you figure out where the computers are that are working?" I asked. "That might tell us where the enemy is."

"Uh, not easily. Uh, like, I'd need a pretty detailed plan showing computer tags. If you had, like, a net administrator's chart of where he put everything, the physical units and stuff—"

"Doc, can you get that?"

"If it's available, sure."

The security room lay beyond the auditorium in another bunker. The response teams had the exterior door covered, but getting in would not be easy—it had been designed to withstand an attack by a bomb similar in size to the one that rocked the Beirut airport barracks and killed our Marines, sailors, and soldiers back in 1983.

Rest in Peace, brothers.

I left Doc and Shunt to work on that themselves while Hulk and I checked out the auditorium. Hulk was a half stride from the steps down to the doors when I grabbed him, stopping him just before he entered the beam of the electronic eye guarding the short flight down.

"They rigged a bomb," I said, pointing to the sensor. It was hooked into a wire that ran to a stack of brown boxes near the door.

The eye was the only sensor I could see. It looked like it had been intended only to take out the careless and slow down the careful. Of which I was neither.

"Down!" I yelled to Hulk, grabbing the kid and pushing him to the floor as a Degtyarev RPD machine gun began raking the lobby.

Machine-gun fire at very close range definitely discourages daydreaming. Something about a stream of lead smashing through the air a few inches from you concentrates your thoughts rather effectively. You don't worry about car payments or the last time you screwed your girlfriend, let alone your wife. You either return fire or you get the hell out of there, or both.

The ambush had been well-prepared, and if it

had kicked off thirty seconds earlier, we would have been fried. The most logical place to go was the well in front of the auditorium entrance, which of course was booby-trapped. The next most logical place was back the way we had come, but the machine gun had been set up to make that impossible. The least logical direction to go in was straight ahead.

So, naturally, that was the way I went.

The RPD is typically fired from a V-shaped bipod at the front, which helps stabilize the weapon when fired from a prone position. The design is simple and effective; you're talking about two short pieces of metal that are light and sturdy. The one weakness—which in most combat conditions would not be a weakness at all—is the difficulty of lowering the point of the barrel past a certain point to fire at very close range—say, six or seven feet in front of you. The shooter has to raise his body or at least his shoulder to narrow the angle. Not impossible, certainly, but not intuitive and not necessarily easy when you're already firing at very close range.

I'm not saying I thought of all of this as we were being fired on. I didn't think at all; I just did what comes naturally, and what had been pounded into my sorry ass back in the prehistoric cave-hunting days by people like Ev Barrett, seadaddy and chief par excellence. Call it a character flaw—when under attack, I counterattack. Always.

I managed to crawl and scramble to the side of the display case. If this had been Vietnam—which, obviously, Shadow had gotten her inspiration from—the sucker in the case would have been dead meat. I would have slipped an MK3A2* concussion grenade through the hole they'd cut in the glass for the gun and waited for the thud.

But this wasn't Vietnam, I didn't have a grenade, and the bullets were coming hot and heavy. I blasted my MP5 blind through the slit, emptying a clip on the bastard without any effect. Bullets continued to pour out of the ancient weapon, chewing everything in the lobby except for me, the kid who was frozen in place, and Hulk, who has a bigger butt than I do and had a harder time squeezing it low enough to avoid getting it shot off. By the time he managed to scoot up on the other side of the case, I'd already emptied my clip and reloaded.

The bullets stopped just as Hulk lifted his gun to add to the spray. I yelled to him to stay down.

He never heard me—my warning was drowned out by the sound of the booby-trapped machine-gun nest exploding.

* The MK3A2 is used in close-quarters combat because the effect of its blast is confined to a small area, unlike a fragmentation grenade (say, the M61), which does most of its damage by showering shrapnel all over the place. You still want to get out of the way.

22

Claymore mines make a distinctive sound right before they go boom. Not that many people can tell you about it, though, because most times you hear it, the next thing you hear is a choir of angels singing. If the ball bearings packed into the sucker don't kill you, the people who planted it usually will, since one of the best uses of the mine is to open an ambush.

Click, oops, boom. Or maybe more like ccc-luck-k, oops, boom.

Kkkkukkkck, oops, whaboooom!

The structure of the display area where the gun had been set up saved my ass. Steel frames had been used to hold the corner together there and they caught most of the explosive force and the shrapnel that headed in my direction. Some of the glass and other crap blown out by the mine rebounded crazily and cut the side of my face and hit my arm, but otherwise the little bent grenade with its cute "front toward enemy" script on the body missed me.

The same could not be said for Hulk, or the cigar-selling kid.

I didn't have to go over to the bodies to see that they were dead, and I didn't. And to tell you the truth, the fact that I'd lost someone who'd been working with me pretty closely didn't really register at that moment—the grief, I mean. I am a cold, heartless son of a bitch in combat. That's the way it is.

It does *suck*, yes. It sucks shit.

I crawled through the debris of the display area, past the machine gun. The entire thing had been rigged to fire on remote control—there was a small receiver box with an antenna at the side—but I couldn't find what they'd used to spot us. The shop sold clothes; it took me more than a minute to make sure all the mannequins were made out of plastic.

"Dick?" shouted Trace from the front of the store.

"I'm here," I yelled back.

I told her what had happened. She relayed the information that the Delta team had made some progress upstairs and down, but there was no way to get to the security bunker from this direction; it was blocked off by a set of the steel crash doors.

"Cavalry's on the way, Dick," said Doc, checking in. Danny and the rest of our people were moving in on the loading platform with the help of some shooters in protective NBC gear. (NBC stands for "nuclear-biological-chemical." The suits are bulky and hot as hell, but they do keep a lot of bad shit off you.)

Shunt groaned when I asked him for an update. "Computer on floor two at the back of the complex, beyond that area they call the 'Star Cruiser.' Like a restaurant or something? There's offices across a hall, according to the map. Somebody's issuing encrypted commands from there. I can't get into them."

The Star Cruiser was a two-story restaurant off the side of the mall where we were. It overlooked a garden that had been pimped up to look like something on another planet. There were two entrances from the mall, along with an elevator shaft that came onto the floor from a parking garage below. The elevator opened into a service area in the kitchen. We decided to take a shot at using the shaft, if possible, because both the other entries were close to the office where the computer was. The elevator was on the mall level and open, which made the move easy. It had a trapdoor at the top right-hand corner. I boosted Trace up and had her stand on my shoulders so she could reach the lock mechanism at the side. There was a large mechanical lever there to open the doors in an emergency. Pulling the lever released a lock on a set of gears; to open the doors themselves, you had to pry them apart. As she wrestled with that, I began climbing up one of the cables. I was just about to her level when the elevator started to move.

For a second or so, I couldn't figure out what the hell was going on. Then I realized that I was about to become a Marcinko pancake, squished into the small service area above the car. I suppose I might have been able to swing back and drop through the trapdoor into the car, but why go backward when you can go forward? I swung feet-first into the rear of the restaurant kitchen. Trace beat me by about a third of a second—long enough to heat up her submachine gun on the two assholes near the stove.

Which left me to take care of the jerk who'd punched the button on the elevator. He was on my right, or more accurately, on my neck, diving on top of me with his bare hands in a misguided show of courage.

One-two-three, stomp.

Then a double tap into the forehead.

Tango on ice for table two. I'd recommend a nice red wine to go with that, the color of his blood.

A double set of doors led from the kitchen to the dining area. One had been locked open, but there was no one in the dining area covering it—a ray of sunshine in an otherwise stormy day. We cleared through the dining area, ducking around serving stations that had been designed to look like space station consoles. The far end of the room opened onto the lower level and garden; the office with the computer sat on the far end of a long walkway almost directly across from the rail, but obstructed by the wall as it jutted out. There was no cover along the walkway; if we took it, we'd be exposed the whole way.

Much quicker to jump across.

"You're jumping a hundred feet?" asked Trace.

The word skeptical would not begin to describe the tone she used.

"Actually, I was thinking you'd go first," I said, pulling off my backpack. I had a nylon climbing rope coiled into the bottom. "Pretend you're Tarzan."

"This fucking rope isn't long enough."

And some women say size isn't everything. I unfolded a small grappling hook and tossed the rope toward one of the pipes holding the laser lights above. It took three tosses to connect. I pulled hard on the pipe and nothing happened, which I figured meant this was as good an idea as any.

I got about two-thirds of the way when the rope started to slip; by then I had all the momentum I needed. I crashed against the rail a bit lower than I'd intended, though fortunately not low enough or hard enough to turn me into a soprano. Trace had shouldered her submachine gun and started firing at the doorway; if I'd've needed any more motivation, the sound of bullets crashing all around me would have done the job nicely. Motivation was not my problem, however; gravity was. And gravity doesn't give a shit about desire. The railing started to give way, and I just barely managed to get my fingers locked on the ledge. I shifted my weight and threw my feet up, getting just enough leverage to roll up onto the walkway.

Trace stopped firing. I crawled around the wall, pulled up my weapon, and peeked around the corner. I couldn't see anything inside. I crossed without drawing fire. While Trace came round the long way, I eased through the threshold, trying to get a better idea of the layout. Doc had described it as three interconnected rooms with the door in the middle, but rather than a wall on the far side, I saw glass and the exterior.

"They want us to wait for the Delta team," hissed Trace behind me when she caught up. "They're on their way."

"We may be in little pieces by then," I said, leaping up and in.

Whoever had built Starship Vegas had altered the plans, at least as far as this room went. Where the blueprint had called for three rooms there was now only one. A large conference table sat on the immediate right; there was a receptionist's desk on the left. Another much larger desk sat off to the right on a raised platform.

There was no one in the room, but the computer was on. A screen saver tossed words around the screen:

DOOM ON YOU, DICKIE.

"Bad news, Dude," said Shunt. "There's another connection somewhere. Unknown player. It's looped in through one of the ports but I can't lock it out. I keep erasing it but it's still there."

"What are you talking about, Shunt? Speak English."

"You have to find another computer, Dude. It may be wireless, like a laptop or even a handheld. I think they're using it to control the shields and environmental system, stuff like that."

"Not the bomb?"

"I don't think so. I have a window open watching it. I don't think it's connected."

"You sure?"

"No."

"Can you find that other computer?" I asked.

"I'm trying."

"All right."

Trace and I heard a steady beat of explosions downstairs and in the hotel area to the left as the Delta and SWAT teams continued to clear out the hotel. We took a breather on the walkway in front of the office and were looking over the rail as the first of the Delta boys came in. I gave them a big wave; they told me to hold my hands out and not try anything funny, motherfucker!

Once we cleared up that little miscommunication, Trace and I took one of the stairways down. The Delta boys estimated that there were three hundred people up in the rooms, along with everyone still trapped in the auditorium. One of the SWAT teams was working on an alternative way into the theater. The emergency exits had been chained and booby-trapped, and the walls were solid cement and rebar, so the job wasn't quite a no-brainer. They had taken some heavy-duty saws to the roof and were hoping to cut a passage.

"You think one of the people we got coming out of the elevator was Shadow?" asked Trace.

"No. Shadow's a she."

"Not necessarily. The voice was a woman's, but that doesn't mean it belonged to Shadow. There's no proof of that at all. It might be another one of the bastard's misdirection plays."

She was right, but even so, I knew she was wrong. I'd spoken to Shadow. That was her. What I didn't know was whether she was in the hotel. From what Shunt had said, it was possible that she was pulling the levers by remote control somewhere nearby—or not even all that nearby.

Doc reported that the Delta shooters were ready to launch the assault on the security bunker but decided to wait until the hotel had been evacuated before taking their shot.

"Probably do best just to let the assholes blow themselves up at that point," I told him.

"That's not much of a joke, Dick."

"It's not meant to be."

"Any more ideas on where the bomb might be?" I asked.

"Thinking now is it's in the security bunker with them."

That didn't make sense—not because I didn't think the assholes would kill themselves but because the bunker's walls would lessen the impact of the blast on everyone else. They wanted a *serious* boom.

Trace and I decided to split up. She'd go and check with the team taking on the auditorium, while I cut back around and hooked up with Danny, who was in the process of securing the loading dock area. So far, they hadn't found any of the mustard gas, nor had any of the fancy chemical sniffers the Delta people had with them.

I passed down a wide staircase through a hall lined with crystal and metal sculptures. There were more laser lights and machines that were used to generate holograms all along the floor and side of the steps. The power failure had taken them off-line. The fact that they weren't working made the place look even more futuristic and bizarre. I felt like I was walking through the back end of a saucer headed out to Alpha Centauri and beyond. The hall opened into another gambling area, this one reserved for higher-stakes games. The backup lights were starting to dim and flicker; I paused for a moment to let my eyes adjust. The MP5 was still in my hand, fully loaded; I had one more clip in my backpack.

I had just picked up the radio to double-check the layout with Doc when I heard something crashing at the far end of the room. I spun around and dropped to my knee as a set of double doors at the far end of the room burst open. Three or four dozen people burst through the doorway.

"Stop!" I yelled. "Down."

A quick burst from my gun got the attention of the few people who hadn't heard me or understood. They fell quickly, toppling against one another. I got Doc on the radio, telling him to get one of the Delta teams down quickly. While I waited, one of the people on the floor explained that they were all casino guests who'd been herded into the bar area by the security people right before the kickoff of the parade, supposedly because they wanted to sweep the gambling room after a bomb alert. Once they were inside, the doors had been locked. They'd watched quite a bit of the festivities on the televisions in the room—which had turned out to be a bar.

If you have to be a hostage, there are worse places to be kept.

The people who'd been inside the bar had no other useful information. When the Delta people arrived, I excused myself and went back down the hallway. I got about halfway through another gaming room when I heard pounding to the right. I turned and saw a set of glass doors with six or seven people behind them; it was another bar.

I'm not too good at lip-reading, but a reasonable guess at what they were saying would have been: "Let us out." I waved at them, then pulled out my radio to call another team down. As I did, one of the larger hostages picked up a table and attempted to crash it through the glass. He rebounded back and crumpled to the floor, falling backward with the table right on top of him.

As I started to laugh, I felt the tip of a gun pressing hard against the back of my head.

23

"The first thing you're doing is dropping your machine gun," said a male voice that sounded vaguely British. "Very slowly or you die right here."

"What's the difference where I die?"

"Your choice."

I held out the MP5 and let it drop to the ground. "I hope I chose wisely."

"And the pistol. The P7 and the Glock 26. I read the books, Dick; I know you carry a little Glock besides your everyday cannon."

"Well, fuck you very much." I dropped the H&K P7, then started to reach down for the Glock at my ankle. He jabbed hard with his pistol. I held my hands out, demonstrating that I intended to be compliant. Then I reached down and removed the gun.

Only the one. That's why I don't put *everything* in the books.

I smiled for the audience behind the doors, hoping that one of them had a cell phone and was smart enough to use it. As it turned out, the casino had installed devices to prevent people from using cell phones in the gaming areas. The idea was to kill any quick calls from Churchill Downs a millisecond before the tape delay, I guess. Tuned to specific frequencies, it only affected cell phones and was still operating with the backup power.

I think the alien holding the gun saw my reflection in the glass, and something about it pissed him off. Or maybe he just felt awful ornery at that moment. Whatever—he pulled the gun back and went to jab it harder in my neck.

He missed, though.

How could he miss when the distance was what? Three inches? My elbow in his rib had something to do with it. That and the pivot that brought me around into his back, helping me to use his own momentum to push him forward. I flew down after him, pounding him into the glass door as the gun went flying. It took a couple of hard thwacks before he stopped trying to get away, and another two before he stopped writhing completely. It must not have been pretty, because the people on the other side of the glass door were cringing when I looked.

Moral of the story: never stick a gun in Demo Dick's neck. If you get the drop on him, stand a goodly distance away, or he'll drop you.

A moral taken to heart by the runt I saw standing across the room with a dumb-ass smirk on his face when I turned after picking up the pistol the alien had so conveniently dropped.

"Everything you say about yourself is true," said the man.

I didn't know him, but I'd seen his ugly Asian

face before. Wiry and athletically built, he could have been anywhere from thirty to forty-five years old. He was the French agent who'd had his head chopped off in Tell-Me-Dick's territory to start this little misadventure.

They are doing *wonders* with reconstructive surgery these days.

Being that he was a French agent, I had a reasonable chance that he might be on my side. Of course, being that he was French, I had just as reasonable a chance that he wasn't.

"You want to drop the gun, Dickie," he said, erasing any doubt about whose side he was on. He raised his hand, revealing an Ingram MAC-10. Not a very big gun as guns go, but certainly capable of complicating my dinner plans.

Of course, I had a decent weapon myself. The alien had come to the party with a Beretta 92F, the basic Italian Stallion stopper adopted, with some slight mods, by the U.S. military as the M9.

"I'd say it's more like a standoff," I told Frenchie. "If anything, I have a height advantage."

"If your gun were loaded, I might agree."

Was the gun a little on the light side? Did it feel empty?

"Go ahead and take a shot," said the Frenchman. "Go ahead."

I'm standing across the room from a guy with a MAC-10 who's daring me to shoot him. There was only one thing to do—dive to the ground while squeezing the trigger as many times as possible, landing next to one of my own weapons and scooping it up in case he wasn't lying.

A great plan. Unfortunately, the man with the MAC decided to demonstrate that his weapon *was* loaded. He sent my weapons sailing well out of reach, and I was lucky to stop short of his gunfire.

For the record, he hadn't been lying; my gun was empty.

Doom on me.

"This way, stepping around the guns and the body, please. There were thirty rounds when I started, yes. I'd say I have more than half left, wouldn't you?"

Probably more, but what's a few hunks of lead between friends, right?

"What'd you do, Pierre?" I asked. "Kill somebody about your age and size so the Frenchies wouldn't come looking for you?"

"You're not as dumb as your books make you out to be," he said.

Ouch.

"I saw your apartment back in Virginia," I told him, walking out as he directed. I glanced at the folks behind the glass, back to hoping they had working cell phones. "And the pictures in the apartment in Paris. If I were you I'd start shopping for a new decorator."

"That was my sister's handiwork. If it were up to me I would have simply killed you and been done with it."

"I hope I meet your sister."

"You will. She's particularly sadistic."

"Sounds like my kind of girl."

"Walk faster," said Pierre. "Or I'll simply kill you here."

He had me go down the hallway to a stairwell where the door had been propped open. I thought as I approached it I might be able to kick the door free, but he closed the distance between us quickly, and it didn't feel like I could break away cleanly enough to escape being shot. He barked at me to go up. I started climbing the metal steps; this was a utility area and the fancy laser shit and the gee-whiz chrome were noticeably absent. I didn't have a good schematic of the hotel in my head, and so it seemed to me that I was going upstairs into the areas the Delta boys were sweeping. That wasn't a bad thing, so on I trudged, until by the sixth or seventh flight I realized I'd miscalculated. We weren't in the main part of the hotel; we were in the space needle—the opposite end of the complex from my SpecOp buddies.

Pierre trailed me by a half staircase. Every time I slowed the bastard growled at me to keep going, and if I picked up my pace he kept right with me. It was damn annoying.

The one thing I was able to do was reach into my pocket and lock the transmit button on the backup radio as we rounded the final turn. I could at least give Doc the play-by-play.

"At the landing, go through the door," Pierre told me as we reached the last set of steps. "Then climb the ladder."

"You got to be kidding me. You're not going to make me climb that way, are you? Can't we take the elevator or something?"

"You're getting old, Dickie. Very old."

"That's the truth."

Whining had no effect. Pierre *had* read the books, or at least enough of them to know that if we were locked in a close space together he wouldn't stand a chance. I opened the door and started climbing—and climbing, and climbing. The ladder was in an access tunnel that rose through the core of the narrow building, probably between the elevators, though from where I was I couldn't tell. Battery-powered backup lights lit the space every twenty or thirty feet, but they were dimming and in several cases already out. After a few minutes of climbing, my arms started to feel tired and my shins threatened to cramp. I don't want to compare it to the training I went through during my UDT days—that was rigorous bullshit in every dimension, not pansy-ass climbing up to the sky with handy rungs for your hands and feet. But I was younger then and completely crazy. Getting older and being only half insane takes a little adrenaline out of you.

I kept going, hoping to put enough distance between Pierre and me to grab my hideaway and pop a few caps through his crown. I couldn't get my second Glock while I was moving, not easily anyway. I figured I would sprint ahead, feign fatigue—hell, I didn't have to *act*—hunch over, and pretend to rest while I fished out the gun. But Pierre must've eaten his Wheaties that day; he stayed practically on my boots the whole way.

The Space Needle was 1,473 feet tall—supposedly designed to top the Stratosphere Tower farther down the Strip by more than 10 percent. There was some local debate over whether the needle at the very top above the observation deck should be counted in the official measurement, but, either way, that's a ridiculous height, even if you don't get aboard the starship ride that whips around the outer shell near the top.

That wasn't our destination. We weren't going to the restaurant, either. Frenchie had me climb all the way to the very top of the tower. Finally a shaft of light caught me as I climbed, the proverbial light at the end of the tunnel. Someone leaned over the side and laughed. The sound echoed weirdly.

The sister, obviously. Shadow herself.

Good-looking woman, the kind who looks prettier at thirty-five than she did at fifteen. Asian features like her brother, short dark hair, trim body, and sarcastic sneer.

Plus she had an assault rifle in her hand. Gotta love a woman who knows how to accessorize.

I paused, leaning toward the ladder to see if I might be able to take a chance and get the gun. But Pierre was too close.

"You guys aren't going to tell me I'm your father, right?"

"You wish. Keep moving, Dickie."

"What'd you do, work together? Play kind of a tag team to make sure you were always where I was?"

"I'll plug you right here, Dick. All the same to me."

"You shoot me I'm going to fall on you and you'll go down, too."

"Keep moving."

"I get to find out what the story is, right? How come you guys want to blow up Las Vegas."

"Don't you think it deserves to be blown up?" asked the girl above.

"Hell, no. I like Vegas."

"Cox did," she said.

"That why you killed him?"

"Keep moving, Dickie," said Pierre.

The girl laughed at the top of the ladder. "We don't give a shit about Vegas, Dick. Or Cox. He started to get in the way at the end, and so we took care of him. If it had been up to him, you wouldn't be here. We don't even care about the Muslim rag-heads who set this all up. It took them years, Dickie. Years. But as far as we're concerned, this is just a convenient place for you to die."

"The way you were arranging it, I would have thought you'd lure me all the way over to Nam," I told her. "What's that about?"

This struck Pierre as being funnier than shit and he started laughing and repeating it as I climbed the last twelve or so feet to the roof. His words started echoing in the small space the way ideas bounce around in your head when you have a fever.

What's that about? What's that about?

One piece of slang I vowed never to use again in my life. Unfortunately, at that particular moment, it looked like a very easy promise to keep; my life expectancy could be measured by an egg timer.

"So this is the part where you tell me what's going on, right?" I asked as I climbed up into the light at the top.

French girl laughed. Pierre—

Pierre screamed. Because as I stepped into the light I stumbled slightly, and my boot caught the side of his hand. I'd aimed for his face, but at that point I wasn't in a position to be particularly choosy. I stomped and he tried to shoot me with the MAC-10. A fatal mistake—it made it too easy to kick at his hand again. He slipped and rebounded two or three times as he fell; I heard the clatter and the thuds. The gun stopped firing as I rolled to the ground, fishing out my mini-Glock and rolling to my feet on the roof.

French girl was standing there, smiling, holding an AK-47 on me. If you're a connoisseur, you might want to note that it was a model with a folding stock, and that stock had been folded down—an AKMS—which I do not recall being a very popular model in Vietnam, though I'll leave it to others to judge French girl's devotion to period accuracy.

We stood across from each other, separated by maybe twenty feet. It was impossible for me to miss. From everything I had seen so far, I doubted she would, either. The helicopters that had been patrolling were nearby. I hoped there was a sharpshooter aboard at least one of them—and that they realized I was the tall one.

"Just you and me now, huh, Dick?" said Shadow.

"Sorry about your brother."

"It's all right. We're blowing up the hotel, anyway. He wouldn't have lived much longer." Still holding the gun in one hand braced against her side, she reached to her belt and held up a PDA. I gathered it was the other device Shunt had mentioned earlier. And contrary to what he had said, my bet was that it would detonate the bomb.

"Why are you going to kill yourself?" I asked.

"Because once you're dead, the game's over. You're the only reason my brother and I are still alive, Dick Marcinko. I should call you Rick; that's how my father knew you."

"Your father North Vietnamese?"

I wouldn't give a dog the look she gave me at that.

"He was an *American.*"

"I don't get it."

She raised the hand with the small computer.

"You go through all this trouble and then you kill me without savoring my look of bitter realization when you tell me what the hell is going on?"

"Fuck you, Marcinko," she said, moving her thumb to the PDA's touch screen.

I had one shot, and I took it—aiming squarely at the PDA.

I fucking missed. The bitch had stepped back and jumped off the building.

Fortunately, I only missed by a half inch. My shot carried through her hand before she could touch the screen.

Shadow dropped the PDA as she fell. The PDA fell onto the deck's patio below, smashing into a dozen pieces as she plunged toward the ground.

Excuse me if I don't shed a tear.

24

The girl's name was Yi Chi du Boc, and her brother's name was Luc. They were Vietnamese refugees who'd managed to get to France with their mother roughly twenty years before—boat people who'd gotten out by spending several weeks on the deck of an overloaded fishing boat, tossed by the waves. It's not clear exactly how they managed to get to France, or how their mother swung the paperwork. She claimed that her father was French, and that the French colonial authorities had recognized her citizenship. It was an extraordinary claim—but her papers proved it. She was granted admission to the country and recognized as a citizen, as were the kids.

The mother was named Lili. She was the daughter of a Frenchman, and he had acknowledged her, but he'd left with no papers to prove it. The Vietcong had killed him when Lili was ten or eleven; she liked to think that he would have formalized the paperwork if he'd the time.

Lili had managed to get legitimate-looking papers because of another Westerner she met, this one an American. The Westerner was her lover and the father of the two children she brought to France with her in the late Seventies. His name was Horace. He did know me back in Vietnam. And I suppose, in a strange way, I did have something to do with his death.

Horace—his full name was Horace S. Alston—worked liaison with the CIA. He was ex-military, not a career agent, one of the people the CIA hired as "contract agents" when they need someone who understood the meaning of "tactical intelligence"—and when the Agency purebreds didn't want to get their white collars bloody.

Horace was the contact agent for operational units in Vietnam working the Phoenix Program and Provincial Reconnaissance Units, which were called "PRUs" back in the day. He personally delivered payroll to these units and collected intel reports throughout his region. Horace's territory was the Delta—my area of interest during Vietnam as well. I guess we had run into each other a time or so.

Maybe a little more than that.

Horace had a pretty steady little milk route, going out of Saigon, west to Cambodia, and all along the river there, making contact with the local PRUs and keeping tabs on a program called "Coyote Walks." A bit of Coyote Walks came out to the public as the Phoenix Program; to this day, I believe the orders forbidding me to talk about its details remain in force.

So we'll skip the details. The general idea was that the locals would collect information, take out bad guys, and everything would work out in the end. Horace had helped oil the machine. Besides the regular payments he delivered, Horace paid extra for weapons captured and especially valuable intel collected. Not coincidentally, the information tended to be collected off DEAD targets of opportunity.

I was not happy with American intelligence in Vietnam; you can check out the whys and wherefores in *Rogue Warrior,* which lays out as much as I legally can say about what happened in the lovely Southeast Asian jungles. So, after a while, I began collecting my own intelligence. I ran my own nets and placed my own people in PRU units; eventually I got my people assigned to Coyote Walks. The advantages were that I got "real" intel from the bad guys' mouths. It was a two-way street; the program and PRUs got U.S. firepower from my patrols and "on call" artillery and TAC Air when I was with them.

Horace and I weren't enemies. We weren't friends, but we weren't enemies. Among the things I didn't like about Horace was the fact that he always stuck to his same stinking schedule for his milk runs. He went to village A on Monday, village B on Tuesday, and on and on. Now, if he'd been a milkman, that would have been commendable. But out in the jungle, dealing with people who were damn good at picking up on patterns, it was foolish. I'd yelled at him a time or two about it and even changed scheduled meets at the last minute when my intelligence or gut warned me away.

A few weeks before I was supposed to go home, Horace and I scheduled a little exchange that featured something a little special—a live North Vietnamese POW. Horace came north on his usual run, flying in an Air America helo. (Air America was the CIA's own private airline.) But I had gotten hung up with my prisoner due to some other action a little farther down the Delta and never made the meet. Horace showed, spent a little time taking my name in vain, then took off to make his next appointment. That was the last time anyone ever saw Horace S. Alston alive.

The CIA suspected that Horace took off with the dough. That wasn't quite true. The wreckage of the helo was found a few weeks later. Both the pilot and Horace were dead; the money was gone. Had he been killed because of the payroll he was carrying, which was never recovered? Because of the NVA POW? Because of simple stupidity called PATTERN?

Probably all three.

It's even possible his kids were right. He might have been killed because of me, in a way. There was a price on my head, and the local Vietcong and North Vietnamese were extremely interested in collecting it. My POW had been extremely talkative and not too hard to capture. Was he part of a setup?

It never occurred to me to ask, and I wouldn't have had the chance if it did. A day after the pickup didn't come off, the POW tried to blow me up with a hand grenade. He took himself out instead.

Horace's mama-san had a one-year-old girl at home and a boy in the oven. The mama-san was Lili. You've already met her progeny.

I found this all out, or most of it, when I went to France right after we got Las Vegas straightened out. I went over partly to tell the French in person what had happened so they could turn their security apparatus upside down—and kick the asshole in the butt who'd put my would-be assassin on his payroll. But I also wanted to talk to Lili, who'd been tracked down by one of the Frenchmen working on Doc's tips. I wanted to know why the pair hated somebody they'd never met and never had any reason to hate. Hating somebody so bad you want to kill him is one thing. Hating him badly enough to want to kill yourself in the process—that's something else again. So I went to see her.

The old lady lived in an apartment out near the Catacombs. The Catacombs lie on the southern edge of Paris; they're old quarries lined with bones removed from the French cemeteries and stacked there for people to gawk at. If you're over sixty, they let you in for free. The French have that kind of sense of humor.

Lili didn't recognize me, of course, but she knew who I was when I told her. She let me in, made some tea, and outlined her life, and theirs.

They'd heard a lot about me. I was a ridiculously trivial part of the story of their father's life, but every time his death was mentioned, I was there. As the story was told over and over, I got stuck with being the bad guy—if it weren't for me, their father would have taken them to America. If it weren't for me and my reports about the lousy intelligence Coyote Walks provided, the CIA might have called him a hero. They wouldn't have had to scrape by near the Catacombs of France. They wouldn't have had to live in poverty. They wouldn't have had to shiver at night, or eat a half cup of noodles every day of the week. It wouldn't have rained; their shit would never have stunk. I became everything that was wrong in the world by the time they were teenagers.

Somewhere along the way, the fact that it was the VC who popped Horace got lost. But I guess you could be philosophical about it and say it wasn't me they hated. It was fate, or Mr. Murphy, or whatever fancy word you want to use. I was just a stand-in.

Had Lili done it? Was she the one who transferred the need for vengeance to her kids? That would have made sense, right? The viper poisoning her young. But no venom came through in her voice or her eyes when we spoke. And if she hated me—if she felt *anything* toward me, it didn't come through. As a matter of fact, if she felt concern for her children, remorse for their deaths, sadness, anything—it wasn't evident that afternoon, or in the apartment. She had two small photos of them on the television, old pictures that hadn't been dusted in months.

On the other side of the room, she had a small altar honoring the dead of her family. Her children hadn't made it to the altar yet; you have to be dead for a certain period of time before you get your own sacred tokens and offerings.

The altar thing is a Buddhist tradition throughout Asia; families make offerings to the souls of their ancestors who have gone on. Exactly what the offerings are depends on the tradition, but the idea is that you feed the dead and they help you. If you don't, they become hungry ghosts, haunting humans, seeking vengeance. Some of the ghosts haunt specific people who have wronged them in life or even in death; their family usually, though not necessarily. Others just haunt whoever happens to be handy.

The French were clueless when I told them about Pierre. They'd checked the kid out nine ways to Sunday and couldn't find a flaw. I'm not totally sure they believed what I told them, either. At one point, one of the Frenchmen asked if I thought Pierre and his sister were secretly Muslims, as if you had to be Islamic to be crazy enough to want to kill people.

Asshole.

But thinking back, maybe he wasn't *that* far wrong. For Pierre and Yi, killing me *was* a religion. It gave them all the meaning they needed.

I think they probably deliberately helped the Muslim terrorists make their connections in America because that's where I was. One group of crazies helping another. There was no proof, though. There seldom is.

"Oh," said Trace when I told her the story. "Now I see."

"See what?"

"I thought the coyotes were a metaphor. But the image was literal."

"What the fuck are you talking about?"

"The coyotes in my dream. The brother and sister—the CIA project Horace was involved in was called Coyote Walks."

Don't ask me how she knew, because the damn program is *still* under wraps, but I have it on reliable authority that she's right.

I knew some of what Cox had done by then, though it took an FBI investigation for the rest of the details to come out. Cox hated Las Vegas for the reasons mostly articulated by the newspaper story. Not that you should think his father's only flaw was gambling. His interest in commercial fishing exposed him to the opportunities of fair market trading on the high seas. Buried in one of the police reports that wasn't released about his death is a line about "at-sea transfers of contraband and/or drugs" that may have provided some seed money for the older Cox to subsequently lose in his Las Vegas investment program. Only the gambling was documented as the culprit in the family. Can't blame them, I guess, even if it did skew their view of the world.

Bureaucratic sled dog that he was, Cox spent quite a lot of effort every day just trying to keep his job; he wasn't the brightest pup in the litter. He ended up being used by smarter people with agendas, as I had seen with the NSA and bank adventure. Somewhere along the way, Shadow and her brother glommed on to him through the terrorist connection. They started feeding him information, which helped him look good. I'm not precisely sure how that got started—not even Karen could find out, and if she can't find something out, it can't be found—but they must have supplied him with something related to a drug deal in the City of Sin, and I suspect that at that point he reacted with so much enthusiasm about screwing Las Vegas that they knew they had their man. They just had to reel him in.

Was he dirty? Or just a dupe?

Can't tell you. I think he probably thought he could play both ends against the middle. I think he honestly wanted me at the port because he didn't want the place blown up. I think he hated Las Vegas, but I don't know that he hated it *enough* to fall in line with a terrorist plot to blow it up. I think he did realize that the terrorists were running drugs and smuggling all sorts of things like weapons in and out of the country, and I think he wanted to do something about it. He just wasn't smart enough to do the *right* thing about it.

But that's my opinion; you'll have to form your own on that.

This much I know, because they told me: one of the du Bocs, or maybe both, killed him in Vegas. And the whole story of what happened between him and them died that night as well.

The FBI shut down the Bosnian company after the dust settled in Vegas. That's the Fucked-up Bureau of Incompetents for you; they spring into action once it's safely too late. Any day now they'll be telling us that Abe Lincoln's been shot and they think they know who did it.

The French were right about how the cells worked. What the French didn't understand was how long these people had been working on this. Nearly a ton of Semtex had been installed in Starship Vegas, apparently by cells completely unrelated to the ones that tried to detonate it. In fact, if it hadn't been for the du Bocs infiltrating the system and trying to use it for their own personal vengeance, it's likely the radical ragheads would have succeeded. There would have been no dramatics on the top of the tower, no hesitation pushing the button. Two of the drivers of the gas-rigged trucks blew themselves up rather than let themselves be captured. Another gave it a good try, but the asshole hadn't wired himself properly. I promise to do it for him as soon as he returns from whatever rock they're going to hide him under for the next fifty or sixty years.

All of the cells that were involved were rounded up. That wasn't a huge accomplishment: a good portion, including everyone who'd infiltrated the hotel's security staff, were already dead, killed either by me or during the assault or in a last suicide pact in the bunker. Not one of the people who took over the hotel had been on any sort of watch list at all.

The funding network, the infrastructure that made this all possible—was still there, untouched. Inconvenienced a bit, with the import-export business down and the agency that doesn't exist now wise to their methods, but the bottom line is: they're still there. Osama, or whichever crazy asshole beyond him is calling the shots . . . still there.

In my view, their big mistake was importing the old gas. Tests the Army conducted on the canisters after the fact found that the stuff, though still nasty, had lost a good portion of its potency. There's a lot worse stuff in train yards and truck depots and nuke plants all across America. Nobody wants to hear about it, though.

"It's too damn depressing, Dick."

"You're becoming a pessimist."

Let me be optimistic for a second; let me put on my positive-thinking hat: I am a mean, wrathful son of a bitch, and I am sure that's the way the world really works.

Doom on us if we don't get wise to it. *Ah, for the peace and quiet of a small war!!!*

Index

Atria Books
Proudly Presents

HOLY TERROR

Richard Marcinko
and Jim DeFelice

Coming soon in hardcover from
Atria Books

Turn the page for a preview of
HOLY TERROR. . . .

Part One

Italian Holiday

1.

A piece of advice in case you ever find yourself on top of the dome of St. Peter's Basilica in Vatican City—watch out for the cross at the very top of the spire. It is a hell of a lot sharper than you'd think.

The roof tiles are pretty slippery, too, particularly the ones with the pigeon shit on them.

On the other hand, the view is to die for. Especially if you're up there with a maniac who's waving a Beretta Model 12S 9mm submachine in your face.

Yeah, I know what you're thinking: That Beretta's a great gun, but the frame tends to crack under the weight of too many hot rounds. The maniac would have been much better off with an H&K MP5; a lot less chance of a misfire.

I would have pointed this out myself but he didn't seem in the mood for constructive criticism. He had a shitass grin on his face, the sort that says "Eat lead and die, Marcinko."

The tips of my fingers started to sweat. They say the dome over St. Peter's is the biggest in the world, but at that moment it felt extremely small. When he swung the business end of the 12S toward me, it felt absolutely claustrophobic.

My own weapon lay on the roof below, out of ammo. It looked like I had two options—throw myself at him in the vain hope of somehow wrestling the gun from his paws before he managed to kill me, or . . .

I couldn't think of an *or,* actually.

But maybe I should explain how I came to be in such an exalted position in the first place. It's not every day that you get a private tour of the most famous rooftop in Christendom. And what got me out into the Roman sunshine wasn't your typical goatfuck . . . it was a truly *artistic* one, the sort of thing that would have made Michelangelo proud. So let's go back to the beginning. . . .

This particular adventure began with a fax that arrived at Rogue Manor on Christmas Eve a few months before. The sheet was blank except for a web address in the middle of the page. It was a bit past ten p.m. and Rogue Manor was empty except for yours truly. With nothing else to do but await the arrival of Ol' Saint Nick, I turned on the computer and typed in the address, which mostly consisted of numbers and backslashes. I vaguely recall thinking I'd see a picture of Santa and one of his elves in a compromising position. Instead, I found myself looking at a page filled with type so small I had to hit the magnifier button three times. It turned out to be a turgid dissertation on the coming end of the "Crusader Epoch," the inevitable clash of "a great civilization with a decript (SIC) one," and the unstoppable rise of the True People of the Book. Clement Moore, or whoever wrote "'Twas the Night Before Christmas," has nothing to worry about.

We get tons of emails, faxes, and letters from wacko crazies at Rogue Manor, and this one probably would have faded into the hazy recesses of my mental round file except for the signature at the bottom of the Web page. The "communiqué of fervor" had been signed with the name "Saladin."

In case obscure, failed world leaders doesn't happen to be your favorite Jeopardy category, here's a quick info dump on Saladin: Also known as Salah al-Din and a half-dozen similar variations, Saladin was an eleventh-century Egyptian warrior who took Jerusalem from the crusaders. He built the wall that surrounds the old city and was the first pan-Arab to try to consolidate all Arab people under the green banner of Muhammad. He failed—not for want of trying or low body count—but has remained a source of inspiration ever since. Many an Arab leader has used him as a role model, reinterpreting history and the legend through his own distorted glasses. Nasser, Saddam Hussein, even the Shah of Iran viewed him as an inspiration. Osama bite-my-butt Laden didn't use the name, but it isn't hard to see parallels between his aims and Saladin's goal of a pan-Arab empire.

Over the years I've had various encounters with would-be Saladins, some of whom were actually credible opponents. Probably the most notable was in Cairo during the 1990s. I won't bore you with more back story than necessary here; suffice it to say that the name piqued my interest. The Web page was on a site that belonged to an international drug company. Clearly, it had been hacked into. When my computer guy checked with the firm the day after Christmas, they expressed complete surprise.

At least that's how he interpreted the words "Holy shitfuck—what the hell is this?"

(My self-anointed "computer dude" and all-around tech expert is a tech-head wop dweeb named Paul Guido Falcone, a wiseass known to us as "Shunt." Shunt has shunts in his head. They're some sort of metal inserts placed into his skull because he was born with water in his skull; I think of them as brain gutters. He's loads of fun with metal detectors.)

A few days later, another fax arrived with a new Web address. Here was posted a new dissertation repeating the main points of the first—history was on the side of the schizophrenics, etc. It concluded by making some predictions: a new leader would arise to knit together the worldwide network of murdering assholes, and his name was—guess now—Saladin.

And by the way, as a display of the new leader's power, a small incident would occur the next day as a signal to the brothers of faith and insanity that the time for war would begin.

The time was given as 00–00–01 but no place was specified. Even though it was an open-ended and nonspecific threat, I reported it anyway, filing the information with both Homeland Security and the CIA (also known as the Christians In Action). I also forwarded a bunch of heads-up to a number of friends and acquaintances in the terrorist threat business, figuring one more wild-goose chase would just make the holiday season that much more enjoyable.

At roughly the same time I was burning up the phone lines, a fax similar to mine arrived at *al-Jazeera,* the mouthpiece long favored by crazies and psychos wrapping themselves in the word of Muhammad, blessed be his name. The fax was turned over to the reporter in charge of wacko ramblings, who dutifully plugged the address into his browser and began reading Saladin's communiqué, which in this case was written in Arabic. While most of the rant was familiar—war of civilizations, death to the crusaders, etc.—this one contained more specific predictions relating to mayhem, promising uprisings across the globe, especially in that holy wasteland known as Afghanistan. It also mentioned that a certain liquefied gas ship on its way from Malaysia to a new port in China would be blown up to start the new millennium of Allah's Paradise. Once more the time was given as 00:00:01.

The reporter considered the matter, then decided to report it, only to find that the ship had been blown up. He subsequently determined that the time of the explosion was correct or at least close enough to count—assuming your watch was set to the time in Mecca, Saudi Arabia, arguably the center of the worldly universe if you're Muslim. The reporter wrote a story, and for maybe twenty-four hours the world's intelligence agencies spent considerable resources trying to profile Saladin. I received not one, not two, but three separate calls from analysts at the Christians In Action about Saladin, the Web pages, and the faxes. I told them everything I knew, which wasn't much. The NSA—"No Such Agency," the ultra-secret eavesdropping and electronic snoops over at Fort Meade—did a frantic search through its archives to see what it had snooped out on Saladin without knowing who he was. The Chinese loaded a group of special agents aboard a destroyer and shipped them over to interview the survivors. Forensics specialists from six or seven different countries flew out to the wreckage, most of which was at the bottom of the Pacific and out of reach.

The sum total of all this work was a big fat zero. Nothing that the crew members said proved conclusively that a bomb had caused the explosion. The safety record of the company involved was rather lackluster, and while it would have taken extraordinary incompetence to cause an accidental explosion—well, let's just say that extraordinary incompetence was not in short supply.

The experts concluded that the explosion had occurred *before* the faxes were sent. Because of this, they decided, it was possible that Saladin had heard of the disaster and was trying to take credit for it to boost his own standing in the community of crazies. This especially made sense given that they could find no other evidence of his existence before the fax I received. And in fact there was almost no evidence that he did exist, except for the faxes and Web site.

I agreed to let the NSA baby-sit my fax line for a few days; nothing came in other than some long-shot predictions on the Super Bowl. Saladin quickly slipped off their radar scope.

And mine. The lack of follow-up over the next few days convinced me that this was just one more Osama Wannabe looking to become caliph on the cheap. Any asshole with a computer and some rudimentary knowledge can hack his way into most corporate systems, and visions of grandeur are as common among Muslims as they are in the rest of the world's population.

It wasn't as if I didn't have other things to do. Red Cell International—my security consulting firm, a successor of sorts to SOS Temps—had been awarded several contracts the previous summer and fall. While we continued to do some training for Homeland Insecurity and the Defense Department, more and more of our business was with private industry. Most of these were very straightforward assessment gigs, where yours truly and his various minions earned big bucks telling corporate security types why their procedures weren't worth the paper they weren't written on. The *best* jobs involved simulating terrorist and corporate espionage attacks against the conglomerates. Not only did these pay absurdly well, but they were a *hell* of a lot of fun. One of our favorite ploys involved kidnapping the company CEO the day before our assignment was supposed to officially begin. We'd take him to the fanciest restaurant in town while his head of security frantically searched for him, enjoying a ten-course dinner while keeping tabs on the Keystone Kop response via video and audio bugs we'd planted at corporate HQ. The only downside was that most of these corporate fat cats were embarrassingly small tippers; it got so I had to intercept the bill and add the amount myself before having them sign. Otherwise the wait staff never would have served my team if we returned.

These domestic assignments led to additional work overseas, training and in a few cases providing choirboy services in foreign pleasure resorts, like beautiful Kandur and lovely Baghdad. We sang, we hummed, we disposed of the garbage when necessary. Our standard contracts include nondisclosure clauses about as long as this book; the lawyers say they mean I can neither name the companies we work for nor say what we did. The lawyers can suck turds, as far as I'm concerned, but since a lot of these assignments are ongoing, in the interests of protecting my people I'd prefer to keep discussion of methods and means to a minimum. Suffice it to say that we did what had to be done, reaping the appropriate rewards but also occasionally suffering the sort of hits that made such rewards a necessary incentive.

As far as this particular yarn is concerned, the most important contracts were in Afghanistan, where three different Western companies required our assistance to varying degrees. Sometime that February—weeks after Saladin's faxes had begun to fade and curl at the edges—we noticed an uptick in operations directed at the companies we were working with. And, eventually, at Red Cell International itself. There wasn't a pattern that we could put our fingers on, but we were interested enough to call a companywide conference to discuss it. For various reasons, including the quality of the beer, we picked a date in March in Germany.

Which fit in nicely with my own schedule, as I was supposed to be in Italy right around the same time to address an annual NATO meeting on the new realities of terrorism.

For me, Italy will always be a land of romance, tomato sauce, and women with very short tempers. I was stationed in Naples in southern Italy in the late 1950s and early '60s. I blame a lot of my subsequent development on the horrors of working for the fattest, laziest UFO (Ugly Female Officer) in the Navy; the horror of that early assignment propelled me to frogman training, and far exceeded any combat situation I faced in later years. If ever I lack motivation for a PT session, the mental image of her butt cheeks flapping in the breeze never fails to get me in gear.

I returned to the Land of Garlic and Oregano several times in my Navy career, both with the SEALs and Red Cell, running training operations, security drills and a few things I can't tell you about unless I shoot you first. All in all, I love Italy, especially when someone else is paying for me to be there.